LEGENDS OF THE SPACE MARINES

THE SPACE MARINES are the last bastion of mankind against the destructive powers threatening the Imperium – their traitorous brethren, the Chaos Space Marines, warp-born daemons, and unending hordes of hateful xenos.

Each Space Marine is a relentless warrior, a fearless bringer of righteous destruction, a champion in their defiance of the hostile universe. But on a battlefield where tales of sacrifice and courage are written every day, legends may still be born. Among thousands of heroes, only those most skilled with bolter and blade will be remembered and revered, those who led their brothers to the most unlikely of victories in the face of vast hordes of foes.

This anthology gathers together some of the stories of those legends, featuring some of the Black Library's leading authors including Aaron Dembski-Bowden, Nick Kyme, Graham McNeill and James Swallow.

WARHAMMER 40,000 STORIES

LEGENDS OF THE SPACE MARINES

Edited by
Christian Dunn

A BLACK LIBRARY PUBLICATION

First published in Great Britain in 2010 by
BL Publishing,
Games Workshop Ltd.,
Willow Road, Nottingham,
NG7 2WS, UK.

10 9 8 7 6 5 4 3 2 1

Cover illustration by Hardy Fowler.

A CIP record for this book is available from the British Library.

ISBN13: 978 1 84416 552 0

Distributed in the US by Simon & Schuster
1230 Avenue of the Americas, New York, NY 10020, US.

This is a work of fiction. All the characters and events portrayed
in this book are fictional, and any resemblance to real people or
incidents is purely coincidental.

See the Black Library on the Internet at
www.blacklibrary.com

Find out more about Games Workshop
and the world of Warhammer 40,000 at
www.games-workshop.com

Printed and bound in the US.

It is the 41st millennium. For more than a hundred centuries the Emperor has sat immobile on the Golden Throne of Earth. He is the master of mankind by the will of the gods, and master of a million worlds by the might of his inexhaustible armies. He is a rotting carcass writhing invisibly with power from the Dark Age of Technology. He is the Carrion Lord of the Imperium for whom a thousand souls are sacrificed every day, so that he may never truly die.

Yet even in his deathless state, the Emperor continues his eternal vigilance. Mighty battlefleets cross the daemon-infested miasma of the warp, the only route between distant stars, their way lit by the Astronomican, the psychic manifestation of the Emperor's will. Vast armies give battle in His name on uncounted worlds. Greatest amongst his soldiers are the Adeptus Astartes, the Space Marines, bio-engineered super-warriors. Their comrades in arms are legion: the Imperial Guard and countless planetary defence forces, the ever-vigilant Inquisition and the tech-priests of the Adeptus Mechanicus to name only a few. But for all their multitudes, they are barely enough to hold off the ever-present threat from aliens, heretics, mutants – and worse.

To be a man in such times is to be one amongst untold billions. It is to live in the cruellest and most bloody regime imaginable. These are the tales of those times. Forget the power of technology and science, for so much has been forgotten, never to be re-learned. Forget the promise of progress and understanding, for in the grim dark future there is only war. There is no peace amongst the stars, only an eternity of carnage and slaughter, and the laughter of thirsting gods.

CONTENTS

Hell Night *by Nick Kyme*   **9**

Cover of Darkness *by Mitchel Scanlon*   **77**

The Relic *by Jonathan Green*   **157**

Twelve Wolves *by Ben Counter*   **209**

The Returned *by James Swallow*   **239**

Consequences *by Graham McNeill*   **295**

The Last Detail *by Paul Kearney*   **331**

The Trial of the Mantis Warriors
by CS Goto   **377**

Orphans of the Kraken *by Richard Williams*   **429**

At Gaius Point *by Aaron Dembski-Bowden*   **505**

HELL NIGHT

Nick Kyme

It can't rain all the time…

The trooper's mood was sullen as he helped drag the unlimbered lascannon through the mire.

The Earthshakers had begun their bombardment. A slow and steady *crump-crump* – stop – *crump-crump* far behind him at the outskirts of bastion headquarters made the trooper flinch instinctively every time a shell whined overhead.

It was ridiculous: the deadly cargo fired by the siege guns was at least thirty metres at the apex of its trajectory, yet still he ducked.

Survival was high on the trooper's list of priorities, that and service to the Emperor of course.

Ave Imperator.

A cry to the trooper's right, though muffled by the droning rain, got his attention. He turned, rivulets

teeming off his nose like at the precipice of a waterfall, and saw the lascannon had foundered. One of
its carriage's rear wheels was sunk in mud, sucked
into an invisible bog.

'Bostok, gimme a hand.'

Another trooper, Genk, an old guy – a *lifer* – grimaced to Bostok as he tried to wedge the butt of his
lasgun under the trapped wheel and use it like a lever.

Tracer fire was whipping overhead, slits of magne-
sium carving up the darkness. It sizzled and spat
when it pierced the sheeting rain.

Bostok grumbled. Staying low, he tramped over
heavily to help his fellow gunner. Adding his own
weapon to the hopeful excavation, he pushed down
and tried to work his way under the wheel.

'Get it deeper,' urged Genk, the lines in his weathered face becoming dark crevices with every distant
flash-flare of siege shells striking the void shield.

Though each hit brought a fresh blossom of
energy rippling across the shield, the city's defences
were holding. If the 135th Phalanx was to breach it
– for the Emperor's glory and righteous will – they'd
need to bring more firepower to bear.

'*Overload the generators,*' Sergeant Harver had said.

'*Bring our guns close,*' he'd said. '*Orders from Colonel
Tench.*'

Not particularly subtle, but then they were the
Guard, the Hammer of the Emperor: blunt was what
the common soldiery did best.

Genk was starting to panic: they were falling
behind.

Across a killing field dug with abandoned trenches, tufts of razor wire protruding like wild gorse in some untamed prairie, teams of Phalanx troopers dragged heavy weapons or marched hastily in squad formation.

It took a lot of men to break a siege; more still, and with artillery support, to bring down a fully functioning void shield. Men the Phalanx had: some ten thousand souls willing to sacrifice their lives for the glory of the Throne; the big guns – leastways the shells for the big guns – they did not. A Departmento Munitorum clerical error had left the battle group short some fifty thousand anti-tank, arrowhead shells. Fewer shells meant more boots and bodies. A more aggressive strategy was taken immediately: all lascannons and heavy weapons to advance to five hundred metres and lay void shield-sapping support fire.

Bad luck for Phalanx: wars were easier to fight from behind distant crosshairs. And safer. Bad luck for Bostok, too.

Though he was working hard at freeing the gun with Genk, he noticed some of their comrades falling to the defensive return fire of the secessionist rebels, holed up and cosy behind their shield and their armour and their fraggin' gun emplacements.

Bastards.

Bet they're dry too, Bostok thought ruefully. His slicker came undone when he snagged it on the elevation winch of the lascannon and he swore loudly as the downpour soaked his red-brown standard-issue uniform beneath.

There was a muted cry ahead as he fastened up the slicker and pulled his wide-brimmed helmet down further to keep out the worst of the rain – a heavy bolter team and half an infantry squad disappeared from view, seemingly swallowed by the earth. Some of the old firing pits and trenches had been left unfilled, except now they contained muddy water and sucking earth. As deadly as quicksand they were.

Bostok muttered a prayer, making the sign of the aquila. Least it wasn't him and Genk.

'Eye be damned, what is holding you up, troopers?'

It was Sergeant Harver. The tumult was deafening, that and the artillery exchange. He had to bellow just to be heard. Not that Harver ever did anything but bellow when addressing his squad.

'Get this fraggin' rig moving you sump rats,' he barracked, 'You're lagging troopers, lagging.'

Harver munched a fat, vine-leaf cigar below the black wire of his twirled moustache. He didn't seem to mind or notice that it had long been doused and hung like a fat, soggy finger from the corner of his mouth.

A static crackle from the vox-operator's comms unit interrupted the sergeant's tirade.

'More volume: louder Rhoper, louder.'

Rhoper, the vox-operator, nodded, before setting the unit down and fiddling with a bunch of controls.

The receiver was amplified in a few seconds and returned with the voice of Sergeant Rampe.

'*…Enemy sighted! They're here in no-man's land! Bastards are out beyond the shield! I see, oh sh–*'

'Rampe, Rampe,' Harver bellowed into the receiver cup. 'Respond, man!' His attention switched to Rhoper.

'Another channel, trooper – at the double, if you please.'

Rhoper was already working on it. The comms channels linking the infantry squads to artillery command and one another flicked by in a mixture of static, shouting and oddly muted gunfire.

At last, they got a response.

'*…aggin' out here with us! Throne of Earth, that's not poss–*'

The voice stopped but the link continued unbroken. There was more distant weapons fire, and something else.

'Did I hear–' Harver began.

'Bells, sir,' offered Rhoper, in a rare spurt of dialogue. 'It was bells ringing.'

Static killed the link and this time Harver turned to Trooper Bostok, who had all but given up trying to free the lascannon.

The bells hadn't stopped. They were on this part of the battlefield too.

'Could be the sounds carrying on the wind, sir?' suggested Genk, caked in mud from his efforts.

Too loud, too close to be just the wind, thought Bostok and took up his lasgun as he turned to face the dark.

Silhouettes lived there, jerking in stop-motion with every void impact flare – they were his comrades, those who had made it to the five hundred metre line.

Bostok's eyes narrowed.

There was something else out there too. Not guns or Phalanx, not even rebels.

It was white, rippling and flowing on an unseen breeze. The rain was so dense it just flattened; the air didn't zephyr, there were no eddies skirling across the killing ground.

'Sarge, do we 'ave Ecclesiarchy in our ranks?'

'Negative, trooper, just the Emperor's own: boots, bayonets and blood.'

Bostok pointed towards the flicker of white.

'Then who the frag is that?'

But the flicker had already gone. Though the bells tolled on. Louder and louder.

Fifty metres away, men were screaming. And running.

Bostok saw their faces through his gun sight, saw the horror written there. Then they were gone. He scanned the area, using his scope like a magnocular, but couldn't find them. At first, Bostok thought they'd fallen foul of an earth ditch, like the heavy bolter and infantry he'd seen earlier, but he could see no ditches, no trench or fire pit that could've swallowed them. But they'd been claimed all right, claimed by whatever moved amongst them.

More screaming; merging with the bells into a disturbing clamour.

It put the wind up Sergeant Harver – Phalanx soldiers were disappearing in all directions.

'Bostok, Genk, get that cannon turned about,' he ordered, slipping out his service pistol.

The lascannon was well and truly stuck, but worked on a pintle mount, so could be swivelled into position. Genk darted around the carriage, not sure what was happening but falling back on orders to anchor himself and stave off rising terror. He yanked out the holding pin with more force than was necessary and swung the gun around towards the white flickers and the screaming, just as his sergeant requested.

'Covering fire, Mr Rhoper,' added Harver, and the vox-operator slung the boxy comms unit on his back and drew his lasgun, crouching in a shooting position just behind the lascannon.

Bostok took up his post by the firing shield, slamming a fresh power cell into the heavy weapon's breech.

'Lit and clear!'

'At your discretion, trooper,' said Harver.

Genk didn't need a written invitation. He sighted down the barrel and the targeting nub, seeing a flicker, and hauled back the triggers.

Red beams, hot and angry, ripped up the night. Genk laid suppressing fire in a forward arc that smacked of fear and desperation. He was sweating by the end of his salvo, and not from the heat discharge.

The bells were tolling still, though it was impossible to place their origin. The void-shrouded city was too far away, a black smudge on an already dark canvas, and the resonant din sounded close and all around them.

Cordite wafted on the breeze; cordite and screaming.

Bostok tried to squint past the driving rain, more effective than any camo-paint for concealment.

The flickers were still out there, ephemeral and indistinct… and they were closing.

'Again, if you please,' ordered Harver, an odd tremor affecting his voice.

It took Bostok a few seconds to recognise it as fear.

'Lit and clear!' he announced, slamming in a second power cell.

'Not stopping, sir,' said Rhoper and sighted down his lasgun before firing.

Sergeant Harver responded by loosing his own weapon, pistol cracks adding to the fusillade.

Casting about, Bostok found they were alone; an island of Phalanx in a sea of mud, but the advanced line was coming to meet them. They were fleeing, driven wild by sheer terror. Men were disappearing as they ran, sucked under the earth, abruptly silenced.

'Sarge…' Bostok began.

Onwards the line came, something moving within it, preying on it like piranhas stalking a shoal of frightened fish.

Harver was nearly gone, just firing on impulse now. Some of his shots and that of Genk's lascannon were tearing up their own troops.

Rhoper still had his wits, and came forwards as the heavy weapon ran dry.

'F-f...' Harver was saying when Bostok got to his feet and ran like hell.

Rhoper disappeared a moment later. No cries for help, no nothing; just a cessation of his lasgun fire and then silence to show for the end of the doughty vox-officer.

Heart hammering in his chest, his slicker having now parted and exposing him to the elements, Bostok ran, promising never to bemoan his lot again, if the Emperor would just spare him this time, spare him from being pulled into the earth and buried alive. He didn't want to die like that.

Bostok must've been dragging his feet, because troopers from the advanced line were passing him. A trooper disappeared to his left, a white flicker and the waft of something old and dank presaging his demise. Another, just ahead, was pulled asunder, and Bostok jinked away from a course that would lead him into that path. He risked a glance over his shoulder. Harver and Genk were gone – the lascannon was still mired but now abandoned – fled or taken, he didn't know.

Some of the Phalanx were staging a fighting withdrawal. Gallant, but what did they have to hold off? It was no enemy Bostok had ever seen or known.

Running was all that concerned him now, running for his life.

Just reach the artillery batteries and I'll be fine.

But then a hollow cry echoed ahead, and Bostok saw a white flicker around the siege guns. A tanker disappeared under the earth, his cap left on the grille of the firing platform.

The fat lump of numbing panic in his chest rose into Bostok's throat and threatened to choke him.

Can't go back, can't go forward...

He peeled off to the left. Maybe he could take a circuitous route to bastion headquarters.

No, too long. They'd be on him before then.

In the dark and the rain, he couldn't even see the mighty structure. No beacon-lamps to guide him, no searchlights to cling to. Death, like the darkness, was closing.

The bells were tolling.

Men screamed.

Bostok ran, his vision fragmenting in sheer terror, the pieces collapsing in on one another like a kaleidoscope.

Got to get away... Please Throne, oh pl–

Earth became swamp beneath his feet, and Bostok sank. He panicked, thinking he was about to be taken, when he realised he'd fallen into an earth ditch, right up to his chin. Fighting the urge to wade across, he dipped lower until the muddy water reached his nose, filling his nostrils with a rank and stagnant odour. Clinging to the edge with trembling, bone-cold fingers, he prayed to the Emperor for the end of the night, for the end of the rain and the cessation of the bells.

But the bells didn't stop. They just kept on tolling.

* * *

Three weeks later…

'FIFTY METRES TO landfall,' announced Hak'en. The pilot's voice sounded tinny through the vox-speaker in the Chamber Sanctuarine of *Fire-wyvern*.

Looking through the occuliport in the gunship's flank, Dak'ir saw a grey day, sheeting with rain.

Hak'en was bringing the vessel around, flying a course that would take them within a few metres of Mercy Rock, the headquarters of the 135th Phalanx and the Imperial forces they were joining on Vaporis. As the gunship banked, angling Dak'ir's slit-view downward, a sodden earth field riddled with dirty pools and sludge-like emplacements was revealed. The view came in frustrating slashes.

Dak'ir was curious to see more.

'Brother,' he addressed the vox-speaker, 'open up the embarkation ramp.'

'As you wish, brother-sergeant. Landfall in twenty metres.'

Hak'en disengaged the locking protocols that kept the Thunderhawk's hatches sealed during transit. As the operational rune went green, Dak'ir punched it and the ramp started to open and lower.

Light and air rushed into the gunship's troop compartment where Dak'ir's battle-brothers were sat in meditative silence. Even in the grey dawn, their bright green battle-plate flashed, the snarling fire-drake icon on their left pauldrons – orange on a black field – revealing them to be Salamanders of the 3rd Company.

As well as illuminating their power armour, the feeble light also managed to banish the glare from their eyes. Blazing red with captured fire, it echoed the heat of the Salamanders' volcanic home world, Nocturne.

'A far cry from the forge-pits under Mount Death-fire,' groaned Ba'ken.

Though he couldn't see his face beneath the battle-helm he was wearing, Dak'ir knew his brother also wore a scowl at the inclement weather.

'Wetter too,' added Emek, coming to stand beside the hulking form of Ba'ken and peering over Dak'ir's broad shoulders. 'But then what else are we to expect from a monsoon world?'

The ground was coming to meet them and as Hak'en straightened up *Fire-wyvern* the full glory of Mercy Rock was laid before them.

It might once have been beautiful, but now the bastion squatted like an ugly gargoyle in a brown mud-plain. Angular gun towers, bristling with auto-cannon and heavy stubber, crushed the angelic spires that had once soared into the turbulent Vaporis sky; ablative armour concealed murals and baroque columns; the old triumphal gate, with its frescos and ornate filigree, had been replaced with something grey, dark and practical. These specific details were unknown to Dak'ir, but he could see in the structure's curves an echo of its architectural bearing, hints of something artful and not merely functional.

'I see we are not the only recent arrivals,' said Ba'ken. The other Salamanders at the open hatch followed his gaze to where a black Valkyrie gunship had touched down in the mud, its landing stanchions slowly sinking.

'Imperial Commissariat,' replied Emek, recognising the official seal on the side of the transport.

Dak'ir kept his silence. His eyes strayed across the horizon to the distant city of Aphium and the void dome surrounding it. Even above the droning gunship engines, he could hear the hum of generatoria powering the field. It was like those which protected the Sanctuary Cities of his home world from the earthquakes and volcanic eruptions that were a way of life for the hardy folk of Nocturne. The air was thick with the stench of ozone; another by-product of the void fields. Even the constant rain couldn't wash it away.

As *Fire-wyvern* came in to land with a scream of stabiliser-jets, Dak'ir closed his eyes. Rain was coming in through the hatch and he let it patter against his armour. The dulcet ring of it was calming. Rain – at least the cool, wet, non-acidic kind – was rare on Nocturne, and even against his armour he enjoyed the sensation. There was an undercurrent of something else that came with it, though. It was unease, disquiet, a sense of watchfulness.

I feel it too, a voice echoed inside Dak'ir's head, and his eyes snapped open again. He turned to find Brother Pyriel watching him intently. Pyriel was a Librarian, a wielder of the psychic arts, and he could read people's thoughts as they might read an open book. The psyker's eyes flashed cerulean blue before returning to burning red. Dak'ir didn't like the idea of him poking around in his subconscious, but he sensed that Pyriel had merely browsed the surface of his mind. Even still, Dak'ir looked away and was glad when the earth met them at last and *Fire-wyvern* touched down.

THE COLD SNAP of las-fire carried on the breeze as the Salamanders debarked.

Across the muddied field, just fifty metres from the approach road to Mercy Rock, a commissarial firing squad were executing a traitor.

An Imperial Guard colonel, wearing the red-brown uniform of the Phalanx, jerked spastically as the hot rounds struck him and was still. Tied to a thick, wooden pole, he slumped and sagged against his bonds. First his knees folded and he sank, then his head lolled forward, his eyes open and glassy.

A commissar, lord-level given his rank pins and trappings, was looking on as his bodyguards brought their lasguns to port arms and marched away from the execution site. His gaze met with Dak'ir's as he turned to go after them. Rain teemed off the brim of his cap, a silver skull stud sat in the centre above the peak. The commissar's eyes were hidden by the shadow the brim cast, but felt cold and rigid all the same. The Imperial officer didn't linger. He was already walking away, back to the bastion, as the last of the Salamanders mustered out and the exit ramps closed.

Dak'ir wondered at what events had delivered the colonel to such a bleak end, and was sorry to see *Fire-wyvern* lifting off again, leaving them alone in this place.

'Such is the fate of all traitors,' remarked Tsu'gan with a bitter tang.

Even behind his helmet lens, Tsu'gan's stare was hard. Dak'ir returned his glare.

There was no brotherly love between the two Salamander sergeants. Before they became Space Marines, they had hailed from opposite ends of the Nocturnean hierarchy: Dak'ir an Ignean cave-dweller and an orphan, the likes of which had never before joined the ranks of the Astartes; and Tsu'gan, a nobleman's son from the Sanctuary City of Hesiod, as close to aristocracy and affluence as it was possible to get on a volcanic death world. Though as sergeants they were both equals in the eyes of their captain and Chapter Master, Tsu'gan did not regard their relationship as such. Dak'ir was unlike many other Salamanders, there was a strain of humanity left within him that was greater and more empathic than that of his brothers. It occasionally left him isolated, almost disconnected. Tsu'gan had seen it often enough and decided it was not merely unusual, it was an aberration. Since their first mission as Scouts on the sepulchre world of Moribar, acrimony had divided them. In the years that followed, it had not lessened.

'It leaves a grim feeling to see men wasted like that,' said Dak'ir, 'Slain in cold blood without chance for reparation.'

Many Space Marine Chapters, the Salamanders among them, believed in order and punishment, but they also practised penitence and the opportunity for atonement. Only when a brother was truly lost, given in to the Ruinous Powers or guilty of such a heinous deed as could not be forgiven or forgotten, was death the only alternative.

'Then you'd best develop a stronger stomach, *Ignean*,' sneered Tsu'gan, fashioning the word into a slight, 'for your compassion is misplaced on the executioners' field.'

'It's no weakness, brother,' Dak'ir replied fiercely.

Pyriel deliberately walked between them to prevent any further hostility.

'Gather your squads, brother-sergeants,' the Librarian said firmly, 'and follow me.'

Both did as ordered: Ba'ken and Emek plus seven others falling in behind Dak'ir; whilst Tsu'gan led another same-sized squad from the drop-site. One in Tsu'gan's group gave Dak'ir a vaguely contemptuous look, before turning his attention to an auspex unit. This was Iagon, Tsu'gan's second, and chief minion. Where Tsu'gan was all thin-veiled threat and belligerence, Iagon was an insidious snake, much more poisonous and deadly.

Dak'ir shrugged off the battle-brother's glare and motioned his squad forwards.

'I could see his attitude corrected, brother,' hissed Ba'ken over a closed comm-link channel feeding to Dak'ir's battle-helm. 'It would be a pleasure.'

'I don't doubt that, Ba'ken,' Dak'ir replied, 'but let's just try and stay friendly for now, shall we?'

'As you wish, sergeant.'

Behind his battle-helm, Dak'ir smiled. Ba'ken was his closest ally in the Chapter and he was eternally grateful that the hulking heavy weapons trooper was watching his back.

As they marched the final few metres to the bastion gates, Ba'ken's attention strayed to the void shield on the Salamanders' right. The commissar lord, along with his entourage, had already gone inside the Imperial command centre. Overhead, the skies were darkening and the rain intensified. Day was giving way to night.

'Your tactical assessment, Brother Ba'ken?' asked Pyriel, noting his fellow Salamander's interest in the shield.

'Constant bombardment – it's the only way to bring a void shield down.' He paused, thinking. 'That, or get close enough to slip through during a momentary break in the field and knock out the generatoria.'

Tsu'gan sniffed derisively.

'Then let us hope the humans can do just that, and get us to within striking distance, so we can leave this sodden planet.'

Dak'ir bristled at the other sergeant's contempt, but kept his feelings in check. He suspected it was half-meant as a goad, anyway.

'Tell me this, then, brothers:' added Pyriel, the gates of the bastion looming, 'why are they falling back with their artillery?'

At a low ridge, just below the outskirts of the bastion, Basilisk tanks were retreating. Their long cannons shrank away from the battlefield as the tanks found parking positions within the protective outer boundaries of the bastion.

'Why indeed?' Dak'ir asked himself as they passed through the slowly opening gates and entered Mercy Rock.

'VICTORY AT APHIUM will be won with strong backs, courage and the guns of our Immortal Emperor!'

The commissar lord was sermonising as the Salamanders appeared in the great bastion hall.

Dak'ir noticed the remnants of ornamental fountains, columns and mosaics – all reduced to rubble for the Imperial war machine.

The hall was a vast expanse and enabled the Imperial officer to address almost ten thousand men, mustered in varying states of battle-dress. Sergeants, corporals, line troopers, even the wounded and support staff had been summoned to the commissar's presence as he announced his glorious vision for the coming war.

To his credit, he barely flinched when the Astartes strode into the massive chamber, continuing on with his rallying cry to the men of the Phalanx who showed much greater reverence for the Emperor's Angels of Death amongst them.

The Fire-born had removed battle-helms as they'd entered, revealing onyx-black skin and red eyes that glowed dully in the half-dark. As well as reverence, several of the Guardsmen betrayed their fear and awe of the Salamanders. Dak'ir noticed Tsu'gan smiling thinly, enjoying intimidating the humans before them.

'*As potent as bolt or blade,*' old Master Zen'de had told them when they were neophytes. Except that Tsu'gan deployed such tactics all too readily; even against allies.

'Colonel Tench is dead,' the commissar announced flatly. 'He lacked the will and the purpose the Emperor demands of us. His legacy of largesse and cowardice is over.'

Like black-clad sentinels, the commissar's storm troopers eyed the men nearest their master at this last remark, daring them to take umbrage at the defamation of their former colonel.

The commissar's voice was amplified by a loud-hailer and echoed around the courtyard, carrying to every trooper present. A small cadre of Phalanx officers, what was left of the command section, were standing to one side of the commissar, giving off stern and unyielding looks to the rest of their troops.

This was the Emperor's will – they didn't have to like it; they just had to do it.

'And any man who thinks otherwise had best look to the bloody fields beyond Mercy Rock, for that is the fate which awaits he without the courage to do what is necessary.' The commissar glared, baiting dissension. When none was forthcoming, he went on. 'I am taking command in the late colonel's stead. All artillery will return to the battlefront immediately.

Infantry is to be mustered in platoon and ready for deployment as soon as possible. Section commanders are to report to me in the strategium. The Phalanx will mobilise tonight!' He emphasised this last point with a clenched fist.

Silence reigned for a few moments, before a lone voice rang out of the crowd.

'But tonight is Hell Night.'

Like a predator with its senses piqued, the commissar turned to find the voice.

'Who said that?' he demanded, stalking to the front of the rostrum where he was preaching. 'Make yourself known.'

'There are things in the darkness, things not of this world. I've seen 'em!' A gap formed around a frantic-looking trooper as he gesticulated to the others, his growing hysteria spreading. 'They took Sergeant Harver, took 'im! The spectres! Just sucked men under the earth... They'll ta–'

The loud report of the commissar's bolt pistol stopped the trooper in mid-flow. Blood and brain matter spattered the infantrymen nearest the now headless corpse as silence returned.

Dak'ir stiffened at such wanton destruction of life, and was about to step forward and speak his mind, before a warning hand from Pyriel stopped him.

Reluctantly, the Salamander backed down.

'This idle talk about spectres and shadows haunting the night will not be tolerated,' the commissar decreed, holstering his still-smoking pistol. 'Our enemies are flesh and blood. They occupy Aphium and when this city falls, we will open up the rest of the continent to conquest. The lord-governor of this world lies dead, assassinated by men he trusted. Seceding from the Imperium is tantamount to an act of war. This rebellion will be crushed and Vaporis will be brought back to the light of Imperial unity. Now, prepare for battle…'

The commissar looked down his nose at the headless remains of the dead trooper, now lying prone.

'…and somebody clear up that filth.'

'He'll demoralise these men,' hissed Dak'ir, anger hardening his tone.

Two infantrymen were dragging the corpse of the dead trooper away. His bloodied jacket bore the name: Bostok.

'It's not our affair,' muttered Pyriel, his keen gaze fixed on the commissar as he headed towards them.

'The mood is grim enough, though, Brother-Librarian,' said Ba'ken, surveying the weary lines of troopers as they fell in, marshalled by platoon sergeants.

'Something has them spooked,' snarled Tsu'gan, though more out of contempt for the Guardsmen's apparent weakness, than concern.

Pyriel stepped forward to greet the commissar, who'd reached the Salamanders from the end of the rostrum.

'My lord Astartes,' he said with deference, bowing before Pyriel. 'I am Commissar Loth, and if you would accompany me with your officers to the strategium, I will apprise you of the tactical situation here on Vaporis.'

Loth was about to move away, determined to send the message that he, and not the Emperor's Angels, was in charge at Mercy Rock, when Pyriel's voice, resonant with psy-power, stopped him.

'That won't be necessary, commissar.'

Loth didn't looked impressed at he stared at the Librarian. His expression demanded an explanation, which Pyriel was only too pleased to provide.

'We know our orders and the tactical disposition of this battle. Weaken the shield, get us close enough to deploy an insertion team in the vicinity of the generatoria and we will do the rest.'

'I– that is, I mean to say, very well. But do you not need–'

Pyriel cut him off.

'I do have questions, though. That man, the trooper you executed: what did he mean "spectres", and what is Hell Night?'

Loth gave a dismissive snort.

'Superstition and scaremongering – these men have been lacking discipline for too long.' He was about to end it there when Pyriel's body language suggested the commissar should go on. Reluctantly, he did. 'Rumours, reports from the last night-attack against the secessionists, of men disappearing without trace under the earth and unnatural denizens prowling the battlefield. Hell Night is the longest nocturnal period in the Vaporan calendar – its longest night.'

'Tonight?'

'Yes.' Loth's face formed a scowl. 'It's sheer idiocy. Fearing the dark? Well, it's just damaging to the morale of the men in this regiment.'

'The former colonel, did he supply you with these… *reports?*'

Loth made a mirthless grin.

'He did.'

'And you had him shot for that?'

'As my duty binds me, yes, I did.' Loth had a pugilist's face, slab-flat with a wide, crushed nose and a scar that ran from top lip to hairline that pulled up the corner of his mouth in a snarl. His small ears, poking out from either side of his commissar's cap, were ragged. He was stolid when he spoke next. 'There is nothing lurking in the darkness except the false nightmares that dwell in the minds of infants.'

'I've seen nightmares made real before, commissar,' Pyriel took on a warning tone.

'Then we are fortunate to have angels watching over us.' Loth adjusted his cap and straightened his leather frockcoat. 'I'll weaken the shield, be assured of that, nightmares or no.'

'Then we'll see you on the field, commissar,' Pyriel told him, before showing his back and leaving Loth to wallow in impotent rage.

'You really took exception to him, didn't you brother?' said Emek a few minutes later, too curious to realise his impropriety. They were back out in the muddy quagmire. In the distance, the sound of battle tanks moving into position ground on the air.

'He had a callous disregard for human life,' Pyriel replied. 'And besides... his aura was bad.' He allowed a rare smirk at the remark, before clamping on his battle-helm.

Overhead, the sky was wracked with jagged red lightning and the clouds billowed crimson. Far above, in the outer atmosphere of Vaporis, a warp storm was boiling. It threw a visceral cast over the rain-slicked darkness of the battlefield.

'Hell Night, in more than just name it seems,' said Ba'ken, looking up to the bloody heavens.

'An inauspicious omen, perhaps?' offered Iagon, the first time he'd spoken since landfall.

'Ever the doomsayer,' remarked Ba'ken under his breath to his sergeant.

But Dak'ir wasn't listening. He was looking at Pyriel.

'Form combat squads,' said the Librarian, when he realised he was under scrutiny. 'Tsu'gan, find positions.'

Tsu'gan slammed a fist against his plastron, and cast a last snide glance at Dak'ir before he divided up his squad and moved out at a steady run.

Dak'ir ignored him, still intent on Pyriel.

'Do you sense something, Brother-Librarian?'

Pyriel eyed the darkness in the middle distance, the no-man's land between the bastion and the shimmering edge of the far off void shield. It was as if he was trying to catch a glimpse of something just beyond his reach, at the edge of natural sight.

'It's nothing.'

Dak'ir nodded slowly and mustered out. But he'd detected the lie in the Librarian's words and wondered what it meant.

FALSE THUNDER WRACKED the sky from the report of heavy cannons at the rear of the Imperial battle line. Smoke hung over the muddied field like a shroud, occluding the bodies of the Phalanx troopers moving through it, but was quickly weighed down by the incessant rain.

They marched in platoons, captains and sergeants hollering orders over the defensive fire of rebel guns and the dense *thuds* of explosions. Heavy weapons teams, two men dragging unlimbered cannon, whilst standard infantry ran alongside, forged towards emplacements dug five hundred metres from the shield wall.

Incandescent flashes rippled across the void shield with the dense shell impacts of the distant Earthshaker cannons and from lascannon and missile salvoes, unleashed when their crews had closed to the assault line.

In the midst of it all were the Salamanders, crouched down in cover, at the edges of the line in five-man combat squads.

Librarian Pyriel had joined Dak'ir's unit, making it six. With the flare of explosions and the red sky overhead, his blue armour was turned a lurid purple. It denoted his rank as Librarian, as did the arcane paraphernalia about his person.

'Our objective is close, brothers. There…' Pyriel indicated the bulk of a generatorium structure some thousand metres distant. Only Space Marines, with their occulobe implants, had the enhanced visual faculty to see and identify it. Rebel forces, hunkered down in pillboxes, behind trenches and fortified emplacements, guarded it. In the darkness and the rain, even with the superhuman senses of the Astartes, they were just shadows and muzzle flashes.

'We should take an oblique route, around the east and west hemispheres of the shield,' Dak'ir began. 'Resistance will be weakest there. We'll be better able to exploit it.'

After Tsu'gan had secured the route, the Salamanders had arrived at the five hundred metre assault line, having stealthed their way to it undetected before the full Imperial bombardment had begun. But they were positioned at the extreme edges of the line – two groups east, two groups west – in the hope of launching a shock assault into the heart of the rebel defenders and destroying the generatoria powering the void shield before serious opposition could be raised.

'Brother Pyriel?' Dak'ir pressed when a response wasn't forthcoming.

The Librarian was staring at the distant void shield, energy blossoms appearing on its surface only to dissipate seconds later.

'Something about the shield… An anomaly in its energy signature…' he breathed. His eyes were glowing cerulean blue.

For once, Dak'ir felt nothing, just the urge to act.

'What is it?'

'I don't know…' The psychic fire dimmed in the Librarian's eyes behind his battle-helm. 'Oblique assault; one primary, one secondary. East and west,' he asserted.

Dak'ir nodded, but had a nagging feeling that Pyriel wasn't telling them everything. He opened a comm-channel to the other combat squads.

'We move in, brothers. Assault plan *serpentine*. Brother Apion, you are support. We will take primary. Brother Tsu'gan–'

'We are ready, Ignean,' came the harsh reply before Dak'ir had finished. 'Assault vector locked, I am the primary at the western hemisphere. Tsu'gan out.'

The link was cut abruptly. Dak'ir cursed under his breath.

Taking out his plasma pistol and unsheathing his chainsword, running a gauntleted finger down the flat of the blade and muttering a litany to Vulkan, Dak'ir rose to his feet.

'Fire-born, advance on my lead.'

Emek's raised fist brought them to a halt before they could move out. He had his finger pressed to the side of his battle-helm.

'I'm getting some frantic chatter from the Phalanx units.' He paused, listening intently. 'Contact has been lost with several secondary command units.' Then he looked up. During the pregnant pause, Dak'ir could sense what was coming next.

'They say they're under attack… from *spectres*,' said Emek.

'Patch it to all comms, brother. Every combat squad.'

Emek did as asked, and Dak'ir's battle-helm, together with his brothers', was filled with the broken reports from the Phalanx command units.

'*...ergeant is dead. Falling back to secondary positions...*'

'*...all around us! Throne of Earth, I can't see a target, I can't se–*'

'*...ead, everyone. They're out here among us! Oh hell, oh Emperor sa–*'

Scattered gunfire and hollow screams punctuated these reports. Some units were attempting to restore order. The barking commands of sergeants and corporals sounded desperate as they tried to re-organise in the face of sudden attack.

Commissar Loth's voice broke in sporadically, his replies curt and scathing. They must hold and then advance. The Imperium would brook no cowardice in the face of the enemy. Staggered bursts from his bolt pistol concluded each order, suggesting further executions.

Above and omnipresent, the sound of tolling bells filled the air.

'I saw no chapel or basilica in the Phalanx bastion,' said Ba'ken. He swept his gaze around slowly, panning with his heavy flamer as he did so.

'The rebels?' offered Brother Romulus.

'How do you explain it being everywhere?' asked Pyriel, his eyes aglow once more. He regarded the blood-red clouds that hinted at the churning warp storm above. 'This is an unnatural phenomenon. We are dealing with more than secessionists.'

Dak'ir swore under his breath; he'd made his decision.

'Spectres or not, we can't leave the Phalanx to be butchered.' He switched the comm-feed in his battle-helm to transmit.

'All squads regroup, and converge on Phalanx command positions.'

Brother Apion responded with a rapid affirmative, as did a second combat squad led by Brother Lazarus. Tsu'gan took a little longer to capitulate, evidently unimpressed, but seeing the need to rescue the Guardsmen from whatever was attacking them. Without the support fire offered by their heavy guns, the Salamanders were horribly exposed to the secessionist artillery and with the shield intact they had no feasible mission to prosecute.

'Understood.' Tsu'gan then cut the link.

SILHOUETTES MOVED THROUGH the downpour. Lasgun snap-shot fizzed out from Imperial positions, revealing Phalanx troopers that were shooting at unseen foes.

Most were running. Even the Basilisks were starting to withdraw. Commissar Loth, despite all of his fervour and promised retribution, couldn't prevent it.

The Phalanx were fleeing.

'Enemy contacts?'

Dak'ir was tracking through the mire, pistol held low, chainsword still but ready. He was the fulcrum of a dispersed battle-formation, Pyriel to his immediate left and two battle-brothers either side of them.

Ahead, he saw another combat squad led by Apion, the secondary insertion group. He too had dispersed his warriors, and they were plying every metre of the field for enemies.

'Negative,' was the curt response from Lazarus, approaching from the west.

Artillery bombardment from the entrenched rebel positions was falling with the intense rain. A great plume of sodden earth and broken bodies surged into the air a few metres away from where Dak'ir's squad advanced.

'Pyriel, anything?'

The Librarian shook his head, intent on his otherworldly instincts but finding no sense in what he felt or saw.

The broken chatter in Dak'ir's ear continued, the tolling of the bells providing an ominous chorus to gunfire and screaming. The Phalanx were close to a rout, having been pushed too far by a commissar who didn't understand or care about the nature of the enemy they were facing. Loth's only answer was threat of death to galvanise the men under his command. The bark of the Imperial officer's bolt pistol was close. Dak'ir could make out the telltale muzzle flash of the weapon in his peripheral vision.

Loth was firing at shadows and hitting his own men in the process; those fleeing and those who were standing their ground.

'I'll deal with him,' promised Pyriel, snapping out of his psychic trance without warning and peeling off to intercept the commissar.

Another artillery blast detonated nearby, showering the Salamanders with debris. Without the Earthshaker bombardment, the rebels were using their shell-hunting cannons to punish the Imperials. Tracer fire from high-calibre gunnery positions added to the carnage. That and whatever was stalking them through the mud and rain.

'It's infiltrators.' Tsu'gan's harsh voice was made harder still as it came through the comm-feed. 'Maybe fifty men, strung out in small groups, operating under camouflage. The humans are easily spooked. We will find them, Fire-born, and eliminate the threat.'

'How can you be–'

Dak'ir stopped when he caught a glimpse of something, away to his right.

'Did you see that?' he asked Ba'ken.

The hulking trooper followed him, swinging his heavy flamer around.

'No target,' Ba'ken replied. 'What was it, brother?'

'Not sure…' It had looked like just a flicker of… *white robes*, fluttering lightly but against the wind. The air suddenly became redolent with dank and age.

'Ignean!' Tsu'gan demanded.

'It's not infiltrators,' Dak'ir replied flatly.

Static flared in the feed before the other sergeant's voice returned.

'You can't be sure of that.'

'I know it, brother.' This time, Dak'ir cut the link. It had eluded him at first, but now he felt it, a… *presence*, out in the darkness of the killing field. It was angry.

'Eyes open,' he warned his squad, the half-seen image at the forefront of his mind and the stench all too real as the bells rang on.

Ahead, Dak'ir made out the form of a Phalanx officer, a captain according to his rank pins and attire. The Salamanders headed towards him, hoping to link up their forces and stage some kind of counter-attack. That was assuming there were enough troopers left to make any difference.

COMMISSAR LOTH WAS consumed by frenzy.

'Hold your ground!' he screeched. 'The Emperor demands your courage!' The bolt pistol rang out and another trooper fell, his torso gaping and red.

'Forward, damn you! Advance for His greater glory and the glory of the Imperium!'

Another Phalanx died, this time a sergeant who'd been rallying his men.

Pyriel was hurrying to get close, his force sword drawn, whilst his other hand was free. In the darkness and the driving rain he saw… *spectres*. They were white-grey and indistinct. Their movements were jagged, as if partially out of synch with reality, the non-corporeal breaching the fabric of the corporeal realm.

Loth saw them too, and the fear of it, whatever this phenomenon was, was etched over his pugilist's face.

'*Ave Imperator*. By the light of the Emperor, I shall fear no evil,' he intoned, falling back on the catechisms of warding and preservation he had learned in the schola progenium. '*Ave Imperator*. My soul is free of taint. Chaos will never claim it whilst He is my shield.'

The spectres were closing, flitting in and out of reality like a bad pict recording. Turning left and right, Loth loosed off shots at his aggressors, the brass rounds passing through them or missing completely, driving on to hit fleeing Phalanx infantryman instead.

With each manifestation, the spectres got nearer.

Pyriel was only a few metres away when one appeared ahead of him. Loth's shot struck the Salamander in the pauldron as it went through and through, and a damage rune flared into life on the Librarian's tactical display inside his battle-helm.

'*Ave Imp–*' Too late. The spectre was upon Commissar Loth. He barely rasped the words–

'*Oh God-Emperor…*'

–when a blazing wall of psychic fire spilled from Pyriel's outstretched palm, smothering the apparition and banishing it from sight.

Loth was raising his pistol to his lips, jamming the still hot barrel into his mouth as his mind was unmanned by what he had seen.

Pyriel reached him just in time, smacking the pistol away before the commissar could summarily execute himself. The irony of it wasn't lost on the Librarian as the bolt round flew harmlessly into the air. Still trailing tendrils of fire, Pyriel placed two fingers from his outstretched hand onto Loth's brow, who promptly crumpled to the ground and was still.

'He'll be out for several hours. Get him out of here, back to the bastion,' he ordered one of the commissar's attendants.

The attendant nodded, still shaken, calling for help, and together the storm troopers dragged Loth away.

'And he'll remember nothing of this or Vaporis,' Pyriel added beneath his breath.

Sensing his power, the spectres Pyriel had seen had retreated. Something else prickled at his senses now, something far off into the wilderness, away from the main battle site. There was neither time nor opportunity to investigate. Pyriel knew the nature of the foe they were facing now. He also knew there was no defence against it his brothers could muster. Space Marines were the ultimate warriors, but they needed enemies of flesh and blood. They couldn't fight mist and shadow.

Huge chunks of the Phalanx army were fleeing. But there was nothing Pyriel could do about that. Nor could he save those claimed by the earth, though this was the malice of the spectres at work again.

Instead, he raised a channel to Dak'ir through his battle-helm.

All the while, the bells tolled on.

'THE ENTIRE FORCE is broken,' the captain explained. He was a little hoarse from shouting commands, but had rallied what platoons were around him into some sort of order.

'Captain...'

'Mannheim,' the officer supplied.

'Captain Mannheim, what happened here? What is preying on your men?' asked Dak'ir. The rain was pounding heavily now, and *tinked* rapidly off his battle-plate. Explosions boomed all around them.

'I never saw it, my lord,' Mannheim admitted, wincing as a flare of incendiary came close, 'only Phalanx troopers disappearing from sight. At first, I thought enemy commandoes, but our bio-scanners were blank. The only heat signatures came from our own men.'

Malfunctioning equipment was a possibility, but it still cast doubt on Tsu'gan's infiltrators theory.

Dak'ir turned to Emek, who carried the squad's auspex. The Salamander shook his head. Nothing had come from the rebel positions behind the shield, either.

'Could they have already been out here? Masked their heat traces?' asked Ba'ken on a closed channel.

Mannheim was distracted by his vox-officer. Making a rapid apology, he turned his back and pressed the receiver cup to his ear, straining to hear against the rain and thunder.

'Not possible,' replied Dak'ir. 'We would have seen them.'

'Then what?'

Dak'ir shook his head, as the rain came on in swathes.

'My lord...' It was Mannheim again. 'I've lost contact with Lieutenant Bahnhoff. We were coordinating a tactical consolidation of troops to launch a fresh assault. Strength in numbers.'

It was a rarefied concept on Nocturne, where self-reliance and isolationism were the main tenets.

'Where?' asked Dak'ir.

Mannheim pointed ahead. 'The lieutenant was part of our vanguard, occupying a more advanced position. His men had already reached the assault line when we were attacked.'

Explosions rippled in the distance where the captain gestured with a quavering finger. These were brave men, but their resolve was nearing its limit. Loth, and his blood-minded draconianism, had almost pushed them over the edge.

It was hard to imagine much surviving in that barrage, and with whatever was abroad in the killing field to contend with too...

'If Lieutenant Bahnhoff lives, we will extract him and his men,' Dak'ir promised. He abandoned thoughts of a counter-attack almost immediately. The Phalanx were in disarray. Retreat was the only sensible option that preserved a later opportunity to attack. Though it went against his Promethean code, the very ideals of endurance and tenacity the Salamanders prided themselves on, Dak'ir had no choice but to admit it.

'Fall back with your men, captain. Get as many as you can to the bastion. Inform any other officers you can raise that the Imperial forces are in full retreat.'

Captain Mannheim motioned to protest.

'Full retreat, captain,' Dak'ir asserted. 'No victory was ever won with foolish sacrifice,' he added, quoting one of Zen'de's Tenets of Pragmatism.

The Phalanx officer saluted, and started pulling his men back. Orders were already being barked down the vox to any other coherent platoons in the army.

'We don't know what is out there, Dak'ir,' Ba'ken warned as they started running in Bahnhoff's direction. Though distant, silhouettes of the lieutenant's forces were visible. Worryingly, their las-fire spat in frantic bursts.

'Then we prepare for anything,' the sergeant replied grimly and forged on into the churned earth.

Bahnhoff's men had formed a defensive perimeter, their backs facing one another with the lieutenant himself at the centre, shouting orders. He positively sagged with relief upon sighting the Emperor's Angels coming to their aid.

The Salamanders were only a few metres away when something flickered into being nearby the circle of lasguns and one of the men simply vanished. One moment he was there, and the next... gone.

Panic flared and the order Bahnhoff had gallantly established threatened to break down. Troopers had their eyes on flight and not battle against apparitions they could barely see, let alone shoot or kill.

A second trooper followed the first, another white flicker signalling his death. This time Dak'ir saw the human's fate. It was as if the earth had opened up and swallowed him whole. Except the trooper hadn't fallen or been sucked into a bog, he'd been *dragged*. Pearlescent hands, with thin fingers like talons, had seized the poor bastard by the ankles and pulled him under.

Despite Bahnhoff's efforts his platoon's resolve shattered and they fled. Several more perished as they ran, sharing the same grisly fate as the others, dragged down in an eye-blink. The lieutenant ran with them, trying to turn the rout into an ordered retreat, but failing.

Emboldened by the troopers' fear, the things that were preying on the Phalanx manifested and the Salamanders saw them clearly for the first time.

'Are they daemons?' spat Emek, levelling his bolter.

They looked more like ragged corpses, swathed in rotting surplices and robes, the tattered fabric flapping like the tendrils of some incorporeal squid. Their eyes were hollow and black, and they were bone-thin with the essence of clergy about them. Priests they may once have been; now they were devils.

'Let us see if they can burn,' snarled Ba'ken, unleashing a gout of promethium from his heavy flamer. The spectres dissipated against the glare of liquid fire coursing over them, as Ba'ken set the killing fields ablaze, but returned almost as soon as the fires had died down, utterly unscathed.

He was about to douse them again when they evaporated like mist before his eyes.

An uncertain second or two passed, before the hulking Fire-born turned to his sergeant and shrugged.

'I've fought tougher foes–' he began, before crying out as his booted feet sank beneath the earth.

'Name of Vulkan!' Emek swore, scarcely believing his eyes.

'Hold him!' bellowed Dak'ir, seeing white talons snaring Ba'ken's feet and ankles. Brothers Romulus and G'heb sprang to their fellow Salamander's aid, each hooking their arms under Ba'ken's. In moments, they were straining against the strength of the spectres.

'Let me go, you'll tear me in half,' roared Ba'ken, part anger, part pain.

'Hang on, brother,' Dak'ir told him. He was about to call for reinforcements, noting Pyriel's contact rune on his tac-display, when an apparition materialised in front of him. It was an old preacher, his grey face lined with age and malice, a belligerent light illuminating the sockets of his eyes. His mouth formed words Dak'ir could not discern and he raised an accusing finger.

'Release him, hell-spawn!' Dak'ir lashed out with his chainsword, but the preacher blinked out of existence and the blade passed on harmlessly to embed itself in the soft earth behind him. Dak'ir raised his plasma pistol to shoot when a terrible, numbing cold filled his body. Icy fire surged through him as his blood was chilled by something old and vengeful. It stole away the breath from his lungs and made them burn, as if he had plunged naked beneath the surface of an arctic river. It took Dak'ir a few moments to realise the crooked fingers of the preacher were penetrating his battle-plate. Worming beyond the aegis of ceramite, making a mockery of his power armour's normally staunch defences, the grey preacher's talons sought vital organs in their quest for vengeance.

Trying to cry out, Dak'ir found his larynx frozen, his tongue made leaden by the spectral assault. In his mind his intoned words of Promethean lore kept him from slipping into utter darkness.

Vulkan's fire beats in my breast. With it I shall smite the foes of the Emperor.

A heavy pressure hammered at his thunderous hearts, pressing, pressing...

Dak'ir's senses were ablaze and the smell of dank and old wood permeated through his battle-helm.

Then a bright flame engulfed him and the pressure eased. Cold withered, melted away by soothing heat, and as his darkening vision faded Dak'ir saw Pyriel standing amidst a pillar of fire. At the periphery, Ba'ken was being dragged free of the earth that had

claimed him. Someone else was lifting Dak'ir. He
felt strong hands hooking under his arms and
pulling him. It was only then as his body became
weightless and light that he realised he must've
fallen. Semi-conscious, Dak'ir was aware of a fading
voice addressing him.

'Dragging your carcass out of the fire again,
Ignean…'

Then the darkness claimed him.

THE STRATEGIUM WAS actually an old refectory inside
the bastion compound that smelled strongly of
tabac and stale sweat. A sturdy-looking cantina table
had been commandeered to act as a tacticarium, and
was strewn with oiled maps, geographical charts and
data-slates. The vaulted ceiling leaked, and drips of
water were constantly being wiped from the various
scrolls and picts layering the table by aides and officers alike. Buzzing around the moderately sized
room's edges were Departmento Munitorum clerks
and logisticians, counting up men and materiel with
their styluses and exchanging dark glances with one
another when they thought the Guard weren't looking.

It was no secret that they'd lost a lot of troops in
the last sortie to bring down the void shield. To compound matters, ammunition for the larger guns was
running dangerously low, to 'campaign-unviable'
levels. Almost an hour had passed since the disas-
trous assault, and the Imperial forces were no closer
to forging a battle-plan.

Librarian Pyriel surveyed the tactical data before him and saw nothing new, no insightful strategy to alleviate the graveness of their situation. At least the spectres had given up pursuit when they'd entered the grounds of Mercy Rock, though it had taken a great deal of the Epistolary's psychic prowess to fend them off and make retreat possible.

'What were they, brother?' said Tsu'gan in a low voice, trying not to alert the Guard officers and quartermaster who had joined them. Some things – Tsu'gan knew – it was best that humans stayed ignorant of. They could be weak-minded, all too susceptible to fear. Protecting humanity meant more than bolter and blade; it meant shielding them from the horrifying truths of the galaxy too, lest they be broken by them.

'I am uncertain.' Pyriel cast his gaze upwards, where his witch-sight turned timber and rockcrete as thin as gossamer, penetrating the material to soar into the shadow night where the firmament was drenched blood red. 'But I believe the warp storm and the spectres are connected.'

'Slaves of Chaos?' The word left a bitter taste, and Tsu'gan spat it out.

'Lost and damned, perhaps,' the Librarian mused. 'Not vassals of the Ruinous Powers, though. I think they are… *warp echoes*, souls trapped between the empyrean and the mortal world. The red storm has thinned the veil of reality. I can *feel* the echoes pushing through. Only, I don't know why. But as long as the storm persists, as long as Hell Night continues, they will be out there.'

Only a few metres away, oblivious to the Salamanders, the Guard officers were having a war council of their own.

'The simple matter is, we cannot afford a protracted siege,' stated Captain Mannheim. Since Tench's execution and the commissar's incapacitation, Mannheim was the highest ranking officer in the Phalanx. His sleeves were rolled up and he'd left his cap on the tacticarium table, summiting the charts.

'We have perhaps enough munitions for one more sustained assault on the void shield.' The quartermaster was surveying his materiel logs, a Departmento Munitorum aide feeding him dataslates with fresh information that he mentally recorded and handed back as he spoke. 'After that, there is nothing we possess here that can crack it.'

Another officer, a second lieutenant, spoke up. His jacket front was unbuttoned and an ugly dark sweat stain created a dagger-shaped patch down his shirt.

'Even if we did, what hope is there whilst those things haunt the darkness?'

A patched-up corporal, his left eye bandaged, blotched crimson under the medical gauze, stepped forward.

'I am not leading my platoon out there to be butchered again. The secessionists consort with daemons. We have no defence against it.'

Fear, Tsu'gan sneered. Yes, humans were too weak for some truths.

The second lieutenant turned, scowling, to regard the Salamanders who dwelt in the shadows at the back of the room.

'And what of the Emperor's Angels? Were you not sent to deliver us and help end the siege? Are these foes, the spectres in the darkness, not allied to our faceless enemies at Aphium? We cannot break the city, if you cannot rid us of the daemons in our midst.'

Hot anger flared in Tsu'gan's eyes, and the officer balked. The Salamander snarled with it, clenching a fist at the human's impudence.

Pyriel's warning glance made his brother stand down.

'They are not daemons,' Pyriel asserted, 'but warp echoes. A resonance of the past that clings to our present.'

'Daemons, echoes, what difference does it make?' asked Mannheim. 'We are being slaughtered all the same, and with no way to retaliate. Even if we could banish these... *echoes*,' he corrected, 'we cannot take on them *and* the void shield. It's simple numbers, my lord. We are fighting a war of attrition which our depleted force cannot win.'

Tsu'gan stepped forward, unable to abstain from comment any longer.

'You are servants of the Emperor!' he reminded Mannheim fiercely. 'And you will do your part, hopeless or not, for the glory of Him on Earth.'

A few of the officers made the sign of the aquila, but Mannheim was not to be cowed.

'I'll step onto the sacrificial altar of war if that is what it takes, but I won't do it blindly. Would you lead your men to certain death, knowing it would achieve nothing?'

Tsu'gan scowled. Grunting an unintelligible diatribe, he turned on his heel and stalked from the strategium.

Pyriel raised his eyebrows.

'Forgive my brother,' he said to the council. 'Tsu'gan burns with a Nocturnean's fire. He becomes agitated if he cannot slay anything.'

'And that is the problem, isn't it?' returned Captain Mannheim. 'The reason why your brother-sergeant was so frustrated. Save for you, Librarian, your Astartes have no weapons against these echoes. For all their strength of arms, their skill and courage, they are powerless against them.'

The statement lingered, like a blade dangling precariously over the thread of all their hopes.

'Yes,' Pyriel admitted in little more than a whisper.

Silent disbelief filled the room for a time as the officers fought to comprehend the direness of their plight on Vaporis.

'There are no sanctioned psykers in the Phalanx,' said the second lieutenant at last. 'Can one individual, even an Astartes, turn the tide of this war?'

'He cannot!' chimed the corporeal. 'We need to signal for landers immediately. Request reinforcements,' he suggested.

'There will be none forthcoming,' chided Mannheim. 'Nor will the landers enter Vaporis space whilst Aphium is contested. We are alone in this.'

'My brother was right in one thing,' uttered Pyriel, his voice cutting through the rising clamour. 'Your duty is to the Emperor. Trust in us, and we will deliver victory,' he promised.

'But how, my lord?' asked Mannheim.

Pyriel's gaze was penetrating.

'Psychics are anathema to the warp echoes. With my power, I can protect your men by erecting a psy-shield. The spectres, as you call them, will not be able to pass through. If we can get close enough to the void shield, much closer than the original assault line, and apply sufficient pressure to breach it, my brothers will break through and shatter your enemies. Taking out the generatoria first, the shield will fail and with it the Aphium resistance once your long guns have pounded them.'

The second lieutenant scoffed, a little incredulous.

'My lord, I don't doubt the talents of the Astartes, nor your own skill, but can you really sustain a shield of sufficient magnitude and duration to make this plan work?'

The Librarian smiled thinly.

'I am well schooled by my Master Vel'cona. As an Epistolary-level Librarian, my abilities are prodigious, lieutenant,' he said without pride. 'I can do what must be done.'

Mannheim nodded, though a hint of fatalism tainted his resolve.

'Then you have my full support and the support of the Phalanx 135th,' he said. 'Tell me what you need, my lord, and it shall be yours.'

'Stout hearts and steely resolve is all I ask, captain. It is all the Emperor will ever ask of you.'

TSU'GAN CHECKED THE load of his combi-bolter, re-securing the promethium canister on the flamer element of the weapon.

'Seems pointless, when we cannot even kill our foes,' he growled.

The bellicose sergeant was joined by the rest of his brothers at the threshold to Mercy Rock, in the inner courtyard before the bastion's great gate.

Behind them, the Phalanx platoons were readying. In the vehicle yards, the Basilisks were churning into position on their tracks. Anticipation filled the air like an electric charge.

Only two Salamanders were missing, and one of those was hurrying to join them through the thronging Guardsmen from the makeshift medi-bay located in the bastion catacombs.

'How is he, brother?' Emek asked, racking the slide to his bolter.

'Unconscious still,' said Ba'ken. He'd ditched his heavy flamer and carried a bolter like most of his battle-brothers. Dak'ir had not recovered from the attack by the spectre and so, despite his protests, Ba'ken had been made de facto sergeant by Pyriel.

'I wish he were with us,' he muttered.

'We all do, brother,' said Pyriel. Detecting a mote of unease, he asked, 'Something on your mind, Ba'ken?'

The question hung in the air like an unfired bolt round, before the hulking trooper answered.

'I heard Brother-Sergeant Tsu'gan over the comm-feed. Can these things even be fought, brother? Or are we merely drawing them off for the Guard?'

'I saw the Ignean's blade pass straight through one,' Tsu'gan muttered. 'And yet others seized upon Ba'ken as solid and intractable as a docking claw.'

Emek looked up from his auspex.

'Before they attack, they corporealise; become flesh,' he said, 'Although it is flesh of iron with a grip as strong as a power fist.'

'I had noticed it too,' Pyriel replied. 'Very observant, brother.'

Emek nodded humbly, before the Librarian outlined his strategy.

'Our forces will be strung out across the killing field, four combat squads as before. I can stretch my psychic influence to encompass the entire Phalanx battle line but it will be a comparatively narrow cordon, and some of the spectres may get through. Adopt defensive tactics and wait for them to attack, then strike. But know the best we can hope for is to repel them. Only I possess the craft to banish the creatures into the warp and that won't be possible whilst I'm maintaining the psychic shield.'

'Nor then will you be able to fight, Brother-Librarian,' said Ba'ken.

Pyriel faced him, and there was an unspoken compact in his low voice. 'No, I'll be temporarily vulnerable.'

So you, brothers, will need to be my shield.

The severity of the mission weighed as heavy as the weather. Captain Mannheim had been correct when he'd spoken in the strategium: for all their strength of arms, their skill and courage, they *were* powerless against the spectres. Almost.

Pyriel addressed the group. 'Fire-born: check helm-displays for updated mission parameters and objectives.'

A series of 'affirmatives' greeted the order.

'Switching to tac-sight,' adding Tsu'gan. A data stream of time-codes, distances and troop dispositions filled his left occulobe lens. He turned to Pyriel just as the great gates to Mercy Rock were opening. 'I hope you can do what you promised, Librarian, or we are all dead.'

Pyriel's gaze was fixed ahead as he donned his battle-helm.

'The warp storm is unpredictable, but it also augments my own powers,' he said. 'I can hold the shield for long enough.'

On a closed channel, he contacted Tsu'gan alone.

'My psychic dampener will be low,' he warned. 'If at any moment I am compromised, you know what must be done.'

If I am daemonically possessed by the warp, Tsu'gan read between the Librarian's words easily enough.

A sub-vocal 'compliance' flashed up as an icon on Pyriel's display.

'Brothers Emek, Iagon?' the Librarian asked with the gates now yawning wide. The gap in the wall brought lashing rain and the stench of death.

Emek and Iagon were interrogating overlapping scan patterns on their auspexes in search of warp activity in the shadows of the killing field.

'Negative, brother,' Emek replied. Iagon nodded in agreement.

The way, for now at least, was clear.

Despite the rain, a curious stillness persisted in the darkness of Hell Night. It was red and angry. And it was waiting for them. Pyriel was drawn again to the patch of wilderness, far off in the distance.

Just beyond my reach...

'Into the fires of battle...' he intoned, and led the Salamanders out.

DAK'IR AWOKE, STARTLED and awash with cold sweat. He was acutely aware of his beating hearts and a dense throbbing in his skull. Disorientating visions were fading from his subconscious mind... An ashen world, of tombs and mausoleums lining a long, bone-grey road... The redolence of burning flesh and grave dust... Half-remembered screams of a brother in pain...

...Becoming one with the screams of many, across a dark and muddied field... The touch of rain, cold against his skin... and a bell tolling... 'We are here...' 'We are here...'

The first was an old dream. He had seen it many times. But now new impressions had joined it, and Dak'ir knew they came from Vaporis. He tried to hold onto them, the visions and the sense memories, but it was like clutching smoke.

With the thinning of the unreal, the real became solid and Dak'ir realised he was flat on his back. A wire mattress with coarse sheets supported him. The cot groaned as he tried to move – so did Dak'ir when the daggers of pain pierced his body. He grimaced, and sank back down, piecing together the immediate past. The attack by the spectral preacher came back to him. A remembered chill made him shiver.

'You're pretty well banged up,' said a voice from the shadows. The sudden sound revealed just how quiet it was – the dull reply of heavy artillery was but a faint thudding in the walls. 'I wouldn't move so quickly,' the voice advised.

'Who are you?' rasped Dak'ir, the dryness in his throat a surprise at first.

A high-pitched squeal grated against the Salamander's skull as a Phalanx officer sitting in a wheelchair rolled into view.

'Bahnhoff, my lord,' he said. 'You and your Astartes tried to save my men in the killing field, and I'm grateful to you for that.'

'It's my duty,' Dak'ir replied, still groggy. He managed to sit up, despite the horrendous pain of his injuries and the numbness that lingered well after the preacher had relinquished his deathly grip. Dak'ir was gasping for breath for a time.

'*Lieutenant* Bahnhoff?' he said, remembering; a look of incredulity on his face when he saw the wheelchair.

'Artillery blast got me,' the officer supplied. 'Platoon dragged me the rest of the way. Took *me* off the frontline too, though.'

Dak'ir felt a pang of sorrow for the lieutenant when he saw the shattered pride in his eyes.

'Am I alone? Have my brothers gone to battle without me?' Dak'ir asked.

'They said you were too badly injured. Told us to watch over you until they returned.'

'My armour...' Dak'ir was naked from the waist up. Even his torso bodyglove had been removed. As he made to swing himself over the edge of the cot, enduring still further agonies, he saw that his battle-plate's cuirass was lying reverently in one corner of the room. His bodyglove was with it, cut up where his brothers had needed to part it to treat his wounds. Dak'ir ran his finger over them. In the glow of a single lume-lamp they looked like dark bruises in the shape of fingerprint impressions.

'Here... I found these in a storage room nearby.' Bahnhoff tossed Dak'ir a bundle of something he'd been carrying on his lap.

The Salamander caught it, movement still painful but getting easier, and saw they were robes.

'They're loose, so should fit your frame,' Bahnhoff explained.

Dak'ir eyed the lieutenant, but shrugged on the robes nonetheless.

'Help me off this cot,' he said.

Together, they got Dak'ir off the bed and onto his feet. He wobbled at first, but quickly found his balance, before surveying his surroundings.

They were in a small room, like a cell. The walls were bare stone. Dust collected in the corners and hung in the air, giving it an eerie quality.

'What is this place?'

Bahnhoff wheeled backwards as Dak'ir staggered a few steps from the cot.

'Mercy Rock's catacombs. We use it as a medi-bay,' the lieutenant's face darkened, 'and morgue.'

'Apt,' Dak'ir replied with grim humour.

A strange atmosphere permeated this place. Dak'ir felt it as he brushed the walls with his fingertips, as he drank in the cloudy air.

We are here…

The words came back to him like a keening. They were beckoning him. He turned to Bahnhoff, eyes narrowed.

'What is that?'

'What is *what*, my lord?'

A faint scratching was audible in the sepulchral silence, as a quill makes upon parchment. Bahnhoff's eyes widened as he heard it too.

'All the Munitorum clerks are up in the strategium…'

'It's coming from beneath us,' said Dak'ir. He was already making for the door. Wincing with every step, he betrayed his discomfort, but gritted his teeth as he went to follow the scratching sound.

'Are there lower levels?' he asked Bahnhoff, as they moved through a shadowy corridor.

'Doesn't get any deeper than the catacombs, my lord.'

Dak'ir was moving more quickly now, and Bahnhoff was wheeling hard to keep up.

The scratching was getting louder, and when they reached the end of the corridor the way ahead was blocked by a timber barricade.

'Structurally unsafe according to the engineers,' said Bahnhoff.

'It's old...' Dak'ir replied, noting the rotten wood and the gossamer webs wreathing it like a veil. He gripped one of the planks and tore it off easily. Compelled by some unknown force, Dak'ir ripped the barricade apart until they were faced by a stone stairway. It led into a darkened void. The reek of decay and stagnation was strong.

'Are we going down there?' asked Bahnhoff, a slight tremor in his voice.

'Wait for me, here,' Dak'ir told him and started down the steps.

'STAY WITHIN THE cordon!' bellowed Tsu'gan, as another one of Captain Mannheim's men was lost to the earth.

An invisible barrier stretched the length of the killing ground that only flared incandescently into existence when one of the spectres struck it and recoiled. Like a lightning spark, the flash was born and died quickly, casting the scene starkly in its ephemeral life. Gunnery teams slogged hard to keep pace and infantry tramped hurriedly alongside them in long thin files, adopting firing lines once they'd reached the two hundred metre marker. Las-bursts erupted from the Phalanx ranks in a storm. Barking solid shot from heavy bolters and autocannon added to the sustained salvo. So close to the void shield the energy impact returns were incandescently bright and despite the darkness made several troopers don photoflash goggles. For some, it was just as well that their vision was impeded for shadows lurked beyond Librarian Pyriel's psychic aegis and not everyone was immune to them.

The barrier was narrow, just as Pyriel had warned, and as the Phalanx had tried to keep pace with the Salamanders on the way to the advanced assault line, some stepped out of it. A muted cry and then they were no longer seen or heard from again. By the time the firing line was erected, some several dozen troopers were missing. The Salamanders, as of yet, had not succumbed.

Tsu'gan saw the flickering white forms of the warp echoes through the Librarian's psychic shield. They lingered, angry and frustrated, ever probing to test the limits of Pyriel's strength. Though he couldn't see his face through his battle-helm, Tsu'gan knew by the Epistolary's juddering movements that he was feeling the strain. He was a vessel now, for the near-unfettered power of the warp. Like a sluice gate let free, the energy coursed through him as Pyriel fought hard to channel it into the shield. One slip and he would be lost. Then Tsu'gan would need to act quickly, slaying him before Pyriel's flesh was obtained by another, heralding the death of them all, Salamanders or no.

One of the creatures breached the barrier wall, corporealising to do it, and Tsu'gan lashed out with his fist.

It was like striking adamantium, and he felt the shock of the blow all the way up his arm and into his shoulder, but did enough to force the creature back. It flashed briefly out of existence, but returned quickly, a snarl upon its eldritch features.

'Hard as iron you said,' Tsu'gan roared into the comm-feed as the weapons fire intensified.

Overhead the Earthshaker shells were finding their marks and the void shield rippled near its summit.

Emek battered another of the spectres back beyond the psychic cordon, the exertion needed to do it evident in his body language.

'Perhaps too conservative,' he admitted.

'A tad, brother,' came Tsu'gan's bitter rejoinder. 'Iagon,' he relayed through his battle-helm, 'what are the readings for the shield?'

'Weakening, my lord,' was Iagon's sibilant reply, 'But still insufficient for a break.'

Tsu'gan scowled.

'Ba'ken…'

'We must advance,' the acting sergeant answered. 'Fifty metres, and apply greater pressure to the shield.'

At a hundred and fifty metres away, the danger from energy flares cast by void impacts and friendly fire casualties from the Earthshakers was greatly increased, but then the Salamanders had little choice. Soon the bombardment from the Basilisks would end when they ran out of shells. The void shield had to be down before then.

'Brother-Librarian,' Tsu'gan began, 'another fifty metres?'

After a few moments, Pyriel nodded weakly and started to move forwards.

Tsu'gan turned his attention to the Phalanx.

'Captain Mannheim, we are advancing. Another fifty metres.'

The Phalanx officer gave a clipped affirmative before continuing to galvanise his men and reminding them of their duty to the Emperor.

Despite himself, the Salamander found he admired the captain for that.

The bells tolled on as the Imperial forces resumed their march.

THE STAIRS WERE shallow and several times Dak'ir almost lost his footing, only narrowly avoiding a plunge into uncertain darkness by bracing himself against the flanking walls.

Near the bottom of the stairwell, he was guided by a faint smudge of flickering light. Its warm, orange glow suggested candles or a fire. There was another room down here and this was where the scratching sound emanated from.

Cursing himself for leaving his weapons in the cell above, Dak'ir stepped cautiously through a narrow portal that forced him to duck to get through and into a small, dusty chamber.

Beyond the room's threshold he saw bookcases stuffed with numerous scrolls, tomes and other arcana. Religious relics were packed in half-open crates, stamped with the Imperial seal. Others, deific statues, Ecclesiarchal sigils and shrines were cluttered around the chamber's periphery. And there, in the centre, scribing with ink and quill at a low table, was an old, robed clerk.

The scrivener looked up from his labours, blinking with eye strain as he regarded the giant, onyx-skinned warrior in his midst.

'Greetings, soldier,' he offered politely.

Dak'ir nodded, uncertain of what to make of his surroundings. A prickling sensation ran through his body but then faded as he stepped into the corona of light cast by the scrivener's solitary candle.

'Are you Munitorum?' asked Dak'ir. 'What are you doing so far from the strategium?' Dak'ir continued to survey the room as he stepped closer. It was caked in dust and the grime of ages, more a forgotten storeroom than an office for a Departmento clerk.

The scrivener laughed; a thin, rasping sort of a sound that put Dak'ir a little on edge.

'Here,' said the old man as he backed away from his works. 'See what keeps me in this room.'

Dak'ir came to the table at the scrivener's beckoning, strangely compelled by the old man's manner, and looked down at his work.

Hallowed Heath – a testament of its final days, he read.

'Mercy Rock was not always a fortress,' explained the scrivener behind him. 'Nor was it always alone.'

The hand that had authored the parchment scroll in front of Dak'ir was scratchy and loose but he was able to read it.

'It says here that Mercy Rock was once a basilica, a temple devoted to the worship of the Imperial Creed.'

'Read on, my lord…' the scrivener goaded.

Dak'ir did as asked.

'*"…and Hallowed Heath was its twin. Two bastions of light, shining like beacons against the old faiths, bringing enlightenment and understanding to Vaporis,"*' he related directly from the text. '*"In the shadow of Aphium, but a nascent township with lofty ambitions, did these pinnacles of faith reside. Equal were they in their fervour and dedication, but not in fortification–"*' Dak'ir looked around at the old scrivener who glared at the Salamander intently.

'I thought you said they were not fortresses?'

The scrivener nodded, urging Dak'ir to continue his studies.

'*"–One was built upon a solid promontory of rock, hence its given appellation; the other upon clay. It was during the Unending Deluge of 966.M40 when the rains of Vaporis continued for sixty-six days, the heaviest they had ever been in longest memory, that Hallowed Heath sank down beneath a quagmire of earth, taking its five hundred and forty-six patrons and priests with it. For three harrowing days and nights the basilica sank, stone by stone, beneath the earth, its inhabitants stranded within its walls that had become as their tomb. And for three nights, they tolled the bells in the highest towers of*

Hallowed Heath, saying, "We are here!", "We are here!"
but none came to their aid."'

Dak'ir paused as a horrible understanding started
to crawl up his spine. Needing to know more, oblivious now to the scrivener, he continued.

'"Aphium was the worst. The township and all its peoples
did not venture into the growing mire for fear of their own
lives, did not even try to save the stricken people. They shut
their ears to the bells and shut their doors, waiting for a ces-
sation to the rains. And all the while, the basilica sank,
metre by metre, hour by hour, until the highest towers were
consumed beneath the earth, all of its inhabitants buried
alive with them, and the bells finally silenced."'

Dak'ir turned to regard the old scrivener.

'The spectres in the killing field,' he said, 'they are
the warp echoes of the preachers and their patrons.'

'They are driven by hate, hate for the Aphiums
who closed their ears and let them die, just as I am
driven by guilt.'

Guilt?

Dak'ir was about to question it when the scrivener
interrupted.

'You're near the end, Hazon, read on.'

Dak'ir was compelled to turn back, as if entranced.

'"This testament is the sole evidence of this terrible
deed – nay; it is my confession of complicity in it. Safe
was I in Mercy Rock, sat idle whilst others suffered and
died. It cannot stand. This I leave as small recompense,
so that others might know of what transpired. My life
shall be forfeit just as theirs were, too."'

There it ended, and only then did Dak'ir acknowledge that the old man had used his first name. He

whirled around, about to demand answers... but he was too late.

The scrivener was gone.

THE EARTHSHAKER BARRAGE stopped abruptly like a thumping heart in sudden cardiac arrest. Its absence was a silent death knell to the Phalanx and their Astartes allies.

'It's done,' snarled Tsu'gan, when the Imperial shelling ended. 'We break through now or face the end. Iagon?'

'Still holding, my lord.'

They were but a hundred metres from the void shield now, having pressed up in one final effort to overload it. Without the heavy artillery backing them up, it seemed an impossible task. All the time, more and more Phalanx troopers were lost to breaches in the psychic shield, dragged into dank oblivion by ethereal hands.

'I feel... *something*...' said Pyriel, struggling to speak, 'Something in the void shield... Just beyond my reach...'

Despite his colossal efforts, the Librarian was weakening. The psychic barrier was losing its integrity and with it any protection against the warp echoes baying at its borders.

'Stand fast!' yelled Mannheim. 'Hold the line and press for glory, men of the Phalanx!'

Through sheer grit and determination, the Guardsmen held. Even though their fellow troopers were being swallowed by the earth, they held.

Tsu'gan could not help but feel admiration again for their courage. Like a crazed dervish, he raced down the line raining blows upon the intruding spectres, his shoulders burning with the effort.

'Salamanders! We are about to be breached,' he cried. 'Protect the Phalanx. Protect your brothers-in-arms with your lives!'

'Hail Vulkan and the glory of Prometheus!' Ba'ken chimed. 'Let Him on Earth witness your courage, men of the Phalanx.'

The effect of the sergeants' words was galvanising. Coupled with Mannheim's own stirring rally, the men became intractable in the face of almost certain death.

Tsu'gan heard a deep cry of pain to his left and saw Lazarus fall, impaled as Dak'ir had been by eldritch fingers.

'Brother!'

S'tang and Nor'gan went to his aid as Honorious covered their retreat with his flamer.

'Hold, Fire-born, hold!' Tsu'gan bellowed. 'Give them nothing!'

Tenacious to the end, the Salamanders would fight until their final breaths, and none so fiercely as Tsu'gan.

The battle-hardened sergeant was ready to make his final pledges to his primarch and his Emperor when the comm-feed crackled to life in his ear.

'You may have cheated death, Ignean,' snapped Tsu'gan when he realised who it was. 'But then survival over glory was always your–'

'Shut up, Zek, and raise Pyriel right now,' Dak'ir demanded, using the other Salamander's first name and mustering as much animus as he could.

'Our brother needs to marshal all of his concentration, Ignean,' Tsu'gan snapped again. 'He can ill afford distractions from you.'

'Do it, or it will not matter how distracted he becomes!'

Tsu'gan snarled audibly but obeyed, something in Dak'ir's tone making him realise it was important.

'Brother-Librarian,' he barked down the comm-feed. 'Our absent brother demands to speak with you.'

Pyriel nodded labouredly, his hands aloft as he struggled to maintain the barrier.

'Speak…' the Librarian could scarcely rasp.

'Do you remember what you felt before the first assault?' Dak'ir asked quickly. 'You said there was something about the shield, an anomaly in its energy signature. It is psychically enhanced, brother, to keep the warp echoes *out*.'

Through the furious barrage a slim crack was forming in the void shield's integrity, invisible to mortal eyes but plain as frozen lightning to the Librarian's witch-sight. And through it, Pyriel discerned a psychic undercurrent straining to maintain a barrier of its own. With Dak'ir's revelation came understanding and then purpose.

'They want vengeance against Aphium,' said Pyriel, beginning to refocus his psychic energy and remould it into a sharp blade of his own anger.

'For the complicity in their deaths over a thousand years ago,' Dak'ir concluded.

'I know what to do, brother,' Pyriel uttered simply, his voice drenched with psychic resonance as he let slip the last of the tethers from his psychic hood, the crystal matrix dampener that protected him psychically, and laid himself open to the warp.

'In Vulkan's name,' Dak'ir intoned before the link was overwhelmed with psychic static and died.

'Brother Tsu'gan…' Pyriel's voice was deep and impossibly loud against the battle din. A tsunami of raw psychic power was coursing through him, encasing the Librarian in a vibrant, fiery aura. '…I am about to relinquish the barrier…'

Tsu'gan had no time to answer. The psychic barrier fell and the warp echoes swept in. Thunder split the heavens and red lightning tore across boiling clouds as the warp storm reached its zenith.

Already, the breach Pyriel had psychically perceived was closing.

'Maintain positions!' roared Mannheim, as his men were being taken. 'Keep firing!'

Secessionist fire, freed up from mitigating the Imperial artillery barrage, was levelled at the Phalanx. Mannheim took a lucky las-round in the throat and was silenced.

Tsu'gan watched the officer fall just as Pyriel burst into violent conflagration. Running over to Mannheim, he scooped the fallen captain up into his arms, and watched as a bolt of flame lashed out from Pyriel's refulgent form. It surged through the void shield, past the unseen breach, reaching out for the minds of the Librarian's enemies…

Deep in Aphium rebel territory, in an armoured bunker sunk partially beneath the earth, a cadre of psykers sat in a circle, their consciousnesses locked, their will combined to throw a veil across the void shield that kept out the deeds of their ancestors. It was only around Hell Night when the blood storm wracked the heavens and brought about an awakening for vengeance, a desire for retribution, that their skills were needed.

One by one they screamed, an orange fire unseen by mortal eyes ravaging them with its scorching tendrils. Flesh melted, eyes ran like wax under a hot lamp, and one by one the psyker cadre burned. The heat inside the bunker was intense, though the temperature gauge suggested a cool night, and within seconds the psykers were reduced to ash and the defence of Aphium with it.

Upon the killing field, Tsu'gan detected a change in the air. The oppressive weight that had dogged them since mustering out for a second time on Hell Night had lifted, like leaden chains being dragged away by unseen hands.

Like mist before the rays of a hot sun, the warp echoes receded into nothing. Silence drifted over the killing field, as all of the guns stopped. The void shield flickered and died a moment later, the absence of its droning hum replaced by screaming from within the city of Aphium.

'*In Vulkan's name...*' Tsu'gan breathed, unable to believe what was unfolding before his eyes. He didn't need to see it to know the spectres had turned on the rebels of Aphium and were systematically slaying each and every one.

It wasn't over. Not yet. Pyriel blazed like an incendiary about to explode. The Librarian's body was spasming uncontrollably as he fought to marshal the forces he'd unleashed. Raging psychic flame coursed through him. As if taking hold of an accelerant, it burned mercilessly. Several troopers were consumed by it, the mind-fire becoming real. Men collapsed in the heat, their bodies rendered to ash.

'Pyriel!' cried Tsu'gan. Cradling Captain Mannheim in his arms, he raised his bolter one-handed.

...you know what you must do.

He fired into Pyriel's back, an expert shot that punctured the Librarian's lung but wasn't fatal. Pyriel bucked against the blow, the flames around him dwindling, and sagged to his knees. Then he fell onto his side, unconscious, and the conflagration was over.

'Tsu'gan. Tsu'gan!'

It took Tsu'gan a few seconds to realise he was being hailed. A curious stillness had settled over the killing field. Above them the red sky was fading as the warp storm passed, and the rain had lessened. On the horizon, another grey day was dawning.

'Dak'ir...'

Stunned, he forgot to use his derogatory sobriquet for the other sergeant.

'What happened, Zek? Is it over?'

Mannheim was dead. Tsu'gan realised it as the officer went limp in his arms. He had not faltered, even at the end, and had delivered his men to victory and glory. Tsu'gan's bolter was still hot from shooting Pyriel. He used it carefully to burn an honour marking in Captain Mannheim's flesh. It was shaped like the head of a firedrake.

'It's over,' he replied and cut the link.

A faded sun had broken through the gathering cloud. Errant rays lanced downwards, casting their glow upon a patch of distant earth far off in the wilderness. Tsu'gan didn't know what it meant, only that when he looked upon it his old anger lessened and a strange feeling, that was not to last in the days to come, spilled over him.

Rain fell. Day dawned anew. Hell Night was ended, but the feeling remained.

It was peace.

COVER OF DARKNESS

Mitchel Scanlon

IT WAS A night made for war by stealth. The night sky was moonless, with an opaque covering of clouds hiding the light of the stars. Cresting a ridge on his bike, Sergeant Kergis of the White Scars paused for a moment and scanned the arid landscape spread out before him. Ahead, the twisting maze of gullies and snaking furrows of the region known as Volcan's Cradle were bathed in Stygian blackness. To Kergis's mind, it seemed a favourable omen. Success in their mission was dependent on catching the enemy unawares. Tonight, the darkness would be their ally.

Turning his bike to follow the sinuous curve of the ridge slope as it descended toward the next gully, Kergis spared a glance at the rest of the eight-man squad behind him. His men travelled in single file, the lights of their bikes turned off, their armour covered in a thick layer of dust courtesy of the terrain around them. Occasionally, there was the ominous clatter of falling stones as they dislodged a few small rocks in crossing the slope, but the White Scars negotiated these hazards with the smooth assurance born of a lifetime spent in the saddle.

Reaching the foot of the slope in safety, they pushed on with their journey, following the trail of the gully as it headed northward. Much of Volcan's Cradle was open plain: a vast dusty expanse of dried lava created by millions of years of volcanic activity. But the need for stealth had forced Kergis and his men to take a circuitous route to their target, hugging the zigzag contours of a series of ravines and gullies in the western part of the region, cut by the effect of rain erosion on the yielding surface of the lava plain. It had made their path through the Cradle longer and more difficult, but given the nature of their mission it was vital they stayed clear of enemy patrols.

'I am reading movement,' Kergis heard the voice of Arik, a fellow White Scar, on his helmet-vox as they sped through the gully. 'Several vehicles from the size of the contact. The auspex puts them at six kilometres away, moving towards us on a bearing twelve degrees north-north-west.'

'An interception force?' Kergis voxed back.

'No,' Arik's voice was confident. 'Based on their bearing, I'd say it's a routine patrol. If we stay to our plotted course and maintain our speed, we will be long gone by the time they get here.'

'Good. We can't be more than a kilometre away from the geyser field by now. Take the lead, Arik. You will be our pathfinder. The rest of us will follow behind you.'

Throttling back his bike, Kergis allowed the other man to overtake him. Briefly pressing his right fist across his breast in a salute as he passed, Arik took up the sergeant's position at the head of the line of White Scars and veered eastward as he came to a fork in the gully. Kergis and the others followed suit.

The darkness would have been impenetrable to any normal man, but thanks to their enhanced eyesight and the autosenses of their armour the White Scars could navigate the desolate terrain of the Cradle with equal facility by day or night. The same sharpness of the senses alerted Kergis to the stink of sulphur long before the geyser fields became visible.

During the briefing that preceded the mission, a Techmarine named Goju had attempted to outline the unusual conditions which underpinned the geography of the Cradle. The planetary crust was thin here, he had explained, likening it to a frail wafer laid across a huge broiling sea of lava. In some places, the crust had cracked due to the enormous stresses upon it, creating a path to the surface for red-hot magma.

In the area the White Scars were headed for, the magma had heated the water stored underground in naturally formed aquifers, causing geysers and thermal springs to emerge in place of lava. Such phenomena were relatively common in the unstable volcanic landscape of the Cradle, but Kergis and his men would be travelling through the largest geyser field in the region, riding tens of kilometres through dangerous territory in the hope of keeping their presence hidden from the enemy.

Following Arik's lead, the squad of bikers emerged from the gully and sped on through the short distance of open plain separating them from the geyser field. Ahead, a strange and deadly landscape lay ready to greet them.

'Keep your helmets sealed and respiratus systems engaged,' Arik warned as they entered the geyser field. 'Leave at least five metres between you and the man in front. And stay on my track. The ground is fragile here. If it gives way beneath the weight of your bike, you'll be swimming in boiling water.'

According to the Imperial survey maps Kergis had inspected before making planetfall, it was known simply as Geyser Field Septimus. The prosaic title hid a sinister reality. The entire area was dotted with steaming vents and smoking craters. The colours were mostly concealed by the night, but Kergis knew the ground was covered in a thick multi-hued residue in startling shades of red, green and yellow, alongside vast white carpets of glittering salt crystals. The residue and the crystals were accumulated from the minerals leached from the rocks by the underground heat and brought to the surface as tiny particles over thousands of years every time one of the geysers erupted.

Kergis did not doubt the geyser field would be beautiful by daylight, but it was also treacherous. The vapours rising from the vents included deadly gases as well as scalding superheated steam, while the sluggish liquid bubbling in some of the craters was concentrated acid created by the same leached minerals responsible for the coloured residue. Enemy patrols tended to avoid the geyser field with good reason. By any standard, it was a lethal environment.

Carefully staying to the line of Arik's trail as it twisted between the smouldering vents, Kergis checked his auspex for any sign of the enemy patrol detected earlier. Seeing no trace of them, Kergis was pleased. The range of the auspex on his bike was limited, but even if the enemy were nearby there was little chance of his squad being detected while they were in the geyser field.

The throaty roar of the White Scars' engines was drowned out by the noises of the vents around them. Listening to the hiss of steam and the cackle of bubbling acid, Kergis was reminded of the sounds of breathing. It was as though they had intruded into the domain of a massive, slumbering beast, an illusion underlined by the occasional *whoosh* as one of the geysers erupted. The sound brought to mind the sea-leviathans that inhabited the oceans of Chogoris: gargantuan creatures that emerged periodically from the waves to breathe out through their blowholes, emitting great clouds of spray before returning once more to the deep.

Having never seen a body of open water until he was thirteen years of age and already on the path to becoming a White Scar, Kergis had always regarded the sea and its denizens with awe. He was Astartes, so he did not fear them. Still, they impressed him.

Inside Kergis's helmet, a warning sensor flashed an angry red to draw his attention to the rising levels of poisonous gases in the air outside, already far beyond human tolerance. He ignored it. The geyser field was a labyrinth of death, but the sergeant trusted Arik to guide them through it. Arik had always shown an unerring ability to find the correct trail through any terrain, no matter how difficult.

It was not an uncommon talent on their home world. Countless generations spent navigating the shifting pathways of the endless plains of Chogoris meant that some were born with a special aptitude for finding their way, whatever the circumstance. They were not psykers. It was simply that they took more notice of the subtle clues around them, whether in the landscape, the weather or the stars, relying on the patterns of past experience to guide them onto the best path to their destination.

In Arik's case he was aided by the fact his bike was equipped with a more powerful auspex unit than the others in the squad, but Kergis had no doubt he could have guided them through the geyser field without it. Even if Arik had never left Chogoris, never become Astartes, he would have been a pathfinder to his people, responsible for guiding his tribe to the watering holes for their herds and the best winter pastures.

As the White Scars moved deeper into the geyser field, the clouds of steam and poison grew thicker. Soon, visibility was reduced to a few metres. Still, they pushed onward, each warrior trusting to the man in front to lead him safely through the miasma.

It was no more than Kergis would have expected. The habit of mutual trust was deeply ingrained between his men. Their bonds of brotherhood were strong; bonds forged and tempered across a hundred battlefields. With it came a sense of debt, of obligation. Kergis did not doubt that any man in the squad would be willing to die for his brothers.

Certainly, it was part of the reason he had come to Volcan's Cradle.

'TEPHRA VII,' JURGA Khan had said to him, two days earlier. 'It has been an Imperial world for ten thousand years. Our great Primarch Jaghatai Khan, may his memory always be honoured, played a part in its liberation. But a year ago it was all undone. Chaos has seized this place, Kergis. Now, it falls to us to follow in the footsteps of our primarch. This planet will be liberated again. And the White Scars will be the spearhead, the first among the liberators.'

They were standing on the strategium deck of the strike cruiser *Warrior of the Plains*. A few minutes earlier Jurga Khan had concluded a briefing for the squad leaders under his command, indicating the roles they would be expected to play in the coming invasion. When the briefing was done, the Khan had dismissed everyone except Kergis. Even the Chapter serfs had been sent to perform duties elsewhere on the ship, ensuring the two men's privacy.

Courtesy of the strategium's display units, a shimmering translucent globe hovered in the air showing a hololithic representation of Tephra VII. Kergis noticed part of the planet's power grid had been highlighted, creating a network of fine golden lines that crisscrossed the northern hemisphere.

'We will make our first strike here,' Jurga Khan said, lifting an armoured finger to indicate a city. 'The planetary capital, Chaldis, is the main centre of the enemy's power. If we can defeat them here, in one assault, we will break the backbone of their resistance. But the city is protected by void shields. It will not be easy. We may face heavy losses.'

Kergis nodded. The invasion and re-conquest of Tephra VII was a major undertaking. The *Warrior of the Plains* was one of nearly thirty Imperial ships massing at the edge of the system. As the only Astartes taking part in the invasion, the White Scars could expect to bear the brunt of the fighting in the crucial opening stages when the enemy's defences were first breached.

'But there is a way we can lessen some of the price in blood,' his commander continued.

The Khan moved his finger to point to an area several thousand kilometres to the east of the capital. Responding to the movement, the hololithic globe turned to reveal a low-lying plain, surrounded by mountains to form a massive basin. Significantly, the golden lines of the power network all seemed to lead to the same region.

'The locals call this place Volcan's Cradle,' the Khan said. 'Goju will give you an in-depth briefing on the region and its conditions later, but you can take it for granted it is hard country. It's a desolate, volcanic wasteland. No one would ever go there, except for this...'

The Khan pressed his finger into the surface of the globe. The hololith shimmered and changed as the floating image zoomed in to a three-dimensional representation of a large manufactory complex, evidently based on the data from reconnaissance picts. Studying the image, Kergis realised the facility was situated on the slopes of a smouldering volcano.

'It is some kind of power generating facility?' he said, comparing the design to similar buildings he had seen on other worlds, even fought over, in his time as a White Scar.

'Geothermal,' Jurga Khan told him. 'You are looking at a power plant situated on the Ignis Mons, the largest active volcano in the Cradle region. Goju will explain the particulars to you, but it is my understanding they generate power by harnessing the heat of underground magma. Tephra VII is deficient in promethium and other fuels, so a number of such facilities were built in ancient times to provide for the planet's needs. The Ignis Mons complex supplies power to almost the entire western section of the northern hemisphere, including the void shields protecting the capital.'

'So, if this facility is destroyed, the shields go down?'

'Exactly. There are supposed to be backup power sources to supply the void shields in the event of an emergency. But the systems are old and it is believed the enemy have been lax in their maintenance. To add to its value as a target, the Mons complex also supplies power to the planet's sensor array network. If we destroy it, the enemy will be blind as well as shield-less.'

'But the enemy must also be aware of its value. The target will be well-defended?'

'It is,' Jurga Khan nodded. 'Including the forces manning a series of sentry points surrounding the area, the enemy can call upon at least two thousand warriors to defend the complex. Added to which, the main access ways into the facility are protected by multiple bunkers and other secure emplacements armed with autocannons and anti-tank weapons. The heart of the facility is situated deep underground, so orbital bombardment won't work. It would take a major assault to capture the Mons. And not only would that warn the enemy of our intentions, it would divert manpower away from the main assault on Chaldis.'

'But there is another way?' Kergis asked him. The Khan's briefing seemed to be headed in one direction and he could see its logical conclusion. 'A stealth assault by a small team, ideally to be inserted into the area under cover of darkness. It would be their task to destroy the complex, or at least sabotage it to deny its use to the enemy. Given the importance of the mission, and its risks, it is a task for Astartes rather than Imperial Guardsmen.'

'Very good,' Jurga Khan smiled, the expression highlighting the honour scars crosshatching his features. 'Perhaps you missed your calling with the Stormseers, Kergis. You seem to have read my mind.'

'It was simply that I could see your intention, my Khan. When you assigned tasks to the other sergeants during the briefing earlier, I was surprised when myself and my squad were left without duties. Then, you called me aside to this briefing out of earshot of the others. I have never known you do something without reason. It suggested you had a particular mission in mind for me and my men.'

'Not a psyker, then,' the Khan's smile deepened. 'Simply a man with the mind of a chess master, always able to think several moves ahead of his commander. I said you missed your calling as a Stormseer. Perhaps I was in error, and your true calling was as a savant.'

He raised a hand good-naturedly to stifle Kergis's protests.

'There is no shame in having a sharp mind, Kergis. The histories record that Jaghatai Khan, may he always be honoured, possessed one of the great military minds of his era. Too often we forget our primarch's example in this. We honour our warriors for feats of arms, but we forget it is a man's mind and the character of his heart which wins battles as much as the strength of his sinews. In this case, I chose you for this mission because you are well served in all three of those qualities.'

'My Khan's words honour me.' Kergis bowed in obeisance.

'No more than your character merits it.' The Khan's face became serious. 'Besides, there were other considerations. Before you joined this company, you served with Kor'sarro Khan during the Hunt for Voldorius. I know you fought side by side with the Raven Guard, and learned some of their tricks of stealth. I know you have passed some of these lessons on to the men in your squad. I hear you emphasise to them that the lightning attack is negated in value if the enemy knows which direction it will come from. Such skills may be important on Tephra.'

Raising his hand again, Jurga Khan banished the hololith with a gesture. As the shimmering image of the geothermal complex faded away, the Khan's expression grew darker. He lowered his hand to hover over the manual control of the hololithic generator.

'But there is something else, Kergis. Another reason I chose you for this mission. The same reason I decided to banish the others and hold this briefing in private. You will soon see I had good cause for secrecy.'

Jurga Khan's hand moved over the control system's keypad, inputting a coded sequence of numbers. In response to the code, the hololithic generators hummed to life once more and a new image began to form.

'The attack on Chaldis is scheduled to begin in a little over two days. It will be a dawn assault, meaning you and your men will be expected to infiltrate the complex the night before. But there are other considerations at work here beyond the re-conquest of this world. What I am going to show you is for your eyes alone. It is not to be shared with your squad. In time, when the matter is resolved, the need for such secrecy may pass. But for the present, it is better we keep this between ourselves.'

The new hololith coalesced, revealing a pict-image taken at a distance of an armoured figure standing on top of a plascrete bunker.

'A Naval Lightning adapted for long-range reconnaissance took a series of picts two days ago during a high-speed sweep over the Ignis Mons,' the Khan said. 'The images are grainy, but you can clearly see the commander of the enemy garrison as he oversees the disposition of his troops.'

At a gesture from the Khan's hand, a second pict appeared. It was taken from a slightly different angle, but it showed the same figure. Helpfully, the enemy commander had craned his head up to look skyward, presenting a clearer image of his face. Seeing it, Kergis felt a sick feeling in the pit of his stomach. He barely heard his Khan's next words.

'It is almost as though he knows the spy-ship is there and is looking at it. Impossible, of course. The Lightning was moving at too high an altitude for anyone on the ground to spot it. But you see the reason for secrecy? This is an event of dark moment, Kergis. The honour of our Chapter is at stake.'

Kergis nodded, his mind still reeling at the revelation of the identity of the garrison commander. Standing on top of the bunker was a figure in battered white power armour emblazoned with a lightning insignia. Kergis could hardly believe it, but he saw the face of an old comrade, a man he had believed dead.

He saw the face of a battle-brother, a White Scar.

A friend.

THE RENDEZVOUS POINT was situated seven kilometres from the target. Having successfully navigated though the geyser field courtesy of Arik's pathfinding skills, Kergis and his men reached the meeting place with fifteen minutes to spare. Seeking to stay out of sight, they hid their bikes in a low-lying gully that had once formed the riverbed of a long dead stream. While the rest of the squad stayed with their bikes, Kergis and his second-in-command Gurban climbed the gully's eastern wall on foot to check their surroundings.

'It seems quiet,' Gurban whispered, once he had scanned the area with a handheld auspex. 'I'm not reading any enemy patrols. But there's no sign of Balat and his men, either.'

Balat was a sergeant in the White Scars' 10th Company. When Kergis was told he would rendezvous with a squad of Scouts under Balat's command before making his approach on the target, he had been pleased. He and the Scout-sergeant were old comrades. Before Balat had transferred across to 10th Company, they had served together for several decades. Balat had been the sergeant of the squad Kergis had served in during his early days as a battle-brother. Kergis had always regarded the older man as something of a mentor.

'I would be more surprised if we did see them,' Kergis replied. He raised his hand in a thumb-sideways gesture to signal to the men in the gully that the area was clear but they should remain wary. Then, he turned back to Gurban.

'Keep your eyes sharp,' he told him. 'A broken undulating landscape like this one can play havoc with the auspex. It creates dead spots the sensors can't reach. A platoon could be hiding within fifty metres of us and we wouldn't know it.'

As though in proof of his words, the sound of a birdcall abruptly broke the silence. Kergis recognised it as the cawing of a razorhook, a sharp-beaked carrion eater native to the plains of Chogoris. Having been expecting the signal, Kergis had already removed his helmet. Decades ago, on a world called Quintus, a Raven Guard Space Marine named Melierax had taught him the vox-amplifiers in an Astartes helmet gave an unnatural timbre to attempts to imitate the sound of birds. An unknowing listener hearing the noise would be less likely to assume it was a genuine birdcall and ignore it.

Kergis responded to the razorhook's cawing by whistling three times in imitation of another native

Chogorian bird. In reply, the cawing stopped. After a second, he became aware of dim shapes moving through the darkness towards them. Kergis kept his hand on his bolt pistol, ready in case it was a trick, but as the figures came closer he recognised the face of his old sergeant, Balat.

'It is good to see you again,' he said, clasping Balat's hand once the Scouts had joined them in the gully. 'What is our situation?'

Before answering, Balat made a signal to his men. Silently, they deployed to take up sentry posts around the lip of the gully.

'The immediate area is clear,' Balat said, once the Scouts had moved into position. 'Enemy patrols don't like to come this close to the geyser field in case the wind blows the poison clouds towards them. Still, it is better to be careful.'

Satisfied his men had covered every approach to their location, Balat walked a little distance along the bottom of the gully with Kergis beside him until they were out of earshot of the others.

'I made planetfall with my squad forty-eight hours ago,' the Scout-sergeant said. 'In that time, the enemy have tripled their patrols. This entire region has become a hotbed of activity.'

'Do you think they detected your arrival?'

'Perhaps,' Balat shrugged. 'We were inserted by Thunderhawk, as you were. The pilots did their best to fly us in under the enemy's sensor network, but it is possible we were detected. But, if that is the case, the enemy don't appear to be actively searching for us. We have seen no flyers, nor any sign of auspex sweeps. Rather than being a direct response to our arrival, it seems more likely they have stepped up their patrols because they are expecting trouble.'

'It would make sense,' Kergis agreed. 'They must know an invasion is coming. They may even have detected our reconnaissance flights. And they would realise the power complex is a target. They have probably increased their patrols as a precaution.'

'Even so, it is strange they have not brought in flyers or auspex,' Balat said. 'Why take half-measures if they think the invasion is coming? They must know the landscape of the Cradle makes an attack by stealth a real possibility. You would think they would take every step they could to prevent it.'

Balat shook his head in frustration. He was old, even by Astartes standards. He had nearly four centuries behind him, the years etched as lines on his face as surely as the many honour scars he wore as mark of his deeds. Kergis had heard rumours that Balat had once respectfully declined a promotion to become Master of the Watch back on Chogoris. In its place, he had asked to remain a simple sergeant and transferred to the 10th Company so he could pass on his skills to new generations of White Scars. Having experienced Balat's tutorship himself, Kergis had no doubt the Chapter's Scouts would be better warriors for it.

'Still, we should not be surprised if we find it difficult to divine the enemy's plans,' Balat said. 'It was always the same in the battle with Chaos. Do you remember Cernis? We thought to catch Voldorius unawares there, but he was ready for us.'

'I remember,' Kergis nodded. Briefly, he thought of the battle in the polar wastes. He remembered the race across the ice fields and the monstrous enemy they had fought under the northern lights. His memories brought to mind other battles: he thought of Kavell and icy Zoran, of the underhives of Modanna and the guntowers of Quintus. He thought of his encounter with the Bloodtide. He had come far and survived much. With Balat as his mentor, he had learned lessons in every battle.

'It was always so,' the Scout-sergeant continued. 'Of all the enemies we face, Chaos is the most treacherous, its champions the most cunning.'

Abruptly, Balat fell quiet. Staring intently at Kergis, he grimaced.

'You are smiling. I have said something amusing?'

'Forgive me, arban,' Kergis said, using a traditional Chogorian word for sergeant. Strictly speaking its meaning translated simply as 'leader of ten men', but among the White Scars it had grown to mean much more. The word held no official standing, but it was used commonly when referring to a sergeant whose courage and wisdom were highly regarded. It was meant as a mark of honour, a term of great respect.

'I was reminded of the old days when I served in your squad as a newly promoted battle-brother,' Kergis continued. 'To become a White Scar, I had passed through trials that not one in ten thousand men

could have survived. On my first day, you told me
not to get too cocky.'

'I was right,' Balat scowled. 'Arrogance is a dangerous vice in a warrior. It blinds him to his own
weaknesses and the enemy's strengths.'

'Yes,' Kergis agreed. 'You taught me what it truly
means to be Astartes. You moulded me to be a better warrior, a better servant of the Chapter and our
Khan. I was smiling because the lessons continue.
Despite the passing of a century, I am still the student and you the master. And, to be truthful, I was
also smiling because your motive is transparent. In
discussing Chaos and reminding me of Voldorius,
you were not talking idly. You had a specific aim in
mind.'

'Subtlety was never one of my own vices,' Balat
admitted grudgingly. 'I have been fully briefed on
the details of your mission. Including the identity of
the enemy commander.'

'And you were wary I might need reminding of my
duty?'

'No, not that. Never that.' All through their conversation, Balat had continued to stare at Kergis's
face. Now, his gaze became more searching, more
insightful. 'I simply hoped to remind you that
Borchu is gone. Don't let your hand be slowed by
the memory of past friendship. Strike fast, and
strike to kill. If you hesitate, the enemy will make
use of it.'

'Sound advice,' Kergis nodded again. 'I will follow
it, I promise you.'

He glanced briefly above their heads. The sky was dark and overcast. Night still held its grip over the Cradle.

'But now, my men and I need to make ready. The darkness will not last forever. And we need to be at the Ignis Mons before dawn.'

IT SOON BECAME apparent Balat and his Scouts had made able use of their time on Tephra VII. In their forty-eight hours in the Cradle, while being careful to stay out of sight, they had observed every aspect of the defences surrounding the Ignis Mons.

By the time he and Kergis met at the rendezvous, Balat possessed the kind of in-depth intelligence that might well prove vital to the successful outcome of their mission. While Kergis and his men watched and listened, he sketched out the positions of the ring of sentry points, minefields and hidden bunkers protecting the Mons. He provided an analysis of the enemy's patrol schedules, indicating the route each patrol took through the Cradle. He had even prepared a map outlining a suggested approach to their objective. Checking the approach and finding no flaw in it, Kergis ordered his men to memorise it.

Once Balat had passed on all the intelligence, the two groups took their leave of each other.

The pre-arranged mission plan called for the Scouts to remain behind and cover the line of retreat of Kergis's squad. At the same time, they would guard the mission team's bikes. They were close enough to the target that Kergis and his men could no longer use their vehicles for fear the sound of their engines would give them away. As much as it pained them as White Scars to leave their bikes behind, they had no choice. Henceforth, they would continue their mission on foot.

It was not the only change which had been forced upon them by the needs of the mission. Ordinarily, at least two of the men in his squad would have been equipped with meltas or other heavy weapons. Instead, the nature of their mission in the Cradle meant they had left behind their heavy weapons in order to carry more explosives. Each man in the squad carried a grey, polyleather satchel filled with demolition charges and detonators: necessary equipment to sabotage the power plant. To save on weight, their only other arms were bolt pistols, knives and their normal close combat weapons.

'May the spirits of your ancestors go with you,' Balat said, once preparations had been made and Kergis was ready to leave. The rest of Kergis's squad stood nearby, watching as the two sergeants clasped hands once more in parting.

'May they be your guide and guardians. May they strike the stones from your path and leave your enemies grieving in your wake.'

'And may your ancestors ride with you also,' Kergis responded, completing the form of a traditional Chogorian farewell. 'May they always be beside you.'

To Kergis's surprise, Balat refused at first to release his grip once the goodbyes were done. While their hands were still joined he leaned forward, whispering a few words out of hearing of the others.

'Good luck,' he said. 'I know the choice you have made. It honours you. But do not assume this will be our last meeting. I will see you again, Kergis. I count on it.'

'I hope you are right, arban,' Kergis answered quietly. 'Things will fall where they may. Whatever the outcome, you should know I have always valued your guidance.'

The contact was broken. With nothing more to be said, Kergis turned and took his place at the head of his squad. With a gesture, he set them moving. With half the night gone already, they could not afford to waste an instant. Seven kilometres of hard terrain lay ahead before they reached their target.

Despite that, as he and his men followed a path through the gully, he spared a glance behind him. Balat was consulting with one of his Scouts, his head nodding sagely as he corrected some of his men's positioning. A moment later the line of the gully turned, blocking Kergis's last sight of his old mentor.

Despite Balat's good wishes, he did not expect the two of them would meet again.

IN THE END it was easier to infiltrate his men into the immediate vicinity of the Ignis Mons than Kergis would have expected. Although Balat's warnings of increased activity proved accurate, the sentries and patrols guarding the approaches to the enemy stronghold were surprisingly badly organised and half-hearted in the performance of their duty. Kergis did not doubt that the enemy's troops would fight fanatically to the last man to repel an Imperial invasion. But when it came to the more drudging tasks of soldiery, the night patrols and the long boring hours on watch, the enemy's lack of discipline told against them.

Even as Kergis and his men moved to within sight of the lower slopes of the Mons, the same defects of organisation among the enemy's defences were readily apparent. Any halfway competent commander would have ordered the ground of the lower slopes bulldozed and cleared so as to provide open fields of fire for the defenders' guns. As it was, the entire area was littered with rocky outcrops and dense patches of wiry scrub, as well as the occasional low ridge of dried lava.

The landscape provided Kergis and his men with ample cover as they made their way closer to their target. Similarly, the laxity of the enemy sentries meant they were able to reach the very edge of the slopes without having to once unsheathe their knives.

Suddenly, as Kergis crept onto the foot of the Mons, he heard voices approaching. Careful not to make any noise, he signalled to his men to stay in cover and sought refuge in the shadow of a weathered boulder. As the voices came closer he crouched in the darkness, waiting. His knife was in his hand, the blade smudged with volcanic ash to dull its reflection.

There were two of them. As the enemy sentries drew nearer, he was able to distinguish their voices and footsteps. They were arguing quietly amongst themselves, making no attempt to hide their presence. Listening as he waited, Kergis learned they had been assigned to sentry duty as punishment for failing to recite the litany properly during a rite of offering on a recent day of worship; a collective failure that each one blamed on the other.

As the footsteps came closer, Kergis was struck by the banality of their evil. From their conversation it was clear the rite they were referring to involved the blood sacrifice of innocent victims to the gods of Chaos. Yet, the sentries were more concerned with a petty grievance against their immediate superior in the cult hierarchy.

'It ain't right that Sinner Grell punished us,' the one on the left said. 'The litany's long and the Hierarch speaks so fast it's hard to keep up. I bet Sinner Grell don't know it no better than we do. He had the easy part, holding the salver for catching the blood. He ain't careful, somebody will tell the Hierarch what he does with the sacrifices before we kills 'em.'

They were his last words. Waiting until the sentries had walked past him, Kergis was on him in an instant. Clamping a hand over the man's mouth, he dragged the knife across his throat.

Hearing the sound of movement, the second sentry turned towards his partner. His eyes widening as he saw Kergis, he tried to raise his autogun. He was dead long before he could fire the weapon. Gurban emerged from the darkness behind him to press a hand over the second man's mouth and cut his throat just as Kergis had done to the first.

'We will take the bodies with us,' Kergis whispered to Gurban once he was sure the killing of the sentries had not raised any alarms. 'They are less likely to be discovered if we dump them in the tunnels.'

Gurban nodded. Kergis had made no gesture of thanks to the other man for killing the second sentry, nor would Gurban have expected one. Aware that his squad were nearby, Kergis had assumed that one of them would back him up when he launched his attack. If the position had been reversed and it was one of his men who had been left exposed by the sudden arrival of the sentries, Kergis would have behaved exactly as Gurban had done in supporting him. Such behaviour was taken for granted among the White Scars. As brother Astartes, they relied on each other implicitly.

Nearby, the rest of the squad emerged from cover. Motioning them to him, Kergis waited until they were huddled around him before he issued his orders.

'The entrance to the tunnels is that way,' he whispered, pointing to an area of the slope that was close at hand. Looking at the helmeted faces the men around him, he gave orders to several of the squad members in turn. 'I will take the lead. Osol, you will help Gurban carry the bodies. Doshin, shift some of the dust to cover the blood splatter from the sentries, then take a piece of scrub bush and use it to obscure

our tracks. Arik, you're with me. The rest of you, follow behind us.'

The huddle dissolved as the squad followed his
commands. Climbing the slope with Arik by the side
of him, Kergis kept his senses sharp for any sign of
the enemy. The lower reaches of the Ignis Mons were
little more than a gentle incline, but the slopes of the
volcano soon began to grow steeper.

Ahead, two kilometres above them, Kergis could
see the smoking peak of the Mons. It was lit by a dull
red glow from the lake of lava hidden inside it. They
were on the northern slope, out of sight of the geothermal complex which was situated on the southern
one, but they maintained the same habits of stealth
that, so far, had taken them within striking distance
of their objective. The most dangerous leg of the
journey still lay ahead of them.

'I can see the hatchway,' Arik whispered over a
secure channel on their vox. 'It is in the low depression thirty metres away, at three degrees
south-south-west.'

'I see it, too,' Kergis replied. 'Signal to the others to
stay back in case the enemy have left any unpleasant
surprises waiting for us.'

While Arik communicated his orders to the rest of
the squad by gesture, Kergis made his way cautiously
across the slope.

The cone of the volcano and the ground beneath it
were riddled with man-made tunnels designed to
bleed off the hot magma and prevent the Ignis Mons
from erupting. The same tunnels channelled the

excess magma to heat steam which was then re-directed to drive turbines to create an energy supply for the planet's cities. Based on the information gathered from debriefing some of the Imperial refugees who had escaped the fall of Tephra VII, the invasion forces had learned some of the tunnels beneath the Ignis Mons had not been used for centuries. Assuming the intelligence was right, Kergis and his men could use the tunnels to sneak into the power complex right under the noses of the enemy.

The access hatchway into the tunnels was set in a shallow well of plascrete to help protect it from the elements. Despite such precautions, its surface was pitted and scarred with rust. It was clear it had not been opened for some time.

Checking the surface of the hatchway for heat, Kergis took hold of the wheel-like opening mechanism and experimentally tried to turn it. The hatchway held fast, its inner workings rusted in place through centuries of disuse. Kergis increased the pressure incrementally, wary in case his gene-seed-wrought strength caused the wheel to shear off in his hands. With a protesting squeal of rusted metal, the wheel started to move. Slowly, he managed to turn it half a revolution.

The shriek as the hatch finally came free seemed as loud as a gunshot in the silence of the night. Expecting to see sentries hurrying towards their position, Kergis waited with Arik beside him, carefully scanning their surroundings. To his surprise, there was no sign of activity. Evidently, the remaining sentries had been too far away to hear it.

'Quickly,' Kergis said, easing himself into the tunnel. 'The moment I give the all clear, tell the men to follow me. I don't want to test our luck out here any longer than necessary.'

Inside, the tunnel was dark and quiet. There was a vaguely sulphurous smell in the air; a side-effect, Kergis assumed, of the proximity of a live volcano. It was clear, however, that the intelligence from the refugees had been correct. The air was warm and damp, but it was obvious the tunnel had not been put to work in recent times.

The inner surface of the tunnel was rough with a residue of dried lava, but overlaying it was a thick layer of undisturbed dust. The tunnel itself was over four metres tall. Standing with ease once he had dropped through the hatchway, Kergis signalled to Arik above him that everything was all right.

Soon, the rest of the squad had joined him in the tunnel. As the last man dropped through, Doshin shut the hatchway behind him. Meanwhile, Gurban and Osol dumped the bodies of the dead sentries to one side of the tunnel.

'We will move forward in single file,' Kergis told his men once they were ready to proceed. 'If we meet the enemy, we will fight with swords and knives. We will only use our bolt pistols as weapons of last resort. Remember, the sound of a shot might echo across the whole length of these tunnels, alerting the enemy.'

The squad nodded their understanding. Turning, Kergis faced into darkness. The tunnels were even blacker than the night had been outside.

He and his men carried compact luminators attached to the sides of their helmets. He gave a signal to switch them on. The dull glow of the luminators revealed the shape of the tunnel in their immediate vicinity. Beyond it, there lay yet more darkness.

They had been furnished with a layout of the tunnel network courtesy of an ancient survey blueprint from the planetary archives; one of thousands of such documents the planetary governor and his retinue had taken with them when they fled the fall of their world to Chaos. Ordinarily, Kergis would have expected a governor to spend more time defending his planet and less saving some mouldering parchments, but on this occasion he supposed the man's weak backbone had played in his favour. Always assuming, of course, that the tunnels had not been substantially altered in the millennia since the survey had been completed.

'Move out,' he voxed his men.

As one, they marched forward into the darkness.

AN HOUR LATER, they had made steady progress. The tunnel layout recorded in the survey blueprints had proven to be accurate, allowing the squad to move faster than Kergis had expected. The luminators supplied only limited radiance, but this was not an insurmountable obstacle. Within minutes, the White Scars' eyes had begun to grow accustomed to the gloom. Soon, they could see as well in the tunnels as they had in the moonless night on the approach to the Ignis Mons.

By Kergis's reckoning, they were another three quarters of an hour from their destination.

'We need to pick up speed,' he told his men. 'The assault will be easier if we time our attack to the middle of the workers' shift, when they are likely to be at their most tired and dull-witted. From now on, double-time.'

Uncomplaining, the squad followed his example and broke into a jog.

Their objective was the control room which oversaw the operation of the lava tunnels. It was the most critical part of the facility. The White Scars were carrying a number of demolition charges with them; more than enough, he hoped, to destroy the control systems responsible for directing the movement of lava. Back on the strike cruiser, Goju, the Techmarine attached to their company, had given the squad an in-depth briefing, highlighting what each piece of the control apparatus looked like and where to place the charges to achieve the greatest effect. If the White Scars were successful in their plan of sabotage, the geothermal complex would be destroyed.

It would be harsh medicine for the people of Tephra VII. Assuming the invasion was a success, the newly liberated population in the western regions would be left without power. But the needs of victory outweighed any other consideration. First, Tephra VII would have to be liberated from the yoke of Chaos.

Compared to that noble aim, anything else was of secondary importance.

* * *

THE WHITE SCARS had travelled another half a kilometre before they discovered the tunnels had guardians. Hunters by nature, these guardians did not practise the lax habits of the sentries protecting the slopes of the Mons. They did not announce their presence with loud footsteps or idle conversation. They were not even human.

Kergis and his men had reached a place where the tunnel they were following suddenly opened out into a broad, empty space at least a hundred metres long and an equal distance wide. The ceiling high above was partially hidden in the gloom, but Kergis could see it was gently rounded, while the floor of the chamber was rough and uneven due to a coating of dried lava.

Entering cautiously into the hemispherical expanse, Kergis noted that the walls were dotted with the entrances of dozens of other tunnels, some of them set high above the floor of the chamber.

'What is it, do you think?' Gurban asked as he followed Kergis into the open. In keeping with Chapter tactics, the rest of the squad had stayed back at the mouth of the tunnel, ready to cover them in the event of an ambush.

'Some kind of overflow chamber, perhaps?' Kergis shrugged. 'If Goju was here, we could ask him.'

Summoning up the tunnel blueprints on his helmet display, he checked for the chamber in the layout. There was no sign of it.

'Whatever it is, it was built after the survey blueprints were made. Still, it doesn't look as though it was created recently. The stonework appears ancient. What does the auspex say?'

'The area reads clear,' Gurban said, grimacing as he checked the handheld unit he was carrying. 'But the reading may be unreliable. The tunnel walls are warm, hot even in places. I think some of these disused tunnels run parallel to pockets of lava. The temperature fluxions are confusing the auspex.'

'Understood,' Kergis said. He contacted the rest of the squad by vox. 'The auspex readings are unclear. Gurban and I will remain on point. Osol, you'll cover the others as last man. The rest of you, spread out. We move with caution.'

Blades at the ready, the White Scars fanned out across the chamber. Taking the lead with Gurban at his side, Kergis followed the lessons he had first learned as a Scout, then later as a battle-brother under the tutelage of Balat.

Given the proliferation of tunnels entering into the chamber, there were dozens of places an ambusher could hide. Rather than allowing his attention to become fixated on any particular point, Kergis broadened his perception and tried to take in the totality of his surroundings, relying on his armour's autosenses to supply him with a continuous feed of details. Above all else, he attuned himself to respond to any sign of movement – be it sight or sound – from the various tunnel mouths around him. At the same time, he listened for a warning shout from any of his fellow White Scars, each of whom acted as an extra set of eyes and ears for their brothers.

In the end, it was the smell that warned him of the enemy's presence. He picked up on a rank odour. It was only the merest trace. An animal stench, familiar yet elusive.

'Contact!' Gurban yelled a warning as the proximity alert on the auspex in his hand burst suddenly into noisy life. 'I make a dozen at least. They are all around us…'

The rest of his words were lost as the first of the attackers emerged from their hiding places to ambush the White Scars.

Kergis caught a blurred glimpse of slavering jaws as their owner leapt towards him. He responded with a sweep of his sword, the blade of the power weapon sizzling eagerly through the air as it hurried to meet its target. The blow caught the creature in the flanks in mid-leap. Kergis heard the attacker scream as his armour was splashed with hot alien gore.

Amid the stench of blood he smelled the same rank odour he had sensed before, stronger this time. It was a charnel smell of malice and corruption, one he recognised from bloody encounters on a dozen different worlds.

A second creature emerged from a nearby tunnel and bounded towards him. This time, given more opportunity to ready his defence, Kergis was able to take in the full nature of the creature as it charged. To any man who was not Astartes, it would have seemed a source of terrifying horror; a thing of nightmare given swift and shrieking life.

The beast was perhaps two metres long. Its body was lean and hungry, with powerful rippling muscles and a head that seemed too large for its torso. Its legs ended in sharp claws that gouged scratches into the surface of the ground as it ran. The oversized head ended in a long snout set with a row of massive, interlocking fangs. The first beast had been covered in matted fur, but this one was disturbingly hairless. Its skin was a leprous ashen shade of grey.

As the creature began its death-leap towards him, Kergis saw a pair of bony hooks emerge from concealed sheaths on its shoulders, ready to strike in unison with its jaws. Holding to the last moment with the confident assurance of a skilled swordsman, Kergis waited until the creature was almost upon him before he lashed out with his sword.

The blow caught the beast in the centre line of its skull. The head and brain were split down the middle, killing it.

Propelled by momentum, the dead creature's body continued moving. Sidestepping it with ease, Kergis heard it flop to the ground behind him.

In the brief breathing space accorded by the death of the second attacker, he snapped a quick glance towards his men. Behind him, the rest of the squad were each busy with their own battles, fighting with knives and whirring chainswords against the teeth and claws of a horde of similar monsters.

Kergis turned, intent on offering aid to his brothers. Suddenly, he felt a blow hit his side. Caught unawares, it knocked him from his feet.

Too late, he realised the creatures attacked in *threes*.

Falling to the ground, Kergis found himself looking up at a pair of red, rage-filled eyes. The third beast was bigger than either of its two fellow hunters. It had Kergis on his back, its weight pressing down on his chest. His sword arm was held gripped in its jaws. Kergis tried to pull the arm free, but the creature's hold was too strong.

As he struggled, it bit down harder into his arm. Incredibly, Kergis saw the teeth had made an impression on the ceramite skin of his armour. A minute series of cracks had begun to appear in the armour's surface. Kergis would have hardly thought it possible, but the creature gave every impression of being able to bite through his armour if he gave it long enough. Unable to bring his sword to bear as long as his right arm was in its grip, Kergis's left hand scrabbled to free his knife, then stabbed the creature with all his strength.

He felt a brief moment of resistance as the blade cut through the beast's tough outer skin before sliding deep into its body. The monster seemed indifferent to the blow; if anything, its grip on his arm tightened.

Kergis pulled out the knife and stabbed it again. And again. The blade of the knife arced back and forth in a rapid succession of blows, making a bloody ruin of the creature's side as Kergis fought desperately to kill it.

Abruptly, his efforts were rewarded. Still gripping tightly on his sword arm, the beast closed its eyes and died.

Kergis's view of his fellow White Scars was obscured by the body of the creature on top of him, but as he recovered his breath he became dimly aware the struggle around him had been brought to a close. The noises of war, the battle cries of his men and roars of the creatures had faded. In their place he heard a strange, mournful howl echo in the distance.

Unsure of the sound's origin, Kergis pushed the creature's bulk to one side. Unable to break its death-grip on his arm, he managed to work his power sword free and took it in his left hand. Then, activating the blade, he sliced through the upper and lower jaws of the dead animal's snout just below the point where they gripped his arm.

With nothing left to maintain their hold, the two parts of the severed snout came away. Looking down at the indentations that the beast's fangs had left in his armour, Kergis could not help but wonder how much longer it would have taken the monster to crack through his defences.

Now that the beast was dead, Kergis could see it was different from its fellows. Gazing at the dozen or so creatures lying dead around the chamber, he observed that each individual bore only the vaguest signs of kinship to the others. He saw fur and armoured scales, retractable claws and envenomed fangs, poison-weeping musk glands and iridescent insect eyes; sometimes all combined in the body of a single creature. For all that, however, there was a resemblance between each and every one of them, no matter how slight. It was as though each of the monsters had been badly drawn from memory to the same basic design.

'Ugly beasts, aren't they?'

It was Arik. Looking up, Kergis saw the rest of the squad had gathered around him. He was relieved to see there were no casualties among them. Despite the deadly nature of their opponents, his men had passed through the fight unscathed.

'What were they?' Osol asked. He was the youngest man in the squad, with barely half a decade as a battle-brother behind him.

'A hunting pack,' Kergis replied. 'A Chaos warband may raid on dozens, even hundreds of worlds. Sometimes, they capture particularly fearsome examples of the local animals, predators especially. Some they use for sport, but others they breed together, creating hybrid monstrosities that they train as hunting packs. Making use of the powers of Chaos, they can combine even completely different animals, creating chimera creatures like these. We have fought them before, maybe a dozen times. Each time the creatures look different. But the smell is always the same.'

'They must have left them down here because they knew the tunnels would be a target for infiltrators,' Arik said. 'You realise the noise of the fight may have warned the enemy of our presence?'

'No,' Kergis shook his head. 'It doesn't necessarily follow. We are deep underground, and none of us fired our bolt pistols. The enemy may not have heard the battle at all. Or, if they did, they may rely on the hunting pack to have killed us. What concerns me more right now is the howling.'

The sound had continued, growing louder as the creature making it moved closer to their position. In his long service as an Astartes, Kergis had never heard anything to match it. It was a keening sound, long and ululating, rising and falling in pitch in a harsh, continuous wail. The noise of it was grating, even disturbing.

Kergis would have preferred to believe no human voice was capable of making such a sound, but the howling seemed to speak wordlessly of all too human emotions. Kergis recognised a sound born of rage and insanity. There was a squall of white noise underlying it, which seemed to indicate the howl was issuing from a vox unit, but there was no mistaking the raw seething emotion behind it. Kergis heard tones of outrage, grief and betrayal. Above all else, he heard the sound of madness.

'It started in the middle of the fight,' Arik said. 'When the hunting pack heard it, they fled.'

'Spread out,' Kergis ordered his men. 'It's getting closer. Given that sound, we can assume it's hostile. And if it scared the hunting pack away, it must be dangerous.'

The howling grew louder. Although the sound echoed around the chamber, it was clear which tunnel it was coming from. Taking a step forward, Gurban raised his auspex and tried to gain a reading.

'It's big,' he said. 'From the size of the contact, it must be barely able to fit in the tunnel.'

'All of you, check your bolt pistols and melta charges,' Kergis said as Gurban stepped back to join the line of White Scars standing in the centre of the chamber. 'But only use them if you hear my order. If possible, we will try to use our blades.'

Privately, he doubted the White Scars' swords were up to the task of killing the thing lumbering its way towards them, but he was willing to try so long as there was any chance of maintaining the element of surprise in their mission.

The volume of the howling had risen to an ear-splitting roar. Kergis pressed the activation rune on his power sword as a dark shape emerged from the mouth of the tunnel.

As the creature stepped forward, Kergis saw it clearly for the first time. He realised he and his men were in deep trouble.

His NAME WAS long forgotten. If his current captors referred to him by any name at all they called him Shulok-ahk-alim-neg, a phrase meaning 'he howls without end' in the corrupt argot favoured by the warband's leaders. Or else, they simply called him Shulok.

He did not care. His true name had been lost on the day his brothers betrayed him.

Once, he had been handsome and well featured. He was strong of limb and purpose. He was Astartes. When his brothers rebelled against the Emperor, he had followed their example. Ultimately, they had been defeated in their struggle, but they consoled themselves with the thought they had helped deliver a deathblow to the Emperor and all His works.

The years would prove them wrong. The Emperor's followers refused to accept His demise. They placed Him on a golden throne, a corpse-god effigy to rule over a conquered galaxy. Incredibly, the Imperium He had founded prospered and grew stronger.

Angered by this inexplicable development, Shulok and his brothers had begun to raid the Imperium's territory. Bitter and vengeful after their defeat, they sought to destroy the Emperor's dominions in piece-meal fashion.

In truth, there was no longer any grand strategy or noble aim. Once, they had made war in the name of ideas. But defeat had changed everything. Now, they simply killed for its own sake. They fought to bring destruction to their enemies, with no thought of high ideals or consequence.

To the mind of the creature who would one day become Shulok, they had been wonderful times. His memories had been blurred and darkened by the years, but he remembered the heady sense of free-dom, of licence. He had fought across the stars with his brothers beside him. He had known glory and victory.

Then, one day he died.

He remembered it vividly. They had fought beneath a giant red sun. A warrior with a crimson fist had raised a bolt pistol as the two of them struggled in hand-to-hand combat. Point blank, the barrel opening of the bolt weapon seemed huge, a yawning chasm. He had tried to grab the pistol, to deflect the shot, but it was too late. There was a bright flash from the muzzle and his world passed to darkness.

After that, there came the betrayal. He awoke to find his body felt strangely numb. Puzzled by unfamiliar sensations, he tried to lift his arms to inspect them. What he saw once he did so made him cry out in anguish.

He had been encased in a metal shell. His body, too badly injured to be healed, had been entombed inside a cold sarcophagus, henceforth to serve as the central cortex piloting a hulking war machine.

Raging at his imprisonment, he had screamed for release. Alternating between fury and bouts of pleading, he had called for someone, anyone, to have mercy. Even death would be better than an eternity trapped inside a machine. He had begged to be killed.

His only answer had come with cruel laughter. Focusing on the sound, he had realised several of his brothers stood nearby. Standing at their head was their leader, the warsmith. He smiled, his expression insufferably smug and mocking.

'Kill you? I think not. You are a resource to us now, a valuable one. And, really, you can't complain. We simply took you at your promise all those times you uttered our battle cry. "Iron within, iron without." Now, my friend, you truly are an iron warrior.'

It was then that the creature who would one day be known as Shulok began to earn his name. He started to howl, giving vent to pain and frustration as he strained against the chains his brothers had used to bind him.

From that day on, the howling had never ended. The men who betrayed him were dead and gone, killed in a long ago battle he could barely remember. But even with their deaths his captivity and his torment had not ended. Over the course of thousands of years he had been passed from warband to warband, traded as a chattel or captured as part of the spoils of war.

Through it all, the howling continued.

It had become a reflex. A man of flesh and blood cannot scream forever; he needs rest and sleep. But a machine knows no such limitations. After thousands of years, the vox unit in his war machine body still gave voice to the same keening, strident shriek.

His reason had long since left him, his wits broken in the centuries since his betrayal. If there was one saving grace left to him, it was that he could still take pleasure in killing his enemies.

In particular, he cherished the killing of Astartes, especially the heirs of the loyalist Legions who had taken the Emperor's side in the rebellion. He hated them most of all. They reminded him of all he had lost. Killing them gave him respite, creating a brief moment of joy that drowned out his pain and anguish, even if only for a second.

In recent days he had been accorded little opportunity for killing of any kind. Weary of his howling, his current captors had imprisoned him in the disused tunnels beneath the Ignis Mons. Left to wander alone, he had soon discovered the only creatures other than himself in the tunnels were the warband's hunting animals. He had tried to stalk them, to sate his need for killing, but they proved to be difficult quarry, too quick and wily to be easily caught.

The lack of killing had made his existence even harder to endure. Until, one day, the sounds echoing through his underground domain had brought news of the presence of fresh prey in the tunnels.

Soon, the roar of the hunting animals and the smell of blood had seemed to confirm his hopes, bringing him hurrying to investigate. Stepping forward from the confined space of the tunnels into open territory, he saw nine figures clad in white power armour emblazoned with a lightning insignia.

White Scars.

A thrill of anticipation ran through him.

The pistons of his leg hydraulics hissing like a pit of angry vipers, he strode forward into the chamber and made ready to kill them.

'DREADNOUGHT!'

Forewarned by his auspex a split second before the metal giant emerged from the tunnel, Gurban shouted out a desperate warning.

The war machine was huge. Dust fell where its massive hulking shoulders had scraped against the tunnel walls. Still howling as it moved into the chamber, it advanced with thudding, foreboding footsteps. Its exterior was a dull gunmetal grey in colour, overlaid with riveted Chaos symbols in brass and copper. On one shoulder, Kergis could see an ancient skull insignia indicating the Dreadnought had once belonged to the Iron Warriors. The skull had been crudely scratched out and defaced, but the outline of the insignia was still visible.

Unlike the majority of Astartes Chapters, the White Scars had never made use of Dreadnoughts. To warriors accustomed to the freedom of the plains of their home world Chogoris, the idea of being entombed in a walking sarcophagus seemed like a fate worse than death.

Despite this, as the Chaos Dreadnought advanced on his position Kergis was forced to grant that the machine was impressive. He did not doubt that a group of lesser warriors might have decided to flee rather than face the monster. But he and his men were White Scars. They were made of sterner stuff.

The Dreadnought came closer, eager to begin the fight.

'Switch to bolt pistols!' Kergis called out to his men. 'Rapid fire! Aim for the legs!'

Fanning out to create more room between themselves and their opponent, the men of the squad drew their pistols and began firing. Following their sergeant's order they aimed at the Dreadnought's legs, hoping to knock out the motive hydraulics enabling its movement.

It was an old lesson of the plains that an immobilised enemy was nearly as good as dead. When facing a more powerful opponent, the White Scars would often attempt to hamstring him in order to take the greatest advantage of their manoeuvrability on their bikes. Kergis realised that the tactic was less likely to be successful in the relatively confined space of the overflow chamber, especially as the White Scars were on foot. The most he could hope for was that if they destroyed the Dreadnought's movement capability it would allow them to outflank and overwhelm it.

Despite the hail of gunfire, the Dreadnought was unaffected. Almost contemptuous of the White Scars' efforts, it brandished the plasma cannon fitted to its left arm.

Kergis dived to the ground just in time as a stream of plasma scythed through the air over his head. Going into a roll, he came up and fired his bolt pistol at the war machine again. He aimed for the shadowed recess where its head met his body, hoping to find a weak point in the heavy armour protecting it from the front.

Meanwhile, his men had spread out in a wide circle around their enemy. Adapting their more normal tactics to the situation, they fired on the move, each individual Space Marine alternating between phases of advance, retreat and sideways movement in an attempt to confuse the Dreadnought.

Greeted with multiple, moving targets the Dreadnought seemed briefly stymied. Until, seeking to make use of the opportunity presented by the enemy's uncertainty, Osol moved behind the machine and made a sudden dash for its back. In his hand, he held the round shape of a melta bomb.

Guessing his intent Kergis almost called out a warning, but kept his silence for fear of alerting the Dreadnought. His worst fears were quickly realised. As Osol came within a few paces, the Dreadnought suddenly turned, its legs remaining motionless as it pivoted its upper body around one hundred and eighty degrees on its central axis. Catching Osol by surprise, it smashed him to the ground with a blow from the power claw on its right arm.

Using the heavy gauntlet as a club, it hammered repeatedly on Osol's inert form. Attempting to rescue his battle-brother, Doshin swept into the fray firing his bolt pistol. Turning once more on its axis, the Dreadnought moved with surprising swiftness. It raised its plasma cannon to meet Doshin's attack, leaving the charging White Scar staring down the muzzle of the weapon at nearly point-blank range.

'No!'

Activating his power sword, Kergis charged forward to intervene.

It was too late. The plasma weapon fired with a blinding light. Doshin's head was atomised in an instant, leaving his body still standing, the seared flesh smouldering from the heat of the energy discharge.

Caught in the backwash of the blast as he leapt forward, Kergis's sword strike was deflected. Instead of biting deep into the Dreadnought's arm, he caught it a glancing blow on the shoulder. Shuddering as the crackling energy field surrounding the blade sliced off a layer of its metal skin, the Dreadnought bellowed in rage and hit the White Scar sergeant with a heavy, backhanded blow.

The force of it sent Kergis hurtling bodily across the chamber. He landed with a jarring impact, skidding to a halt beside the cadaver of one of the dead hunting animals. Pulling himself up, he saw his men had increased their attacks against the Dreadnought to distract it from going after their sergeant.

Kergis was about to charge back into the battle when he realised he was no longer holding his power sword. Evidently, it had slipped from his grip when the Dreadnought hit him.

Looking about desperately, he saw it lying on the floor of the chamber near the Dreadnought's feet. Spotting it, he almost cried out in frustration. The sword was the most potent weapon he possessed. In the absence of the heavy weapons his squad had given up to carry explosives, it was the best weapon they had against the Dreadnought. Without it, there was precious little chance that he and his men could even hurt the machine, much less kill it.

For a moment, it appeared to Kergis that he and his men were doomed. He would fight to the last, they all would, but there seemed no prospect of their survival. Worse, their mission would be a failure. At dawn, when their brothers assaulted the city of Chaldis they would find the enemy shields were still in place. The likely result would be a bloodbath. The success of the invasion would be at risk.

Then, abruptly, he spotted something in the chamber floor that changed everything.

There was a spider web of cracks in the surface of the floor around the Dreadnought. With each crunching footstep more cracks appeared, adding to the pattern as the great weight of the war machine pressed down on the stone. More tellingly, Kergis could see tiny wisps of steam and smoke rising from among some of the cracks, almost lost in the thin clouds of dust that hugged the chamber floor. At the same time, he noticed the ground beneath his feet was hot to the touch. Looking down, he saw the floor was not composed of the same stonework as the walls of the chamber. Instead, it appeared almost identical to the rocks he had seen while travelling through the Cradle.

With a sudden burst of inspiration, Kergis realised the chamber he was standing in was a sphere, not a hemisphere. He and his men had mistaken a bed of dried lava for the chamber floor. It seemed likely there was yet more lava beneath it, red-hot and still liquid.

A dangerous plan forming in his mind, Kergis's hands scrabbled in the satchel he carried with him. Then, lifting his bolt pistol to fire a rapid series of shots, he charged across the chamber towards the Dreadnought.

'Pull back!' he yelled to his men as he drew closer to the machine. 'Keep firing, but pull back, all of you! That is an order! Leave this monster to me.'

With no time to explain his plan, he could only hope the habit of obedience was so deeply engrained that his men would follow his orders without question.

Ahead, it was almost as if the Dreadnought was waiting for him. Instead of firing its weapons, it spread its arms wide in a taunting gesture and encouraged Kergis to continue his charge. Sprinting closer as the bolt pistol in his hand ran out of ammunition and fell silent, Kergis let out an emphatic battle cry.

'For the Khan and the Emperor! For victory!'

The Dreadnought leaned its great bulk forward, ready to meet his charge. But instead of facing the monster head-on, Kergis changed tack. At the very last instant before he moved into range of its grasp he threw himself to the ground, relying on the momentum of the charge to carry him forward as his body skidded across the filmy, dusty surface of the lava floor. Catching the Dreadnought by surprise, Kergis slid between its articulated legs and emerged behind the machine. His momentum exhausted, he slowed to a gentle stop a few metres behind the Dreadnought.

The sound of its howling briefly changing timbre to a cry of rage at the trick, the Dreadnought turned on its axis and angrily moved its arm into a firing position. Levelling the plasma weapon at Kergis as he lay on the ground, it prepared to blast him to oblivion. In response, Kergis lifted a small, hand-held remote detonator, making sure the Dreadnought could see it before he pressed the ignition stud.

Too late, the machine realised the White Scar had left something beneath it in his skidding journey underneath its body. Looking down, it saw the dark compact shape of a polyleather satchel lying on the ground at a point almost equidistant between its feet.

The contents of the satchel detonated with a roar that drowned out the Dreadnought's howl of anguish.

The explosion did not penetrate its armour, but it was enough to fatally weaken the ground beneath the monster's feet. With its arms flailing madly, the Dreadnought began to fall screaming as the floor immediately underneath it shattered and gave way, pitching it headlong into a suddenly revealed abyss of burning lava situated below the level of the chamber floor. For the first time in thousands of years the Dreadnought's howls of pain and anguish were replaced by the sounds of fear as it tumbled into a lake of fire. It made a splash as it landed, sending droplets of hissing magma flying into the air as it sank into the red heat of a flowing sea of lava.

Nearby, luck had been on Kergis's side. Although the floor had collapsed to within a few centimetres of his position, the ground had held firm underneath him. Rising to his feet, he saw that his sword lay on the floor barely a metre away. He reached over to pick it up. Behind him, the mouth of the newly created pit was obscured by a pall of steam and rising smoke, as hot air from the lava well met the colder air of the overflow chamber.

Casting a quick glance around him, Kergis could see that his men had followed his orders to pull back. He was the closest man to the edge of the pit. The remaining members of the squad were congregated twenty metres away, on the other side. As he leaned forward to grip the hilt of his sword, he raised his other hand to signal to his men that he was all right.

His presence of mind in immediately seeking out the sword saved his life as one of the Dreadnought's arms suddenly emerged from inside the pit and lashed through the air beside him. Caught by a glancing blow, Kergis was knocked to the ground as the monster's blindly groping claw latched on to his leg and began to pull him into the hole. From the other side of the pit he heard his men call out in horror as they rushed to help him. But they were too far away. With a remorseless strength born of a desire for vengeance, the Dreadnought began to drag him towards the edge of the abyss.

His free hand scrabbling at the floor as he tried to arrest his journey, Kergis turned on his side and attempted to bring the sword to bear. At last, his hand found purchase as the Dreadnought's arm tugged him onto the crumbling lip of the pit. Digging his hand into the relatively soft surface of the floor, Kergis managed to create enough of a hand-hold to resist the monster's strength.

He held on with all his might, his muscles aching with the strain as the Dreadnought fought merci-lessly to pull him into the abyss. Suspended on the edge of the pit, he glanced down and saw the Dread-nought glaring up at him, its body half-submerged in burning lava. Flames and steam billowed from its body as the lava found a way past its defences through the crevices in its armour. The monster was being burned alive inside its own skin. Yet, still, it clung on to Kergis's leg, intent on dragging him to hell with it.

At last, Kergis was able to twist around and bring his sword to bear. He slashed downward, the descending arc of his power sword trailing bright flashes of sparks as the energy field of the blade ignited tiny micro-pockets of flammable gas rising from the lava. Unlike the last time he had struck the Dreadnought, this time the blade hit its mark squarely. It cut through the lava-weakened armour of the Dreadnought's arm, severing it at the elbow.

Its hold on his leg lost, the Dreadnought sank into the boiling lava like a tired swimmer. Its last sound was a final, despairing howl. Then, it was gone.

'Sergeant!' Kergis felt hands at his shoulder. 'Quickly, take my hand! We won't let you fall!'

It was Arik. Together with Gurban, the pathfinder had leapt across the pit to help rescue him. Soon, they had pulled Kergis away from the mouth of the hole. The three of them stood watching the smoke rising from the pit as the other men of the squad rushed to join them.

'That was a close one,' Arik said to Kergis, once he could see the sergeant had regained his breath. 'For a moment, I thought we'd lost you.'

'For a moment I thought the same myself,' Kergis admitted.

He paused for a second to listen. From further ahead he heard the sound of a distant klaxon, echoing shrilly around the tunnels. Evidently, the fight with the Dreadnought had alerted the enemy to their presence.

It seemed they no longer had the element of surprise on their side.

OSOL WAS DEAD. In the aftermath of the fight, it became clear the White Scars had lost two of their number in return for the Dreadnought's death. Kergis had known Doshin had been killed, his head blasted to atoms by the thing's plasma cannon, but the death of Osol came as an unpleasant surprise. He had seen the younger Space Marine fall, but he had still harboured hopes that Osol might have survived the attack.

As it was, those hopes had been swiftly dashed. The Dreadnought's hammering blows had smashed through Osol's helmet and crushed his skull like an eggshell.

The death of both men was a bitter loss to the squad, but Kergis found the death of Osol to be an especial cause for sorrow. The young White Scar had been rough around the edges, but he had showed great promise. Kergis knew he was not alone in expecting that Osol would one day rise high in the Chapter.

Sadly, that promise would never be fulfilled.

'We have lost our brothers,' he said to his men afterwards, once they had taken the weapons and ammunition from the dead men's bodies, along with the explosives and their few personal effects. 'But we know all that was good in them is not lost. They will be remembered in the tales we tell around the campfire, and in the annals maintained by the Chaplains. And their gene-seed has survived their deaths. Through it, they will serve as the forebears of future White Scars.'

His hands were slick with blood as he spoke. As the ranking warrior among his men, it had fallen to Kergis to remove the progenoid glands from Osol and Doshin. He had placed the harvested glands into a cryo-flask and given it to Gurban for safekeeping. In time, the progenoids would be returned to Chogoris where the Chapter Apothecaries would use them in the creation of more new White Scars. Osol and Doshin were dead, but their gene-seed would live on.

While Kergis had performed the bloody work of removing the progenoids, the other members of the squad had removed their helmets as a mark of respect. Now, Kergis looked around at their faces, one by one.

'Remember the teachings of the Stormseers,' he said to his men. 'Even in death, our brothers are still with us. They sit at our shoulder. Their spirits guide us and watch us.'

'In death, their spirits are still with us,' the squad intoned quietly, echoing his words with their heads bowed and their voices as one.

It was a phrase and a sentiment taken from the ancient funerary rites still practised on the plains of Chogoris. The pressure of time meant that Kergis could do little except say a few words over the bodies of his dead brothers. If they had been on Chogoris, things would have been different. As warriors fallen in battle, Osol and Doshin would have been accorded the highest of honours. Instead, the current situation meant the best Kergis and his men had been able to do was to set booby traps to kill any enemy or scavenger who might try to defile their dead brothers' remains.

'We should be on our way,' Gurban said, once their preparations were done. 'The enemy will be looking for us, but they'll have a hard time searching all these tunnels. We'll have the best chance of reaching our objective if we push on now, before they can get the search properly organised.'

'Agreed,' Kergis nodded. 'But there has been a change of plan. I won't be going with you.'

If he had claimed the Emperor had appeared to him in a vision, he doubted it would have had more of an effect on his men. Their faces looked thunderstruck.

'I cannot explain the whole of it,' Kergis said, lifting a hand to stifle the squad's protests. 'I can only say that there is more to our mission here than you were told. I was given a second secret task, to be accomplished alongside the main objective of our mission. I had hoped to complete the main objective first, but events have become our master in this. Now the enemy knows we are here, the only way to achieve both tasks is to split our forces. Gurban, you will lead the squad to the main objective and complete the sabotage as planned. As for the second task, I will continue alone and complete it by myself.'

'But sergeant…' Arik's expression was aghast. 'You can't leave us now. At least let us know what is going on. If you have to leave, let us know it serves some reason.'

'I'm sorry,' Kergis turned to Gurban. 'The mission falls to you now. Remember the importance of what we were sent to do here. If the power supply to the void shield isn't interrupted the assault on Chaldis may fail. Our brothers are counting on you, Gurban. I have every faith you will not let them down.'

'I will not allow us to fail,' Gurban nodded, solemnly. 'But what of you, sergeant? When we are attacking the main objective, where will you be?'

'I will be hunting for the master of this place,' Kergis said. 'He has business with the White Scars that cannot be allowed to go unfinished.'

THE OVERFLOW CHAMBER was a juncture point in the tunnels, so it was there that Kergis took his leave of the squad. Using the survey blueprint to guide him he chose a tunnel that brought him closer to the

main body of the power complex while his comrades followed a path deeper into the bowels of the
facility. Their objective was the control room over-
seeing the operation of the lava tunnels, while his
lay in the higher reaches of the complex.

All through the journey the sound of the klaxon
reverberated through the tunnels. Evidently, the
sounds of the battle against the Dreadnought and the
explosion that tipped it into the lava pit had stirred
up a hornets' nest of enemy activity. All too aware that
this might make things harder for Gurban and the
others, Kergis decided he would do what he could to
ease his brothers on their path through the complex.

It was not difficult. The fact an alarm had been
raised meant there were sentries and search parties
moving throughout the area. Some of them would
be in Kergis's way. By killing them as swiftly and
noisily as possible he could achieve two aims at
once: clearing the pathway to his own objective
while simultaneously drawing the enemy away from
the rest of the squad. If luck was on his side every
enemy in the complex would soon be chasing him,
leaving Gurban and the others with a relatively clear
path to the control room.

Given the sheer number of enemy troops now
swarming throughout the facility, it was not long
before he was able to put his plan into practice.

'We have found the intruder!' the search party
leader screamed into his vox. 'He is Astartes... wearing white armour like the blessed one... he...'

Kergis ended the man's words with a shot from his bolt pistol, the round hitting him in the middle of his forehead and detonating inside his skull.

There were five other men in the group, one of dozens of such search parties currently scouring the Mons. They were armed with autoguns and wore robes indicating their membership in one of the many foul cults which had flourished on Tephra VII since it had fallen to Chaos.

Even by the standard of the scum that frequently attached itself to Chaos warbands, they were poor warriors. They were actively searching for an intruder, supposedly on their guard, but Kergis had been able to get behind them with ease. He had encountered them a little while after he emerged from the lava tunnels into the complex proper. By then, they were the sixth or seventh group of guards he had encountered. He had killed so many he had begun to lose count.

The rest of the search party quickly followed their leader into death. Armed with his power sword, he made short work of them.

'Search Group Nine, are you still there? Nine, can you hear me?'

The leader's vox had fallen to the ground and continued to squawk long after its owner and his comrades were dead. Treading on it, Kergis crushed it.

Turning away from the carnage he had just wrought with barely a thought, Kergis hurried his steps and pushed on through the complex. Still guided by the survey blueprints he had been given as part of the mission, he travelled a twisting trail through the Mons, frequently punctuated by bloody encounters with small parties of the enemy garrison.

Wary of the danger he might be overwhelmed by sheer weight of numbers, he was careful to stay away from the main areas of the complex that were likely to feature the greatest concentrations of the enemy's strength. Instead, he stayed to the byways, relying on a network of maintenance tubes and access hatchways to take him through the complex. In this, the facility's very nature worked in his favour.

Inside, the power complex was a vast and uncoordinated maze of rooms and corridors, open spaces and storage areas. It had quickly become clear the enemy lacked the same blueprints that he possessed. Without them, they could only trail in confusion in Kergis's wake while he journeyed unerringly to his target.

His objective was situated in the higher levels of the complex, in the area the warband's leaders had set aside as their quarters. As Kergis followed a twisting path through the tubes and hatchways, he noticed the sentries and guard posts appeared to thin in numbers as he rose higher through the facility.

To his mind it seemed curious that the enemy had chosen to leave their leaders' quarters relatively unprotected. A small, quiet voice in his mind wondered whether he was missing something. It was almost as if the enemy had left the path to their leaders' quarters clear, though any motive they might have had to do so eluded him.

Dismissing his thoughts as idle fancies, he continued on his journey.

Before long he found himself within sight of his objective. Moving quietly down a long corridor on one of the upper floors of the complex, he peered around a corner and saw two sentries standing outside a closed doorway. Based on the survey blueprints, and the intelligence gathered from Imperial refugees who had escaped Tephra after its fall, Kergis knew the doorway was the entrance to the private quarters of the leader of the warband responsible for garrisoning the Mons. Through those doors, he would find his target.

Watching the sentries from cover, he waited until their heads were turned away from him. Then, he struck. He ran towards them, all too aware of the sound of his footsteps as they boomed off the metal surface of the floor. It could not be helped. The time for stealth had passed, replaced by the need for quick, decisive action.

Hearing the footsteps running towards them, the sentries turned and raised their autoguns. Their response came too late. Having crossed the distance to their position in barely the time it took them to lift their guns, Kergis lashed out twice with his power sword. In those two movements, the sentries were dead.

Cautiously, Kergis tried to open the doors into the warband leader's quarters and found them unlocked. Pushing them ajar as quietly as possible, he advanced silently into the chamber beyond. He saw a room decorated in a strangely Spartan manner. There were almost no furnishings, beyond a metal cot at one end of the room and a chair situated in the centre. Kergis noticed they were sized for Astartes rather than ordinary humans. The rest of the room was bare. There was evidence the walls had once been decorated with friezes and mosaics, probably Imperial in nature, but they had been roughly gouged and chopped from the surface, leaving a detritus of dust and plaster sitting on the floor.

His sword and bolt pistol at the ready, Kergis moved further into the room.

'Hello, arban,' a familiar voice said behind him.

'BORCHU?' KERGIS HAD said two days earlier as he stood with Jurga Khan in the strategium, staring at the reconnaissance pict of the armoured figure.

'Yes, it is him,' Jurga Khan agreed, nodding. 'You see now why I thought it best to give you this mission? Borchu was in your squad.'

'But he is dead,' Kergis said, his voice disbelieving. 'He was killed in the caverns of Nephis-Ra. I saw him die myself.'

'His body was never recovered,' the Khan reminded him. 'I have read your battle report. His body was lost in a cave-in after he had been felled by enemy fire. That section of the caverns was destroyed three days later when the enemy unleashed a captured Deathstrike armed with a plasma warhead. It was assumed Borchu's body was annihilated in the blast with everything else.'

The Khan's expression darkened.

'It now seems that assumption was in error.'

'But he was dead,' Kergis said. 'I saw him fall myself. He was hit in the chest by a lascannon. It was at close range and the beam went straight through him, emerging from his back. There is no way anyone could have survived it – otherwise, I would have tried to rescue him. But it was pointless. The heat of the beam would have cooked his internal organs instantly.'

At first, Jurga Khan did not answer. Instead, he made a gesture with his hand and caused another pict to appear. It was taken at the same angle as the previous one, but it showed a close-up of the armoured figure's chest. Despite the grainy nature of the image it was clear the chest plate of the armour had been repaired by an unknown hand. The workmanship was poor and it was readily apparent to Kergis's trained eye that the damage which had occasioned the repair work had been caused by something which had drilled a fist-sized hole through the armour's ceramite surface. Even if he had not seen the wound inflicted himself, his decades spent on the battlefield would have told him precisely which weapon had created the hole.

A lascannon.

'It is impossible,' Kergis said quietly. 'I don't want to believe it, but I must accept the evidence of my own eyes. It is Borchu. Still, I cannot believe he would turn against us. It was his nature to be loyal.'

'He may not have turned on us,' the Khan replied. 'Despite appearances, Borchu may well have died on Nephis-Ra. We have fought enemies who have been possessed by Chaos daemons in the past. Normally, the daemons can only possess a living body, but all things are possible for the creatures of the warp. Perhaps Borchu's body was recovered by the enemy after he died and a daemon now uses it. Or perhaps Borchu's body really was destroyed and a daemon or some xenos creature has shifted its appearance to resemble him. Whatever the truth, it is an abomination. Our Chapter is dishonoured as long as a creature of the enemy wears the face of one of our fallen brothers.'

'Then, the dishonour must be avenged,' Kergis said, lifting a hand to indicate the figure in the pict. 'I will seek him out. Whether it truly is Borchu, or a daemon using his appearance, I will kill him. The Chapter's honour will be restored.'

'You understand the full ramifications of what you are saying?' Jurga Khan asked him. 'I have already agreed, on behalf of our Chapter, that we will lead the assault on Chaldis. I have also agreed to send a mission to sabotage the power complex on the Ignis Mons. I agreed to both these tasks before I saw these picts and spotted Borchu, but that hardly matters. As Khan my words must be iron. If not, if we fail in either mission, our company will be dishonoured. Similarly, whatever his true nature may be, we will also be dishonoured if we fail to act against this "Borchu".'

'I understand,' Kergis said, his voice hard and unyielding. 'And I know there may be a price to be paid. But no matter the price or what it costs me, I promise you I will kill Borchu – whoever or whatever he may be.'

'HELLO, ARBAN,' THE thing wearing Borchu's face said. 'What, no smile of greeting? No warm words of welcome for a comrade you had thought lost? I am disappointed.'

Somehow, it had gotten behind him. Kergis had been sure he had checked every corner of the room before advancing, but the creature that was not Borchu had managed to find a hiding place all the same.

Cautiously, Kergis turned to face it. The room was gloomy, with few sources of illumination, but even as he stared at the armoured figure half-hidden in the shadows he knew at once it was not his former comrade. The face and the armour were the same, but the skin held a blue-white pallor Kergis associated with the recently deceased. At the same time, the creature's eyes rippled with seething and unearthly energies as though its physical form was barely able to contain the maelstrom inside it.

Even without these signs, Kergis would never have mistaken it for Borchu. In life his friend had been a good-natured, hearty fellow, always laughing. The creature before him now might wear Borchu's likeness but it was unable to copy his bearing.

'What is the matter, arban?' the thing said, taking a step forward. 'Don't you know me? Don't you recognise your old friend?'

'You are not Borchu,' Kergis replied, his expression severe. 'You may wear his face, but I know your real nature. You are a daemon, some carrion thing that stole his body. Nothing more.'

'Yes,' the creature smiled. For the moment it stayed where it was, not moving closer, but Kergis saw it carried a power axe in its hands. 'To be honest, I didn't think I'd fool you by pretending to be Borchu. But I had to try. Really, you'd be surprised how often even the clumsiest pretence will work. There is something weak in the heart of man. Show them the face of a friend, even one thought long dead, and they will believe almost anything. But you are stronger than that. Aren't you, *Kergis?*'

In response, Kergis was silent. He knew better than to be lulled by the daemon's words. His senses were alert, carefully reading the thing's stance for any sign it was about to attack. The magazine of his bolt pistol was full, but he was aware it would take almost a miracle to kill the thing with that weapon. His best chance would be to take the head from its shoulders with his power sword, but to do that he would need to move within range of the axe. He watched for an opening, waiting for the moment to strike.

'Aren't you curious as to how I knew your name?' the daemon's mocking smile grew broader. 'You must have wondered? Ordinarily, I'd tell you I learned it from Borchu himself. I'd explain I cap-tured his soul as it was leaving his body, a split second before I entered his physical remains and made them my new home. It would be a lie, of course. But, again, you'd be surprised how often such simple untruths are effective.'

Under cover of its words, the daemon had moved one of its feet fractionally forward of its partner. Recognising the change as evidence it was preparing to attack him, Kergis waited for the daemon to shift its weight from one foot to the other. Once it did so, he knew the attack would not be long in coming.

'It is all a matter of how you play it,' the daemon continued. 'Typically, I'd say something like "Borchu always hated you, you know". And you'd wonder whether I was telling the truth or not. It is the nature of human beings to always wonder whether their fellows secretly despise them. If I told you Borchu really did hate you, it would only confirm your worst suspicions. I would not even have to sell the lie too hard. You would convince yourself I was telling the truth. Humans are such easy marks.'

For all Kergis's watchfulness the daemon nearly killed him then. Even as the White Scar waited, it attacked suddenly without having to shift its weight first.

Too late, Kergis realised his error. He had let the fact the daemon was wearing Borchu's body gull him into thinking it would act like a mortal opponent, not a daemonic one.

Leaping effortlessly across the room towards him, the daemon brought its axe down in a deadly arc. Kergis barely managed to dodge the blow in time. Unbalanced, he struck out with a sideways slash of his blade. The daemon parried it easily, before delivering a counter-blow with the butt of his axe-shaft that sent Kergis staggering backward.

The daemon charged forward to press home its advantage, but Kergis was ready. He lashed out once more with his sword. The daemon blocked it, but by doing so it had left the repaired section on the chest plate of its armour exposed. Even as the sword and axe locked together, Kergis lifted his bolt pistol and fired a salvo of shots into the daemon's chest at point-blank range.

The daemon screamed in rage and pain. Striking again with the butt of its axe it hit the bolt pistol and knocked it from Kergis's hand. It tried to follow the strike with another attack from the blade of the axe, but Kergis saw it coming. He leapt backward, landing with catlike agility as he put several metres between himself and his enemy.

'You know, that actually almost hurt me,' the daemon said, lifting a hand to inspect the damage.

The salvo of bolts had blown away the patchwork repair to the armoured plate, revealing a dark wound in the chest of the daemon's host body. Instead of blood oozing out, Kergis saw sparks of eldritch fire leak from the hole. For an instant, the sparks played around the daemon's probing fingers. Then, they were gone.

'Still, there's no real damage done,' the daemon grinned insidiously. 'Not like the last time we met. You think of it often no doubt, Kergis. The good old days, eh?'

Kergis found he was beginning to hate the creature's smile, not to mention its habit of making insinuating, viperous asides every time it spoke. At the same time, he realised he might be able to play the daemon at its own game; using words to distract it in the same way as it was evidently trying to distract him.

'We have met before?' he asked.

'Surely you're not trying to claim you don't remember?' The daemon's grin deepened as his Astartes opponent took the bait. 'Granted, it was decades ago. But really, I thought you'd remember. Of course, my name was different then. I called myself *Nullus*.'

'Nullus?' Despite his awareness that the daemon would say anything to trick him, Kergis felt a shock run through him. 'I encountered a possessed Traitor Marine on Quintus who called himself by that name. He served as a lieutenant to the daemon prince Voldorius.'

'Indeed, I did,' the daemon said. 'Of course, I did look different in those days, so I can understand that you were slow to recognise me. You remember, Kergis? You killed my host body on Quintus. Sometimes, it feels like it took an eternity for me to find another one. It can be a difficult business finding a suitable body. Which is why I was so happy when I came upon your dear, departed former comrade.'

'And that's why you stole Borchu's body? Revenge?'

'It was part of the motive, I'll grant you.' The daemon's voice was like a satisfied oily purr. 'I had already attached myself to the invasion of this world, close to Chogoris. It occurred to me if I made myself visible enough it was bound to bring the White Scars to me. Naturally, I had no way of knowing it was you they'd send. That was an unexpected bonus.'

'And you did this because I cut you down on Quintus?'

'Hardly.' The daemon rolled its eyes in a curiously human gesture. 'Oh, I'd hoped I would get to settle accounts with you one day. But my aim here goes far beyond any such petty annoyances. I have been an enemy of the White Scars for thousands of years. Does that surprise you, Kergis? I have stalked your Chapter from its earliest days. I was there in the very beginning, on the plains of Chogoris, even before the Emperor came. I know your planet of old, and I knew your primarch.'

'Now I know you are lying,' Kergis told the daemon. 'If you really were such a formidable enemy, I would have heard of you. You forget, the White Scars have their own way of dealing with their foes. If you truly ranked as an ancient enemy of the Chapter, you would have been targeted long ago by the Masters of the Hunt for destruction. You would have been killed and your skull would be sitting on a pike along the road to Khum Karta. Your name would be known from the roster of the hunt.'

'My name? You don't know my name. Not my true name, at any rate. I didn't always call myself Nullus. I'll admit you won't find me mentioned in the annals of your Chapter or in the tales the Chaplains tell, but everything I have told you is true. I am an old enemy of the White Scars, perhaps the *oldest*. I fought against Jaghatai Khan on Chogoris, just as I had fought against many other petty chieftains on your home world. In the old days, the days before the Imperium, your people knew me, Kergis. They called me *Kagayaga*. You know *that* name, I'm sure.'

Again, Kergis felt a shock run through him. The daemon was right. The name was familiar to him, although he had not heard it for over a century.

Kagayaga. It was a word from the old Chogorian dialect. Literally, it meant 'the whisper in the darkness'. It was a name to conjure nightmares. In the ancient folklore of Kergis's home world, Kagayaga had been the title given to a mythical monster. According to the tales he was an invisible, bodiless horror; a malicious spirit who haunted the plains and sometimes stole into the hearts of men while they were sleeping in order to compel them to perform evil acts.

Even today, it was still common for mothers on Chogoris to warn their offspring that Kagayaga would come for them if they did not behave themselves. Kergis had heard the same tales himself in his own childhood at his mother's knee.

Kagayaga. It was impossible. Kergis did not know how the daemon had come to know the name, but he did not believe the creature's claim for an instant. Kagayaga did not exist. He was a fictional figure used to frighten children. A figment of his people's ancient imaginings.

It was clear the daemon was trying to trick him, to frighten him by evoking the terrors of his childhood. It would not work. Kergis was a White Scar. He was Astartes. He was beyond such fears.

'I see you know the name,' the daemon said. 'I thought you would.'

'You are lying,' Kergis replied coldly. 'Kagayaga is a name to frighten children, nothing more. He does not exist.'

'By all means tell yourself that if you find it gives you comfort.' The daemon's smile had grown even more smug and insufferable. 'But, really we both know the truth, don't we? I am Kagayaga. But then, I have used so many names it hardly makes a difference. I am Borchu. I am Nullus. I am no one. I am the voice inside your mind. The whisper in the darkness.'

The daemon moved a step closer to him, shifting the great weight of the axe lightly from hand to hand as though making a game of it.

'For reasons of my own I have a need for the body of a White Scar,' the daemon said. 'Poor Borchu's body is so badly damaged I won't be able to use it for much longer. If only you knew the effort I have to expend just to hold it together and stop his damaged organs from spilling all over the floor like rotten fruit. No, I need something *fresher*. Not too fresh, naturally. It's true I can possess a living host, but it is difficult. One has to find the moral flaw, a chink in the victim's soul, in order to gain entrance. No, what I really need is the body of a recently killed victim. Your body, for example.'

Without warning, the daemon suddenly leapt forward to attack him again.

Kergis was ready for it. He dodged the first blow, counter-attacking with a low strike towards his opponent's legs. The daemon sidestepped it easily, responding with an axe-head strike aimed at Kergis's chest. The fight continued, the blows raining back and forth only to be blocked or eluded as they struggled without either being able to best the other.

They were evenly matched in terms of skill, but Kergis realised the odds were stacked against him. The daemon held all the advantages. As yet none of its blows had connected, but Kergis did not need to feel the force of them to know the warp-abomination was physically stronger than he was. At the same time, it was tireless and seemingly immune to pain.

Kergis was Astartes, with all the benefits it entailed. At the root, though, he was only a mortal man, while the daemon was something darker, ancient and more powerful. Given enough time, he knew it would wear him down.

The monster had shown him its weakness, though. While it baited and mocked him, Kergis had seen the daemon's arrogance. Experience told him it was a flaw he could use to create an opening.

'I believe you are getting slower, Kergis,' the daemon said as the duel between them continued. 'That last parry was hardly of the standard I'd expect from an Astartes. You're getting tired, aren't you?'

'I am feeling a little extended, it is true,' Kergis replied, trying to keep the strain from his voice as he blocked another strike from the axe. 'But it is only to be expected. I had a bike beneath me last time I killed you. The extra running involved in this battle has taken its toll.'

'The bike was the only reason you won last time,' the daemon commented acidly. He might be immune to physical pain, but evidently Kergis's words had struck a nerve. 'This time, it will be different.'

'I agree,' Kergis came back at him. 'This time, I am not part of a larger White Scar army. I am not accompanied by the best part of a company of warriors, most of them on bikes. I am on my own, on foot, at a disadvantage. Yet still, I am holding my own against you. I see now my Khan was right in sending me here alone. It would have been a waste of resources to have sent a bigger force after you, when one sergeant on his own is equal to the task.'

Kergis let his barbed words hang in the air for a moment before twisting the knife.

'Perhaps you are Kagayaga, after all. A bogeyman whose name is invoked to frighten children. Scaring children would seem to be all you are good for.'

His words provoked an immediate response. Its face a mask of rage, the daemon swung its axe in a powerful two-handed strike intending to cut Kergis in half. Expecting the reaction, the White Scar dodged the clumsy blow and responded with a low, rising cut while the daemon was still off-balance.

His blow caught the daemon's host body in the midriff, slicing through armour and exiting just below the shoulder. Showing the first real sign of pain, the daemon briefly lost its balance and fell to its knees. Trying to regain its feet, it lifted its axe to defend itself. But, as it looked up, it saw the bright flash of Kergis's sword arcing towards it as the White Scar prepared to deliver the coup de grace.

'For Borchu,' Kergis said, as he brought the sword down and took the daemon's head from its shoulders.

It felt like a benediction.

AFTERWARDS, KERGIS WOULD never know how long he stood over the headless corpse. With the destruction of its host body, the fell light of the daemon's eyes had been immediately extinguished. Nullus, or Kagayaga, had been banished back to wherever it was daemons went when their physical forms were destroyed. Kergis was left alone with the body of a friend.

Ordinarily, Kergis would have felt pride or exultation in the aftermath of victory. This time, he felt only sorrow. He had defeated the daemon, but though he had driven the thing from Borchu's body he was acutely aware of a loss to his Chapter.

Unlike Osol or Doshin, Borchu's gene-seed would never be used to create new White Scars. For all Kergis knew, the progenoid glands inside Borchu's corpse were still intact. But that same body had been possessed by a daemon, a thing of Chaos. It did not matter that the daemon was gone. Borchu's body was irredeemably tainted.

Similarly, Kergis suspected the record of Borchu's deeds would be quietly purged from the tales the Chaplains told to remind the White Scars of their fallen brethren. No one would want to be reminded of Borchu now. Whatever his achievements in life, his body had suffered ignominy and dishonour after his death. It did not matter that Borchu himself had been innocent of that dishonour. The tales the Chaplains told were as much lessons as anything else. There seemed no good lesson to be learned from Borchu's post-mortem disgrace.

It could not be helped, but to Kergis it felt like he had lost his old comrade a second time.

Abruptly, he felt a tremor run through the floor beneath his feet, bringing him back to the present. It was followed by another tremor, and another, each one more insistent than the last.

Kergis knew at once what it meant. Gurban and the others had succeeded in their mission of sabotage. They had destroyed the control systems responsible for holding the eruptions of the Ignis Mons in check. Once the damage had been done it was only a matter of time before the magma pressure built up to a critical level, resulting in an eruption that would engulf the power complex in a rising wave of red-hot lava. After being kept under artificial control for so long, it was likely the eruption would progress quickly. At most, Kergis supposed he might have ten minutes to escape the complex before it was destroyed.

Ten minutes. It was barely enough time for him to find his way out from the complex, never mind the fact it was teeming with enemy troops, none of whom would take it well that he had just killed their leader.

In all likelihood, Kergis expected to die on the Ignis Mons. He had suspected as much from the very beginning. He had known it was the most probable outcome once he had volunteered for his part of the mission. Jurga Khan and Balat had both said as much to him, at different times and in their own individual ways.

Yet, Kergis had accepted the potential sacrifice ahead of him gladly. The fact that the daemon-possessed Borchu was the leader of the garrison guarding the Mons had left the White Scars facing a conflict between duty and honour.

On one hand, the honour of the Chapter dictated the creature had to be destroyed. On the other, they were already committed to destroying the power plant – a mission vital to the success of the coming invasion. Unable to see any other way to achieve this dual purpose, and unwilling to let more of his brothers be put at risk, Kergis had accepted the mission knowing it would probably be his last. It was a suicide run from the very beginning.

Still, if he was to die on this strange world far from home, he would die fighting. Retrieving his bolt pistol and igniting the blade of his power sword once more, Kergis took a last glance at Borchu's body and turned for the door leading from the chamber.

Expecting to find dozens of enemy warriors waiting for him on the other side, he prepared for the onslaught, opened the door and stepped out into the corridor.

Unexpectedly, it was quiet.

It was empty except for the bodies of the two sentries he had killed earlier. Surprised at his good fortune, Kergis hurried on down the corridor. No matter how far he went there was no sign of the massed ranks of enemy fighters he had expected. The upper levels of the complex seemed almost eerily deserted.

Then, Kergis turned a corner and saw dozens of bodies lying strewn across a broad, open hallway. They were cultists, like the ones he had met earlier, and they had died with great violence. From the amount of autogun casings littering the floor it was clear they had fought savagely, but their killer had cut through them like a scythe through wheat.

'Hello, sergeant.' A smiling figure stood waiting for him in the centre of the hallway. 'I had hoped to catch up with you earlier. But it took longer to kill this scum than I expected.'

It was Arik. Staring at him in disbelief, Kergis realised he was the reason there had been no enemies waiting when he left the daemon's quarters.

'I discussed the matter with Gurban after we planted the charges in the control room,' Arik said.

'We decided it really didn't need all five of us to fight our way out of the complex once the job was done. And Gurban thought you might need a pathfinder. I realise, strictly speaking, we violated your orders. But I hoped you might forgive us if I helped you escape before the volcano erupts.'

'Perhaps I will forgive you,' Kergis smiled back. 'Always assuming you actually have a plan to escape and you aren't just hoping for a miracle.'

'A miracle couldn't hurt,' Arik shrugged. 'But I notice on the blueprints there's a landing pad at the top of complex. If we can reach it before the whole place is destroyed, we might be able to seize a shuttle.'

As though underlining his words, another tremor shook through the walls around them.

'All right,' Kergis said. 'You're the pathfinder. Find us a path out of this hellhole.'

Together, they ran down the hallway.

THE SUN WAS rising by the time they reached the landing pad, the first glimmerings of dawn painting the sky a vibrant red.

Having taken advantage of the confusion caused by the worsening tremors rumbling through the complex, Kergis and Arik fought their way to an ancient shuttle sitting on the landing pad. It was a light cargo lifter of the kind designed to ferry supplies and the occasional passenger to distant outposts.

Boarding the shuttle before the crew could lift off, the two White Scars killed them without breaking stride. Kergis took the controls, while Arik searched through the channels on the shuttle's vox for the telltale comms-chatter that would indicate the invasion of Tephra VII was underway.

Kergis had seen a fuel tanker parked beside the shuttle when they came on board. As he triggered the engines, he found himself hoping the tanker had finished its work rather than not yet started it.

In the event, the engines purred into life smoothly. Except for a few desultory bursts of autogun fire plinking against their hull, they took off without incident. Hurtling through the vast smoke cloud now billowing from the summit of the Mons, Kergis sped westward as the tremors shaking through the complex reached a final crescendo.

Sparing a glance behind him, he saw the eruption of the Ignis Mons. Lava issued from the summit and poured down the slopes, an inexorable and slow moving blanket of death.

There was no question their primary mission had been successful. The power complex, along with the body of Borchu, would be engulfed and destroyed. The void shields protecting Chaldis would come down.

After much adjustment of the unfamiliar controls of the shuttle's vox, Arik found a great welter of encrypted chatter across a dozen channels on Imperial wavelengths. Hearing it, they smiled in satisfaction.

The invasion had begun.

Somewhere, out in the desolate Cradle, Gurban and the other men from the squad would be on their way to rendezvous with Balat and his Scouts, before heading for a pre-arranged extraction point where a Thunderhawk would be waiting to take them back to the *Warrior of the Plains*. With any luck, Kergis and Arik would be there before them.

Kergis's smile grew broader when he thought of the surprised looks his comrades would be sure to wear when they arrived and saw him and Arik already waiting for them.

Today, at this time and place, it was a good day to be alive. The mission had achieved its aims. Hopefully, soon, Tephra VII would be free. A daemon had been slain. An old comrade laid to rest.

Kergis did not fool himself his current mood of contentment would last for long. Experience told him to enjoy it while he could, for he knew such times were fleeting. Soon, there would be new conflicts, new dangers, new battles. The galaxy was not made for times of peace.

In the grim darkness of the forty-first millennium there was only war.

THE RELIC

Jonathan Green

THE HORDE SPREAD across the unsullied blue-white wilderness of the ice fields like an oily black stain. Filthy clouds of greasy smoke rose from the exhausts of fossil fuel-guzzling machines, sending sooty trails into the frozen air to mark their passing. Every war-bike and cobbled-together trukk left a petrochemical smear across both land and sky behind it, marking the horde's progress across the polar wilderness as another region of the planet fell to the furious predations of the alien invaders.

An unstoppable tide of savage, growling machinery poured out across the riven glacier. Before it, still a league or more away, the stalwart line of armour that the Emperor's chosen had decreed would not be breached approached. Today – at this time and in this place, amidst the desolate ice fields of the Dead

Lands of Armageddon – the Astartes would make their stand against the green tide.

Warbike outriders gunned their throttles excitedly, while those boyz clinging to the sides of guntrukks, wartraks and battlewagons cannibalised from captured vehicles of Imperial design fired off round after round from their heavy calibre shootas in their overeagerness to engage with the enemy.

The drop-pod fell from heaven like the wrath of the Emperor Himself. The force of its landing sent shuddering tremors through the iron-hard ice sheet, a network of treacherous crevasses fracturing outwards from the point of impact.

The echoing gunshot retort of the pod's landing still rumbling across the fractured face of the glacier, the armoured landing craft opened and from it emerged the instrument of the Emperor's holy vengeance.

Autoloaders clattered into operation as the barrels of an assault cannon noisily cycled up to speed. The four blunt digits of a huge robotic fist, easily large enough to crush an ork's skull, flexed and whirred, servo-motors in each finger giving it a crushing force equal to that exerted by a crawling glacier.

With heavy, pistoning steps, the revered Dreadnought emerged from the cocoon of its drop-pod, some monstrous metal beetle birthing from its adamantium shell, roused and ready for war.

Bio-linked sensors scanned the rapidly-advancing line of greenskin vehicles, the Dreadnought's machine-spirit-merged sentience processing the constant stream of information – everything from average velocities to weapon capabilities to wind shear – and waited. Experience won on a thousand battlefields across a hundred worlds – including this Emperor-forsaken rock in particular – came into play, recalled from the depths of mind-linked implants. The orks weren't going anywhere. He could afford to be patient. Revenge was a dish served best cold, after all.

Heavy munitions fire chewed the frozen ground in front of him. The foul xenos had seen him fall from the heavens on wings of fire like some avenging angel and now that he was in their sights they were directing everything in their crude arsenal directly at him.

Shells threw chips of ice the size of Predator shells from the bullet-pitted surface of the glacier, many raining back down to strike against the Dread-nought's ancient adamantium armour. It had stood up to much worse over the centuries. The ice shards shattered harmlessly against its hull, some explod-ing into powder.

As the orks drew closer still and their haphazard targeting devices found their range at last, the green-skins let fly with rockets, high calibre shells and even smoky flamethrowers in their eagerness to engage with the ancient.

The Dreadnought disappeared amidst clouds of sooty smoke and roiling flames, the glacier reverber-ating now to the explosions and impacts of the orks' weapons which were, in general, noisy and heavy on the pyrotechnics, but not all that accurate or effective.

And all the time the ork line surged forwards, steadily closing on the Dreadnought's position.

Preceded by a torrent of cannon and bolter fire, the Dreadnought stepped from the smoke of its supposed destruction, swivelling about its waist axis, raking the hurtling ork vehicles with its arm-mounted weapons. The standard that hung from its banner-pole was scorched black and still smouldering at the edges, the halo of iron spikes surmounting its armoured body glowing orange in the oily flames lapping at its pockmarked hull.

Three times the height of a man, larger than many of the ork machines and as heavy as a warbuggy, armoured with adamantium plates and carrying an arsenal that rivalled the firepower of a battlewagon, it would take more than that to halt this juggernaut's advance.

It took the Dreadnought's symbiotic machine-spirit mere nanoseconds to divine the ancient's position relative to the speeding ork vehicles and select a succession of suitable targets. The Dreadnought opened up with its assault cannon and storm bolter again, a hail of hard shells reaping their own whirlwind of death and destruction.

'Death to the invaders!' Brother Jarold of the Black Templars Solemnus Crusade bellowed, his augmented voice booming from vox-casters built into his Dreadnought body-shell. What little of him that was still flesh and blood spasmed in fury, thrashing and sloshing within the amniotic fluids of his sarcophagus-tank. 'Cleanse this place of the xenos taint, in the name of the primarch and the Emperor. Death to the defilers of Armageddon!'

The squadron of warbikes leading the Kult of Speed in its attack was the first to taste his wrath. Burning rubber shredded under the attention of the Dreadnought's assault cannon, sending several bikes and their riders cart-wheeling over the ice, as sheared axles and wheel-less spokes stabbed into the ice, flipping the screaming machines through the air to land in broken piles upon the iron-hard glacier.

Those orks unfortunate enough to land at Jarold's feet had limbs and skulls crushed beneath his relentless, pounding footfalls.

A burst of storm bolter fire found a promethium barrel lashed to the side of wartrak. The fuel inside touched off, blowing the vehicle apart, spreading pieces of wartrak up to twenty-five metres away across the ice field.

With a series of hollow pops, the rocket launchers arrayed across the Dreadnought's broad shoulders sent a fusillade of mortar shells arcing into the pack of vehicles behind the disintegrating line of warbikes.

Unable to stop in time, some of the ork bikes skidded past the Dreadnought, and having already missed one target chose instead to rev their engines and plough on towards the advancing line of Astartes armour.

Three bikes crashed and burned as Brother Jarold's weapons-fire took them down, and just as many again collided with the wrecked vehicles.

Many of the ork drivers were horrified to discover that the Dreadnought still stood after their concerted bombardment of it, and swerved at the last moment to avoid the immovable hulk. But one wasn't quick enough and cleared the choking exhaust trail of another bike to find itself directly on top of the Dreadnought.

The warbike hit Brother Jarold with the force of an ork rokkit. Even as the bike hit him, Jarold grabbed hold of it with his huge power fist, the vehicle swinging up into the air in his grasp as its momentum spun them both around. The ork rider was still clinging to the wide handlebars when a direct hit from Brother Jarold's storm bolter ignited the contents of the bike's fuel tank, as he released the vehicle at the height of its rising arc. The bike spun through the air above him and became a fiery comet, annihilating another ork rider that was rounding on the Dreadnought as the bike crashed back down to earth.

The Dreadnought's deep strike insertion and deadly combination of cannon and bolter fire had decimated the front line of the ork Speed Freeks. And all the while, unheard over the roar of bike and trukk, assault cannon and bolter, as well as the concussive booms of fuel-tank explosions, Brother Jarold called down the wrath of the Emperor and His primarchs on the heads of the xenos filth.

The promethium roar of crude ork engines was joined by the well-tuned growl of the superior Astartes armour as the bikes of the Black Templars' rapid deployment force and its supporting land speeder squadron closed on the drop-pod's homing beacon.

If the orks had been surprised by the fury of the Dreadnought's initial attack, it proved to be only a foretaste of what was to come as Ansgar's Avengers – the strike force mustered in memory of the fallen Emperor's Champion – engaged the enemy.

Clouds of bittersweet incense swirled and ascended into the vault of the battle-chapel, filling the cathedral space with a sparkling aromatic mist. Shapes swam in and out of the constantly shifting vapours, giving glimpses of fluted columns a hundred metres tall, skull and cross adorned buttresses and statues commemorating the fallen of the Chapter.

The skull-set glow-globes had been dimmed and the forests of candles were in the process of being snuffed out by a trundling cenobyte servitor while its partner, following on behind, proceeded to trim their wicks and clear away the crusted wax that coated the black iron candelabra, like a series of frozen cataracts.

The sound of the pitted oak doors opening – the doors so old now the wood was black – resounded throughout the battle-chapel like the boom of distant gunfire. Chaplain Wolfram opened his eyes, finishing the prayer that was on his lips. He rose to standing from where he had been kneeling before the Solemnus Shrine, his eyes

*falling once again upon the empty indentations where the
Black Sword, the Champion's laurel-wreathed helm and
the lovingly ornamented Armour of Faith should have
lain.*

*Wolfram turned, one armoured hand – every knuckle
of the gauntlet embossed with the Templars' black cross
and white skull insignia, a permanent memento mori to
the one charged with watching over the souls of the crusaders – closing around the haft of his crozius arcanum.
The ancient artefact was both a Chaplain's badge of
office and a potent weapon in its own right. A disruptor
generator was concealed within the wooden shaft of the
relic, that one simple addition turning the flared blades
of the Templar cross that surmounted it into a lethal
power axe.*

*The sound of echoing footfalls on the stone-flagged floor
of the cathedral space carried to the Chaplain through the
muffling clouds rising from the glowing nuggets of flame-
flecked incense smouldering within their braziers.
Chaplain Wolfram relaxed his grip on his crozius.*

*The booming footsteps came closer, the incense smoke
parting as a colossal shape, that was neither man nor
machine but something of both, something greater than
either, stepped into the light of the candles that guttered
in the breeze of its advance.*

*Wolfram noted the battle-damaged banner pole and
the deeply etched gothic lettering upon the Dreadnought's
hull and bowed.*

*'In the name of Him Enthroned on Holy Terra, well
met, Brother Jarold,' he said. 'And what brings you to this
place of sanctuary, still an hour from matins?'*

'May the Emperor's blessings be upon you, Brother-Chaplain,' the machine-tempered voice of the ancient responded.

'You are not slumbering with your brother Dread-noughts aboard Forgeship Goliath?'

'Now is not the time for rest.'

'But our recent endeavours on Armageddon have cost us dear,' the Chaplain warned. 'Rest is what is needed now.'

'I cannot sleep, brother, not when there is still so much of His holy work left undone. And besides, I have slept for long enough already.'

'Then what can I do for you, brother?' the Chaplain asked.

'I would seek your counsel,' the Dreadnought said in a voice like the slamming of sepulchre doors.

'From me, brother?' Wolfram asked, caught off guard for a moment by Brother Jarold's honesty. Ancients were usually the ones who shared their hard-won wisdom with the rest of the Chapter; they were not the ones who came seeking it from others. 'You are troubled?'

'Yes, I am troubled, Brother-Chaplain.' The Dread-nought broke off.

'Speak, brother. You have nothing to feel ashamed of.'

'But I do.'

'I see. You speak of the loss of Brother Ansgar.'

'I do, brother. When the Emperor's chosen one needed me most, I was found wanting.'

'You have prayed about this?'

'I have sat in penitent vigil ever since my return to the fleet. I have thought on Brother Ansgar's fate and nothing else.'

'I too have spent time in prayer and contemplation on the same matter,' Wolfram admitted.

'You have, brother?'

'I have. You cannot blame yourself for what happened. Blame the beast, the heretic xenos that blight the world below still. Purge yourself of your guilt in the crucible of war. Smite the xenos with bolter and fist and cannon, all in the name of vengeance. Use the rage that the Emperor has placed within your soul to bring down His wrath upon the greenskin. Show no remorse. Show the alien no pity and you will have nothing to fear.'

Silence descended between Chaplain and Dreadnought as the latter considered the former's words.

'So you believe that this is all part of some greater plan? His divine plan for Armageddon? For our crusade? For me?'

'I do not know, Brother Jarold,' Wolfram admitted with a shake of his head, 'but what I do know is that no one has come forward since to take on the mantle of champion, having received His divine inspiration, and there are plenty who would be ready for such a role.'

'So you believe Brother Ansgar is still alive.' The Dreadnought's augmented voice suddenly sounded strangely like that of a young petitioner, yet to be admitted to the brotherhood, desperate for reassurance.

'That is what I know. Somewhere, and perhaps only barely, but the Emperor would not leave us without a source of inspiration to lead us at a time such as this, with the conflict to decide the fate of this world still raging around us. And Brother Ansgar does not have to fight alongside us to inspire we of the Solemnus Crusade to great deeds.'

Incense-smoke coiled about the motionless form of the monolithic Dreadnought. When Brother Jarold spoke again, the vibrations of his vox-casters sent ripples through the curling smoke, creating new eddying patterns within it.

'Then my course is plain,' he said.

Chaplain Wolfram looked up at the scrollwork decorations of Jarold's Dreadnought-locked sarcophagus.

'This day I vow that I shall not rest until Brother Ansgar has been found and we bear him back in triumph, or that we might lay his body to rest and reclaim the relics of our Chapter – the sanctified weapons that are the most potent symbols of his office.

'I shall petition Marshal Brant to muster an army that we might avenge Brother Ansgar and our Chapter against the orks of the Blood Scar Tribe,' the Dreadnought said. 'And then we shall return to Armageddon.'

BROTHER JAROLD SURVEYED the wreckage that was all that remained of the Speed Freeks expeditionary force. The kult's predilection for speed had proved their undoing. Stronger armour and better armament would have perhaps given them a better fighting chance against the inviolable armour of the Black Templars battleforce.

Sensors that saw in wavelengths ranging from infra-red to ultraviolet scanned the devastation searching for life-signs. If any greenskin had survived the Black Templars' rout they would not remain alive for long.

The once pristine white wilderness was now befouled with the gouged ruts of tyre tracks, blackened mounds of snow and ice thrown up by the artillery shells of both sides, promethium spills and fossil-fuel slicks turning the ice desert black. Some puddles still burned, the oily smoke rising from them adding their own acrid pollution to the devastated wilderness. Impact craters pockmarked the glacier where some heavy shells had missed their targets; where others had hit, debris from large ork vehicles lay strewn across the snow.

The kult's battlewagon had met its end when the machine-spirit of Techmarine Isendur's personal Razorback transport targeted the battlewagon's primary weapon power cell. A single, directed pulse from the Razorback's twin-linked lascannon and the resulting detonation had not only taken out the gun-bristling battlewagon itself, but also a guntrukk, a warbuggy and three assorted warbikes.

This had also been the turning point in the battle, a devastating blow from which the orks never recovered. All that was left of them now were piles of burning debris, blackened craters in the ice and piles of crushed and eviscerated carcasses.

Brother Jarold stood at the centre of the devastation, amidst the splintered axle-shafts, buckled wheel-housings and twisted chassis of the orks' ramshackle vehicles.

Behind the imposing presence of the watchful Dreadnought massed the Black Templars of the Solemnus Crusade. That same crusade had set out twelve years before to avenge the atrocity perpetrated against the Templars' Chapter Keep on the world of

Solemnus by the greenskins that fought under the banner of the Scarred Ork.

There were injuries among the crusaders, the most severe being the loss of a limb sustained by Brother Baldulf under the wheels of an ork warbike, although it wouldn't stop him from marching to battle alongside his brethren, his chainsword held high. But there were no brothers to mourn that day, to be marked on the roll of the fallen, maintained within the battle-chapel at the heart of the Solemnus fleet's flagship battle barge, the *Divine Fury*.

The Emperor was truly smiling upon their endeavours that day; for sixty-three verified enemy kills not one Black Templar had fallen to the kult of speed. It was all the proof Brother Jarold needed to feel vindicated that their search for their lost champion was the will of Him Enthroned on Holy Terra.

Brother Jarold gave thanks to the Emperor, the Primarch Dorn and Lord Sigismund, their Chapter-founder, that their sanctified boltguns had functioned fully during their battle with the greenskins and that not one of their war machines had been damaged beyond repair during the conflict.

The Black Templars land speeder squadron had decimated the ork bikes and trukks, the Rhinos and Razorbacks finishing off what Typhoon and Tornado had started, while the Space Marines bike squadron and two-manned attack bikes had harried those orks that attempted to flee the battlefield.

The bark of a storm bolter firing echoed across the ice field like the retort of a heavy artillery piece. It had a number of the Black Templars raking the mounds of debris and bodies with boltgun and flamer, seeking the source of the sound, ready to bring the fight to the enemy once again. Instead they found Brother Jarold, blue smoke coiling from the muzzles of his heavy storm bolter – a weapon so large it would not look out of place mounted on one of the fleet's precious Predators or Vindicators. The body of a greenskin Jarold had targeted spasmed as it was blown in two by the mass-reactive rounds.

Techmarine Isendur approached Jarold. The Dreadnought dwarfed even the crimson-armoured Techmarine, whose twitching servo-arm – which seemed to move with a life all of its own – made him appear even taller than the average superhuman Space Marine. Behind him, Isendur's servitor team were making repairs to superficial damage sustained by the Razorback in the battle, or keeping an unstinting watch over those working on the machine, depending on their designation and degree of sentient programming.

Sensing the Techmarine's presence before he had a chance to speak Jarold asked, 'Are our brothers ready to move on the objective again?'

'Affirmative, brother,' the other replied in that familiar emotionless way of his, that was so out of character when compared with the passion and zeal exhibited by the rest of the crusade's fanatical warriors. 'At your command.'

'How far do you judge us to be from our target?

'Twelve point zero-seven-six kilometres,' the Tech-marine intoned. It had been remarked upon on more than one occasion that Isendur was more akin to the machines to which he ministered than his brother Space Marines.

'And the nature of the signal,' Jarold said. 'Is it still as it appeared from orbit?'

'More so,' Isendur said. 'As hypothesised, the anomalous readings detected from orbit are indicative of some form of primitive teleportation technology.'

Grim satisfaction warred with Jarold's overriding sense of guilt and barely-supressed rage. The memory of the moment Jarold witnessed the mech-enhanced greenskin warboss teleport out of the devastated mekboy's lab blazed within his mind as hot and red as the moment when he had been cut down by a rusting cybernetic claw, that had earned him the privilege of being encased within the Dreadnought shell that had formerly been the living tomb of Ancient Brother Dedric.

The moment Emperor's Champion Ansgar had been taken from right in front of him re-played itself through his mind for what seemed like the thousandth time...

He saw himself closing on the alien tyrant again, a sphere of crackling emerald light surrounding the ork and his unconscious prisoner. He watched again as the green glare of the crackling shield intensified.

And then, just as his crashing steps brought him within reach of the xenos brute, with a sub-sonic boom the

*sphere of light imploded, plunging the ruins of the labo-
ratory into sudden darkness. Only a retina-searing
after-image remained, trapped within the sensor-linked
optic nerves of Jarold's physical body, but of Emperor's
Champion Ansgar and the alien warboss Morkrull Grimskar there was no sign...*

'Then the command is given,' Jarold said simply.

Wherever the orks were using their wildly unpredictable teleportation technology, there was the
possibility that the re-constructed Grimskar, nemesis
of the Solemnus Crusade, would be there too. And if
the greenskin warboss *was* there, there was also the
possibility that they would find Ansgar too.

Isendur made an adjustment to the signum he
held out before him in one crimson gauntlet. Servo-
motors whined as the Dreadnought turned to
observe the Techmarine with its faceless sarcophagus
front. 'Brother Isendur? Is there something else?'

'I am picking up another signal,' the Techmarine
said.

'Another teleport signal?' Jarold asked.

'No. It is weak, like a resting pulse.'

'What is its source?'

'Bearing zero six-seven point three.'

'And what would you hazard is the nature of this
signal?'

'There is a fifty-two per cent probability that it is
electromagnetic interference caused by isotopes
buried in the bedrock beneath the glacier,' the Techmarine explained. 'But there is also a twenty-three
per cent probability that it is interference caused by

the disruption of the planet's magnetic field by the teleportation matrix. One way or the other, probability tells us that it probably is not worth pursuing.'

'But what of the other twenty-five per cent?' Jarold enquired.

'There is a possibility that it is a signal from a dormant power source. But it is unlikely.'

'What sort of power source?' Jarold pressed.

'Like that of a dying power cell.'

'As might be found inside a Deathwind automated weapons system. Or a Dreadnought.'

'It is increasingly unlikely but still a slim possibility,' Isendur persisted, not prepared to have his logic refuted. 'If our mission is to find the source of the teleport signal I would recommend that we move on that target forthwith and ignore this weaker signum reading.'

The knowledge that there was a possibility – no matter how slim – that the signal was the last sign of a lost brother Dreadnought, whether Templar or otherwise, played on Jarold's mind. Dreadnoughts were potent weapons of the Astartes Chapters and revered relics. An entire battleforce would willingly fight to reclaim a fallen Dreadnought brother. Only in the direst circumstances would a Space Marine commander abandon such a sacred relic to the field of battle.

To recover such a potent treasure, whatever Chapter it might belong to, would be of incalculable value to the war effort. Just one Dreadnought could help bolster the Astartes forces on one of

Armageddon's numerous war-fronts, and who knew what impact that could have in the long term on the struggle for the contested planet.

'I respect your opinion, Brother-Techmarine, you know that. You and your brethren of the Forge have tended to me on numerous occasions, but you see only the logic of variables and algorithms. I have the benefit of experience and the wisdom of years and I disagree. We shall investigate the source of this other signal and then, when we have resolved what it is, we will press on towards our primary objective.'

'Very well, brother,' Isendur conceded. 'As you wish.'

The Dreadnought turned to survey the re-ordered ranks of the Black Templars' strike force.

'Brothers,' he declaimed, his voice booming over the burning battlefield, flurries of snow hissing as they melted in the licking flames of the promethium fires. 'The word is given. In the name of the Emperor, Primarch Dorn and Lord Sigismund, move out.'

'Is this the place?' Jarold asked, scanning the blizzard-scoured ice valley. The ice sheet rose up before them to meet the frozen slopes of a ridge of razor-edged peaks beyond which curious green corposant flickered and danced across the sky.

'Affirmative,' Techmarine Isendur replied, consulting the signum in his hand once more.

The hulking black Dreadnought and the crimson-armoured Techmarine stood before a wall of blue ice as solid and as impenetrable as rockcrete.

'So where, precisely, is the source of the signal?'

'Six point eight-nine metres downwards. If we are to discover the source of the signal we are going to have to dig.'

'Then we dig,' Jarold stated bluntly.

'Leave it to me, brother,' Isendur said. The Techmarine signalled the waiting column. 'Brothers Larce and Nyle,' he said, summoning those two crusaders. Jarold understood what it was he had in mind.

Larce, flamer in hand, and Nyle, bearing his thrice-blessed meltagun, joined them before the wall of blue ice.

'Brothers,' Jarold said, 'let the Emperor's holy fire cleanse these xenos-blighted lands.'

Techmarine Isendur directing their fire, Larce and Nyle hit the glacier with everything their weapons could muster.

Initiate Tobrecan brought his bike up to join them and directed a series of searing blasts from the plasma gun mounted on the front of his machine at the glacier. When the steam and mist cleared, Brothers Larce and Nyle stepped up again, while Initiate Isen drove his attack bike forwards, Gunner Leax turning his multi-melta on the metres thick ice.

The Space Marines' flamers and plasma weapons swiftly melted a shaft through the ice to the source of the signal Isendur had located via his signum. Steaming geysers of cloud rose from the hole in the glacier as the boiling water bubbling at the bottom of the pit re-condensed as it came into contact with the cold air.

'Now then, Brother-Techmarine,' Jarold said, standing at the edge of the cone-shaped shaft, 'let us see what lies buried here.'

Using his servo-arm to assist him in his descent, Techmarine Isendur clambered into the steaming shadows of the ice pit. The rest of the strike force waited in tense anticipation to see which would be proved right; the Techmarine or the Dreadnought.

Bracing himself within the shaft Isendur looked down at the shadow still locked beneath one last remaining layer of ice.

'You were right,' his voice rose from the bottom of the pit. There was no hint of annoyance or praise in its tone.

'I was right,' the Dreadnought rumbled with righteous satisfaction.

'Do we wake him?' the Techmarine asked, something like awe tingeing his words, as he stared down at the statuesque creation of frost-rimed adamantium beneath him. A faint red glow pulsed weakly behind the ice, and yet as regular as a heartbeat.

'He is a brother Space Marine.'

'He is a Crimson Fist,' the Techmarine testified.

'But our brother nonetheless. So we wake him.'

He remembered...

Thunder rumbled over the ice fields and frozen, broken peaks of the Dead Lands. It was the crack and boom of heavy artillery fire. The iron-hard ground shook with the force of an earthquake, more so than it did at his own wrathful steps.

He remembered…

Rank upon rank of Space Marines, squad after squad of his fellow battle-brothers, marching against the enemy, their Chapter banners flying proudly above them. Magnificent in their regal blue power armour, their left hands blood-red – recalling the ceremony conducted at the initiation of new Chapter Masters in the former Imperial Fists Legion – their battle-consecrated boltguns cinched tight to their chest plates ready to deliver the Emperor's ultimate justice to the enemy.

And he remembered…

The war machine. A stompa, the rank and file troops of the Armageddon PDF had called it. A mobile war-altar dedicated to the hated greenskins' brutal heathen gods. An icon to thoughtless bloodshed and mindless destruction.

He remembered…

Marching to war across the bitter wastes, shoulder to shoulder with his battle-brothers, the ork host charging to meet them, the glacier's surface fracturing beneath the greenskins' advance, the freezing wind as sharp and as cold as a blade of ice slicing the air between them.

He remembered…

Faced with insurmountable odds, a new strategy had to be formed, shaped within the heat of battle.

He remembered volunteering, proud that he should be the one to bring an end to this conflict. He remembered sound and heat and light. He remembered dying a second time.

And then, amidst the clamour of battle and the cataclysmic roar of destruction, he heard a voice.

'Brother,' it said. 'Awake.'

THE DULL RED glow behind the visor of the Dreadnought's sarcophagus helm pulsed more brightly with every word the Dreadnought spoke. Its voice was phlegmy and cracked from age and lack of use.

'I am sorry, brother, but what did you say?'

A sound like vox-distorted coughing crackled from the ancient. Then the Dreadnought tried again.

'You are on Armageddon, brother,' Jarold replied. 'You are here, within the Dead Lands.'

The coughing resumed, rose to a crescendo and then subsided at last.

'No. When is it?' the venerable asked. 'My internal chronograph appears to be malfunctioning.'

Techmarine Isendur answered in terms precise to three decimal places.

The Crimson Fist was silent for several long moments.

'How long have you been here, brother?' Jarold dared to ask at last. 'Since the conflict began?'

'You mean to tell me that Armageddon has been a contested world all this time?' the venerable said with something like disbelieving incomprehension.

'Yes, since the abomination Ghazghkull Mag Uruk Thraka fell upon this world for a second time.'

'A second time?'

Jarold regarded the ancient suspiciously.

'Tell me, brother, how long have you been trapped here, entombed within the ice?'

Several moments more passed before the venerable was able to speak again. 'Fifty years, brother Templar. I have been trapped here, lost, for fifty years.'

THE VEHICLES HAD been parked up and the massed force of Brother Jarold's avenging angels had formed a circle of unbreakable armour. All were included, from the newest neophyte to the oldest initiate. The formation of the praying Space Marines served as a barricade against the biting winds that swept across the Dead Lands, stabbing at any exposed flesh with knives of ice. It affected the neophytes – Gervais, Feran, Eadig and Galan – worst, for they were yet to earn the right to wear the full power armour as worn by their brethren and their heads were exposed. But if the freezing wind caused them any discomfort they didn't show it. Weakness of the flesh was not permitted of a Space Marine.

Brother Jarold stood on one side of the circle and opposite him loomed the Venerable Rhodomanus of the Crimson Fists.

The latter's crimson and regal blue paintwork was in stark contrast to the predominantly black and white power armour of the Templars – although some of the older, more ornamented suits worn by those veterans among the battleforce were traced with gold and red as well.

The moaning wind whirled flurries of snow around them but over the voice of the blizzard, Brother Jarold's booming prayers could be heard quite plainly.

'We shall bring down His almighty wrath and fury upon the xenos and drive the greenskin from the face of this planet!' Jarold bellowed. 'For the Emperor and the primarch!'

'For the Emperor and the primarch!' his battle-brothers responded with fervent zeal.

'For the Emperor and the primarch,' Venerable Rhodomanus echoed.

Brother Jarold had not needed to ask the ancient whether he would deign to join the Templars on the continuation of their mission. To awaken to a world fifty years into his future and so unchanged despite the passage of time, and yet finding his brother Crimson Fists with whom he had fought shoulder to shoulder against the greenskins gone, the prospect of fighting alongside the Templars had given him a noble purpose. Here was a chance to finish what he and his brothers had started.

For what purpose could there be for a Space Marine, other than eternal service? If he were denied the right to serve Him Enthroned on Holy Terra, a Space Marine's long life, and all the battles he had fought, everything he had achieved in His holy name would count as naught.

The Black Templars and Crimson Fists – two Chapters formed in the aftermath of the Heresy ten thousand years before – were both successor

Chapters of the original Imperial Fists Legion, created from the very genetic material of the Primarch Rogal Dorn. Templar and Fist owed their very existence to the lauded Rogal Dorn, so there had never been any question as to whether Rhodomanus would join the Black Templars of the Solemnus Crusade. They were brothers-in-arms; that was all that mattered.

Brother Jarold surveyed the assembled Templars, the ancient Fist and the ice-clad vista beyond.

'It is time,' he said, scanning the ridge of sickle-shaped peaks on the horizon. 'Whatever the source of the anomalous signals detected by the fleet, it lies beyond that ridge.

'Today we show the greenskins why they should fear us. We let them see why we are fear incarnate. Today we take the fight to the enemy. Today we purge the Dead Lands of the xenos plague that blights this world.

'Move out!'

THEIR ACT OF worship concluded, with renewed steel in their hearts, shielded by the armour of their faith as much as by the ceramite of their power armour, the circle broke up as the Space Marines returned to their vehicles. With a roar of mighty engines, like the wrathful prayers of Brother Jarold himself, Ansgar's Avengers moved out.

The force progressed slowly, so as to never leave the Dreadnoughts far behind. Brother Jarold had deployed into the heart of the Dead Lands by drop-pod and the

Templars had not anticipated having another ancient join them in their quest to find the source of the anomalous readings. There was no means of transporting them, other than for them to continue under their own propulsion.

But it still did not take them long to climb the icy slopes of a pass between the jagged obsidian-black peaks. Initiate-pilot Egeslic took his land speeder on ahead, to scout out what lay in wait for them on the other side of the ridge. He returned presently, guiding his speeder deftly over the ice, compensating for wind shear as he descended from the crest of the pass, and brought the vehicle to a hovering halt beside the clumping Dreadnought.

'Brother Jarold,' Egeslic said, 'you should see this for yourself.'

'THAT,' SAID TECHMARINE Isendur, pointing into the heart of the crater that had been dug into the ice, 'is the source of the anomalous readings.'

From the Space Marines' position at the mouth of the pass, sheltered by the shadows of the looming wind-scoured ice sculptures that surmounted the ridge in impossible overhangs, Brother Jarold surveyed the rift in the ice below them.

The ork-dug crevasse was a hive of seemingly disorganised industry. Everywhere he looked he saw orks. The foul xenos covered the glacier in a thick, dense green carpet as they swarmed over the dig site, the clamour of their mining machines ringing from the ice walls around them. There were customised digging machines, and other ork vehicles had been pressed into strange service here too. Some of these machines bore banner poles, bearing the iconography that demonstrated the ork tribe's loyalty. The sight of the Scarred Ork again – the ugly steel-cut tribal glyph bearing a rust red lightning bolt scar that bisected its crude simulacra features – filled Brother Jarold with both righteous satisfaction and indignation in equal measure.

They had found the one tribe that Jarold had hoped they would. The orks labouring within the ice pit were of the Blood Scar tribe. Truly the Emperor was smiling upon their endeavours that day.

But focusing again upon the coarse alien totem Jarold felt rage burn within him like he had not known since the moment the re-constructed warboss Morkrull Grimskar had made his cowardly escape, taking the body of the Emperor's Champion Ansgar with him as he teleported out of the mekboy's crumbling lab smothered within the foetid green depths of the equatorial jungle.

'Is there a teleportation device somewhere here?' Jarold demanded of the Techmarine, watching the waves of green corposant rolling across the underside of the thick clouds that covered the arctic valley. He had to be certain.

'I have recalibrated the signum and fine-tuned the signal, brother,' the Techmarine said. 'And there is.'

Excitement pulsed through the husk of Jarold's mortal remains locked within the life-preserving amniotic tank of the Dreadnought's sarcophagus.

Had they really tracked down their long-sought-for quarry at last? Was the warboss here? And if he was, was Brother Ansgar with him?

Jarold gazed down into the crater again and treacherous doubt began to creep between his thoughts of righteousness revenge. But it was not the size of the ork horde that filled Brother Jarold's mind with appalled awe and wonder but the effigy that they had virtually finished digging out of the solid ice of the glacier that had spilled between the frost-chiselled peaks into this valley like some great frozen and fractured river.

Venerable Rhodomanus saw it too. And remembered.

The war machine. An appalling amalgamation of scavenged weapons and armour, the product of unholy alien engineering and genetically pre-programmed habit, the living embodiment of ork savagery and the relentless desire for war.

The monster – for it was a monster – crashed across the glacier, decimating the Crimson Fists' frontline. The Space Marines brought their armour and heavy weapons to bear but it was too little compared to the might of the monstrous god-machine that now marched to war before them.

Desperate times called for desperate measures and Rhodomanus had never known them more desperate. Something had to be done to bring about the destruction of this angry god.

And so, supported by his noble brethren Fists, he had strode forth to conquer the beast in one final act of self-sacrifice. His battle-brothers falling one by one at his side, giving their lives – all of them – that he might complete his final mission, weathering shoota, kannon, gatler and a storm of rokkits, the ancient was able to breach the stompa's shields and place the thermal charges at its very feet.

'The Emperor protects,' he intoned, quietly resigned to his fate.

Then all was white noise, heat and light.

For one brief moment the ice of millennia became a torrent of liquid water again and the blazing stompa sank beneath the sudden waves. The force of the blast hurled Rhodomanus across the sky like a blazing comet and he thought he heard the Emperor calling him to serve at his side in the next world…

'THE IDOL LIVES,' Rhodomanus breathed.

It was clear to all – and not just Techmarine Isendur's practised eye – that the orks had finished carving the remains of the war machine from the body of the glacier and were now busy attempting to re-activate it; re-fuelling it, testing its growling motive systems and firing off bursts of random weapons-fire from its many and varied weapon emplacements.

There was a hungry roar of pistons firing and thick billows of greasy black smoke gouted from the proliferation of smoke-stacks and exhaust flues that rose from the back of the alien war idol.

'That, I take it, is not the source of the signal we have been tracking, is it?' Jarold quizzed the Techmarine standing beside him.

'No, brother. That is.' Isendur pointed with his power axe.

'I see it,' Rhodomanus said.

Jarold looked again, refocusing his optical sensors, and then he saw it too.

It was a vast assemblage of iron beams and girders, crackling brass orbs and endless spools of cabling. It was supported by an immense scaffold and yet the whole massive structure had been hidden by the blizzard and the bulk of the ork effigy standing before it.

The device culminated in a huge gun-barrelled probe that Jarold imagined to be a beam transmitter, supported on strong gantry arms.

'By Sigismund's sword!' Jarold gasped.

'Its designation in this warzone is an ork tele-porter, I believe,' Isendur said.

'We should warn the fleet,' Jarold said. 'We cannot allow the xenos filth continued access to such weaponry or technology,' he added as he pondered the matter in hand. It was clear to Jarold now that the orks intended to teleport their scavenged stompa out of the ice-locked Dead Lands to be used on another war front and bolster their forces there. Such a rein-forcement could turn the tide of battle in the orks' favour. Such a thing could not be allowed to happen.

'Yes, brother,' Isendur replied.

Tense moments later, with Jarold watching the heavens as if he expected the *Divine Fury* to deliver a thunderbolt directly from heaven against the stompa, the Techmarine made his report. 'The interference being generated by the teleporter that we detected from orbit is now preventing my signal from getting through to the crusade fleet,' he said, delivering his bad tidings without any obvious emotion.

They were alone down there.

'We are going to have to deal with the stompa and the teleporter ourselves,' Rhodomanus declared. 'We cannot allow the greenskins to make it away from here with their idol intact. It is against the will of the Emperor.'

'Then we shall face the enemy in battle once again; fight them hand to hand if that is what it takes,' Jarold said, his assault cannon whining as it began to run up to speed. 'Just the way we like it.'

WITH THE ROAR of bike engines and heavy armour running at maximum speed, the Black Templars poured through the ridge pass and into the carved crevasse in the ice before the orks had any warning as to what was happening.

'No pity! No remorse! No fear!' Brother Jarold boomed as he tramped down the glacial slopes towards the great ork-gouged hole, the toe-hooks of his Dreadnought feet locking him securely in place on the treacherous ice.

'There is only the Emperor!' Rhodomanus joined, urging the crusading Space Marines on. 'He is our shield and our protector!'

First came the bikes and attack bikes, pouring over the lip of the ridge, past the clumping Dreadnought.

Then came the Razorbacks and the Rhinos, the heavy armour grinding over the ice of the glacier, pounding it to shards beneath their tracks, heavy bolter fire riddling both the ice sheet and those orks that had mustered enough awareness to try to do something about the approaching Space Marines.

The land speeder squadron hurtled over the ridge after the rest of the Templar armour past the advancing battleforce, the *whub-whub-whub* of their engines thrumming through the ice, the Tornado's assault cannon rattling off hard rounds into the milling orks as they hurried to respond to this new threat.

With a whooshing roar, the Typhoon fired off a barrage of missiles. The rockets corkscrewed through the air and impacted in a series of scathing detonations amidst the moving ork armour. Bodies, armour plating and wheels were thrown into the air to land in broken burning piles.

With a searing scream, the lascannon mounted on Techmarine Isendur's Razorback fired, a blinding spear of light burning through the constant snow flurries and illuminating the crevasse like an incendiary shell-burst. A moment later the crater was illuminated again as an ork halftrakk exploded in a sheet of flame, the las-blast having hit both its fuel tank and the rokkits loaded into the back of it.

There was the *crack* and *crump* of frag grenades detonating amidst the greenskin horde, and orks fell in their dozens.

Some of the orks had climbed aboard their trukks and bikes again. They revved their engines as they turned their vehicles to face the oncoming Black Templars armour.

The orks were rallying. Jarold's crusaders had made the most of the advantage that stealth and the blessings of the Emperor had brought them but now the enemy were starting to organise a cohesive defence.

As war trukks and heavy orkish bikes began to converge on the advancing Templar armour, those battle-brothers piloting the fleet's venerated vehicles urged them forwards, Techmarine Isendur making supplication to the Omnissiah in the same unmodulated tone, over and over.

At the bottom of the crater, in the shadow of the dug-out idol, the two sides met with a roar of over-revving engines and the scream of shearing metal. Sparks flew, armour plating buckled, axles sheared and fuel tanks ruptured. Orks were thrown over the hulls of Rhinos and land speeders. Milling grots were crushed under the tracks of Rhinos and ork bikes alike. Others among the horde were gunned down by the blazing, blessed bolters of the Templars, the ork guns unable to match the reliability or accuracy of the Space Marines' arsenal.

But despite their primitive design there was one thing that the ork guns had over the Templars' weapons; there were more of them. Far more. It was becoming painfully apparent that the Templars were drastically outnumbered, at least twenty to one. Although the Emperor's chosen were renowned for their fighting prowess, those were odds that tested even a Space Marine. There was a very real danger that sheer weight of numbers would see them overwhelmed, if the orks were able to unify their attack.

But Brother Jarold – now part of the rearguard, finishing off those greenskins that had evaded the Templars' guns – had realised this would be the case before he had committed his fighting force to this action.

It was clear that the Blood Scar orks were planning on teleporting the stompa from this location, to deploy elsewhere on Armageddon. Jarold's plan had always been to infiltrate the dig site and bring down the war-effigy or, failing that, seize and hold the colossal ork teleporter until Isendur found a way to destroy it.

With a scream of failing engines, Initiate-Pilot Egeslic's land speeder ploughed into the surface of the glacier: an ork shokk attack gun had made a lucky hit. A gaggle of snarling boyz piled onto the downed speeder, burying Egeslic and Initiate-gunner Fraomar beneath a flurry of thumping axes and stabbing serrated knives.

The two Rhinos slewed to a halt in the middle of the crater, dropped their hatches and the troops they were carrying poured out in a tide of funereal black and gleaming white. Boltguns barking and chainswords screaming, they met the milling rabble head on. They might be outnumbered, but they were in the thick of battle, which was the only place where a Templar might hope to win his honour-badges.

Venerable Rhodomanus' multi-melta pulsed, and a swarm of orks died as their blood boiled and their own bodily fluids broiled their internal organs.

The ice field was lit up again, this time as a sphere of actinic light exploded into life like a miniature sun at the periphery of the Templar lines. The explosion pushed a great wave of concussive force before it as the land speeder Typhoon and its remaining payload of missiles were obliterated by a direct hit from the stompa's now active deth kannon.

Brother Jarold stood firm, as ork bikes tumbled end over end past him, carried before the bow-wave of explosive force. He then turned his assault cannon on the surviving greenskins now running from the epicentre of destruction, holy wrath pounding through what little remained of him that was still flesh and blood.

'Brother Jarold,' Techmarine Isendur's voice crackled over the comm-net, the interference caused by the orks' unstable teleporter technology affecting even close range communications.

'What is it, brother? Report.'

'We have our objective.' Isendur declared with something dangerously like emotion tingeing his words. 'The teleporter is ours.'

'YOUR OBJECTIVE IS the teleporter; reconvene there,' Jarold commanded, his battle-brothers hearing him through the comm in their helmets, his words also carrying to them over the bestial roars and bolter fire of the battlefield. 'Repeat, rally at the teleporter.'

The device was huge, on a monumental scale that even an ancient such as Venerable Rhodomanus had never witnessed before. It was too big a target to miss. The Templars had teleport technology themselves, of course, hidden within the bowels of the Forgeship *Goliath* where it was carefully tended and operated by the Techmarine Masters of the Forge and their servitors, but they had nothing approaching the size of this brutal piece of esoteric machinery.

Techmarine Isendur felt something approaching heretical awe on seeing the monstrous device arrayed before him in all its terrible, alien glory.

THE TEMPLARS WERE brutally outnumbered by the thuggish orks, but by launching a surprise attack, the vengeful Space Marines had been able to penetrate far into the dig site; the either arrogant or idiotic orks having failed to post anything like enough sentries to create an effective defensive perimeter. They had probably not thought to be interrupted out here in the trackless frozen wastes of the Dead Lands for little could survive in these bitter wastes other than the alien orks. But then, from what Jarold had witnessed first-hand, it seemed that orks could survive pretty much anywhere.

The Templars' fast-moving, heavy armour had been able to penetrate the ork crater that held the ice-locked stompa with ease, the Razorbacks and Rhinos ploughing into the aliens and their scratch-built vehicles as if sainted Sigismund himself were smiting the foul xenos from beyond the stars, where he now stood at Primarch Dorn's right hand.

But now the initially bewildered orks had rallied and were mounting an effective counter-attack against the Black Templars' lightning assault.

Despite the crusading Chapter's prowess in hand-to-hand combat, even hardened fighters such as Brother Jarold's avenging warriors would be hard-pressed to overcome when facing such impossibly overwhelming odds.

The best they could hope for was to sell themselves dear. They might not have found their lost Brother Ansgar or their nemesis the warlord Morkrull Grimskar, but they could end their crusade here, denying the ork host the war machine that the greenskins had fought so hard to win again.

Bikes – in both the black and white livery of the Templars and the scruffy red kustom paint jobs of the orks – roared past Brother Jarold as he stomped across the battlefield. He took aim and fired. The front wheel of a warbike that was pursuing a Space Marine attack bike – its gunner whooping wildly as it took pot-shots at the noble Templars – disintegrated in a hail of cannon fire. The wheel struts dug into the ice, halting the bike's forward motion. The vehicle flipped over, hurling the ork gunner into the path of a hurtling land speeder – the surprised-looking greenskin bouncing off the hull with the unmistakable sound of breaking bone – while the bike's driver was crushed beneath the great weight of the bike landing on top of it and crushing its spine.

Jarold turned his bolter on a gaggle of greenskins that charged him, large-calibre shootas and clumsy chain-bladed weapons in their meaty paws. A burst of flesh-shredding gunfire and then he was through. Nothing now stood between him and the ork teleporter.

And he wasn't the only one to have made it to the objective. Sergeant Bellangere had led the men under his command by example – bolt pistol in one hand, chainsword in the other dripping with alien gore – and hadn't lost a single member of his squad in the process. He and his troops were even now finishing off the last of the resistance being put up by the orks that crawled all over the vast gantries of the teleporter, an augmented mekboy falling to Bellangere's gutting chainblade.

Jarold turned to survey the smoking craters and tight knots of fighting that characterised the battlefield dig-site. The crumpled wreckage of a devastated Rhino lay nearby, as did the smouldering remains of a bike. Most of the Templar armour had made it through to the objective, but not all. Jarold caught glimpses of scratched black and blistered white amidst the bodies of the slain between billows of smoke from burning wrecks strewn across the combat zone.

On seeing his fallen battle-brothers Jarold felt his blood boil. The machine-spirit that resided with him inside his Dreadnought body informed him of the names of each and every one of the fallen – Initiate Garr and Gunner Heolstor, Brother Derian, Brother

Eghan and Brother Clust of Squad Garrond, Clust's heavy bolter lying useless on the ice under his eviscerated body.

Brother Jarold was shaken from his enraged reverie by what felt like an earthquake.

The ground shook, splinters of ice twenty metres tall breaking free of the glacier as the stompa began to move. The orks had finally coaxed their idol into unnatural life once more.

Like Brother Rhodomanus it had lain locked in the ice for the last fifty years. Like Brother Rhodomanus it now had a second chance to finish what Ghazghkull Mag Uruk Thraka's hordes had started half a century ago.

At the growl of the effigy's engines, filthy smoke poured from its chimney-exhausts, filling the cerulean blue sky with stinking black clouds.

The stompa's wrecking ball attachment – the krusher itself looking like a huge rusted boulder – came whirling around over the top of its pintle arm mount, crashing down on top of a Rhino with all the force of a meteorite impact. The tank's adamantium plates buckled under the force of the wrecking ball blow, sending the troop transport bouncing off the uneven ice-gouged bedrock that had lain buried beneath the glacier until the orks had dug it up.

As Jarold watched, what was left of Neophyte Feran rocketed skyward as an ork skorcha engulfed his body in flame, detonating the krak grenades he carried at his waist.

Raging to the heavens at the death of another battle-brother, and one who had not yet had the chance to prove himself in glorious battle to his brethren's satisfaction, the Dreadnought turned his blazing weapons on the ork responsible.

The barrels of his assault cannon glowing red hot, his mind-linked machine-spirit informed him that his auto-loaders would soon be out of ammunition. But if today was his day to die a second death then he would make it his vow to take as many of the Blood Scar orks with him as possible.

Jarold surveyed the scorched glacier around him. The remaining Black Templar armour had formed a cordon around the teleporter, every vehicle's guns pointing outwards towards the enemy now pouring over the ground towards their position. The aliens' fury at the audacity of the Templars in taking the teleporter spurred them on, the savage brutes giving voice to harsh barks and hoots of wild abandon.

'Brothers!' Jarold declared, his voice echoing strangely from the derricks and hoists of the corposant-sheathed structure. 'This day we show the xenos filth that Armageddon is not theirs for the taking. This day we show the orks that we will leave no wrong unavenged, no slight unchallenged. This day we will deliver the Emperor's divine retribution upon the heads of the greenskin defilers of this world in the name of Primarch Dorn and his servant Lord Sigismund.'

Jarold turned his storm bolter on another charging ork and took its head off with one mass-reactive round.

'Brothers! Today we sell ourselves dear in the name of the Emperor that we might deny the orks another victory upon the shores of Armageddon. We have a new mission. We will not depart this world until we have ensured that they may never make use of their teleporter or their war-idol again. Today is a good day to die!'

With a scream of rending metal, lightning-drenched claws tore through the chugging engine of an ork wartrak as its armour plating melted under the intense heat-blast of a multi-melta.

As the smoke and flames died back again, the Black Templar Dreadnought watched with grim satisfaction as the still more imposing and ornamented form of Venerable Rhodomanus strode through the devastation to reach the protection of the cordon of crusader armour, crushing a flailing ork beneath one colossal foot whilst snatching the mangled body of another from the wrecked wartrak and quartering its head between the crimson talons of his colossal power fist.

'No, brother,' the ancient boomed. 'I am sorry to contradict you, but today is not your day to die.'

As he reached the Templar line, Rhodomanus turned his multi-melta on an ork bike, igniting its fuel tank; the vehicle and its rider disappeared in a sheet of incandescent flame.

'It is not your destiny that you give your lives in sacrifice to stop this blasphemy,' the venerable went on, as if making his decree. 'Your mission is not yet done. You must live to fight another day.'

Jarold did not interrupt, but listened, considering Rhodomanus's words as he targeted the ork manning the flamethrower mounted on the back of a rumbling halftrakk.

'This is my battle, brother,' Rhodomanus continued. 'It is up to me to accomplish what I and my brother Fists tried to fifty years ago.'

The ancient was right. This was not the Templars' battle. The destruction of the ork war machine had never been their objective. Brother Ansgar still awaited them, somewhere. And it was up to Jarold and the others to find him. It was as they had sworn it.

But none of that changed the fact that they were severely outnumbered and completely surrounded, with little hope of being able to turn the tide of battle in their favour now, unable to even call for extraction by the fleet.

The superstructure of the incomparable ork device in whose shadow they now sheltered hummed and twanged as orkish hard rounds and crackling energy beams spanged off its pylons and girders.

'Do you think you can fathom the workings of this teleporter?' Jarold asked his Techmarine.

'All ork machines are primitive and alien,' Isendur replied, 'but I would predict a seventy per cent chance of success.'

'Then set to work,' Jarold instructed. 'By the Emperor, I want this thing operational and locked onto the fleet in orbit as soon as is humanly possible.'

* * *

WITH A DULL crump the speeding guntrukk exploded, obliterated by the massed barrage of heavy weapons that pounded it.

Standing side by side against the horde, the Dreadnoughts Jarold and Rhodomanus locked onto a new target and a warbike disintegrated into shrapnel.

Only a matter of metres away, Brother Huarwar died as he was decapitated at close quarters by a heavily mekanised ork. Roaring in grief-stricken pain, Jarold broke from the circle, advancing on the creature responsible, litanies of hate spouting from his vox-casters like bile as he shredded the alien's augmented body with raking bolter and cannon fire.

'Brother Isendur!' he bellowed over the howls of the orks and the savage chatter of their guns, ignoring the succession of hard rounds that rattled off his own adamantium body-shell as if they were no more than the stings of rad-midges. 'Give me some good news!'

'I have subjugated what passes for the device's machine-spirit, patching a link via one of my servitors and dominating it with a liturgical subroutine, and, through its transmitter array, have located the fleet in orbit and Forgeship *Goliath*–'

'Brother!' Jarold boomed, bisecting an ork from midriff to neck with a barrage of bolter fire. 'Is it ready?'

'Aye, brother,' Isendur replied. 'It is ready.'

'Then begin the evacuation.'

As the two Dreadnoughts held back the press of the ork horde with bolter and fist, cannon and melta, at Jarold's command the strike force moved back beneath the beam emitter of the huge gantry, never once turning their backs on the enemy, claiming a dozen ork lives for every step they took in retreat.

It was not the Templars' way to retreat in the face of greater numbers of the enemy. But for the brethren of the Solemnus Crusade, this was their last action. They could not afford to sacrifice their lives so freely, not when their holy work remained undone. They were yet to recover Brother Ansgar's body and repay the warboss Morkrull Grimskar for all the monster had taken from them when the orks of the Blood Scar tribe razed the Chapter Keep on Solemnus.

They had all sworn it – every crusading battle-brother, from neophyte to initiate, Techmarine to Apothecary, Dreadnought to Marshal, Chaplain to Champion – and they could not relinquish the fight until their vow had been fulfilled, not when a way out of this impossible situation had presented itself.

So large was the ork teleporter – it having been intended to beam something as gargantuan as the stompa to another arena of battle – that the entirety of the survivors of Jarold's battleforce could fit within the circumference of the projection plate beneath the enormous beam emitter.

They would go together. That was how Brother Jarold wanted it. Whether their plan worked, and the teleporter returned them to the Forgeship *Goliath*, or scattered their component atoms to the stars, they would go together. The only ones they would leave behind were one tech-servitor to initiate the firing sequence of the teleporter's beam-gun, and Venerable Brother Rhodomanus of the Crimson Fists.

'Brother Jarold,' came Techmarine Isendur's voice with something almost like urgency in his usually unexcitable tone. 'Our departure now waits only on your presence upon the plate.'

Jarold turned to Rhodomanus, swivelling about the pivot of his waist bearing, as if he were about to address the venerable, blasting a leaping axe-wielding ork out of the air with a single, well-placed shot.

'Go, brother,' Rhodomanus said, before the other could speak. 'Go to meet your destiny and leave me to face mine.'

'It has been an honour,' Jarold stated stoically.

'Aye, it has been that,' the ancient agreed.

'Die well, brother. For the primarch.'

'For Dorn. Now go.'

Rhodomanus directed another blast from his multi-melta into the press of the ork pack, the heat blast clearing ten metres around him in every direction.

Taking his leave, Brother Jarold defiantly turned his back on the orks and marched to join his battle-brothers at the heart of the humming teleporter, the venerable laying down covering fire behind him, like some colossal avatar of the Emperor's retribution.

And as he did so, he began to intone Dorn's litany of service.

'What is your life?' he began. 'My honour is my life.'

An ork fell to scything fire from his storm bolter.

'What is your fate? My duty is my fate.'

Another was impaled on the crackling blades of his lightning fist.

'What is your fear? My fear is to fail.'

As he retreated behind Rhodomanus, Brother Jarold gave voice to the defiant battle cry in one last act of defiance directed at the alien orks.

'No pity!' Brother Jarold boomed.

'No remorse!' his battle-brothers responded, taking up his battle cry.

'No fear!' they bellowed in unison, clashing their weapons against their holy armour in a clattering cacophony of defiance.

Corposant crawled over and around the superstructure of the ork teleporter in writhing serpents of sick green light. With an apocalyptic scream like the sundering of the heavens, the beam-emitter fired.

Rhodomanus did not look back. He knew the Templars were gone.

'And what is your reward?' he asked, his voice rising like a challenge against the ravening greenskins. 'My salvation is my reward!'

Three orks fell to a withering hail of bolter fire.

'What is your craft? My craft is death!'

The multi-melta put an end to another ork bike.

'What is your pledge?'

The venerable hesitated. He could see the stompa advancing on him now, and him alone, belching smoke into the air from its exhaust-stacks, its colossal mass shaking the ground with its every step.

'My pledge is eternal service!'

As the stompa closed on the teleporter at last, with heavy, purposeful steps that sent tremors skittering through the bedrock that lay beneath the glacier, an inescapable fact wormed its way into the spirit-linked mind of the ancient. This was to be his last stand, but even the glorious sacrifice of a venerable Dreadnought might not be enough to stop the stompa.

Rhodomanus and his brother Fists had been unable to destroy it fifty years before, during the Second War for Armageddon, only managing to delay the inevitable by trapping it within the glacier. And now, fifty years on, what hope was there for him as he stood before the devastatingly powerful war machine?

But still he kept firing, directing blast after blast of his multi-melta at the gun emplacements that bristled from the effigy's carapace, at the stompa's armour itself, and its crew, when his spirit-linked targeter could lock onto them.

The stompa loomed before him, blocking his view of the crater and the rest of the horde, the macabre god-machine filling his world. Nothing else mattered now. There was only the ancient and the idol, two relics from another battle for Armageddon, ready to make the final moves of a power play begun five decades before.

Sparkling emerald flame consumed the ork teleporter once more, power relays humming as the device came online again. Rhodomanus's optical sensors homed in on the roasted remains of the tech-servitor fused to the esoteric device by its last firing. The servitor was dead, so how was it that the teleporter was powering up to fire at all?

It was only then that Rhodomanus realised that in his face-off with the stompa he had backed himself onto the empty platform and now stood directly beneath the beam emitter.

A nimbus of actinic light formed at the centre of the teleporter, also directly beneath the focusing beam of the vast construction, surrounding him with its suffused essence. Something was being beamed back to the teleporter.

He felt the tingle of it at his very core, in every fibre of his body that was still flesh and blood. And the machine-spirit of his Dreadnought body felt the exhilarating rush of a trillion calculations as the impossible machine read and recorded the position of every atom within his body, the connection of every synapse, the binary pattern of every recollection-code stored within his memory implants. He was beaming out.

Framed by the skeletal structure of the alien device, the stompa seemed to peer down at him with the telescoping sights of its cannon-barrel eyes.

Through his one remaining mortal eye Rhodomanus saw adamantium, steel, ceramite and flesh become first translucent and then transparent. At the same time he saw something else taking shape within the sphere of light with him, becomingly steadily more opaque as it solidified around his departing form.

For the briefest nano-second he and the object shared the same space – his machine-spirit merging with its primitive programmed consciousness. Fifty metres long and weighing a hundred tonnes – the energy build-up already taking place within its plasma reactor perilously close to the point of critical mass and detonation – the torpedo was capable of blowing a hole in the side of an ork kill krooozer with armour plating several metres thick. The venerable's own machine-spirit continued the countdown to destruction.

Five.

Four.

Three.

Two.

Suffer not the alien to live, he thought.

And then actinic light blinded his optical sensors and the bleak white wastes of the Dead Lands, the collapsing structure of the teleporter and the impotently raging stompa. Everything vanished, melting into black oblivion, and Brother Rhodomanus was gone.

THE BATTLE-BARGE *Pride of Polux* hung in high orbit above Armageddon's second largest landmass.

All was still within the reclusiam. Captain Obiareus, Commander of the Crimson Fists 3rd Company, was alone with his thoughts and his strategium. There were not many minutes in the day when he could say that, and he savoured those times when it was the case. But such precious moments made all the difference to his command. They were those times when he could step back, reflect, consider and plan.

He sat, the elbows of his power armour resting on the cuisses of his armoured legs, gauntlets locked together before his face. His lips touched the reliquary that hung from his neck on its golden chain and which he held within his hands as reverentially as he might a newborn. He stared out of the roof-high windows of the reclusiam at the silent void beyond, pondering again his Chapter's gains and losses on the planet below, alone with his thoughts and the stars.

Footsteps disturbed the captain's contemplations, the sound of ceramite ringing from the stone-flagged floor shattering the silence of the reclusiam. Obiareus looked up in annoyance.

Brother Julio approached the strategium, head bowed respectfully.

'What is it?'

'My lord,' Julio began. 'We have received a hail from Marshal Brant of the Black Templar Solemnus Crusade. He wishes to speak with you, my lord.'

'The Templars wish to speak with us?'

'Yes, my lord.'

'Regarding what matter?' Obiareus probed further.

'They have news, my lord.' Brother Julio faltered, as if hardly able to believe what he himself was saying.

'Yes? What news?'

'News of Venerable Rhodomanus,' Brother Julio said hesitantly.

'Brother Rhodomanus?' Now it was Obiareus's turn to express his disbelief. 'Brother Rhodomanus lost to us these fifty years past since the Second War fought against the xenos for this world?'

'Yes, my lord,' Julio confirmed, 'but lost no longer. Venerable Rhodomanus has returned.'

TWELVE WOLVES

Ben Counter

THE SONS OF Fenris look not only to the future, but also to their noble past and so my task is a most arduous one. Think not that the saga I speak comes to this tongue easily, or that to bend the ear of a mead-soaked Blood Claw is a task any less worthy than bringing the bolter and chainsword to the Emperor's foes! No, indeed, to tell these tales of the past, and to have them listened to by the Brothers of the Wolf, is a task whose difficulty is matched only by the weight of the duty I bear in telling them.

I hear you now, throaty and raucous, demanding to hear a saga of some great battle or feat of arms that will fill your hearts with fire. Lord Russ fighting the One-Eyed traitor, you cry! The many crimes of the Dark Angels, you demand, so that we might feast and drink and remember our grudges! But my purpose here is not to serve this feasting throng with whatever bloody tale they desire. No, I have gathered you by this roaring fire, in the grand hall of the Fang where generations of Space Wolves have celebrated their victories and toasted their dead, because there is a lesson I have to impart.

I do not need an Astartes' augmented senses to hear your sighs. What use, you whisper to yourselves, is a saga not dripping with the blood of foes and thundering with the sound of chainblade on heretic flesh? Fear not! There will be blood. Could an old thrall like me, a broken, haggard thing kept in pity by the Chapter whose standards I failed to reach in my youth, hope to survive if he spoke of anything but battles and glory to a roomful of Astartes? It is from the Wolf Priests themselves, the guardians of your spirits, that I learned this tale, and they know better than to impart lessons that will not be heeded.

IT IS IN a great battle of the past, then, that our tale takes place. Those attentive young wolves will know of the Age of Apostasy, one of the direst lessons that mankind has ever had to learn, during which the corrupt clergy of the Imperial Creed sought to seize power for themselves. It is a long and grim story in its own right that I will not tell here. Suffice it to say that it was a time of blindness, fear and chaos, when the Imperium of Man sought to crumble in a way not threatened since the dark times of Horus. Among the many tales of sorrow in this time, our story concerns that of the Plague of Unbelief, when a wicked man named Cardinal Bucharis carved out an empire of his own, throwing off Imperial authority to rule as a king!

Bucharis, while a cunning and fearless man, was a fool. For as his empire grew, conquered by renegades of the Imperial Guard and armies of mercenary cutthroats, he came to the threshold of Fenris. Arrogant in the extreme, Bucharis did not halt there and turn back, afeared of the Space Wolves who called it their home then as you do now. No, he sent his armies to Fenris, to conquer its savage peoples and force the Space Wolves to cede their world to him!

Ah, yes, you laugh. Who could have thought that an Apostate Cardinal and a host of mere men could defeat the Space Wolves on their home world? But it happened that at this time very few Space Wolves were at the Fang, with most of them having joined the Wolf Lord Kyrl Grimblood on a crusade elsewhere in the galaxy. The Space Wolves left there to face Bucharis's villains numbered little more than a single Great Company, along with the newly-blooded novices and the thralls who dwell within the Fang. Bucharis, meanwhile, bled the garrisons of his empire white to flood Fenris with soldiers and lay siege to the Fang. Do not think that the Fang was impregnable to them! Any fortress, even this ancient and formidable mountain hold, can fall.

In the third month of this siege two Space Wolves were abroad in the valleys and foothills around the Fang. They were patrolling to disrupt and observe the enemy forces, as the sons of Fenris were wont to do at that time in the battle. One of them, and his name was Daegalan, was a Long Fang such as those battered, leather-coloured Astartes who watch us even now from the back of the hall. They have heard this tale many times, but take note, young Blood Claws and novices, that they still listen, for they understand its lesson well. The other was much like you. His name was Hrothgar, and he was a Blood Claw. Daegalan was wise and stern, and had taken Hrothgar as a student to teach him the ways of war that, with the Fang and the Chapter in great peril, he had to learn very quickly.

Imagine a mountain ridge at night, bare flint as sharp as knives clad in ice that glinted under the many stars and moons of mother Fenris. It overlooked a wide, rocky valley, cleared of snow by tanks and shored up by engineers, like a black serpent winding between the flinty blades of the Fang's foothills. Now you are there, the story can begin.

Two Astartes made their way up to the lip of this ridge. One of them wore a wolf skin cloak about his shoulders, and across his back was slung a missile launcher. This was Daegalan. His face was like a mask of tanned leather, so deeply lined it might have been carved with a knife, his grey-streaked hair whipping around his head in the night's chill wind. He wore on his shoulder pad the symbol of Wolf Lord Hef Icenheart, who at that time was directing the defence of the Fang from its granite halls. The other, with the red slash marks painted on his shoulder pad, was Hrothgar. The scars, where the organs of an Astartes were implanted, were still red on his shaven scalp. His chainsword was in his hand, for it rarely left, and his armour was unadorned with markings of past campaigns.

'See, young cub,' said Daegalan. 'This is the place where our enemy creeps, like vermin, thinking he is hidden from our eyes. Look down, and tell me what you see.'

Hrothgar looked over the edge of the ridge into the valley. The night's darkness was no hindrance to the eyes of an Astartes. He saw a track laid along the bottom of the valley, along which could be wheeled the huge siege guns and war machines which Bucharis's armies hoped would shake the sides of the Fang and bring its defences down. Slave labour on the worlds the Cardinal had captured had created countless such machines and they filled the bellies of spacecraft supplying his war on Fenris. Indeed, it was the mission of the two Astartes to locate and disrupt the bringing of these war machines to a location where they could fire on the Fang.

Many Guardsmen, from the renegade Rigellian regiments who had thrown their lot in with Bucharis, guarded the tracks, knowing that soon the precious war machines would come trundling along it.

'I count twenty of the enemy,' said Hrothgar. 'Imperial Guard all, they are reasonably trained – not the equal of a Space Wolf, of course, but dangerous if they can fire upon us in great numbers. See, Long Fang, they have assembled defences of flak-weave and ammunition crates, and they seem ready for an attack by such as us. They know the importance of their mission.'

'Good,' said Daegalan, 'for a first glance. But our task here is to destroy these enemies. What can you see that will ensure they fall?'

'This one, 'said Hrothgar, 'is the officer that leads them. See the medals and badges of rank on his uniform? That silver skull on his chest is granted by the heretic Cardinal to followers who show great ruthlessness in leading the troops. Upon one sleeve are the marks of his rank. In his hand is a map case, surely marking out the route of these tracks. This man must die first, for with their leader dead, the others will fall into disarray.'

Daegalan smiled at this, and showed the grand canine teeth that are the mark of a true Long Fang. May you who listen to this one day sport such fangs as these, sharp and white, to tell the tale of your years spent fighting with the Sons of Russ! 'Young Blood Claw,' said Daegalan, 'can it be that even with the eyes of an Astartes you are so blind? You must learn the lessons of the Twelve Wolves of Fenris, those great beasts who even now hunt through the mountains and snowy plains of our world. Each wolf is taken as the totem of one of our Great Companies, and for good reason.' Daegalan here tapped the symbol of his Great Company on his shoulder pad. 'I wear the symbol of Wolf Lord Icenheart. He took as his totem Torvald the Far-Sighted, the wolf whose eyes miss nothing. This wolf of Fenris teaches us to observe our enemy, much as we would love to get our claws around his throat first, for it is in looking ahead that the victory can sometimes be won before a blow is struck.

'Look again. The man you see is indeed an officer, and no doubt a ruthless one at that. But there is another. There, seated on an ammunition crate, his lasgun propped up by his side. See him? He is reading from a book. Even these old eyes can read its title. It is the *Collected Visions*, a book written by the Apostate Cardinal himself, serving as a collection of his madness and heresies. Only the most devout of his followers, when the night is this cold and the mission is this crucial, would read it so earnestly. This man may not be the officer who leads these soldiers on paper, but he leads them in reality. He is their spiritual heart, the one to whom they turn for true leadership. This man must die first, for when it is shown that the most devout of them is no more than meat and bone beneath our claws, then all their hope shall flee them.'

Hrothgar thought upon this, and he saw the truth in the Long Fang's words.

'Then let us fight,' said the Blood Claw. 'The reader of books shall die first, beneath these very hands!'

'Alas, I have but two missiles left,' said Daegalan, 'otherwise I would sow fire and death among them from up here. I shall fight alongside you, then. When you tear the heart from them, I shall slay the rest, including that officer to whom you paid so much attention.'

With this Hrothgar vaulted down from the ridge and crashed with a snarl into the heart of the enemy. He charged for the spiritual leader, and was upon him before the other Guardsmen had even raised their lasguns! At that time the Space Wolves were sorely lacking of ammunition for their guns and power packs for their chainswords, and so it was with his hands that Hrothgar hauled the reader of books into the air and dashed his brains out against the rocks.

'He is dead!' came the cry from the Guardsmen. 'He who assured us that the divine Cardinal would deliver us, he whose survival proved to us the sureness of our victory! He is dead!' And they wailed in much terror.

Daegalan was among them now. He was not as fast as the Blood Claw, but he surpassed him in strength and cunning. He fought with his knife, and plunged it up to the hilt in the skull of the first Guardsman who faced him. Another died, head cracked open by the swinging of his fist, and then another, speared through the midriff. The officer, who was shouting and trying to steel the hearts of his men, fell next, knocked to the ground and crushed beneath Daegalan's armour-shod feet.

It was, but the space of a few heartbeats, as a non-Astartes might reckon it, that the enemy were torn asunder and scattered. Those that were not dead cursed their fates and fled into the snowy wilderness, eager to face the teeth and claws of Mother Fenris rather than spend another moment in that blood-spattered valley.

The hot breath of the two Astartes was white in the cold as they panted like predators sated from the hunt. But this hunt was not finished. For from down the tracks came the sound of steel feet on the rocks, and the roaring voice of an engine. And before the Astartes could ready themselves, from the frozen darkness lumbered a Sentinel walker.

Many of you have seen such a thing, and perhaps even fought alongside them, for they are commonly used by the armies of the Imperial Guard. This, however, was different. Its two legs were reinforced with sturdy armour plates and its cab, in which its traitor driver cowered, was as heavily plated as a tank. It had been made with techniques forgotten to the masters of the forge worlds today, and it bore as its weapon a pair of autocannon. This was no mere spindly scouting machine! This was an engine of destruction.

'Despair not!' shouted the headstrong Hrothgar as this monster came into view. 'You shall not have to face this machine, old man, wizened and decrepit as you are! I shall ensure this traitor's eyes are on me alone. All you need do, venerable one, is fire that missile launcher of yours!'

Daegalan had it in mind to scold the Blood Claw for his insolence, but it was not the time for such things.

Hrothgar ran into view of the Sentinel. He fired off shots from his bolt pistol, and the Sentinel turned to hunt him through the valley's shadows. But Hrothgar was fast and valiant, and even as the Sentinel's mighty guns opened fire he sprinted from rock to rock, from flinty fissure to deep shadow, and every shell spat by the Sentinel's guns was wasted against unyielding stone. At that time it happened a flurry of snow was blown up by Mother Fenris's icy breath and Hrothgar ventured closer still, diving between the metal feet of the Sentinel, knowing that he was too fast and his movements too unpredictable for the machine's pilot to fire upon him with accuracy.

So infuriated was the pilot of the Sentinel that he forgot, as lesser soldiers than Astartes are wont to do, the true threat he was facing. For Daegalan the Long Fang had indeed taken aim with his missile launcher, the only weapon the Astartes had between them that might pierce the machine's armour. With a roar the missile fired, and with a vicious bark it exploded. The rear of the Sentinel was torn clear away, and the pilot mortally wounded. Exposed to the cold night, the blood from his many wounds froze. But he did not have long to suffer this fate, for Hrothgar the Blood Claw climbed up the legs of the Sentinel and tore out the traitor's spine with his bare hands.

'You may think,' said Daegalan, 'to have angered this old Long Fang with your insolence, but in truth you have expounded the lesson of another of Fenris's wolves – or rather, two of them, for they are Freki and Geri, the Twin Wolves who were companions of Leman Russ himself. See how this enemy, a match for both of us, was destroyed by the fruits of our brotherhood! When wolves fight as a pack, as one, they slay foes that would confound them if they merely attacked as individuals. You have learned well, though you did not know it, the lesson of the Twin Wolves!'

With that, the two Astartes set about destroying the tracks, and for many days as a result the walls of the Fang were spared the bombardment of Bucharis's war machines, and the lives of many Space Wolves were surely spared.

Now, it was about this time that the Apostate Cardinal, accursed Bucharis himself, was upon Fenris directing the siege of the Fang. You already know that he was a man possessed of great arrogance and blindness to the rage he inflamed in those who suffered under his conquest. He was also a wrathful man, much given to extravagant punishments and feats of cruelty when angered. Having heard from a subordinate that his war machines (which he expected to shatter the Fang and slay all those within) would be delayed by the actions of the Astartes, he flew into a rage. He supposed that a great host of Space Wolves had done this deed, and that with their destruction the defenders of the Fang would be greatly weakened in number. A foolish man, I hear you cry. Indeed he was, but he was also a very dangerous man, whose foolishness lay not in an inability to achieve his goals but in ignorance of the consequences his cruelty would have. You know, of course, that Bucharis was eventually to meet an end as befits a man like him, but that is a story for another time.

Many units of the Imperial Guard were sent to punish the host of Astartes that Bucharis believed to be abroad in the foothills of the Fang. They were men picked by Bucharis's warmaster, the renegade Colonel Gasto, from the regiments of Rigellians he commanded. They had been well versed in the beliefs of Bucharis, which were heretical in the extreme and shall not be spoken of by this humble tongue. They believed Bucharis's lies that the Imperium had fallen and that only by obeying Bucharis could they hope to survive its collapse. Gasto gave them tanks and heavy weapons, and the kind of murderous cutthroat mercenaries that Bucharis had swayed to his cause to lead them.

These men and machines left the great siege encampment of the Rigellian Guard and headed for the Fang, ordered on pain of death to destroy the Astartes.

MEANWHILE, DAEGALAN THE Long Fang and Hrothgar the Blood Claw were making their way back to the Fang, for their mission was completed. Though it was now daylight a storm had fallen over the area and Mother Fenris was breathing ice across the flinty hills. Terrible gales blew and showers of ice fell like daggers.

'Remember,' said Daegalan as he led Hrothgar up the slippery slope of a barren hill, 'that it is cruel weather such as this that makes every blasted and inhospitable place the domain of Haegr, the Mountain Wolf. For he endures all, indeed, he thrives in such inhospitable climes. It is to him that we must look, for is it not so that the physical endurance of an Astartes is a weapon in itself, and that by taking this hazardous path we make better time towards the Fang and further confound our enemies?'

Hrothgar did not answer this, for while he was young and vigorous, the Long Fang was so much inured to hardships and gnarled by Fenris's icy winds that the old Astartes did not feel the cold as much as the Blood Claw. But he did indeed recall the Mountain Wolf and, knowing that the sons of Fenris are made of stern stuff, he shrugged off his discomfort and the two made good speed over the hills.

It was at the pinnacle of the next hill that a break in the storm gave them a glimpse of the Fang. It was the first time they had seen it in many days. Daegalan bade his companion to stop, and look for a moment upon the Fang itself.

'This tooth of ice and stone, this spear piercing the white sky, does this not fill your heart with gladness, young Blood Claw?'

'Indeed,' said Hrothgar, 'I am now struck by the majesty of it. It gladdens me to think of the despair our foes must suffer when they see it, for those are the slopes they must climb! Those are the walls they must breach!' And all of you have seen the Fang and, I do not doubt, imagined how any foe might hope to silence the guns that stud its sides or climb the sheer slopes that guard its doors more surely than any army.

'Then you feel,' said Daegalan, 'the howl of Thengir in your veins! For he is the King Wolf, the monarch of Fenris, and everything under his domain is alight with glory and majesty. So you see, ignorant and insolent young cub, that another of Fenris's wolves has a lesson to teach us today.'

Hrothgar did indeed hear Thengir, like a distant howl, speaking of the kingly aspect of the Fang as it rules over all the mountains of Fenris.

'And mark also the Wolf Who Stalks Between Stars,' continued Daegalan, 'as you look above the Fang to the moons that hang in the sky. The Stalker Between Stars was the totem of Leman Russ himself, and even now his symbol adorns the Great Wolf's own pack. Our pawprints may be found even on distant worlds and the farthest-flung corners of the Imperium. So long as we, like that wolf, hunt abroad among the stars, then Fenris is not merely the ground beneath our feet but also any place where the Sons of Fenris have trod, where the Space Wolves have brought fang and fire to their enemies!'

Hrothgar's hearts swelled with pride as he thought of the mark the Space Wolves had left upon the galaxy beyond Fenris. But the Astartes could not tarry for long, and quickly made their way on.

Soon Daegalan saw the white tongues of engine exhausts nearby, and knew that the traitor Guard were close. He led Hrothgar into a winding valley, deep and dark even when the sun broke through the blizzards. Many such valleys lead through the foothills of the Fang, chill and black, and within their depths lurk many of the most deadly things with which Mother Fenris has populated her world.

'I can tell,' said Daegalan after some time, 'your frustration, young Blood Claw. You wish to get to grips with the foe and cover your armour with their blood! But remember, if you will, that another wolf stalks beside us. Ranek, the Hidden Wolf, goes everywhere unseen, silent and cunning. In just such a way do we stalk unseen. Do not scorn the Hidden Wolf, young one! For his claws are as sharp as any other, and when he strikes from the shadows the wound is doubly deep!'

Hrothgar was a little consoled by this as he listened to the engines of the enemy's tanks and the voices of the soldiers raised as they called to one another. They could not traverse the foothills of the Fang as surely as a Space Wolf, and many of them were lost as they stumbled into gorges or fell through thin ice. Driven by their fear of Bucharis they made good time but paid for it in lives, and with every step the force became more and more ragged. Hrothgar imagined slaying them as he emerged from hiding, and he smiled.

'Now you think of killing them by the dozen,' continued Daegalan, for he never passed by the opportunity to instruct a younger Astartes. 'But ask yourself, in this butchery you imagine, is there any place for me, your battle-brother? You need not reply, for of course there is not. I do not admonish you this, Blood Claw. Quite the opposite, I commend you to the spirit of Lokyar, the Lone Wolf.

While the Twin Wolves teach us of brotherhood, Lokyar reminds us that sometimes we must fight alone. He is the totem of our Wolf Scouts, those solitary killers, and now he may be your totem, too, for it is Lokyar whose path you tread as you imagine yourself diving into our enemy alone.'

Now our two Astartes came to the head of the valley, where it reached the surface. They espied before them fearsome barricades set up by the traitor Guard, the bayonets of the heretics glinting in the sun that now broke through the storm clouds. Dozens of them were waiting for the Astartes, and they were trembling for they believed that a host of Astartes would stream from the black valley.

'Ah, may we give thanks to Mother Fenris,' said Hrothgar the Blood Claw, 'for she has guided our friends to meet us! What a grand reunion this shall be! I shall embrace our friends with these bloody hands and I shall give them all gifts of a happy death!'

'Now I see the battle favours the youthful and the heedless of danger,' said Daegalan in reply, 'and is content to leave the old and cunning behind. Go, Brother Hrothgar! Bestow upon them the welcome your young wolf's heart lusts for! And remember the Iron Wolf, too, for he watches over the artificers of our Chapter forge wherein your armour was smelted. Trust in him that your battlegear will turn aside their laser fire and their bullets, and run with him into battle!'

Hrothgar recalled, indeed, the Iron Wolf, whose pelt can turn aside even the teeth of the kraken who haunt the oceans of Fenris. And he ran from the darkness of the valley. The soldiers opened fire as one and bolts of red laser fell around the Blood Claw like a rain of burning blood. But his armour held firm, the Iron Wolf's teachings having guided well the artificers of the Fang.

Ah, how I wish I had the words to describe Hrothgar in that bloody hour! His armour was red to the elbow and the screams of his enemies were like a blizzard gale howling through the mountains. He leapt the barriers the traitors had set up and even as he landed, men were dying around him. He drew his chainsword and its teeth chewed through muscle and bone. One heretic he spitted through the throat, throwing him off with a flick of a wrist, and a heartbeat later a skull was staved in by a strike from his gauntleted fist. He cut them apart and crushed them underfoot. He threw them aside and hurled them against the rocks. He took the lasgun from one and stabbed him through the stomach with his own bayonet. Some traitors even fell to their own laser fire as the men around them fired blindly, seeing in their terror Astartes charging from every shadow.

Daegalan followed Hrothgar into the fray. Some leader amongst the traitors called out for a counterattack and bullied a few men into charging at Hrothgar with their bayonets lowered. Daegalan fell amongst them, his combat knife reaping a terrible toll. He cut arms and heads from bodies, and when he was faced by the officer alone he grabbed the heretic fool with both arms. He crushed the life out of the man, holding him fast in a terrible embrace.

The Guardsmen fled, but Hrothgar was not done. Some he followed behind outcrops of rock where they sought to hide. He hauled them out, as a hunter's hounds might drag an unwilling prey from a burrow, and killed them there on the ground. When they tried to snipe at him from some high vantage point he trusted in his armour to scorn their fire and clambered to meet them, holding them above his head and throwing them down to be dashed to pieces against the rocks below.

When the traitors bled, their blood froze around their wounds, for Mother Fenris had granted the Astartes a day bright yet as cold as any that had ever passed around the Fang. Blood fell like a harvest of frozen rubies. Now Daegalan and Hrothgar rested in the centre of this field of bloody jewels, as bright and plentiful as if Mother Fenris herself was bleeding. They were exhausted by their killing and they panted like wolves after the kill, their breath white in the cold. They were covered in blood, their faces spattered with it, their pack emblems and Great Company totems almost hidden. Silently, each gave thanks to Fenris herself for the hunt, and even to Cardinal Bucharis for his foolishness and arrogance, for it was he who had sent them such prey.

Above them loomed the Fang, wherein their battle-brothers waited to receive the news of their success. Prey lay dead all around them, and the majesty of Fenris was all about. What more could a Space Wolf ask for? It was indeed a good day, and may you young pups have many such hunts ahead of you.

'Well fought, my brother,' said Daegalan. 'It is well that the Apostate Cardinal stumbled upon Fenris, for without his ill fortune we would not have such hunts upon our very doorstep!'

'He should have a statue in the Hall of Echoes,' agreed Hrothgar. 'Was there ever a man who did more for the glory of the Space Wolves? I think I shall toast him with a barrel of mead when we celebrate this hunt.'

They laughed at that, and it was to this sound that the rumble of engines grew closer and a shadow fell over them. For the mercenaries who led the Guardsmen were hard-bitten and foul-minded men, well versed in the low cunning of war, and they had prepared a trap for the Astartes.

The force the Space Wolves had slaughtered were just the vanguard of the army sent to punish them. Bucharis had sent in his fear ten times that number, sorely stretching the forces that besieged the Fang elsewhere. They had with them tanks: Reaper-class war machines such as can no longer be made by the forge worlds of the Mechanicus. Six of these machines had survived the journey, and they all rumbled into view now, their guns aiming at the place where the two Astartes stood.

The Guardsmen, though sorely pressed by the harsh journey through the foothills, numbered hundreds, and they had brought many heavy weapons with which to destroy the Astartes from afar – for they feared to face the claws and teeth of the Space Wolves up close, and rightly so. Their leaders, Bucharis's chosen mercenaries, were strong and brutal men who wore pieces of uniform and armour from a dozen places they had plundered, and all wore the scars of war like banners proclaiming their savagery. They, too, were afraid of the Astartes, but they turned their fear into brutality and so the men under them obeyed them out of terror.

One such man addressed the Astartes through the vox-caster of his tank. By the standards of such men, it was a bold thing to do indeed!

'Astartes!' he called to them. 'Noble sons of Fenris! The honoured Lord Bucharis, monarch of his galactic empire, has no quarrel with the Space Wolves. He seeks only to grant protection to those within the fold of his generosity. For the Imperium has fallen, and Terra lies aflame and ruined. Lord Bucharis promises safety and sanity for those who kneel to him!

'But we do not ask you to kneel. How could we, mere men, demand such of Astartes? No, we ask only that Lord Bucharis count Fenris among the worlds of his empire. What do you care for this grim and frozen place, its savage peoples and its bitter oceans? To the Space Wolves, of course, we shall leave the Fang, and the right to rule yourselves, excepting a few minor and quite necessary obeisances to Lord Bucharis's undoubted majesty. So you see, there is no need for you to fight any more. There is nothing left for you to prove. Stand down and place yourselves within our custody, and we shall deliver you safely unto the Fang where you can pass on word of Lord Bucharis's matchless generosity.'

The Astartes, of course, saw through these lies. They knew the Imperium was eternal, and had not fallen, and moreover they believed no more than you do that Bucharis meant to destroy the Space Wolves and take the Fang for himself. No doubt he wished to install himself in our great fortress, and to use as his throne room the hall wherein Leman Russ himself once held court! The only answer to such a speech lies at the tip of a wolf's claws, or in the gnashing of his fangs!

'Now, young wolf,' said Daegalan, 'we face our death. How blessed are we that we can look it in the face as it comes for us. And moreover, we die on Fenris, on the ground upon which we were born, and first ran with our packs in the snow. This is the world that forged us into the Astartes we are, that gave us the strength and ferocity to be accepted into the ranks of the Space Wolves. Now we shall repay that honour by choosing this very ground for our deaths! How blessed are we, Blood Claw, and how blessed am I that it is beside my brother that I die.

'And do not think that we shall die alone. For I hear the snarling of Lakkan, the Runed Wolf, upon the wind. Once Lakkan walked across Fenris, and wise men read the symbols he left in his footprints. These men were the first Rune Priests and those who still follow the path of Lakkan even now watch us from the Fang. They scry out our deeds, and they shall record them, and give thanks as we do that we die a death so fine.'

Daegalan now drew his bolt pistol. He had but a single magazine of bolt shells, for at that time the Astartes were sorely pressed for ammunition with their fortress besieged. Hrothgar, in turn, drew once more his chainsword. Its teeth were clotted with the frozen blood of traitors, but soon, he knew, he would plunge it into a warm body and thaw out that blood so its teeth could gnash again.

'I do not seek death,' said the Blood Claw, 'as easily as you do, old man.'

'Your saga shall be a fine one,' replied Daegalan, 'though it is short.'

'Perhaps you are right,' said Hrothgar, and in that moment the guns of the tanks were levelled at the place where they stood in the field of blood rubies. 'You are a Long Fang, after all, and wise. But I fear that in all you have taught me you have made a single error.'

'And what might that be, Blood Claw?' said Daegalan. 'What omission have I made that is so grave I must hear of it now, in the moment of my death?'

Now a strange countenance came upon Hrothgar the Blood Claw. His teeth flashed like fangs and his eyes turned into the flinty black orbs of the hunting wolf. 'You have spoken of the wolves of Fenris that follow us and impart to us their lessons. Twelve of them you have described to me, each one mirroring an aspect of Fenris or of the teachings the Wolf Priests have passed down to us. These lessons were well earned, and I thank you for them, Brother Daegalan. But I am wiser than you in but one aspect.'

'Speak of it, you cur!' demanded Daegalan with much impatience, for the guns of the traitor tanks were now aimed at them, awaiting the order to fire, as were the heavy weapons of the Guardsmen.

'I have counted twelve Fenrisian wolves in your teachings, each one taken as the totem of a Great Company of the Space Wolves. But here you are mistaken. For I know that in truth, there are not twelve wolves. There are thirteen.'

IT IS TIME, I fear, for this old tongue to lie still and for a draught of mead to warm this thrall's bones. You wish the story to continue? I have no doubt you foresee great bloodshed of the kind you love to hear. And there was bloodshed after that moment, it is true. Terrible it was, perhaps worse than any that fell upon the face of Mother Fenris during the besieging of the Fang. But it is not for me to speak of it. I hear you groan, and a few even flash your fangs in anger! But look to the Long Fangs who sit at the back of the hall. Do they growl their displeasure? No, for they know the truth. A thrall such as I has no place speaking of such things. Even the most ancient among the children of Russ, the mighty Dreadnoughts who have marched to war for a thousand years or more, would not speak of it.

There is, however, a legend told among the people of Gathalamor, the world where the Apostate Bucharis first came to prominence. They are a fearful and religious people, for upon them has fallen the burden of redeeming their world from the stain the Apostate left upon it. But sometimes they speak of legends forbidden by the cardinals of their world, and among them is this one, brought back, it is said, by the few survivors of the armies who fought on Fenris.

Once an army was sent by Bucharis to destroy the Astartes who had been sowing much death and confusion among the besieging forces. The army cornered the Astartes but found, much to their delight, that they faced not a Battle Company or even a single pack, but a single Space Wolf.

In some versions of the tale there was not one Space Wolf, but two. The difference matters not.

Now the soldiers drove their tanks into range and took aim at the Astartes. And they awaited only the order to open fire, which would surely have been given but a moment later. But then they were struck by a great and monstrous fear, such as rarely enters the hearts even of the most cowardly of men.

The Space Wolf was an Astartes no more. In fact, he appeared as nothing that could once have been a man. A bestial countenance overcame him, and the winds howled as if Fenris herself was recoiling in disgust. Talons grew from his fingers. His armour warped and split as his body deformed, shoulders broadening and spine hunching over in the aspect of a beast. The soldiers cried that a daemon had come into their midst, and men fled the sight of it. Even the gunners in their tanks did not think themselves safe from the horror unfolding in front of them.

And then there came the slaughter. The beast charged and butchered men with every stroke of its gory claws. It tore open the hulls of their tanks and ripped out the men inside. In its frenzy it feasted on them, and strips of bloody skin and meat hung from its inhuman fangs. Men went mad with the force of its onslaught. The leaders of that army fired on their own men to keep them from fleeing but the beast fell on them next and the last moments of their life were filled with terror and the agony of claws through their flesh.

The soldiers were thrown to the winds of Fenris and scattered. Some say that none survived, either torn down by the beast or frozen to death as they cowered from it. Others insist that a single man survived to tell the tale, but that he was driven hopelessly mad and the legend of the Beast of Fenris was all that ever escaped his quivering lips.

But this is a tale told by other men, far from the Fang and the proud sons of Fenris who dwell therein, and I shall dwell upon it no more.

Now IT CAME that many days later, when the battle had waxed and waned as battles do, a pack of Grey Hunters ventured forth from the Fang to drive off the traitor Guardsmen who were thought to be encamped in the foothills. There they came across a place like a field of rubies, where frozen blood lay scattered across the snowy rocks with such great abandon that it seemed a great battle had been fought there, though the pack-mates knew of no such battle.

'Look!' cried one Space Wolf. 'Someone yet lives! He is clad in the armour of a Space Wolf and yet he is not one, for see, his bearing is that of an animal and his face bears no trace of the human we all were before becoming Astartes.'

The pack leader bade his battle-brothers to cover him with their boltguns as he went to see what they had found. As he approached he saw countless bodies torn asunder, many with the marks of teeth in their frozen flesh, and still others dead in the ruins of their tanks.

The figure in the centre of the battlefield indeed wore the power armour of an Astartes, but split apart and ruined as if rent from within. He crouched panting in the cold, as if fresh from a hunt. His form was not that of a human, but of a beast.

'He is touched by the Wulfen,' said the pack leader. 'The Thirteenth Wolf of Fenris has walked here, and its inhumanity has found a place to dwell inside this Blood Claw. Some flaw in his gene-seed went unnoticed during his novicehood, and now it has come to the fore in this place of bloodshed.'

Another Space Wolf cried out. 'There lies another of our battle-brothers, dead beside him! What appalling wounds he has suffered! What monstrous force must have torn his armour so, and what claws must have ripped at his flesh!'

'Indeed,' said the pack leader, 'this noble brother was a Long Fang, one of that wise and hardy breed, and he shall be borne by us to a proper place of resting within the Fang. Alas, I knew him – he is Brother Daegalan, I recognise him by his pack markings. But see, the claws of the survivor made these wounds! His teeth have gnashed at the fallen Astartes's armour, and even upon his bones.'

The pack was much dismayed at this. 'What Space Wolf could turn on his brother?' they asked.

'Mark well the path of the Wulfen,' said the pack leader sternly. 'His is the way of deviant and frenzied bloodshed. He cares not from whom the blood flows as long as the hunting is good. This ill-fated Long Fang is testament to that – when this Blood Claw ran out of foes to slay, under the Wulfen's influence he turned upon his brother.'

The pack spoke prayers to mighty Russ and to the ancestors of the Chapter, and all those interred in the Fang, to watch over them and protect them from such a fate as suffered by the two Astartes.

You might think that a beast such as they found should have been put down, but imagine for a moment you were confronted by such a sight. It would surely be impossible for you to kill one such as Hrothgar, for though a warped and pitiable thing he was still a Son of Fenris and to slay him was still to slay a brother. So the pack brought Daegalan's body and Hrothgar, still living, to the Fang. I have heard it said they led him by a chain like an animal, or that they called upon a Wolf Priest to administer a powerful concoction that sedated him long enough to be carried to the Fang.

And so it came to be that Daegalan the Long Fang was given his rightful place among the packmates who had fallen over the decades, and there he lies still. As for Hrothgar, well, he was interred in a similar way, this time in a cell hollowed out from the rock of the Fang's very heart where from the lightless cold none can hope to escape.

Hush! Cease the sound of clinking tankards. Ignore the crackling of the fire. Can you hear it? That scratching at the walls? That is Brother Hrothgar, scrabbling at the boundaries of his cell, for he is now but an animal and yearns to run in the snows of Fenris, hunting beast and brother alike. But sometimes he remembers who he once was, and the Long Fang who fought alongside him, and then he lets out a terrible mournful howl. You can hear it in the longest of Fenris's nights, echoing around the heart of the Fang.

Now, my tale has come to an end. Perhaps now you understand why it was to a lowly thrall that this saga has been given to tell, and not one of the venerable Wolf Priests or well-scarred Long Fangs who uttered its grim words. What true Space Wolf could bear to have such things pass his lips?

And perhaps a few of you have even understood the lesson that lies at its heart. The rest will have to listen for Hrothgar's claws, for Hrothgar's howl, and perhaps the truth will come to you.

Remember always, whether you hunt in the wilds that Mother Fenris tends, or you stalk between the stars, the thirteen wolves hunt beside you.

THE RETURNED

James Swallow

THE SKIES ABOVE the Razorpeak range wept oil. Low cowls of cloud, grey as ancient stone, ranged from horizon to horizon, grudging to allow only a faint glow of sunlight to pierce them from the great white star of Gathis. The clouds moved upon the constant winds, the same gales that howled mournfully through the jagged towers of the mountains, the same heavy gusts that reached up to beat at the figure of Brother Zurus.

The slick rain, dark with the metallic scent of oceans and the tang of rotting biomass, fell constantly upon the landing platform where he stood. Zurus watched it move in wave fronts across the granite and steel. The storms hammered, as they always did, against the constructions men had built high up here in the tallest crags. The platform was only one of many extensions, cupolas and balconies emerging from the sheer sides of the tallest fell among the Razorpeaks. The earliest, most primitive tribes of Gathis II had christened it the Ghostmountain, a name not in honour of its white-grey stone, but in recognition of the many dead that haunted it, so lethal were its slopes. Thousands of years later and the name was, if anything, more fitting.

Once, before men had come from Terra to colonise this world, there had been a true peak atop the Ghostmountain, a series of serrated spires that rose high enough that they could pierce the cloud mantle. Now a great walled citadel stood in their place, the living rock of the peak carved and formed by artisans into halls, donjons and battlements of stark, grim aspect. At each point of the compass, a hulking tower rose, opening into the sculpted shape of a vast raptor screaming defiance at elements and enemies. These warbirds put truth to the name of the great fortress-monastery atop the Ghostmountain: the Eyrie.

One of the great eagles stood at his back, and like the raptor, Zurus was watchful. He peered out from under the hood of his heavy, rain-slick over-robe, waiting for the roiling, churning sky to release to him his responsibility. In the far distance, down towards the settlements of Table City and the lowhill coasts where the tribals lived, great jags of bright lightning flashed, and on the wind the grind of thunder reached his ears a few moments later, cutting through the steady hiss of the falling rains.

Zurus was soothed by the sound. He found it peaceful, and often when he was far from Gathis, perhaps upon the eve of battle at some distant alien battleground, he would meditate upon the sounds of the rainfall and find his focus in it. And so, when he had awoken at dawn this day, he had at once sensed something amiss. Zurus exited his sleeping cell and found only rays of weak sunlight reaching down the passages of the dormitoria; and outside, a break in the clouds, and a silence in the air.

A rare thing. By the ways of the Gathian tribes, an omen of ill fortune when the eternal tears of Him Upon The Throne ceased to fall, and with them the protection the God-Emperor of Mankind provided. After a time, the rain began again, as constant as it ever was, but Zurus had witnessed the moment of silence, and was on some level unsettled by it.

As HE HAD crossed through the gate to venture out to the landing platform, a figure in red-trimmed robes was waiting for him in the lee of the entranceway.

Thryn, the Librarian Secundus. The old warrior's sallow, bleak features always measured Zurus whenever he turned to face him. The look in his eyes was no different from the expression he had shown when the battle brother had first seen the psyker, on the fateful day the Chapter had recruited Zurus into their fold. Many decades ago now.

Thryn nodded towards the open gate and the sky beyond. 'The rain returns,' he noted.

'It never leaves,' Zurus replied. The exchange of words had a ritual quality to them.

The Librarian's lip curled in something that a generous observer might have considered a smile. 'If only that were so. The light of naked sun upon the peaks... It does not bode well.'

Zurus gathered in his robes, unfurling the hood. 'I have no time for omens.'

Thryn's mouth twisted; the old warrior could sense a bald untruth even without the use of his witch-sight. 'You are ready for this, brother?' he asked, turning to stare out at the empty landing pad. 'You did not need to take on this duty alone. Other men–'

'It is right that I do it,' Zurus spoke over the Librarian. 'It is right,' he repeated.

Thryn turned back to study him for a long moment, then stepped away, out of his path. 'As you wish.' The Librarian banged his fist against the inner door of the gateway and halted. Metal gears began to grind as the saw-toothed hatchway drew open. When Thryn spoke again, he did not face him. 'But remember this, Zurus. What comes today, what you go to meet... You have not faced the like before.'

Something in the other warrior's tone chafed on him. 'If you think I will falter when... *if* the time comes, you are mistaken. I do not shrink from death.'

Thryn gave a low chuckle. 'That much is certain. We are Doom Eagles, brother. Death is part of us.'

'I know the difference between friend and foe,' Zurus insisted. 'I know what the Archenemy looks like. I can tell a traitor when I see one.'

The inner gate clanged open. 'I have no doubt you believe that. But Chaos has faces it has never shown to you, kinsman. Do not forget that.' Thryn walked away, back into the fortress.

THE THUNDER WAS closer now, sullen and deep enough to echo in his bones. His companion rains drew hard across the metal decking as if they were scouring it, preparing it for the arrival; and then it came to him that the tone of the storm-sound had changed, a new note growing loud, fast approaching.

Zurus looked up, following his hearing. The oily rain touched his face, streaking over an aspect that was a maze of scars. He saw a shape up there, only the suggestion of it really, a shadowed thing with broad wings and a hooked profile. A vast eagle, falling towards him, talons extending.

The sound was strident, and it opened the cowl of cloud cover for a brief instant. On pillars of orange fire and hard jet-noise, a gunmetal-silver drop-ship suddenly emerged from the haze, dropping fast. Rain sluiced from the steel wings and across the blocky, rigid angles of the Thunderhawk's blunt nose. Zurus's robes snapped and billowed as the thruster backwash buffeted him, but he did not move from his sentinel stance.

The drop-ship landed firmly, the slow impact resonating through the landing platform. Engines

keening as they powered down, the craft settled on
hydraulic skids, lowering itself to the deck as if it
were thankful to have completed its journey. Zurus
saw motion behind the windows of the cockpit, but
nothing distinct. He found he was holding his
breath, and chided himself, releasing it. The Astartes
warrior resisted the urge to throw a glance over his
shoulder, back towards the Eyrie. He had no doubt
Thryn was at some gallery window far above him,
watching.

With a crunch of cogs, the Thunderhawk's drop
ramp unfolded, a mouth opening to show the dark
interior of the transport craft. A servitor was the
first to shamble out, head bobbing as it chewed on
the punchcard containing its command strings.
The machine-slave dragged a wheeled trolley
behind it, half-covered by the tattered remains of a
war cloak.

Zurus's gaze was momentarily drawn to the trolley
as it was pulled past him; he saw the distinct and
unmistakable shape of ceramite armour heaped
within the wheeled container. The silver wargear, the
trim of red and ebon, as familiar to him as the scar-
patterns on his own face. Doom Eagle armour, but
corroded and damaged in a fashion no son of Aquila
would ever willingly countenance.

When he looked back there was a hooded man at
the top of the ramp. He was looking down at his
hands, and the streams of rainwater spattering off
his upturned palms. He resembled a pilgrim accepting a benediction.

The Thunderhawk's sole passenger spoke, after a moment. 'The rains,' he began, in a low, crack-throated voice. 'I thought I might never see them again.' He took in a deep, long breath through his nostrils. 'On the wind. I smell Chamack.' There was a smile in the words.

Zurus nodded. Down in Table City, leagues away from the Eyrie, the great bio-matter refineries that fabricated lubricant oil from the fibres of the sinuous Chamack sea-plant worked night and day, and the heavy, resinous odour was always present in the air. Zurus only ever noticed it by its absence.

The moment passed and the new arrival bowed his head. He began to walk down the ramp, but in two quick steps Zurus had crossed to the bottom of the gangway and stood blocking his path. The other man faltered, then halted.

'Who are you?' said Zurus. 'Let the ghosts of the mountain hear your name.'

From beneath the other man's hood, eyes narrowed and became cold. 'The ghosts know who I am, brother. I am a Gathis-born son, as you are.'

'You must say the words,' insisted Zurus. 'For protocol's sake.'

Hands tightened into fists, before vanishing into folds of the dripping robes. 'The protocols of which you speak are for outsiders. *Strangers.*'

Zurus searched the face concealed beneath the hood for any sign of subterfuge or malice. 'Say the words,' he repeated.

The other man said nothing, and the moment stretched too long. Then finally, with a fall of his shoulders, the new arrival relented. 'My name is Tarikus. Warrior of the Adeptus Astartes. Brother-Sergeant of the esteemed 3rd Company of the Doom Eagles Chapter. And I have returned home.'

Tarikus. Zurus had been there on the day that name had been added to the Walls of Memory in the great Relical Keep. He had watched with due reverence as a helot carved the name into the polished black marble, etched there for eternity among the hundredfold dead of the Chapter. Zurus had been there to hear the Chaplains announce Tarikus's loss, and cement it in the annals of Doom Eagle history. Two whole Gathian cycles now, since he had been declared *Astartes Mortus.* Many seasons come and gone, his life become a revered memory among all the honoured fallen.

The other man drew back his hood for the first time and walked on, down towards the end of the drop ramp.

Zurus took a wary step backwards and met the gaze of a dead man.

'Is it him?'

Thryn did not turn away from the rain-slicked windowpane, watching the two men far below on the landing platform. He saw Brother Zurus step aside and allow the passenger from the Thunderhawk to stride back towards the gate. The Librarian clearly saw the tawny, battle-scarred aspect of the man, lit by a momentary pulse of high lightning. 'That remains to be seen, lord,' said Thryn, at length.

In the shadowed gloom of the observation gallery, Commander Hearon folded his arms across his barrel chest and his ever-present frown deepened. The answer was unsatisfactory to the Chapter Master of the Doom Eagles. 'I allowed him to be brought here on your advice, old friend,' Hearon rumbled. 'I did so because I thought you could give me the answer I wanted.'

'I will,' Thryn replied. 'In time.'

'Not too much time,' said the Chapter Master. 'Voices call for a swift end to the matter of this... return. Chief among them the Chaplains and your senior, Brother Tolkca.'

Thryn nodded. 'Yes, I imagine the Librarian Primus is ill-tempered at the thought of such a thing being placed in my hands.'

Hearon gestured at the air. 'He is at battle a sector distant. You are here. If he's irked by my decision, he may take it up with me on his return.' The commander leaned in. 'There is no precedent for this, Thryn. Death is the closure of all things, the last page in the passage of a life. For that book to be re-opened once we have written the final entry...' Hearon trailed off. 'This man... if that is what he is... must be put to the question. The truth of him must out.'

The Librarian nodded again, musing. Thryn had pored over the battle records and honours listed under the name of Tarikus. A veteran of bloody conflicts and engagements on worlds such as Thaxted and Zanasar, he had risen to the rank of Brother-Sergeant with command of a tactical squad under

Consultus, the current captain of the 3rd Company. The 3rd had a history of ill fate; two commanders in succession had been lost to them during the last Black Crusade of the Archtraitor Abaddon, at Yayor and then again at Cadia, but Tarikus had survived them all – even the great massacre at Krypt, where the Doom Eagles had lost many men on the surface of that brutal, frigid planetoid.

It was only after the destruction of the planet Serek, on a voyage back to the Segmentum Tempestus, that the luck of Brother Tarikus had run dry. The medicae frigate he had been aboard was ambushed by the hated Red Corsairs, and torn apart. Tarikus had not been among the Astartes who made it to the saviour pods before the wrecked ship had plunged into a star. He was given the honour of a worthy end, and declared dead, with all the ritual and rite such a tribute entailed.

But now… Now a ghost walked the halls of the Eyrie.

Thryn was well aware that some brother Chapters of the Doom Eagles regarded their association with matters of death as unusual. *Morbid*, even *macabre*; he had heard these slights from warriors of the Space Wolves and the White Scars, even brothers of the Ultramarines, the very Legion his Chapter had been drawn from. Some viewed the character of the Doom Eagles and saw an *obsession* with fatality; but this was a short-sighted, narrow view.

The Doom Eagles were gifted with an understanding of the universe. They knew the truth, that all life is born dying, moment by moment. What others saw as fatalism, they saw as pragmatism, a manner born out of knowledge that life and joy were transient things, that the only constants in existence were despair, loss – and ultimately the embrace of death. *We are already dead*, so said the first words of the oath of the Chapter. The Doom Eagles understood that death was always close; and so they fought harder, strove longer, to perform their duties before the cloak of Final Sleep came upon them. They had no illusions.

Death was the end of all things. Nothing could come back from the void beyond it. This knowledge was the pillar upon which stood everything the Chapter believed in.

Tarikus, by his presence, his mere existence, challenged that.

Hearon spoke again. 'You have my authority to do as much as required in order to cut to the core of this circumstance.' The Chapter Master turned away. 'I ask you only be certain.'

Thryn felt a tightening in his gut as the full scope of Hearon's command became clear to him. 'And if I cannot be certain, my lord? What would you have me do then?'

'There is no scope for doubts, brother.' Hearon paused at the edge of the chamber's shadows and nodded towards the window. 'End him if you must. Our ghosts remain dead.'

TARIKUS AWOKE, AND his first reaction was one of shock. It faded quickly, to be replaced by a twinge of annoyance; ever since his escape from the prison on Dynikas V, each new slumber ended with the same tremor of fear and uncertainty, and it angered him.

Each time, he expected to find himself back in the searing metal cell, his ash-smeared skin slick with sweat against the hard surface of his sleeping pallet, the humid air about him resonating with heat. It was as if his subconscious mind could not willingly accept that he had found his freedom. He had experienced so many strange tortures during his imprisonment in that Light-forsaken hell that even now, weeks after breaking out of the cursed place, some seed of doubt remained lodged in his thoughts, some tiny part of him too afraid to accept the reality presented to it for fear it would be torn away a moment later.

The stone and steel of the prison on Dynikas V was no more, his tormentors consumed by tyranid swarms, the prison itself scoured to the bedrock by Astartes lance fire; but the walls still stood in Tarikus's mind, and he wondered if they would ever fall.

With a sigh, he pushed such thoughts away, rose and moved to the simple fresher unit in the corner of his room. Perhaps there was an irony in the fact that this small chamber was also called a 'cell', but its function was dedicated to providing silence and peace, not confinement. He ran cold, brackish water over his face, glancing at the small circular window high in the wall. A simple pattern of acid-etching covered the glassaic; the shape of a spread-winged eagle and upon that the lines of a human skull. The sigil of his Chapter. Seeing it made Tarikus's chest tighten; the symbol meant so much to him. It had been his life for so long, and in the darkest moments of his incarceration, he had thought never to lay eyes upon it again.

Men of the steady and dour nature that characterised most of the Astartes of the Doom Eagles Chapter were not often given to moments of open excitement or joy, and yet Tarikus could not deny that he felt something close to those emotions deep within him, a strange elation at being home once more, but tempered with apprehension at what was to come next.

A day now since he arrived on the Thunderhawk. A day, after a sullen greeting from this Brother Zurus; none of his questions answered, mind, only the offer of a Spartan meal and the room and rest. *A place where you can reflect*, Zurus had said. It was not lost on Tarikus that, although the door to his chamber had not been locked, a discreet gun-servitor had been stationed nearby. And he knew without needing to search for them that audial and visi-spectrum aura sensors were concealed in the covings above him.

They were watching him closely. He expected as much.

Should he have been affronted by such surveillance? On some level he was. On another, he understood the motivation behind it. Trust was a precious commodity in the Imperium of Mankind, and it was only in places where bonds of brother-hood and fealty ran strong that it could be spent. The ranks of the Adeptus Astartes were one such place, but when outsiders ventured into that circle – *outsiders and strangers*, Tarikus reminded himself – the wellspring quickly ran dry.

His own kinsmen did not trust him, and for reasons that a cursed fate had forced upon him.

Tarikus grimly considered the unfairness of it, the hard reality of callous outcome that was the way of his bleak universe. After Serek, where he and his squad had engaged a force of Necrontyr and ultimately been compelled to flee a planet in its death throes, he had healed aboard a hospitaller ship. In a narthecia-induced slumber, his enhanced physiology working to repair the damage of a poor teleport reversion, he had slept the voyage away – at least until the Traitor-kin had ambushed them. Too weak to fight them all, Tarikus had been captured even as his brothers escaped, thinking him dead. From there, the whoreson Red Corsairs sold him like chained cattle to the master of the Dynikas prison – and he had remained in that place for month after month, year after year, confined with other Astartes stolen from battlefields or presumed dead. Forgotten men turned into laboratory animals, test subjects for the amusement of the Chaos primogenitor who called himself Fabius Bile.

Tarikus had expected to die there – but then he was a Doom Eagle, and Doom Eagles always expected death. Still, when the chance for freedom came, he embraced it with all his might, aware that his service to the Golden Throne was not yet over. In his soul, Tarikus knew that he was not ready to perish, not on Dynikas, not at the hands of Bile and his freak-army of modificate mutants. He had not been granted permission to die.

He heard footsteps out in the corridor, then a voice. 'Tarikus,' called Zurus, 'will you join me?'

The Doom Eagle gathered in his duty tunic and over-robe, then opened the cell door. 'Are we going somewhere?'

Zurus nodded once. 'I have something I wish you to see.'

THEY WALKED, AND Zurus did his best to observe his charge without making his scrutiny an open challenge. Tarikus seemed no different from the man shown in his file picts, or captured by the imagers of servo-skulls in battle footage. He carried himself like an Astartes should, and with no prompting the warrior showed all the correct fealty and honour towards the sacrosanct statuary ringing the gates of the great circlet corridor, which ran the circumference of the Eyrie. If anything, Tarikus seemed almost moved to see the great carving of Aquila, first of the Doom Eagles and chosen of the Second Founding. Zurus looked up from his own deep bow a moment quicker than usual, examining the curve of the other man's shoulders.

Finally, Tarikus stood and straightened. 'Perhaps you wish to set an hourglass at my side, brother. That might be method enough to gauge my piety.'

'I am not an inquisitor,' replied Zurus, a little too swiftly. In truth, he wondered what the representatives of the Ordo Hereticus might have done if they knew of Tarikus and his circumstances – or indeed that of the other handful of Astartes, who had been liberated from Dynikas by brothers of the Blood Angels Chapter. To spend months, years even, in a gaol ruled by one of the most notorious traitors of the Heresy... Could anyone, even a chosen warrior of the Emperor's Astartes, emerge untouched by the experience? Could a Space Marine survive such a thing and not be tainted in some fashion? Zurus held the question in his thoughts as he spoke again. 'You are among kinsmen here.'

'And who better to judge me?' Tarikus looked around, his hard gaze sweeping the ranges of the curving corridor, the galleries overhead and the gloomy alcoves where lume-light did not fall. 'Where are my other watchers? Nearby, I'd imagine.'

Zurus resisted the urge to look where Tarikus did. He knew full well that the Librarian Thryn was somewhere close at hand, studying them both. He wondered what Thryn thought of them; outwardly, the two Doom Eagles were similar in aspect, although Zurus's hairless scalp was paler – the legacy of his origin in the sea-nomad tribes, unlike Tarikus, who was a son of the high-mountain kindred. They were both as good an example of the aspect of a Son of Aquila as one could hope to find on the Ghost-mountain; but it was what lay beneath that aspect that could not be quantified.

That which could not be valued in the weight of coin; this was what Zurus had to quantify. If Tarikus was found wanting, it would mean ignoble death – the worst of fates for a Doom Eagle to suffer.

A party of Scouts passed close, and Zurus guessed by their garb and weapons they had returned from a training sortie out in the equatorial island chains. He gave the youths a terse nod that was returned, but none of them acknowledged the presence of Tarikus, passing him by without making eye contact. Zurus saw him stiffen at the slight, but he said nothing. After a moment, he nodded to himself, as if accepting something.

'Where are my men?' said the other warrior, without meeting his gaze. 'It has been two years since I last saw them, and this question I have asked more than once. Do they live still?'

Zurus had been ordered not to speak of Tarikus's former comrades-in-arms, but the command sat poorly with him. He could not in good conscience remain silent on the matter. At length, he gave a nod. 'They live,' Zurus admitted. At Serek, Tarikus had led a number of good, steadfast Space Marines – Brothers Korica, Petius and Mykilus – each of whom had survived the Red Corsair attack on the medicae frigate.

'I wish to see them.'

Zurus shook his head. 'Perhaps later.'

Tarikus shot him a glare. 'Do not lie to me, brother. Grant me that, at least.'

He sighed. 'What do you expect me to say, Tarikus? What did you think would happen when you returned here?' Zurus gestured around. 'Did you think we would welcome you with open arms? Take you in as if nothing had happened? You said it yourself. Two years, brother. A long time in the heart of darkness.'

The other man's gaze dropped to the ornate stone floor, and despite himself, Zurus felt a pang of sympathy for him. 'I'm a fool, then,' said Tarikus. 'Naïve to think that I could return and pick up where I left off.' He shook his head. 'I only want to return. That is all.'

Zurus frowned and walked on. 'Come,' he told Tarikus, 'you must see this. You'll understand better when you do.'

THE EYRIE'S CENTRAL feature was a great octagonal tower, tallest of the citadels that reached for the sky, deepest of those that plunged levels down into the heart-rock of the Ghostmountain. The Reclusiam was a million memorials to countless deaths across the galactic disc. Entire floors were given over to relics recovered from the sites of terrible battles and brutal wars across the entire span of the Imperium. Many were from conflicts in which the Doom Eagles had taken a direct part, but others were from atrocities so soaked in despair and fatality that warriors of the Chapter had been drawn to visit them.

The Doom Eagles were born from the Legion of the Ultramarines in the wake of the Horus Heresy, in the shadow of Great Aquila. He had been a warrior of Guilliman during the Siege of Terra, and along with the rest of the Ultramarines, battles fought during the race to reinforce humanity's home world waylaid them at a most crucial moment. As Chapter history told it, Aquila had been so wracked with guilt and despair at arriving too late to protect the Emperor from his mortal wounds at the hands of Horus, that he had sworn an oath never again to delay in defence of the Imperium. When the time of the Second Founding came, Aquila willingly broke away to forge the Doom Eagles and make his belief manifest in them. The first Master made it a tenet of his new Chapter that every Son of Gathis would understand the cost of hesitance, of failure – and with it, the great guilt that came in step.

He would have them see these things, know them first-hand. And so, the relics; gathered by brothers on pilgrimages to places of battle and failed wars, each item a piece of despair and calamity made solid and real.

Many levels of the Reclusiam were such grim museums, halls reverent with shards of stone and bone, glass and steel. Armageddon, Rocene, Malvolion, Telemachus, Brodra-kul, and countless other war-sites, all represented here. And in the hallowed core, brought to this place by Aquila himself, the silver-walled chamber where pieces of shattered masonry from the Imperial Palace lay alongside a feather from the wing of Sanguinius and a shard of the Emperor's own battle armour.

It was said that those with the witch-sight could hear the ghost-screams in the tower. If that were so, if these relics could indeed contain a fraction of the pain and anguish that had enveloped them, then Zurus was glad the great chorus of sorrow thundering silent in the air was hidden from him.

This was not their destination, however. With Tarikus quiet at his side, the Space Marine rode the grav-car that ran the brass rails following the length of the tower. They rode up and up, beyond the ranges of the death-relics of strangers and into the Hall of the Fallen.

The largest open space inside the Eyrie, the vast walls, floor and ceiling were sheathed in great tiles of polished obsidian, each the size of a Land Raider. Hanging at right angles from complex armatures, some from floor to ceiling, others suspended at differing heights, there were free-floating panels of the same dark stone. At a distance, the glassy black panes seemed clouded somehow, but as one drew closer, definition unfolded.

Each panel was perfectly laser-etched into thin strips; each strip sported a half-globe of glass, behind which lay a random item. Upon the strip, the name of a Doom Eagle claimed by death. Next to each name, inside the glass, a relic: a fragment of armour, an eye-lens, a bolt shell, an honour-chain. Every artefact, something touched by the dead. A piece of them, to be held in trust for as long as the Chapter existed.

The grav-car changed tracks, joining a conveyor that took them across the span of the hall, down and across in zigzag motions toward one of the tallest of the panels.

Zurus looked down towards the floor far below. Somewhere down there was the memorial of Aquila, and beside it a cracked helmet under glass. It had no dressing, no great and ostentatious detail to set it aside from every other marker. The First Master had ordered it so, knowing that in death, all men were in unity.

He glanced up and saw that Tarikus was also looking downward. *Mimicking me,* he wondered? *Or is he feeling the reverence that I feel?*

At last, the grav-car rattled to a halt some distance up the face of a suspended wall and Zurus gestured towards the pane that hung before them. Behind a glass bubble, an Astartes combat blade was visible, the fractal edge still bright and sharp even though the length of the knife was dirty and pitted with use.

Tarikus saw the weapon and took a half step towards it, then stopped dead. 'It's mine,' he said. The tone of his voice was peculiar; there was something like fear in it.

Zurus nodded and indicated the memorial panel. 'Look here, brother.'

There in gothic script, etched by the hand of some machine-slave stoneworker, letters lined in heavy silver. As if he had no control over the action, Tarikus reached out and ran his fingers over the shape of his name. 'No...' began the other Astartes, shaking his head.

Zurus nodded again. 'You were lost, brother. You know our laws and diktats. Your name was cast from the rolls. The ceremony of loss completed and sanctified. Your name, carved here, in memoriam. By the lights of the Chapter and all of Gathis–'

The other Doom Eagle turned abruptly to face him, a curious shade of emotion in his dark eyes. 'I am dead,' he said, finishing Zurus's sentence for him. 'I no longer exist.'

TARIKUS STRODE FROM the gates of the Reclusiam across the processional bridge with such pace and intent that it was a long moment before he realised he had nowhere to go. He slowed and the grief he had tried to outrun caught up with him, as if it were only his swift tread that had kept it at bay.

In his darkest moments, trapped in that hated prison cell, Tarikus had encountered a great dread within himself that had shocked him with its potency. He had feared that he was *forgotten*; that after he was lost in deep space, the many sorties and battles he had fought, the honours he had earned, all would count for nothing among his brethren. He feared that all he had done would be meaningless.

But now he saw that the greater horror was this – that he had been *remembered*, in so final and damning a way as to make each breath he drew now a phantom. In the eyes of Great Aquila and his Chapter, Brother-Sergeant Tarikus had perished aboard that lost medicae frigate, years past. His kinsmen had counted him gone and made their peace with that fact.

Was it any wonder the Scouts had looked away from him, unsettled by his presence? For a Chapter so intimate with the manners of death, to see a warrior return from it must have shaken them to their core. *Our ghosts remain dead*, Tarikus thought, recalling the words written in the *Prayer Mortalis*.

Zurus called his name and he turned as the other Doom Eagle approached him, his pale face set like ice.

'This must be undone,' Tarikus began, but Zurus waved him into silence.

'Do you understand, brother?' Zurus demanded of him. 'You see now why your reappearance is... problematic?'

Tarikus felt a swell of anger inside him, and let it rise. 'Don't speak to me as if I am some whining neophyte. I am a battle-brother of this Chapter with honour and glory to my name!'

'Are you?' The question slipped from Zurus's lips.

He glared at the other warrior. 'Ah. I see. At first I thought you were concerned that my wits might have been dulled by my confinement, that perhaps you suspected my spirit damaged by my experiences... But it's more than that, isn't it?' Tarikus made a spitting sound and advanced on the other Doom Eagle. 'Can it be that you doubt the evidence of your own eyes, *brother*?' He put savage emphasis on the last word.

'The truth—'

Tarikus's anger was strong now, and he refused to let Zurus speak. 'What do you presume?' He spread his hands. 'Are you waiting for me to shed my skin, to transform into some hell-spawned Chaos daemon? Is that what you think I am?'

Zurus's gaze did not waver. 'That question has been asked.'

He took a quick step forward and prodded Zurus in the chest with his finger. 'I know what I am, kinsman,' snarled Tarikus. 'A warrior loyal to Holy Terra!'

'Perhaps,' said Zurus, 'or perhaps you are only a thing which believes that to be true. Something that only resembles Brother-Sergeant Tarikus.'

Muscles bunched in his arm, and for a long second Tarikus wavered on the verge of striking the other Space Marine across the face. That another Doom Eagle would dare to impugn the honour of a kinsman lit his fury still higher, reasons be damned.

And in that moment, through the lens of his cold anger, Tarikus discerned something else: a greasy, electric tingle across his skin and the sense of a hundred eyes staring at him. He relaxed his stance and turned away, glaring about across the length of the high marble bridge. The only sound was the clatter of heat exchangers working far below in the depths of the Ghostmountain.

To the air he spoke a demand. 'Show yourself, witch-kin.' Tarikus shot a look at Zurus, and the other warrior's expression confirmed his suspicions. He turned away again, ranging around. 'Come, brother. If you wish to damn my name, at least do me the courtesy of looking me in the eye when you do so.'

'As you wish.' The voice came from behind him, close and low. Tarikus found a figure in the lee of a carved support, swamped by red-trimmed robes. The

Doom Eagle had looked in that direction only moments earlier, and there had been nothing there. Only shadows.

The psyker walked closer, dropping his hood. Cold, hard eyes bit into Tarikus, searching for any sign of weakness. He betrayed none.

'I am Thryn,' said the Librarian. 'My name is known.'

Tarikus nodded once. 'I have heard of you. A chooser of the faithful.'

'But not you,' Thryn replied. 'It was not my duty on the day you were picked from the aspirants to join this Chapter, all those decades ago. Perhaps, if it had been, this question would already be answered.'

'There is no question,' Tarikus retorted. 'What you see before you is all that I am. Doom Eagle. Adeptus Astartes. Son of Gathis.'

Thryn cocked his head. 'The enemy hides in plain sight. A tactic the followers of the Ruinous Powers are quite fond of. They have warped many a mind in the past. It is only sensible that we must be certain that has not happened here.'

Tarikus met Thryn's burning gaze and refused to look away. 'Do you know what kept me centred for all those months inside that hellhole, witch-kin? It was my faith in my brothers, my Chapter and my Emperor. Was I wrong to believe that? Have I been forsaken?'

'That is the question we must ask of you, Tarikus,' said Thryn.

'You dare ask me to prove myself?' The fury boiled inside him. 'After all that I have done in Aquila's name, you question *me*?' He advanced on the psyker until they were face to face. He could feel the prickling aura of the Librarian's controlled mind-force pressing on his flesh. 'This is your greeting for a lost brother, who by the grace of He That Is Most Mighty, has had the temerity to survive. Nothing but disdain and isolation. Accusations and disrespect.'

'This is the universe we live in,' offered Zurus.

Tarikus paused, holding Thryn's gaze. 'Perhaps you would have preferred it if I allowed myself to die in confinement.'

Thryn cocked his head. 'That would have brought a definite end to this matter, to be sure.'

'Then I apologise for daring to live,' Tarikus shot back. 'It must be very inconvenient for you.'

'There is still time,' said the psyker. 'But not much time.'

Tarikus was silent for a long moment, and with an effort, he calmed himself and shuttered away his annoyance. That there was some logic in the challenge posed by Zurus and Thryn only made matters worse; but rather than resist it, Tarikus drew in a breath and looked to his heart, to the soul and spirit that made him a Doom Eagle.

'So be it,' he said grimly. 'If I must be questioned, then I must be questioned. This is the way of things. I will face it and not flinch. Tell me what must be done to put this challenge to its end.'

'You're certain?' asked Zurus. 'It will be difficult. Some have been broken by less.'

'Tell me,' repeated Tarikus, glaring at the psyker.

Thryn looked back at him with a level, even gaze. 'There are rituals of purity. Rites of passage. You will be tested.' The psyker turned to leave. 'Tomorrow, at dawn–'

Tarikus's hand shot out and grabbed the Librarian's forearm, halting him instantly. 'No,' said the Doom Eagle. 'We will begin this now.'

Thryn studied him. 'You understand what you will face?'

'*Now,*' repeated Tarikus.

THEY BEGAN WITH the Talons.

A mechanism made of bright, polished steel, and as cold as polar ice, it wrapped around Tarikus and held the Doom Eagle in its grip. It resembled an artificer's vice, scaled up to the size of a giant. A great oiled screw turned, bringing knurled blocks of metal towards one another in an inexorable approach. From each block grew a fan of wicked barbs, claws modelled on the talons of the great raptors that rode the thermals of the Razorpeak range.

Tarikus stood between them, clad only in thin exercise robes. The muscles of his arms and legs bunched and became iron-solid as he settled in against the blocks. Only his strength and fortitude held back a crushing death. He breathed evenly, pacing himself, marshalling his strength rather than spending it all in a single effort.

The Talons pressed in. They never tired. The slow-turning gears pushed against the Space Marine's resistance, daring him to falter for just a moment;

and there was the insidious thing about the trial. If the warrior relaxed, even for an instant, the blocks would lurch forward by a full hand's span, reducing the space between by a good measure – but in doing so, giving him a moment's respite from the struggle. Thus, the Talons preyed on fatigue and inattention. After hours, days between the blocks, a warrior might consider letting them close the distance a little, just to take a precious second of rest before they reached their stops and started to press in once again; but that was the route to failure. So it was said, Hearon himself once managed a lunar month in the Talons and never gave any quarter.

Tarikus was there for days. With no windows in sight, he could only make the most basic reckoning of the passing hours. And unlike Hearon's trial, Tarikus was not left alone with his struggle. From the shadows about the Talons, figures moved and called out to him, bombarding him constantly with questions and demands. They asked him to recite lines of catechism and Chapter rote, or they hectored him over every last point of the story he told of his confinement in Bile's prison. The interrogation went on and on, without end, circling his thoughts until he felt his mind going numb.

Thryn was among his questioners; perhaps he was only one of them, perhaps he was all of them, but as sweat dripped from Tarikus's limbs and acid slowly filled his veins, the warrior did not give the answers the Librarian wanted. He told the same story over and over, he recited his hymnals and prayers as he should have, all the while resisting the constant, blinding pressure. Denied food, denied water, denied release, he stood his ground.

Then without warning, a week into the trial, it ended. The Talons retracted, and Tarikus fell to the deck, his muscles twitching and cramping. It took him a moment to get back to his feet. Dimly, he was aware of figures in the cowled robes of Chapter serfs crowding towards him.

He frowned. This could not be the end of it. He had not suffered enough.

He was correct.

TARIKUS WAS STRIPPED naked and put into the hold of a rotorflyer. The aircraft left the Ghostmountain with a sudden upward lurch, and almost as quickly it began a steep downward arc. The Doom Eagle had barely enough time to register the howl of winds over the hull of the craft before the deck beneath him parted and he fell.

Tarikus landed hard on a shelf of icy rock, a harsh bombardment of sleet angling across it towards a sudden, sheer drop into the mist. He glanced up to see the flyer power away on flickering blades and caught sight of the Eyrie beyond it. They had deposited him on one of the nearby peak sides, little more than half a kilometre distant from the Ghost-mountain as the eagle flew, but uncrossable without a jet pack or a wing-glider.

He cast around, searching for something to shield himself from the punishing weather, and found only a canted slab of rock. Aching from the strain of the Talons, Tarikus made it into the poor cover and found mud and lichen in the lee. The fungus he ate, the mud he smeared over his flesh to hold in his body heat.

He wondered if this was some kind of punishment. Had he failed the first test in some way that had not registered in his mind? Or had Thryn and those who sat in judgement of him tired of the game and made their choice, left him out here to die of exposure? Both seemed unlikely; a bolt shell to the back of his head would have ended him far faster than starvation or hypothermia, and the Doom Eagles were not given to cause suffering where it need not occur – there was enough of that to go around in the universe, without adding to the volume of it.

As he half-dozed behind his rough shelter, Tarikus imagined the scrutiny of distant eyes, watching him from the windows of the fortress-monastery he thought of as his home. He felt darkness crowd in on him, a numbness spreading through his body. Still they questioned him, only now it was without words, now it was with the force of ruthless nature. Now it was Gathis itself, the voice of the Ghost-mountain and the Razorpeaks, that challenged him.

And still, the answer that was sought was not given. By the following dawn, Tarikus had died.

THRYN SENSED HIS master's displeasure before he entered the observation gallery. It filled the space around him like a cold fog, present in everything and ready to become an ice-storm at a moment's notice.

Within he found Hearon at the heavy window, and off to one side the figure of Brother-Captain Consultus. The warrior was clad in his wargear, and he stood at stiff attention, eyes focused on a distant point beyond the far wall. Consultus looked like carved stone, immobile and rigid; but Thryn saw past that, reading the steady churn of emotions inside the captain of the 3rd.

The Luckless 3rd, so the other company commanders called them, but never to their faces. Thryn considered this and saw truth in it; the return of Tarikus was just one more piece of ill fortune laid at the boots of Consultus and his men.

Hearon threw a glance at the Librarian. 'You have an answer for me?'

'I do not, lord,' he replied.

'Where is he now?'

The psyker gestured with a nod. 'In the Apothecarion. He was recovered before brain death could occur. He will live.'

'For what that is worth.' Thryn's master made a negative noise. 'Does your witch-sight fail you? Look into his soul, tell me what you see.'

'I have,' admitted the psyker, 'and I can draw no conclusion. Resilient as he is, his psyche was tormented by imprisonment and suffering, but that is to be expected. But this is not a case of black and white. There are many shades of grey.'

'I disagree,' Hearon replied. 'The question is a direct one. Is Tarikus to be trusted? Yes or no?'

'He has endured the trials,' ventured the captain. 'Survived, once again.'

'I know your opinion already,' Hearon snapped. 'Repeating it serves no purpose.' He looked back at Thryn.

'The captain is quite correct,' said the Librarian. 'His flesh withstands great punishment. He does not waver beneath chastisement that would kill a warrior of lesser courage.'

Hearon grimaced. 'That is a thing of meat and blood,' he said, with a terse gesture. 'And we know those can be controlled.' The Chapter Master shook his head. 'No, it is the question of Tarikus's spirit that tasks me. His soul is where the question lies.'

'His faith in the Emperor is strong.' Thryn paused, framing his words. 'His faith in his Chapter also.'

'*Even after we have done this to him,*' Hearon was looking at Consultus as he said the words. 'I don't need Thryn's powers to pluck that thought from your mind, brother-captain.'

'It is so, lord,' Consultus replied.

'Let no man here labour under the mistaken belief that I take pleasure in this,' Hearon grated. 'But Tarikus is one man. My responsibilities are to a Chapter one thousand strong, to a heritage of ten millennia. The Doom Eagles are my charge, and if I must shoulder the guilt of persecuting a single kinsman in order to protect them, I will do so without hesitation. It is only a grain of sand against the weight of Aquila's holy remorse.'

Thryn was silent for a moment. He knew full well why he had been called to this meeting, and why too Consultus, as Tarikus's former commanding officer, had been brought in as a witness. 'There is word from the Council of Eagles?'

Hearon nodded. Modelled after the High Council of Terra, the Doom Eagles encompassed a commission of men of highest rank who would draw together on matters of import facing the Chapter. The group would offer advice to the Chapter Master, and while ultimately Hearon held the sanction over all commands, he drew upon the knowledge and advice of all his company captains, his senior Chaplain, Apothecary, Forge Master and Librarian. 'The greater body of my warriors question the need to prolong this matter. The risk outweighs the gain. The damage that might be wrought by a single turncoat among our number is huge when compared against the value of one veteran sergeant.'

'Is it?' Consultus said quietly. 'Do we not damage the Chapter ourselves if we reject a warrior whose only crime was a failure to die?'

'The others believe he is tainted?' asked Thryn.

'The others suggest that Tarikus be put down,' said the captain, with no little venom.

Hearon ignored Consultus's interruption. 'I... am not convinced.'

'My lord?'

The Chapter Master returned to the window. 'The Doom Eagles have always been the most pragmatic of the Adeptus Astartes. We have no time for vacillation. That we may never again delay... Those words are etched on our hearts.' He paused. 'Some of our battle-brothers say we should excise this man and move beyond. End him, and confirm what has already been laid to stone; that Tarikus of the 3rd is dead and gone.'

Thryn cocked his head. 'And yet?'

'And yet...' repeated Hearon, glancing toward Consultus, 'I cannot in all good conscience end this in so cursory a manner. When death comes to claim me, I find myself asking how I could go to the Emperor's side and answer for this. That I would allow a Son of Gathis to meet the sword's edge all because of an unanswered question?' He shook his head. 'That will not stand.'

Thryn's eyes narrowed. 'There is another way, lord. A method I have yet hesitated to employ. A weirding, if you will. '

'Do what you must.' The Chapter Master looked over his shoulder at Thryn. 'You *will* bring me an answer, Librarian.'

'Even if Tarikus is destroyed by it?' said Consultus.

'Even if,' Hearon replied.

ZURUS EXITED THE south range after morning firing rites, and found the three of them waiting for him. He hesitated, for a moment uncertain how to respond, then beckoned the Space Marines to follow him. They moved to a worktable in the far corner of the arming hall, and he took the only stool and sat upon it. With careful, spare motions, Zurus dismantled his bolt pistol and set about the work of cleaning the weapon.

As he expected, it was Korica who spoke first. 'Lord,' he began, tension thick in his tone, 'we have talked amongst ourselves of… of this matter, and we have questions.'

'Indeed?' said Zurus, taking apart the trigger assembly. 'Questions seem to be the matter of the day.' From the corner of his eye, he saw the other two Doom Eagles exchange glances; one of them, his face dark and intense with old fire scarring, the other sallow of features with a single silver ring in his ear and the helix electoo of an Apothecary upon his neck. He read conflict in their aspects. It came as no surprise; he felt the same thing they did, to some degree.

'There is much talk in the galleries,' Korica went on, gesturing with his carbon-and-steel augmetic arm. 'Rumour and hearsay. We would know the truth.'

Zurus stopped and studied the pieces of his gun. 'Would you?' he said, a warning in his manner. 'Tell me, brother, would you also have me go against the express orders of the Chapter Master?'

'We would never disobey a legal command, brother-sergeant,' said the Apothecary. 'You know that.'

He nodded. 'Aye, Petius, I do.' Zurus glanced at the scarred warrior. 'Mykilus? As your kinsmen have spoken, I trust you must have something to venture as well?'

The other Doom Eagle gave a slow nod. 'Sir,' he began, 'you have commanded our squad for two cycles and we have been bound in blood and fire together. No disrespect to you is intended... but Tarikus was our sergeant for a long time. He saved each of our lives on one battleground or another. We thought him dead, and now we learn that he still lives...' Mykilus trailed off, unable to find the right words.

'Aquila's remorse runs strong in us,' said Korica. 'We believed Tarikus had been killed at the hands of the Red Corsairs. We brought back his knife. We share the guilt at giving up on him.' He shook his head. 'We let him down. We should have done more. Searched longer.'

Zurus looked up for the first time. 'No,' he said flatly. 'Do not torment yourselves. You could not have known.'

'We want to see him, sir,' said Petius.

'Impossible.' Zurus shot a glance at the Apothecary. 'It is forbidden. He is to remain in isolation until he has been judged.'

Korica's face twisted in anger. 'Tarikus is no traitor. We know the man better than any other battle-brother on the Ghostmountain! He is steadfast!'

Zurus studied the faces of the three men. 'Is that what you all think?' He got a chorus of nods in return – and yet, the warrior could sense some tiny inklings of doubt lurking behind the hard eyes of his men. The very same hesitation he himself experienced. 'I took on the mantle of Tarikus's stewardship for one reason,' Zurus went on. 'Because of what I knew of the man whom I had succeeded. I did it because of what you told me of him.' He didn't add that in truth, Brother Zurus had always felt as if he could not measure up to the shadow of the squad's former commander.

'Then tell us what you think, sir,' said Mykilus. 'If we cannot speak to him ourselves, tell us your thoughts.'

'Aye,' added Petius. 'You have looked him in the eye. What did you see?'

Zurus sighed. 'One of us.' His gaze dropped to the disassembled bolter. 'Or so it seemed.'

'Chaos does not lurk within the heart of Brother Tarikus,' grated Korica. 'I would stake my life on that.'

'Are you sure?' Zurus returned to his work. 'Trapped in the heart of madness, tormented every moment of every day by the foulest traitor-genius hell ever spawned? Could a man not be twisted under such pressure?'

'A man, perhaps,' said Petius. 'But not a Doom Eagle.'

'Not Tarikus,' insisted Korica.

Zurus was silent for a long time, carefully rebuilding the weapon. 'It is no wonder you wish Tarikus to be found pure,' he said, at length. 'Each of you carry the guilt of speaking his death when in fact he had only been lost. But that remorse will pale into nothing if he is proven to be tainted.'

'If that is so,' Mykilus began, his voice leaden, 'then we three will be the ones to send him into oblivion.'

'But it is *not*,' Korica insisted. 'And we three will be there to welcome him back once this mistrust is swept away!'

The gun went back together smoothly, and Zurus tested the action before returning it to his holster. Finally, he rose and walked away.

At the threshold of the chamber door he paused and glanced back at his men. *But not really my men*, he told himself. *Tarikus's men*.

'Are you coming?' he asked.

HE WAS AT peace.

Sleep, pure and real. Tarikus struggled to remember the last time he had rested so well, free from nightmares and horrific recollections. Sluggish amniotic fluid swathed him, and he drifted in a tiny, warm ocean of his own. His fingers brushed the inside of a glassy orb. No sound reached him here.

Peace. And all he had needed to do to find it was to die.

He knew that what he experienced now was not true death; he had known that even as the cold had crept into his flesh, tightening about his bio-implant organs, pushing him towards nothingness. No, this was the little-death of the healing trance, the strange state between where the engines of his Astartes physiology were left to work their chemical magicks. He had been here before. After the battle for Krypt. After the narrow escape from Serek–

Serek. Tarikus suppressed a shudder. Memory of that incident returned to him with harsh clarity. After Serek, he had been in a trance like this, repairing damage wrought by a forced teleport transition. And it had been inside a medicae tank such as this one that he had watched the Red Corsairs come to take him. It came back in hard punches of sense-memory – bolt shells cracking the glassaic, his body sluicing out with the liquid on to the deck, still broken, still unready. The renegades coming in to attack him. Blood mixed with the yellowish amnio-fluid. Fighting and killing; but ultimately, failing.

A shiver ran the length of him. Suddenly the warm liquid was as cold as the mountainside.

Tarikus took a breath of the oxygenated medium and felt the chill bore deeper. Out beyond the walls of the medicae tank shapes moved to and fro. They might have been other Astartes, perhaps come to observe this curiosity, this warrior back from the dead, this soul in limbo – or perhaps they were just servitors, going about their tasks, making sure Tarikus did not perish. Not yet.

He did not have permission to die. Aquila had not granted it.

The Doom Eagle looked inside himself and dared to wonder what a real death might feel like. He had been close to that abyss so many times, but never fallen to it; and now, in this moment of great darkness he dared to wonder if death would be the better end for him. If he had perished aboard the hospitaller ship, or perhaps in the cells of the Dynikas prison, then all that happened now would not have come to pass. Tarikus's Chapter would continue on, untroubled by the aberration of his chance survival. The pestilent questions would not have been asked. Constancy would not be challenged.

He felt hollow inside. In his prison cell, whenever he could snatch a moment away from the eyes of the mutant guards and the modificate freaks, he had prayed to the Golden Throne that he might live to see home once more. And in all that time, he had never once thought that he would not be trusted by his own kinsmen.

Conflict raged inside him. At once he hated Thryn and the others for daring to doubt him, but at the same moment he understood why they did so. If matters had been different, if it had been Zurus returning to Gathis and not Tarikus, then what choices would *he* have made in the same place? What questions would Tarikus have demanded answers for?

It came to him that the only way he would be able to prove himself would be to give up the last breath in his body. In death, truth could not be hidden.

THE DOOR TO the psyker's sanctum opened on oiled pistons and a grave voice issued out from the darkness inside. 'Enter, Zurus. If you must.'

Zurus did as he was bid. Thryn's meditation chamber was little bigger than the accommodation cell where the sergeant laid his head, but it had the illusion of depth thanks to the strange jumble of shadows cast by electro-candles atop a series of iron stands, each at the corner of a mathematical shape carved into the floor.

Thryn rose from a kneeling cushion and pushed aside a fan of imager plates. Zurus glanced at them and saw only unreadable texts and oddly blurred images. He swallowed and failed to hide a grimace. The air in here was strange, almost oily, but with an acid tingle on the bare flesh of his face and hands.

Thryn glared at him. The psyker was in his wargear, and about his head in a blue-white halo, the crystalline matrix of a psionic hood glowed softly. 'You're interrupting my preparations, brother. And you have no good reason.'

Zurus met his hard look with one of his own. 'I have every reason—' he began.

'I'll save you the trouble of explaining yourself to me, shall I?' snapped the Librarian. 'You've been swayed by Tarikus. You've listened to his men, and felt their anxiety for their former commander's fate.' He turned away. 'And as you have never truly felt content as the leader of Tarikus's former squad, you wish to have him return to our fold so you can be free of your conflicts. Is that close to the truth?'

Zurus bristled at the other warrior's tone. 'You make us sound like mewling, weak children! You mock men who dare to show compassion and loyalty to their brothers!'

'Pragmatism is the watchword of the Doom Eagles,' Thryn continued. 'We do not let matters of sentimentality cloud our vision.'

'You think fidelity is something to be dismissed, witch-kin?' Zurus advanced on him. 'Is your warp-touched heart so empty that you forget your bonds of brotherhood?'

'I have forgotten nothing,' Thryn replied. 'But some must bear the burden to voice the questions that no others can utter. Some must dare to speak the hard words that no brother wishes to hear!' He turned to face him, the psy-crystals flickering. 'This obligation is mine. I will see it to its end.'

Zurus's shoulders sagged. 'How much further must this go? You have looked into his mind – tell me, have you sensed the taint of Chaos in his thoughts?'

Thryn shook his head. 'I have not.'

'And the testing of his flesh, first the Talons and then the wind and ice. Did his body belie the touch of the Archenemy at any time?'

'It did not,' intoned the Librarian.

'Then how can you let this go on? Tarikus is not corrupted!'

Thryn nodded. 'I agree.' It was not the answer Zurus was expecting. Before he could speak again, the psyker continued. 'I agree that his mind and his body are sound. But it is not those that I seek to test, brother. It is his soul. That which is the most ephemeral, yet the most powerful element of a life.' Thryn sighed, and something of the bleak aspect of his face softened. 'We know the insidious ways of Chaos, the Emperor blight them. Tarikus may carry a seed of darkness within him and never know it. It has happened before. He may live out a long life, and then one day, at an appointed time, or at some word of command, be transformed into something horrific. All that, if the smallest sliver of warp-stigma lies buried in his aura.'

Zurus frowned. 'The only way to be sure is to kill him, is that what you mean? If you end him and he erupts into some hell beast, you are proven right. If he dies, then he was innocent and just, and goes to the Emperor's side.' He snorted. 'A poor choice for Tarikus on either account.'

'This matter cannot be brought to a close while doubt still exists,' insisted Thryn.

'Then you'll do it?' Zurus snapped. 'And not just the little-death this time, but a cold-blooded murder?'

'Lord Hearon has granted me latitude to do whatever I must to end this uncertainty. And I will end it, this day.' Thryn returned to the centre of the room and knelt once more.

Zurus felt the tingle on his skin of psy-power in the air, the near-storm sense of it growing by the second. 'What will you do?'

Thryn bowed his head. 'Go now, brother. You will know soon enough.'

He lingered at the threshold for a long moment, then stepped through and allowed the hatch to close behind him. Cogs worked and seals fell into place, and Zurus stood outside, staring at the strange hexagrammatric wards etched into the metal, wondering what final trial Tarikus was about to face.

A sound came to him, echoing down the stone corridor. It sounded like thunder, but it could just as easily have been the report of distant shellfire.

TARIKUS AWOKE, AND he was in hell.

He fell hard, the rough metal plating of the floor rising up to slam into his knees and arms. He groaned and coughed up a river of stinging bile and thick amnio-fluid. Black streaks of blood threaded the ejecta from his lips. The warrior felt strange; his body seemed wrong, the impulses from his fingertips somehow out of synchrony with the rest of his nerves. He tried to shake himself free of the sensation but it would not leave him. Tarikus's flesh hung on him like an ill-fitting suit of clothes.

He looked up and blinked, his eyes refusing to focus properly. Lights and shadows jumped around him, blurring into shapes that he could not define. Something hove close and he perceived a hand reaching out to him, offering assistance.

'Here,' said a thick, resinous voice. 'To your feet. Come. There is much work to do.'

He took the grip, and felt peculiar talons where fingers should have been; but he was already rising, legs working, muscles tightening.

Light flashed, too slow to be storm-glow, the thunder-pulse with it too quick, too near. *Gunfire?* The sluggish thought trickled down through the layers of his awareness.

Tarikus jerked his hand away. 'Who are you? What is happening?'

Harsh laughter answered him. 'So many questions. Be still, warrior. All will be made clear.' One of the shadows came closer, looming large. 'Don't fight it, Tarikus. Let it happen.' He heard another low, callous chuckle. 'It will be less painful.'

There was heat at his back, burning and steady like the beating of a pitiless sun; and in the air about him, he perceived motes of dust falling in a slow torrent. He saw steel walls. Chains and broken glass. 'What is happening?' he shouted, but his words were lost in the blazing roar of a weapon. He knew that sound: a heavy bolter cannon on full automatic fire, impacts cutting into flesh and ceramite.

'You have done well,' he was told. 'Better than we could have expected. You opened the way for us.' The shadow-man came closer. 'Our perfect weapon.'

'What?' Tarikus raised his hands in self-defence. 'I do not understand–'

'Then look at me,' said the voice. 'And know the truth.'

The light chose that moment to come again, and in its hard-edged, unflinching glare Tarikus saw a thing that resembled an Astartes, but one made of flayed meat, broken bone and corroded iron. A face of gallows-pale flesh leered at him and twisted in amusement. Beneath it, on the figure's chest, was the design of a star with eight razor-tipped points.

'Traitor!' Tarikus shouted the word.

The corrupted warrior nodded. 'Yes, you are.'

He stumbled backwards, shaking his head. His skull felt heavy and leaden. 'No…'

'Your hands. Look at your hands.'

Tarikus could not help but glance downward. The meat of his hard, calloused fingers was gone, and in its place were arcs of bone that glistened like black oil.

'The change is already upon you. It's coming now. Let it happen.'

Ice filled his gut and Tarikus thrashed at the air, smashing aside a support frame, crashing back into the opened medicae tank where he had been healing. He tried to give a wordless shout of denial, but the sound would not form in his constricting throat. His muscles bunched and he shuddered, losing balance. Tarikus could feel a wave of something terrible billowing up inside him, reordering the meat and blood of his body as it moved. He spat and acid flew from his lips, spattering the walls with tiny smoking pits where the droplets fell. He tried to reject it, and failed.

He could hear battle beyond the doors of the chamber now, fast and lethal. Thunder rumbled all around, echoing through the stone at his feet. The Eyrie was under attack.

The Traitor Marine took a step towards him. When it spoke again, there was almost concern in its words. 'The Primogenitor told me it would not be an easy transformation. But hold on, kinsman. You will be renewed in all but a moment. And then you will join us fully.'

'I am not your kinsman!' Tarikus roared, and the words were ragged animal sounds torn from the throat of some monster, not from his lips, not from the mouth of a Doom Eagle. 'What have you done to me?'

Another chuckle. 'You did this to yourself, Tarikus. Don't you recall?' The room seemed to contract, the walls closing in on them both. 'On Dynikas. When you cast off your master. When you finally understood?'

'Understood… what?' All around him the stone of the medicae chamber flowed like wax into different shapes, and through the haze across his twitching vision the walls momentarily turned into planes of steel, vibrating with heat. The cell. The chains and the walls and the cell. *Did I never really leave? Have I always been there?*

The Traitor cocked its head. 'You understood that you had been discarded. Forgotten. That your corpse-god is ashes and lies. That you mean nothing to the men who tried to make you their slave.'

Tarikus stumbled away, shaking his head, denying every word. 'No!' He tried to launch himself towards the other warrior, but the sudden heat robbed him of every ounce of energy. In place of sweat, oily fluids seeped from his skin, draining his vitality with them.

'Don't you remember?' The Traitor gestured around, and Tarikus saw a distorted liquid mirror shimmer in the air. Upon it he saw himself in rags, kneeling before a towering figure in a coat made of human skin, a giant brass spider emerging from its back.

Fabius Bile.

'No…' he insisted. 'This is a trick! That did not happen! I would never break my oath!' Tarikus lurched back to his feet. 'I would not turn!'

'But you did,' said the voice. 'Because they hated you, forgot you.' The Traitor gestured and Tarikus saw a line of figures in tarnished silver armour standing high behind him. Their proportions were monstrous; they towered like Dreadnoughts, each one jeering and mocking him. They had faces he knew: Zurus and Thryn. At their shoulders: Korica, Mykilus and Petius. And above them all, as tall as a Titan, Aquila himself.

Tarikus reached out his mutating talon-hand and they shrank away; and then the worst of it. As one, all the Doom Eagles turned their backs on him, casting him aside.

Suddenly the room was tight and small about him, the space at the bottom of a pit that stretched up and away, walls too sheer to climb, light too far to reach.

'Poor Tarikus,' said the voice, soothing and unctuous. 'Is it any wonder you accepted the gift?'

Terror filled him at the words, but he could not stay silent. 'What gift?'

The Traitor opened its claw-hand and in it lay a feather, a small curl of plume alike to those that an eagle might leave behind in passing. It was ink-black, a colour so deep and strong that Tarikus immediately knew that to touch it would be poison to him.

No sooner had he laid eyes on the barb than his chest began to burn. Tarikus gasped and clawed at the wet strips of torn tunic shrouding his torso and ripped them away. His transformed talon hands caught the surface of his skin and great rents appeared in the meat of him. From the wounds he had made, no blood flowed; instead cascades of tiny black feathers issued out, spilling from his body. He roared and felt his throat filling with a swarming mass. Tarikus retched and spat a plug of wet, matted quills from his lips.

'Do you see now?' said the Traitor. 'A Chapter that rejected you, left you to perish in the cold, pitiless void. A cadre of false brothers who fled when their lives were in jeopardy. The lies you were told about fealty and honour, but all of it sand. Is it any wonder you were broken?' The other warrior leaned in. 'Is it any wonder you let us remake you in the Primogenitor's name?' He nodded. 'And now the last shroud is released from you, kinsman. Now you are free to be one of us… and our first act will be to grind this Ghostmountain to dust.'

Tarikus could not stop himself from trembling. The worst of it was not the visions, or the perhaps-memories, or the sense of his own body slipping away from him. No, the worst of it was that he could not be sure. The Traitor's words had the edge of truth to them.

How often in those long months in that cell had he lain in torment, one single question desperate on his lips. *Why have I been forgotten?* His every waking moment as an Adeptus Astartes had been in service of something greater than himself, and in return, in exchange for the surety of fate and death the Doom Eagles gave, Tarikus had the priceless gift of brotherhood. The certain knowledge of comradeship among his kindred, the knowing that he would never be lost, not so long as a single son of Gathis still drew breath. *So why did they never come for me? Why did they count me dead and be done, never to speak my name again?*

'Because it is a lie,' said the Traitor. 'And has ever been one.' He gestured around. '*We* will never lie to you, Tarikus. You will always know the truth with us.' The hand extended out to him once more. 'Take it.'

The thunder outside and the flashes of blue-white light coursed all around him. Tarikus looked up and saw the outstretched hand, the turncoat Astartes – and beyond, the shadows of the Doom Eagles.

They were judging him.

Time halted for Tarikus, and the questions that had bombarded him since he had returned to the Eyrie were echoing through his mind. The accusations welled up from within.

He could imagine a shade of himself – a weaker, broken Tarikus – who might have had the flaw of character to yield to the strain of his confinement on Dynikas. This ghost-Tarikus, this pale copy of him, made bitter by his abandonment, clawing in desperation for the one thing every Space Marine wanted... The bond of brotherhood. Without their comradeship, the Astartes were nothing. Everything they were was built upon that foundation. What horror it would be to lose that, to be cast adrift and counted as unkindred. A weakened soul, captured at the lowest moment, might be persuaded to bend the knee to a former foe for just a taste of that blessed bond once again. A fragile spirit, yes, who would willingly hide their new loyalty beneath the cloak of the old, and carry poison back to those who had deserted them. Poison and murder, all in the name of revenge.

Suddenly, events were moving again, and he was aware of the Traitor nodding. 'Yes. You see now, don't you?'

But that shade, that weakling who appeared in his thoughts… Whatever it was, it was not Tarikus, son of Gathis, scion of Aquila. He drew himself up and with a vicious shove, pushed the turncoat aside.

Tarikus glared up at the silent, condemning gazes of his Doom Eagle brethren, peering at the phantoms of their faces. 'I am not a heretic.' He spoke, and with each word that left his mouth, Tarikus felt his vitality returning to him. A sense of righteous power enveloped him, and with it the wrongness of his changed body bled away. Moment by moment, he began to feel *correct*. With every breath, he moved closer to the warrior he had always been – and with a surge of strength, Tarikus realised that he had not felt so certain of anything in years. Not since before he had been taken prisoner. 'Judge me if you will,' he shouted, 'I do not fear it! You will look inside my heart and see only fealty! I am Tarikus!'

The hazed faces of his former squad mates danced there in the wraith-light. Korica: impulsive and brave. Mykilus: steadfast and strong. Petius: taciturn and measured. They did not turn from him. They had not forgotten him.

Behind him, the Traitor was getting to its feet, coming towards him with murder in its eyes. 'Fool–'

He silenced the enemy by grabbing his throat and tightening his grip until the Traitor could only make broken gurgles. Gunfire-thunder rumbled louder and louder in his ears and Tarikus bellowed to make himself heard. 'I am a Doom Eagle! My fidelity will never falter!' He threw his enemy to the ground. 'I did not break! *I will never break!'*

A great pressure, silent but deafening, pushed out from inside his thoughts, and all at once the warped walls around him exploded like glass beneath a hammer.

Tarikus swept around; he was intact, unchanged. Everything that had happened in the phantom room was gone, vanished like shafts of sunlight consumed by clouds. He stood before the open healing tank, then turned and found the Librarian Thryn coming back to his feet. The psyker was nursing an ugly bruise forming at his throat. He spat and eyed the other Astartes.

'You?' said Tarikus. He sniffed the air, scenting the greasy tang of spent mind-power. 'You cast a veil over me… All of it illusions and game-play.'

'Aye,' Thryn replied, rough-voiced. 'And you almost tore the breath from me in the process.'

Tarikus advanced towards the psyker, his hands contracting into fists. Anger burned in his eyes, and the question of Thryn being clad in armour and himself not didn't cross his thoughts. 'I should beat an apology from you, witch-kin.'

'You should be thanking me,' Thryn retorted. 'At last, I finally saw into you. Saw what you hid from us.'

'I hid nothing,' Tarikus spat.

Thryn shook his head. 'Don't lie to me, not now. You hid your fear, Tarikus. The black and terrible fear that came upon you in the darkest moments of your confinement, when just for a moment, you wondered what would happen if you weakened.' The Librarian gave a crooked, unlovely smile. 'How very human of you.'

Gradually, Tarikus's fists relaxed. 'I looked into the darkness, across the edge of the abyss,' he said slowly. 'And I turned away.'

Thryn nodded. 'Indeed you did. And now I have the answer I wanted.' He offered his hand to the other Doom Eagle. 'Your integrity is assured. You are returned to us, brother. In body, mind... and in soul.'

Tarikus shook his hand in the old fashion, palm to wrist. 'I never left,' he said.

'WHEN WILL THERE be an end to this?' grated Korica. He glared at Zurus, and the other warrior nodded slightly.

'I have no answer for you,' admitted the sergeant. He looked away, his gaze crossing the towering black marble fascias of the memorial towers, each reaching up and away towards the ornate ceiling far overhead. He saw something moving; a travel platform, dropping towards them.

Mykilus saw it too, and he pointed. 'Look there.'

Petius took a tentative step towards the edge of the gantryway, then halted. Like all of them, he was unsure of what meaning lay behind the urgent summons that had brought them to the relical.

In the next moment, the platform had arrived and a figure in duty robes stepped off, pushing past them.

'Tarikus?' Zurus could not keep the amazement from his voice. He had truly believed that he would never see the errant Astartes again. Thryn was not known for his lenience in matters of judgement. Then his thoughts caught up with him and Zurus allowed himself a small smile. He had been right about his lost brother; suddenly, all the doubts he had harboured about this duty and his part in Tarikus's ordeal were swept away, and it was as if a great weight fell from his shoulders.

Korica extended his augmetic arm towards Tarikus, but the veteran pushed past him, not slowing. The other Doom Eagles followed Tarikus down the length of the gantryway until he halted before a particular memorial slab.

Zurus knew what would come next the instant before it happened. The veteran's fist shot out and punched through the bubble of glassaic at the end of the panel and then folded around the death-remnant inside.

He watched the other warrior draw out a blood-streaked hand, and in it, a battle-worn combat blade. Tarikus looked down at the knife, and then up at them for the first time. His steady, clear-eyed gaze crossed each one of them in turn, ending with Zurus. The veteran opened his mouth to speak – and then thought better of it. Instead, Tarikus acted.

With a slow, steady draw of blade point over stone, he etched a heavy line through his own name, erasing the record of his death. He reclaimed his life.

Mykilus was the first to speak. 'Welcome back, sir.' He bowed his head. 'If we had only known that the Red Corsairs had not killed you–'

'No.' Tarikus held up his hand. 'You will not speak of that again. And by my order, you will not carry any guilt over what happened.' He stepped forward and moved from brother to brother, tapping each on the shoulder in turn. 'I hold no malice. You did no wrong that day.'

Then he was looking at Zurus. The Doom Eagle sighed, and made a decision of his own. He reached beneath his robes and his hand returned with a fetter of black and silver links pooled in the palm; it was the honour-chain that signified his command of the battle squad. He offered it. 'This also belongs to you, I believe.'

Tarikus showed quiet surprise. 'The squad is yours, brother. You have made it so. These men are your men.'

Zurus shook his head. 'No. It has been my honour to lead them into battle in the name of the Emperor and Aquila, but I have never been their commander, not in the manner you were. I have only been... the caretaker of that post. You have seniority over me, the laurel and the honours. It is your right to reclaim your prior status.'

The veteran came closer, his brow furrowing. 'You are sure you wish to step down, Zurus? I know my brothers would not have followed you if you had not been worthy of it.' He nodded at the chain.

Zurus pressed the links into Tarikus's hand. 'I will not take that which by right is yours.' He stepped away. 'I will find another place in the Chapter.'

'You already have a place, sir,' said Korica. He glanced at Tarikus, and the veteran sergeant nodded.

'Aye,' said the other Doom Eagle. 'I have need of good men, who see clearly and fight well.' Tarikus held up the honour chain. 'I will accept this on condition that you remain in the squad as my second.'

Zurus thought on the offer, then nodded. 'That seems a fair bargain.'

Tarikus was silent for a long moment; then he wrapped the chain about the hilt of the knife and put it into his belt. 'Come, then, kinsmen. The enemy tasks me.' He gestured up towards the distant roof, where glimmers of constant storm-light flickered. 'I have been dead long enough.'

Zurus followed his commander's gaze upward to where the rain fell, steady and ceaseless as the Emperor's wrath.

CONSEQUENCES

Graham McNeill

Author's note
This story is set between the events of Warriors
of Ultramar *and* Dead Sky, Black Sun.

THE COLD WATER pooled in a depression in the centre
of the stone floor of the cell, before spilling through
the cracked stonework to unknown destinations.
This deep beneath the rock of the Fortress of Hera,
water dripped from the rugged ceiling, leached
through thousands of metres of hard granite from
the river that thundered along the length of the Valley of Laponis high above.

Only the thinnest sliver of light from below the
thick, iron door illuminated the cell, but it was
enough for its occupant, due to enhanced vision that
allowed him to see almost as well at night as in daylight. Not that there was anything to see within the
cell's dank confines, merely an iron ring set into the
wall where a prisoner could be kept chained until
such time as he was removed for sentencing or punishment.

The cell's solitary occupant was not chained to the wall or restrained in any way. There would be little point in chaining one whose strength could easily break any such fetters, tear the iron ring from the wall or who secreted an acidic saliva that, given time, would eat away at even the strongest of metals.

The prisoner had already sworn an oath that he would not attempt to escape or hamper his gaolers in any way and his word was accepted as truth.

He sat cross-legged, supporting his weight on his hands, holding his body a centimetre from the cold floor of the cell. An aquila tattoo flexed on his right shoulder as he tensed and released his muscles. Inscribed upon the flesh of his left was a number in the curling script of High Gothic.

The prisoner heard the clip of approaching footsteps over the steady *drip-drip* of the water from the ceiling and lowered himself to the floor, uncrossing his legs and standing in one smooth motion. His hair was dark and short, though longer than he kept it normally, and his thundercloud eyes smouldered with promised threat. Two golden studs glittered on his forehead and, though he was powerfully muscled, taller and broader than the mightiest of humans, he knew he was much weaker and leaner than he should be.

A knotted mass of scar tissue writhed across his flat stomach, paler than the rest of his skin, but it was merely the largest of an impressive collection of scars: battle wounds that criss-crossed his skin in a macabre web.

He heard the rattle of keys and the heavy door groaned open, spilling warm light into the cell. He squinted briefly, before his eyes quickly adjusted to the increased illumination and saw a blue-robed helot dressed in the garb of a gaoler with a dark hood covering his face.

Behind him, two giants in brightly polished Terminator armour stood with golden-bladed polearms carried across their chests. Their bulk filled the wide corridor, braziered torchlight flickering across the blue ceramite surfaces like fiery snakes. The prisoner bowed to his gaoler and said, 'Is it time?'

The helot nodded – it was forbidden for one such as he to address the prisoner – and indicated that he should leave the cell.

The prisoner bowed his head below the level of the stone lintel and stood in front of the Terminators, before marching through the fire-lit tunnels towards whatever fate the Master of the Ultramarines had decreed for him.

As he made his way up the rough-hewn steps of the detention level, Uriel Ventris wondered again at the path that had led him to this place.

SIX DAYS EARLIER, the battered and war-weary form of the Ultramarine strike cruiser *Vae Victus* limped towards the blue jewel of Macragge. Her armoured hide seemed to hang loose on her frame, like a beast starved of food and entering its dying days. The journey through the warp from Tarsis Ultra had taken the better part of six months, though upon re-entering real space and calibrating the ship's chronometers against local celestial bodies, it was noted that a time dilation of a year and a half had passed. Such anomalies in the apparent flow of time while travelling through the fluid medium of warpspace were not uncommon; rather, they were an accepted price to be paid for a method of travel that allowed a ship to cross the galaxy without spending generations in the journey.

Indeed, such a relatively minor time dilation was remarkable given the vast distance travelled by the *Vae Victus*. Tarsis Ultra lay to the north of Segmentum Tempestus, while Macragge orbited her star in the eastern reaches of Ultima Segmentum, half the galaxy away.

In the forward hangars of the ship, three Thunderhawk gunships were securely tethered to the deck – one in dire need of the ministrations of a Techmarine and a team of mono-tasked servitors before it would fly again, so stripped of its armaments and armour was it. Here, a lone Space Marine knelt in prayer between two parallel rows of corpses covered in sky-blue sheets. Another Space Marine, armoured in black, with a skull-faced helm, stood at the end of the rows of bodies, chanting a soft mantra to the fallen and calling upon the Emperor to guide each man to His side.

The bodies lined up on either side of him were the dead of the 4th Company, the cost to the Ultramarines for honouring an ancient debt sworn by their primarch to aid the people of Tarsis Ultra in times of need. Such a price was high, terribly high, but it was a price the Ultramarines willingly paid for the sake of honour.

The Space Marine kneeling between the corpses raised his head and smoothly rose to his feet. Captain Uriel Ventris hammered his fist twice into his breastplate in the warrior's Honour to the Fallen. These were his men, his warriors. They had followed him into battle on Pavonis against traitors and a monstrous alien star god and thence to Tarsis Ultra where they had fought with courage and honour against the terrifying threat of the extra-galactic predators known as the tyranids. They had saved Tarsis Ultra, but had paid a heavy blood price for the victory.

There, Uriel had fought shoulder to shoulder with brother Space Marines, the Mortifactors, an honourable Chapter whose lineage could be traced back to the Blessed Guilliman, but whose doctrines and belief structure had changed so radically as to make them unrecognisable from their parent Chapter.

To the Mortifactors, death was venerated above all things, and the wisdom of the dead was sought through the visions of their Chaplains. Blood rites and the worship of those who had passed through this life in ages past was the norm for the Mortifactors and, though initially horrified by such deviation from the pages of the *Codex Astartes*, Uriel had found that he had more in common with the warriors of the Mortifactors than he cared to admit.

It was not a pleasing revelation.

Astador, the Chaplain of the Mortifactors, had said it best: 'You and I are both Angels of Death, Uriel.'

But it had taken him many months of hard fighting and harder choices to realise the truth of this. Despite the protests and outrage of Sergeant Learchus, Uriel had followed Astador's vision quests and emerged triumphant, where a strict adherence to the *Codex* would have seen them defeated in the earliest stages of the war. Pulled between two opposing philosophies, Uriel had made his choice and had found the balance between following the spirit and the letter of the *Codex*. He knew such behaviour marked him out amongst his brethren, but his former captain, Idaeus, had taught him the value of such insights and he knew in his heart that he had done the right thing.

Uriel looked along the line of corpses and felt a great weight settle upon him.

He had almost died in the belly of the tyranid hive ship, an insidious alien poison causing his blood to clot throughout his body. Only the devotion of his oldest friend and comrade, Pasanius, had saved his life, the veteran sergeant almost bleeding himself dry to save his captain's life. The wounds he had suffered in the conflict had mostly healed, though the mass of plasflesh that sealed the gaping wound in his torso was a constant dull, throbbing ache. Techmarine Harkus and Apothecary Selenus had reconstructed his left shoulder and clavicular pectoralis major with augmetic sinews and muscle grafts following a battle with a tyranid guardian organism, and his blood still underwent regular transfusions to ensure its purity.

But he had not died, he had triumphed and through his and countless others' sacrifice, Tarsis Ultra had been saved, though it would never be the same again. Uriel had seen enough on Ichar IV to know that once a planet was infected with the taint of these vile xeno creatures, it would forever be impossible to remove.

The bodies had been prepared for transport to the crypts beneath the Fortress of Hera; Chaplain Clausel was performing the *Finis Rerum* and Selenus had reverently removed the progenoid glands from the fallen. Upon their return to Macragge, each battle-brother would be interred in his own sepulchre and Uriel himself would go to the Shrine of the Primarch in the Temple of Correction and carve the names of the dead onto the bronze-edged slabs of smooth black marble that ran along the curved inner wall of the sanctum.

Clausel's chanting came to an abrupt end and Uriel turned to face the skull-visaged Chaplain, reflecting that perhaps the Mortifactors were not so different after all. For wasn't a Chaplain nothing more than a vision of Death incarnate? Frequently the last face a warrior saw before passing from this mortal coil was that of a Chaplain, the warrior who prepared his body before its journey to the halls of the dead.

He nodded to Clausel, feeling a tonal shift in the vibrations running through the hull as the ship's main engines powered down. The *Vae Victus* had achieved orbit and they were ready to descend to Macragge.

Awe. Humility. A sense of history that stretched back ten thousand years. All these feelings and more flooded Uriel's body as he entered the Temple of Correction once more. He remembered the last time he had set foot in this mighty marble edifice before he had set off for the world of Tarsis Ultra. Then he had been but a newly tested captain, with the weight of his next command heavy on his shoulders and a life of service before him. Everything had seemed simpler back then, before the burden of choice had entered his life.

As always, the Temple was thronged with pilgrims and the faithful, many of whom had journeyed further than he to be here. Many women carried babes in swaddling clothes and Uriel knew that a great many would have been both conceived and born during the pilgrimage to Macragge. Heads bowed as he passed and shouted blessings followed him. There were whispered prayers of thanks that one of the Emperor's chosen had come to this place to worship with them.

Uriel marched through the marble corridors, the dazzling white of the walls veined with thin traceries of gold and sepia and the floor paved with stone from the rocks at the base of Hera's Falls.

Finally, he entered the inner sanctum, beams of multicoloured light spearing from the gargantuan dome above. Refracted by cunning artifice through the crystals that made up its structure, each beam interwove with the others to create a dazzling internal rainbow. Hundreds of people knelt before the gently glowing Sepulchre of the Primarch, their voices raised in songs of praise to his memory. The sense of wonderment and rapture in the chamber was palpable and Uriel dropped to one knee, feeling unworthy of gazing too long on the face of his Chapter's founding father.

Being in the presence of such a magnificent hero of the Imperium, even though his heart had ceased to beat nearly ten thousand years ago, was a humbling experience, made all the more so for his own sense of unworthiness after the battles on Tarsis Ultra. Had he not cast aside this legendary warrior's teachings in favour of his own initiative and the primitive rites of a death-worshipper? Such arrogance, such hubris. Who was he to second-guess the wisdom of this hero, who was the flesh and blood progeny of the Emperor himself?

'Forgive me, my lord,' whispered Uriel, 'for I am unworthy of your love. I come before you to honour the names and deeds of your sons who fell in battle. They fought with courage and honour, and are deserving of a place at your side. Grant them surcease of their sorrows until they are ready to be reborn in your image through the holy mysteries of their gene-seed.'

He stood and made his way to the marble slabs set into the inner circumference of the wall, finding the section designated for the members of the 4th Company. So many slabs, so many names of those who had given their lives for the Chapter. He moved to the last slab with names upon it and, though he had seventy-eight names to carve, he needed neither list nor record to remember each warrior. Each face and name was indelibly etched on his memory and even if he lived to see out his days as one of the Chapter's Masters, he would never forget those who had died under his command.

He fished out a small chisel and hammer from his belt and began delicately chipping the marble to fashion the first name. He smoothed the inner edges of each letter with a hard-edged sanding stone, ready for those more skilled than he to apply the gold leaf to each name.

Name followed name, and Uriel lost track of time as he relived each warrior's character and personality through the simple act of carving their name. Daylight dimmed: the dome's rainbow fading and vanishing before rising anew the following morning. Days passed, though Uriel stopped for neither food nor water. Helots tasked with the care and maintenance of the temple enquired at regular intervals if he wished for anything, but were dismissed with a curt shake of the head. After three days they stopped asking.

As the rainbow crept down through the air to the stone floor of the temple on the fifth day of Uriel's vigil, he smoothed the last edge of the final name. His arms ached from the precise and painstaking movements of carving, but he was pleased with the results. All seventy-eight warriors would now remain part of the Chapter's heritage forever more and he felt their silent acceptance of his vigil as light and warmth filled the temple.

He pushed himself to his feet, pocketing his craftsman's tools, and made his way back to the centre of the temple. Though he had not eaten, drunk or slept these last days, he felt more refreshed than ever, as though a cool spring flowed through his veins, washing away the old Uriel and leaving only a dedicated warrior of the Emperor in his stead. The songs of the many pilgrims echoed in his skull and Uriel felt a great welcoming embrace.

Uriel closed his eyes and prayed, giving thanks for being afforded the chance to serve his Chapter and the Emperor. He joined in song with the pilgrims and many were the rapturous faces that beamed radiantly from the assembled congregation as his voice joined theirs.

They sang of duty, of courage and of sacrifice. They sang until they were hoarse and could raise their voices no more. They sang until tears spilled from their eyes and a swelling sense of brotherhood filled the temple. A choking tide of emotions welled within Uriel's chest as more and more voices joined the choir of praise.

As the latest hymn came to a rousing climax, ending in an exhilarated round of exultation, Uriel saw a trio of Space Marines in burnished blue armour enter the temple. That in itself was nothing unusual, but then Uriel realised the leader of the group was none other than Captain Sicarius of the 2nd Company, Commander of the Watch and Master of the Household. Uriel also saw that the Terminators who followed him were armed, something normally unheard of within the sanctum of the primarch.

Sicarius stopped before Uriel and said, 'Ventris.'

Though both were captains, Sicarius was still senior to him, and thus Uriel bowed his head, saying, 'Captain Sicarius, it is good to see you again.'

Sicarius's granite features were harder and colder than Uriel had ever known.

'Uriel Ventris of Calth,' said Sicarius formally. 'By the power invested in me by Lord Calgar and by the Emperor of Mankind, you are to surrender yourself into my keeping, that I might render you into the custody of your peers and effect their judgement upon you.'

Uriel suspected he knew the answer already, but asked, 'On what charge?'

'Heresy,' spat Sicarius, as though the word itself were repugnant to him. 'Do not offer any resistance, Ventris, there are more warriors without and it will do no good to create discord before these people.'

Uriel nodded and said, 'Thank you for letting me finish my work here. I know you could have come sooner.'

'That was for the dead, not for you,' snapped Sicarius.

'Thank you anyway.'

Sicarius nodded to the Terminators.

'Take him to the dungeons.'

THE HALLS OF Marneus Calgar, Master of the Ultra-marines, were set atop the highest peak of the mountains, amidst the golden domes and marble-pillared temples of the Fortress of Hera. Though the day was hot, the air here was temperate, a fine mist of water from Hera's Falls sapping the worst of the heat. A perfectly symmetrical structure, the Chapter Master's chambers enclosed a central, sunken court-yard that was open to the azure sky above, its cloisters wrapped in cool shadows, its balconies draped in ancient, gold-stitched battle honours.

At its centre, a foaming fountain splashed. Carved in the likeness of Konor, the first Battle King of Macragge, it was surrounded by statuary depicting long-dead heroes of Macragge, artfully arranged so that they gave homage to their ancient king.

The last time Uriel had set foot here, it had been to receive his orders to depart for Pavonis and it had been a momentous occasion for him. Now, after a night in the dungeons and stripped of his armour, it was the scene of his disgrace.

And worse, it was the scene of his oldest friend's disgrace.

Pasanius stood beside him, similarly manacled and dressed in a blue chiton.

His own fall from grace he would accept, but to see Pasanius dragged down with him was almost too much for him to bear.

Surrounding Lord Calgar were the various Masters of the Chapter present on Macragge, in whose hands his ultimate fate lay. Captain Sicarius, Master of the Watch, sat to his left, next to Captain Galenus, Master of the Marches, who in turn flanked Fennias Maxim, the Master of the Forge. Opposite them sat Captain Ixion, Chief Victualler, Captain Antilochus, Chief of Recruits and the heroic Captain Agemman of the 1st Company. The great and good of the Ultramarines sat in judgement of him and at their head sat Lord Calgar, his liege lord and Chapter Master.

Calgar looked older than Uriel remembered him, his piercing gaze sadder and his stern, patrician features more careworn than he remembered. The disappointment in his lord's eyes was too much and Uriel dropped his gaze, shame burning hot in his breast.

And last of all, seated beside Calgar, was Learchus.

Veteran sergeant of the 4th Company, Learchus had fought beside Uriel and, though it broke his heart, he knew now the source of the accusations against Pasanius and himself.

He should have seen it coming. In the final hours of the war on Tarsis Ultra, Learchus had as good as told him that he would seek redress for Uriel's flagrant disregard of the *Codex Astartes*. Much as he wanted to feel anger towards Learchus for this, Uriel could not bring himself to feel anything but pride in his sergeant. He was an Ultramarine through and through and had done nothing wrong. Indeed, had the circumstances been reversed, Uriel might well have found himself where Learchus was now.

At some unseen signal, Captain Sicarius rose from his seat, his long red cloak billowing around him as he stepped down into the sunken courtyard. He stared at Uriel and Pasanius with a look of loathing, pulling a wax-sealed vellum scroll from beneath his cloak.

He looked towards Calgar, who nodded solemnly.

'Uriel Ventris. Pasanius Lysane. On this, the nine hundredth and ninety-ninth year of the tenth millennium of his Imperial Majesty's rule, you are hereby charged with seventeen counts of the crime of heresy. Do you understand the gravity of these charges?'

'I do,' said Uriel.

'Aye,' said Pasanius, in a tone that made no secret of his contempt for this hearing. 'Though to drag us here after the great victory we won at Tarsis Ultra does nothing but shame the memories of those who died there. We fought the Great Devourer with courage, honour and faith. No man here can ask more than that!'

'Be silent!' thundered Sicarius. 'You will answer only those questions I ask of you and you are to volunteer no more information than that. Do you understand me?'

Pasanius's lip curled, but he said nothing and merely nodded.

Apparently satisfied, Sicarius circled the fountain and stood before Uriel, his gaze boring into him, as though he were attempting to force him to admit his guilt by sheer force of personality.

'You are a protégé of Captain Idaeus, are you not?'

'You know I am, Captain Sicarius,' answered Uriel evenly.

'Answer the question, Ventris,' retorted Sicarius.

'My rank is captain, you have not found me guilty yet and will address me by my title until such time as I may be convicted by this body.'

Sicarius pursed his lips, but knew it would do him no good to press the point and reluctantly conceded.

'Very well, captain. If we may proceed?'

'Yes, I served in the 4th Company under Captain Idaeus for ninety years, before rising to its captaincy following his death on Thracia.'

'Could you describe the circumstances of his death for us?'

Uriel took a deep breath to calm his rising temper. The tale of Idaeus's final battle was well known to every man here and he could see no purpose in reiterating it.

'Captain Ventris?'

'Very well,' began Uriel. 'The world of Thracia was one of a number that had rebelled against the lawful rule of the Emperor's representatives in the Ulenta sector and it was rumoured that the uprising had been instigated by followers of the Dark Powers. We were attached to the crusade forces of Inquisitor Appolyon and had been tasked with several surgical strikes against key enemy positions to facilitate the advance of Imperial Guard units closing on the capital city of Mercia.'

'And what was your final mission in this crusade?' asked Sicarius.

'Guard units were advancing along a narrow frontage, with one flank open to assault across a number of bridges. Squads of the 4th Company were tasked with their destruction.'

'An easy task surely?'

'In theory, yes. Intelligence indicated that the bridges were lightly held by poor quality opposition.'

'But that proved not to be the case, did it not?' asked Sicarius.

'No, bridge two-four was held by inferior troops, and we easily dealt with them without loss. Once the bridge was ours, we began rigging it for destruction, under the direction of Techmarine Tomasin.'

'May he always be remembered,' intoned Fennias Maxim from the edge of the courtyard.

'And then what happened?'

'As we prepared the bridge for destruction, the weather deteriorated markedly and we received fragmentary reports of the enemy moving in our direction. Within minutes we were under attack from a battalion-sized force of enemy units intent on seizing the bridge.'

'A fearsome prospect,' observed Sicarius.

'Not in this case,' said Uriel. 'Though this opposition was of a higher calibre than that tasked with holding the bridge, we were able to keep them at bay, though in the course of the fighting, our Thunderhawk gunship was shot down by enemy flak tanks.'

'So you were trapped,' stated Sicarius. 'Truly a desperate situation. At what point did the enemy attack again?'

'Just before dawn we were attacked by warriors of the Night Lords Legion.'

A collective gasp went around the courtyard. Though every warrior knew of the fallen Legions, to hear their name spoken so brazenly was still a shock. To mention such things was as unseemly as it was unbelievable.

'We were able to hold them off, but as the battle dragged on, it soon became clear that we would not be able to hold our position.'

'So what did you do?'

'The explosives were rigged, but Techmarine Tomasin had died in the initial attack. Without his detonator mechanism, we had no way of triggering the charges to destroy the bridge. During the night, Captain Idaeus had sent our assault squads to attempt to detonate the explosives manually using krak grenades. They were unsuccessful, but the principle was sound.'

'I'm sorry, Captain Ventris, I don't understand,' said Sicarius, cocking his head to one side.

'Don't understand what?'

'This plan of Idaeus's, it is obviously one that does not refer to the tactica of the *Codex Astartes*. Are you sure it was his plan?'

Uriel was about to answer that of course it was, when he was seized by a sudden memory of the frantic battle on bridge two-four. Sicarius smiled and Uriel saw how deftly he had been manoeuvred into this admission of guilt. Slowly he shook his head.

'No, it was not Captain Idaeus's plan,' he said. 'It was mine.'

Sicarius stepped back, arms raised at his sides.

'It was your plan,' he said triumphantly.

'But it worked, damn it,' roared Pasanius. 'Don't you see that? The bridge was destroyed and the campaign won!'

'Irrelevant,' responded Sicarius. 'A victory is not a victory unless it is won with the principles of the primarch. We have all read of the Mortifactors in Captain Ventris's after-action reports from Tarsis Ultra. We all see where the path of deviance from the *Codex* leads. Tell me, sergeant, would you have us become the Mortifactors?'

Pasanius shook his head. 'No, of course not.'

'But you would have us follow their methods?'

'No, that's not what I said,' growled Pasanius. 'I just meant that whatever breaches of the *Codex* we made, they were only small.'

'Sergeant,' said Sicarius, as though speaking to a small child, 'our faith in the *Codex* is a fortress, and no crack in a fortress can be accounted small. If we take small steps down their path, each tiny indiscretion becomes that little bit easier, doesn't it? After a hundred such breaches of the *Codex's* teachings, what matters another ten, or a hundred? That is why you must be punished, Captain Ventris, for where you tread, others follow. You are a captain of the Ultramarines and must comport yourself appropriately.'

Uriel glared as Sicarius climbed the steps back to his seat and the Master of the Forges, Fennias Maxim, descended to the courtyard. His leather-tough skin was the colour of aged oak and completely hairless. Dark, hooded eyes, one replaced with a blinking red metriculator augmetic, transfixed Uriel as Fennias circled them, his hands laced behind his back. A hissing servo-arm, folded into a recumbent position on his back, wheezed as it flexed in time with his breath and his heavy, metal legs thumped on the stonework of the courtyard.

'I have spoken to Techmarine Harkus,' he barked suddenly.

Uriel knew where Maxim was heading and said, 'I ordered him to strip the Thunderhawk down to its bare bones. He was only obeying my orders and no blame should be attached to him for his actions on Tarsis Ultra.'

Maxim stepped close and lowered his thunderous face into Uriel's.

'I know,' he hissed. 'Did you think I would not know that?'

'No,' replied Uriel, 'I merely wished to be clear on the subject.'

'Tell me why you desecrated such a holy machine, one that had seen honourable service for almost a millennium and had carried you into battle on occasions too numerous to count. How could you turn your back on such a noble spirit and treat it so cruelly?'

'I had no choice,' said Uriel simply.

'No choice?' scoffed Maxim. 'I find that hard to believe.'

'I do not lie, Master,' said Uriel darkly. 'To destroy one of the tyranid's hive ships we had to get the planet's defence lasers firing again, and the only way we could do it was to transport fresh energy capacitors to a site that had the best chance of killing it. The only craft available that stood any chance of reaching this site and making it back was the Thunderhawk. Even then I was forced to order the gunship stripped down to its minimum weight to ensure we would have enough fuel to get us there and back.'

'You angered its war-spirit. I have since ministered to it and great is its wrath. Were I you, I would not trust my life to it again until you have begged its forgiveness and performed the necessary rites of obeisance.'

Maxim turned his back on Uriel and returned to his seat as, one by one, each of the Chapter's Masters came forward to highlight an example of Uriel's disregard for the teachings of the *Codex Astartes*.

They knew everything from both the Pavonis and Tarsis Ultra campaigns, the events on the space hulk, *Death of Virtue*, and the battle with the dark eldar on the return leg of the journey.

His frustration grew as example after example of his recklessness was paraded before him. While he could not deny the veracity of these claims, he could refute with reason and proof of their merit, but as the day wore on, he saw that the Chapter Masters were not interested in his truth. He had deviated from the *Codex Astartes*, the most heinous crime imaginable, and nothing could atone for such a breach of trust and faith.

As the sun dipped below the tiled roof of Lord Calgar's chambers, Uriel's temper was fraying and he knew he was in danger of losing it completely. These men did not want truth; they wanted a scapegoat for the dead of Tarsis Ultra and to set an example to the rest of the Chapter that there was no other way than the *Codex*.

He wanted to scream in frustration, but pursed his lips and bit down on his anger.

Purple shadows lengthened on the floor of the courtyard. Evening moths gathered around the torches that were hung from the balconies.

Marneus Calgar stood and swept his gaze around the assembled Masters before striding into the centre of the courtyard to face Uriel and Pasanius. He stared into Uriel's eyes and Uriel met his gaze unflinchingly. Whatever his fate, he would face it on his feet like the warrior he knew himself to be, and damn the consequences.

At last, Lord Calgar said, 'It saddens me to see what has become of you both. I saw greatness within you and hoped that one day you might have taken your place amongst this Chapter's mightiest heroes. But nothing in this life is set in stone and you stand before me accused of the darkest of crimes. Tomorrow you shall have your chance to refute your accusers and present your defence. Think well on what you wish to say. I urge you to spend this night in prayer. Look to the Emperor for guidance and remember your oaths of allegiance to this Chapter and all that once meant to you when next you stand before me.'

The first slivers of moonlight crested the roof as Uriel and Pasanius were led back to their cells.

THE CELL WAS dark and filled with a musty odour of damp and helplessness. A chain dangled from a ring set in the wall and water dripped from the ceiling to disappear down a crack in the stone floor.

'Do I need to chain you?' enquired one of the Terminators, his voice hissing through his helmet-vox.

'No,' said Uriel. 'You have my word I will give you no trouble.'

'The Terminator nodded as though he had expected as much and closed the cell's door, bolting and locking it with thick chains and mechanical wards.

Uriel bunched his fists and paced the cell like a caged animal. He would not try to escape, but tomorrow, he would hurl every one of the accusations levelled at him back at those who stood in judgement over him. They had not witnessed the circumstances that had driven him to this point.

Where were they on the walls of Tarsis Ultra? Where were they when he had stood defiant before the might of an ancient star god and allowed its vile xeno taint into his mind? Where were they when he had almost died in their name? He knew he was reacting with his heart and not his head, but couldn't help himself. The injustice of it all made him sick and he slumped on the floor of the cell, listening to the dripping water and framing what he would say.

SOME HOURS LATER, as he lay sprawled on the cold, damp floor, Uriel heard the soft pad of footsteps approach. Furtive steps, like those of a man afraid of being discovered, drew near, and even through the thickness of the stone walls and iron door, Uriel's enhanced hearing could tell that whoever was approaching his cell was a Space Marine.

He swivelled upright and sat with his back to the wall opposite the door. Keys rattled and the door swung inwards, a hooded figure blocking the light. The figure stepped into the cell and pulled back his hood.

'It is good to see you, Captain Ventris,' said a deep voice, rich with age and experience.

'Captain Agemman?' said Uriel, recognising the voice. Agemman was the Captain of the 1st Company: the veterans, the best and bravest of the Chapter. Amongst his titles was Regent of Ultramar, the man to whom the Master of the Ultramarines entrusted the safety of Macragge in his absence. After the death of Captain Invictus, hero of the 1st Company who had died fighting the tyranids of Hive

Fleet Behemoth, Agemman had taken on the role of rebuilding the destroyed company. Only now, two hundred and fifty years after its complete destruction, was it returned to full strength and the Banner of Macragge unfurled once more.

Agemman had been an inspiration to them all while training at Agiselus and all through their elevation to the ranks of the Adeptus Astartes at the Fortress of Hera. His noble bearing and courage of spirit were shining lights amid the darkness. What could he want with Uriel?

'Aye,' replied Agemman, holding out his hand. 'Courage and honour.'

'Courage and honour,' said Uriel, accepting Agemman's hand.

Agemman folded his arms within his robe and glanced around him in distaste at the bleakness of the cell.

'It is galling to see a warrior of such courage treated so,' he said.

'You pick a strange time to come and see me, captain. What are you doing here?'

'I come on behalf of Lord Calgar, Captain Ventris.'

'Lord Calgar? I do not understand–'

'I know all about you, Uriel,' interrupted Agemman. 'I followed your progress all the way through Agiselus. I recognised your potential and I rejoiced when you were selected to come to the Fortress of Hera and become an Ultramarine. I gave thanks for the victory on Vorhn's World and mourned with you after Black Bone Road. I know all of what you did while serving with the Deathwatch and I know why you will never speak of it.'

'Why are you telling me this?' asked Uriel, suddenly wary.

'So that you will know that I speak true, Uriel Ventris,' explained Agemman. 'You stand accused of the gravest crime an Ultramarine can commit and your life hangs by the most slender of threads. You would do well to heed my words.'

Agemman closed the cell door.

'Much depends on it...'

DAWN BROKE CLEAR and bright over the mountains, casting long shadows over the pale rocks and highland forests. A cool breeze blew down the length of the Valley of Laponis, and Uriel felt a curious light-headedness as he marched up the smooth-worn steps carved into the rock that led to the chambers of Marneus Calgar. Despite the armed guards escorting them, his step was lighter and his heart unclouded by anger or resentment. He knew now what he had to do and, with the choice so clear before him, there was no more doubt or uncertainty.

He was saddened that Pasanius would be tarred with the same brush, but there was little he could do to prevent that now.

Captain Agemman had spoken simply and clearly for an hour and Uriel had been struck by his simple honesty and the force of his words. When he had finished, they had shaken hands in the warrior's grip, wrist to wrist, and said their

farewells. Agemman had wished him well and
departed, no doubt to take the same message to
Pasanius. As they climbed the stairs to their fate,
one glance at Pasanius's face told Uriel that he had
accepted Agemman's words and chosen the same
path. Uriel was humbled by his comrade's loyalty
and managed a wan smile as they reached the
esplanade at the top of the steps and approached
the many-pillared portico that led to the chambers
of Marneus Calgar.

They passed between the Terminator guards into
the shadowed vestibule before emerging once more
into the sunlit courtyard. Though they had been
taken from their cells at first light, the Masters of the
Chapter were already gathered, their ceremonial
cloaks of office draped around their shoulders and
laurels of judgement wreathing their skulls.

They took their place before the statue of Konor,
facing Lord Calgar and standing at parade rest, with
their arms ramrod straight at their sides. The armed
warriors retreated from the courtyard and not a soul
moved until the echoing clang of the bronze doors
rang out.

Marneus Calgar stepped down into the courtyard
to stand before Uriel and Pasanius. His augmetic eye
burned a steady red, his features unreadable. Uriel
knew that Calgar had sent Agemman to their cells
last night and, though he knew it meant his undoing, could find no anger in his heart for this act, just
a simple understanding of what it meant to be a true
Ultramarine.

The Lord of the Ultramarines strode around the fountain, addressing the assembled Masters.

'Brother Ultramarines, today is a day of judgement. We have heard much that condemns these warriors in the eyes of our brethren, but we are men of honour and would not think of deciding their fate without first giving them a chance to refute these charges and answer the accusations against them.'

Calgar completed his circuit of the gurgling fountain and stood before Uriel, locking his gaze with him.

'Captain Ventris, you have the right to speak and defend yourself.'

Uriel took a deep breath and said, 'I waive that right and accept the judgement of my lords upon me.'

A ripple of surprise rose from the masters and hurried glances were exchanged as Lord Calgar gave an imperceptible nod of his head to Uriel. Calgar then asked Pasanius the same question and received the same answer. Uriel saw Learchus's face harden and knew it pained the sergeant to have brought this upon him, but Uriel now knew that Learchus had no choice but to do so. He nodded to Learchus in a gesture of peace and respect between them.

Uriel faced the Master of the Ultramarines as he spoke again to him. 'You do not wish to give an account of yourself and enter a plea to your peers?'

'No,' said Uriel. 'I willingly submit myself to your judgement.'

Lord Calgar turned from Uriel and ascended to his throne, arranging his cloak about him before addressing the assembled masters.

'These men have broken faith with the *Codex Astartes*, and by their own admission admit to abandoning its teachings,' began Calgar. 'Their fate is now in my hands and on the morrow I shall render my verdict. We shall convene again at dawn tomorrow at Gallan's Rock where judgement will be passed.'

Though he had known they were to be punished, Uriel felt his heart sink as Calgar spoke.

Gallan's Rock was a place of execution.

THE NOISE OF Hera's Falls was deafening. Torrents of water fell hundreds of metres to the jagged rocks below, cascading into a spume-covered pool of glacially cold water. The sharp white rocks glistened and sparkled with quartz, and emerald green highland fir grew right up to the edge of the cliffs. Sunlight crept over the mountaintops and bathed everything in the glow of molten gold. It was, thought Uriel, one of the most beautiful vistas he had been privileged to lay his eyes upon, as though nature, realising that this might well be the last thing he saw, had striven to produce the most wondrous vision for him to take into the next life.

He and Pasanius marched in silence after the Chapter's Masters, their chains removed and armour stored in the 4th Company's armourium. Both wore unadorned black chitons, their bare feet warmed by the sun-kissed earth.

No guards accompanied the sombre column. Though guilty, they were still Ultramarines and would meet their fate with courage and honour. The climb from the Fortress of Hera had taken two hours and they stood now before Gallan's Rock, an angular slab of black marble that speared out from the valley side.

In ancient times, convicted criminals had been hurled to their deaths on the rocks below and it had been on this very spot that the sword of Roboute Guilliman had cut the head from the traitor king, Gallan, who had murdered his adopted father with an envenomed blade and attempted to take control of Macragge.

The Masters gathered at the edge of the cliff, a thin veil of water soaking their armour, and as he approached them, Uriel felt the fabric of his chiton cling to his skin as it became saturated.

Without any words being spoken, Uriel and Pasanius marched onto the rock and slowly inched their way towards the end. Uriel experienced a moment's vertigo as he lost sight of the cliff edge in his peripheral vision. The black rock was slippery underfoot, but he supposed it didn't much matter whether he fell now or not.

They reached the end of the rock and knelt, the stone hard and cold against their skin. Uriel looked over the edge, the drop dizzyingly high and the rocks below indelibly stained with the blood of the condemned. His own would soon join it and, strangely, the thought did not trouble him overmuch. Agemman had made it clear what was at stake and Uriel was Ultramarine enough to grasp the truth of his words and make the right decision.

He felt a hand grip his shoulder and glanced over at Pasanius. His friend and comrade in arms was stoic and stared across the valley, savouring the beauty of their surroundings.

'I regret nothing of what we have achieved,' said Pasanius. 'We acted with courage and honour and no man can ask more of us than that.'

Uriel felt his chest tighten and nodded, too over-come with admiration for his friend to speak. He nodded as he heard footsteps behind him, bowing his head and closing his eyes as he awaited the push that would send him plummeting to his death.

He felt armoured gauntlets take hold of his chiton and heard the voice of Lord Calgar.

'A true judgement has been returned against you and the *Codex Astartes* has but one punishment for your crimes. Though you are warriors of courage and it pains me to lose such valiant fighters, I have no choice in my verdict.

'Just as we all are, I too am bound by the *Codex* and must obey its teachings in sentencing you to death.'

The grip on Uriel's chiton tightened.

'There are many ways one can achieve death, many ways to meet your fate. To waste a life that may yet bring retribution to the enemies of the Emperor is a sin in and of itself. It is therefore my judgement that you be bound by a Death Oath, and take the light of the Emperor into that abominable region of space where many a true warrior has met his end – the Eye of Terror. I bind you to take your fire and steel into the dark places until such time as you meet your destiny.'

URIEL STOOD MOTIONLESS in the torch-lit gatehouse as the Masters of the Chapter circled him. Fully clad in his armour, his golden-hilted sword sheathed at his side, he felt a lightness in his heart he had not felt in many months. Though to journey into the Eye of Terror, that region of space where the madness and corruption of the warp spilled into real space, was as certain a death sentence as if had they been pushed from Gallan's Rock, Uriel knew that this was somehow right.

Pasanius stood beside him, also fully armoured, his customary flamer held tightly in his silver bionic arm. Chaplain Clausel read from an ancient leather-bound tome with gold edged pages and a musty aroma of a book that had sat unopened for many centuries.

Verses from the *Book of Dishonour*, words that had not been spoken in over six thousand years, were uttered in time with the Masters' footsteps as they removed everything that marked them as Ultramarines from their armour and weapons.

His company tattoo had been burned from the skin of his left shoulder and the Chapter symbols of the Ultramarines had been painted over, leaving his shoulder guards an unblemished blue. The golden eagles were removed from his breastplate and waist and the purity seals and honour badges were unclipped and placed in a sandarac reliquary box.

Learchus would lead the 4th Company in his absence and Uriel could think of no one he would rather have commanding his surviving warriors and rebuilding the company.

Marneus Calgar watched them having their insignia removed from their armour impassively. Uriel knew Lord Calgar did not want to have to do this, but the Chapter Master had no choice but to place the Death Oath upon them. It had been that or an ignominious end on the rocks at the foot of Hera's Falls.

He remembered Agemman's words, spoken in a calm and even voice in his cell as though they were being whispered in his ear even now. Agemman had spoken of the great and good name of the Ultramarines, a name that stood for truth, courage and faith in the Emperor. No truer Chapter of Space Marines existed, and to plant any seeds of doubt of that in the minds of its own warriors was to damn it as surely as if it were to embrace the Ruinous Powers. A Chapter's strength came from its belief in itself, a power that devolved from the force of its Chapter Master and was embodied within those he appointed beneath him.

The Chapter was held together by such valour and to allow any one man to undermine that was to erode the very foundations of the Ultramarines. Each warrior looked up to his superiors as embodiments of the *Codex* and to see a captain flaunt its teachings was to invite disaster.

The rot of dissention had to be cut out before it infected the entire Chapter and brought about the ruin of the Ultramarines. There could be no other way. The strength in Agemman's voice had cut through the bitterness and frustration consuming Uriel, and he had seen the ramifications should his methods and actions become widespread. The Ultramarines would become little more than roving bands of warriors, visiting such vengeance as they deemed appropriate upon whomever they chose. Before long, there would be little to distinguish them from the renegades who gave praise to the Dark Gods and Uriel was gripped by a horrifying vision of a future where blood-soaked Ultramarines were as feared and reviled as those who trod the path of Chaos.

Agemman had not ordered either of them in what they must do, but had left them to choose the right path.

Uriel had known what that choice must be: accept the judgement of Lord Calgar and show the Chapter that the way chosen by the Ultramarines was true. They must accept the Death Oath so that the Chapter might live on as it always had.

At last, Clausel closed the book and bowed his head as Uriel and Pasanius marched past him towards the doors of the gatehouse.

'Uriel, Pasanius,' said Lord Calgar.

The two Space Marines stopped and bowed to their former master.

'The Emperor go with you. Die well.'

Uriel nodded as the doors swung open. He and Pasanius stepped into the purple twilight of evening. Birds sang and torchlight flickered from the high towers of the outermost wall of the Fortress of Hera.

Before the door closed, Calgar spoke again, his voice hesitant, as though unsure as to whether he should speak at all.

'Varro Tigurius spoke with me last night,' he began. 'He told me that he had been granted a vision of you and Pasanius upon a world taken by the Dark Powers. A world that tasted of dark iron, with great wombs of daemonic flesh rippling with monstrous, unnatural life. As he watched, fell surgeons – like monsters themselves – hacked at them with blades and saws and pulled bloodstained figures from within. Though appearing more dead than alive, these figures lived and breathed, tall and strong, a dark mirror of our own glory. I know not what this means, Uriel, but its evil is plain. Seek this place out. Destroy it.'

'As you command,' said Uriel and walked into the night.

Ahead was a wide, cobbled esplanade, two parallel lines of Ultramarines lining the route they would take towards the main gate of the Fortress. The entirety of the Chapter's strength on Macragge awaited them, over five hundred Space Marines, their weapons clasped across their chests and heads held high.

Uriel and Pasanius marched between the lines of fellow Space Marines, each warrior snapping to attention and smoothly turning his back on them as they passed. The outer wall of the Fortress towered above them and Uriel could not help but look over his shoulder at the glittering marvel of the Fortress of Hera as he strode from its majesty.

The hundred-metre-high golden gate swung smoothly open, and Uriel felt a tremendous sense of stepping into the unknown seize him. Once they passed through that gate, they would no longer be Ultramarines, they would be stepping into the vastness of the galaxy to fulfil their Death Oath on their own, and the thought sent a realisation of what they had lost through him.

As the gateway drew closer, he saw Learchus in the line of Space Marines ahead of him. He reached his former sergeant and saw that Learchus was not turning his back as every other Ultramarine had.

Uriel stopped and said, 'Sergeant, you must turn your back.'

'No, captain, I will not, I will see you on your way.'

Uriel smiled and held out his hand to Learchus, who shook it proudly.

'I will look after the men of the company until you return,' promised Learchus.

'I know you will, Learchus. I bid you farewell, but now you must turn from us.'

Learchus nodded slowly and saluted before turning his back on his former captain.

Uriel and Pasanius continued on their long walk, finally passing into the shadow of the massive wall and leaving the Fortress of Hera behind.

And the gates slammed shut.

THE LAST DETAIL

Paul Kearney

THE MONSOON RAINS came early that year, as if the planet itself were tugging down a veil to hide its broken face. Even cowering in the bunker, the boy and his father could hear them, thunderous, massive, a roar of noise. But the rainstorm was nothing to that which had gone before – in fact even the bellowing of the monsoon seemed almost like a kind of silence.

'It stopped,' the boy said. 'All the noise. Perhaps they went away.'

The man squeezed his son's shoulder but said nothing. He had the wiry, etched face of a farmer, old before his time, but as hard as steel wire. Both he and his son had the sunken, hollow look of folk who have not eaten or drunk in days. He passed a dry tongue over his cracked lips at the sound of the rain, then looked at the flickering digits of the comms bench.

'It'll be dawn soon. When it comes, I'm going to look outside.'

The boy clenched him tighter. 'Pa!'

'It'll be all right. We need water, or we won't make it. I think they've gone, son.' He ruffled his boy's hair. 'I think it's over, whatever it was.'

'They might be waiting.'

'We need the water. It'll be all right, you'll see.'

'I'm coming with you.'

The man hesitated a second, and then nodded. 'All right then – whatever we find out there, we'll meet it together.'

A SUMMER DAWN came early in the planet's northern hemisphere. When the man set his shoulder to the bunker door only a few hours had passed. The heavy steel and plascrete door usually swung light and noiseless on its hinges, but now he had to throw himself at it to grind it open centimetre by centimetre. When the opening was wide enough for a man's bicep, he stopped, and sniffed the air.

'Get the respirators,' he snapped to his son. 'Now!'

They tugged on the cumbersome masks, and immediately their already enclosed world became tinier and darker still. They breathed heavily. The man coughed, took deep breaths.

'Some kind of gas out there, a chemical agent – but it's heavy. It's seeped down the stairs and pooled there. We've got to go up.' He looked round himself at the interior of the bunker with its discarded blankets, the dying battery-fed lights and useless comms unit. A pale mist was pouring in through the opened door almost like a kind of liquid, and with it, the gurgling rainwater of the passing monsoon.

'This place is compromised,' he said. 'We have to get out now, or we'll die here.'

They pushed together at the door. It squealed open angrily, until at last there was a kind of light filtering down on them from above. The man looked up. 'Well, the house is gone,' he said calmly.

They clambered over wet piles of debris which choked the stone stairs, until at last they stood at the top.

Inside a ruin. Two walls still stood, constructed out of the sturdy local stone, but that was all. The rest was blasted rubble. The clay tiles of the roof lay everywhere, and the boy saw his favourite toy, a wooden rifle his father had carved for him, lying splintered by what had been their front door. The rain was easing now, but he still had to rub the eye-pieces of his respirator clear every few seconds.

'Stay here,' the man said. He walked forward, out of the shadows of their ruined home, his boots crunching and clinking on broken glass and plastic, splashing through puddles. Around them, the pale mist was receding. A wind was blowing, and on it the rain came down, washing everything clean. The man hesitated, then pulled off his respirator. He raised his face to the sky and opened his mouth, feeling the rain on his tongue.

'It's all right,' he said to his son. 'The air is clean now. Take it off, boy, but don't touch anything. We don't know what's contaminated.'

All around them for as far as the eye could see, the countryside which had once been their farm, a green and pleasant place, was now a stinking marsh of shell-holes. The trunks of trees stood up like black sword-blades, their branches stripped away, the bark burnt from their boles. Here and there, one of their cattle, or a piece of one, lay bloated and green and putrid. Smoke rose in black pillars along the horizon.

Such was their thirst that they had nothing to say, but stood with their tongues out trying to soak up the rain. It streamed into the boy's mouth, reinvigorating him. Nothing in his life had ever felt so good as that cold water sinking into his parched mouth. He opened his eyes at last, and frowned, then pointed skywards, at the broken wrack of clouds which the wind was lashing across the sky.

'Pa, look,' he said, eyes wide with wonder. 'Look at that– it's like a cathedral up-ended in the clouds.'

His father looked skywards, narrowed his eyes, and curled a protective arm about the boy's shoulders. Many kilometres away, but still dominating the heavens, a vast angular shape hung shining above the earth, all jagged with steeples and adornments and improbable spikes. It broke out in a white flash as the sun caught it turning, and then began to recede, in a bright flare of afterburners. After a few seconds they caught the distant roar of its massive engines. As the sun rose higher, so they lost sight of it in the gathering brightness of the morning.

'It's moving out of orbit,' the man said.

'What is it – is the God-Emperor inside it, Pa?'

'No, son.' The father's arm curled tighter about his son's shoulders. 'It is the vessel of those who know His face. It is the Emperor's Angels, here in our sky.'

The man looked around him. At the reeking desolation, the craters, the puddled steaming meres of chemicals.

'We were their battleground,' he said.

THEY RANGED OVER what was left of the farm during the next few days, setting out containers to catch rainwater, gathering up what remained of their canned goods, and throwing away anything which the man's rad-counter began creaking at. At night they made camp in the ruins of the farmhouse and coaxed fire out of the soaked timbers which had once upheld its roof.

'Is the whole world like this?' the boy asked, gazing into the firelight one night, huddled under an old canvas tarp that the rain beat upon.

'Could be,' his father said. 'Perreken is a small place, not much more than a moon. Wouldn't take much to trash the whole thing.'

'Why would the Emperor's Angels do this to us?' the boy asked.

'They do things for reasons we can't fathom,' his father told him. 'They are the Wrath of the Emperor made real, and when their anger sweeps a world, no-one escapes it, not even those they are sworn to save. They are our protectors, boy, but also, they are the Angels of Death.'

'What are they like – have you ever seen one, Pa?'

The man shook his head. 'Not I. I did my spell in the militia same as most, and that's as far as my knowledge of things warlike goes. I don't think they ever even came close to this system before. But that was a big Imperial ship in the sky the other morning, I'm sure of it – I seen pictures when I was your age. Only they ride in ships like that – the *Astartes* – the Angels of the God-Emperor.'

THREE DAYS LATER the boy and his father were trudging through the black shattered crag north of their farm which had once been a wooded hillside, looking to see if any of their stock had by some chance survived the holocaust. Here, there had been a rocky knoll some two hundred metres in height, which gave a good view down the valley beyond to the city and its spaceport. It seemed the hill had been bombed heavily, its conical head now flattened. Smoke still hissed out of cracks in the hillside, as molten rocks cooled underground. Out towards the horizon, the city smoked and flickered with pinpoints of flame.

'Pa! Pa!' the boy shouted, running and tumbling among the rocks – 'Look here!'

'Don't touch it!'

'It's – it's – I don't know what it is.'

Looming over them was a hulk of massive, shattered metal, a box of steel and ceramite broken open and still sparking and glowing in places. It had legs like those of a crab, great pincers, and the barrels of autocannon on its shoulders. Atop it was what might once have been a man's head, grotesquely attached, snarling in death. It was a machine which was almost an animal, or an animal which had become a machine. Carved onto the bullet-pocked carcass of the thing were unspeakable scenes of slaughter and perversity, and it was hung with rotting skulls, festooned with spikes and chains.

'Come away,' the man told his son hoarsely. 'Get away from it.'

They backed away, and were suddenly aware that all down the slope below them were other remnants of battle. Bodies, everywhere, most of them shaven-headed, snarling, mutilated men, many with a pointed star cut into their foreheads. Here and there a bulkier figure in heavy armour, horned helmets, dismembered limbs, entrails underfoot about which the flies buzzed in black clouds.

'They fought here,' the man said. 'They fought here for the high ground.'

The boy, with the curiosity of youth, seemed less afraid than his father. He had found a large firearm, almost as long as himself, and was trying to lift it out of its glutinous glue of mud and blood.

'Leave that alone!'

'But Pa!'

'That's an Astartes weapon.' The man knelt and peered at it, wiping the metal gingerly with one gloved hand. 'Look – see the double-headed eagle on the barrel – that's the badge of the Imperium. The Space Marines fought here, on this hill. These are the dead of the great enemy lying around us, heretics cursed by the Emperor. The Astartes saved us from them.'

'Saved us,' the boy repeated grumpily. He pointed at the burning city down in the valley. 'Look at Dendrekken. It's all burnt and blown up.'

'Better that than under the fist of the Dark Powers, believe me,' the man said, straightening. 'It's getting dark. We've come far enough for one day. Tomorrow we'll try and get down to the city, and see who else is left.'

THAT NIGHT, SHIVERING beside their campfire amid the bodies of the dead, the boy lay awake staring at the night sky. The clouds had cleared, and he was able to see the familiar constellations overhead. Now and again he saw a shooting star, and now and again he was sure he saw other things gliding in the dark between the stars. New constellations glittered, moving in formation. He found himself wondering about those who lived out there in that blackness, travelling in their city-sized ships from system to system, bearing the eagle of the Imperium, carrying weapons like the massive bolter he had found upon the battlefield. What must it be like, to live like that?

He got up in the middle hours of the night, too restless and hungry for sleep. Stepping away from the fire, he clicked on his little battered torch, an old wind-up contraption he had had since he was a toddler. He walked out upon the rocky, blasted slope upon which the bodies of the dead lay contorted and rotting, and felt no fear, only a sense of wonder, and a profound restlessness. He picked his way down the slope and apart from his yellow band of torchlight there was no other radiance in the world save for the stars.

And one other thing. Off to his left he caught sight of something which came and went, an infinitesimal red glow. Intrigued, he made his way towards it, sliding his knife out of the sheath at his waist. He crouched and padded forwards, as quiet as when hunting in these same hills with his father's old lasgun. Several times the light died altogether, but he was patient, and waited until he could see it again. It was at the foot of a looming, broken crag which stood up black against the stars.

Something half-buried in rubble, but still with a shine to it that reflected back the torchlight. It was a helmet, huge, fit for a giant. It looked almost like a massive skull. In the eye-sockets were two lenses, one cracked and broken, and the other with that flickering scarlet light oozing out of it. The boy knelt down and gently tapped the helmet with the butt of his knife. There was a hiss as of static, and the thing moved slightly, making him spring backwards in fright. He saw then that it was not just a helmet. Buried in the fallen stone there was a body attached to the helm. Off to one side lay a massive hemispherical shape – the boy could have sat in it – and painted upon it in white was the symbol of a double-headed axe. A shoulder-guard made for a giant.

The boy scraped and scratched frantically at the stones, levering away the looser ones, uncovering more and more of the buried figure. There was a gleam of silver below the helm, and he saw that he had unearthed shining wings engraved upon a mighty breastplate, and in the centre of the wings, a skull emblem. He stared, open-mouthed. This was no Chaos fiend, no armoured heretic. He had found one of *them*, one of the Astartes his father talked about.

A fallen angel, he thought.

'Pa!' he shouted. 'Pa, come here quick and see this!'

IT TOOK THEM most of the remainder of the night to uncover the buried giant. As dawn broke, and the relentless rain began again, so the water washed the mud and caked filth and blood from its armour, making it gleam in the sunrise. Dark blue metal, as dark as an evening sky, save for the white silver wings on the chest. The boy and his father knelt, panting before it. The armour was dented and broken in places, and loose wiring sprang out of gashes in the metal. There were bullet-holes in the thigh, and here and there plates had been buckled out of shape by some inconceivable force, bent out of place; the heavy dark paint scraped off them so they could see the bare alloy underneath.

The boy's father wiped his brow, streaking it with mud. 'Help me with the helmet, boy – let's see if we can get a look at him.'

They felt around the helmet seal with their finger-tips, that savage visage staring up at them, immobile. The boy's quicker fingers found the two pressure points first. There were two clicks, and a hiss, then a loud crack. Between the two of them they levered up the mass of metal, and eased it off. It rolled to one side, clinking on the stones, and they found them-selves staring at the face of an Astartes.

The skin was pale, as though it seldom saw the sun, stretched tight across a huge-boned skull, long and somehow horse-like. It was recognisably human, but out of scale, like the face of a great statue. A metal stud was embedded above one colourless eyebrow. The head was shaved, criss-crossed with old scars, though a bristle of dark hair had begun to regrow on it. The right eye was gone – he had been shot through the lens of his helmet – but the hole was already healed, a ragged whorl of red tissue.

Then the left eye opened.

The boy and his father tumbled backwards, away from the glare of the eye. The giant stirred, his arm coming up and then falling back again. A rasping growl came up from somewhere deep in the barrel-wide chest, and the legs quivered. Then the giant groaned, and was still again, but now his teeth were bared and clenched – white, strong teeth which looked as though they could snap off a hand. He spoke, a slur of pain-filled words.

The boy's father approached the giant on hands and knees. 'You're among friends here. We're trying to help you, lord. The fighting is over. The enemy is gone. Can you hear me?'

The eye, bloodshot and as blue as midwinter ice, came to rest on the boy's father. 'My brothers,' the giant said. 'Where are they?' His voice was deep, the accent so strange that the boy could barely understand him.

'They've gone. I saw the great ship leave orbit myself, six days ago.'

A deep snarl, a cross between rage and grief. Again, the helpless movement of the massive limbs.

'Help me. I must stand.'

They tried, tugging at the cold metal armour. They managed to get him sitting upright. His gauntleted hand scrabbled at the rubble.

'My bolter.'

'It's not here – it must be buried, as you were. We had to dig you out.'

He could not raise himself. The single eye blinked. The Astartes spat, and his spittle spattered against the rocks, bright with blood.

'My armour is dead. We must get it off. Help me. I will show you what to do.'

The rain came lashing down. They struggled in the muck and gravel around the giant, clicking off one piece after another of the armour which enclosed him. The boy could not lift any of them, strong though he was. His father grunted and sweated, corded muscles standing out along his arms and chest, as he set each piece of the dark blue carapace to one side. The massive breastplate almost defeated them all, and when it came free the giant snarled with pain. As it fell away, slick, mucus-covered cables slid out of his torso along with it, and when they sucked free, the boy saw that his chest was pocked with metal sockets embedded in his very flesh. The armour had been part of him.

He had been shot through the thigh, but the wound was almost closed. It was a raised, angry lump, in the midst of which was a suppurating hole. The Astartes looked at it, frowning. 'Something's in there. My system should have fixed it by now.' He probed the hole with one finger, teeth bared against the pain, and raised his bloody pus-covered digit to his face and sniffed at it. 'Something bad.' He put a knuckle to his empty eye-socket. 'It feels hot. I have infection in me.' His voice held a note of incredulity. 'This should not be.' He thought for a moment. 'They used chemical agents in the fighting. Maybe biological too. It would seem my system has been compromised.'

The Astartes looked at the man who knelt by him. 'I must rejoin my brethren. I need a deep space comms link. Do you know where there would be such a thing?'

The boy's father tugged at his lower lip. 'In the city, at the spaceport I suppose. But the city is pretty much destroyed. There may be nothing left.'

The Astartes nodded again. Something like humanity came into his surviving eye. 'I remember. Our Deep Strike teams made planetfall not far from the landing fields. The Thunderhawks took out positions all up and down the pads. They had drop-ships there, three of them. We got them all.'

'Who were they, lord, if I might ask?'

The Astartes smiled, though the effect was less humorous than ferocious on that massive, brutal face. 'Those who brought us here were the enemies of Man – a Chaos faction my Chapter has been charged with eradicating for decades now. They call themselves the *Punishers*. They meant to take over your world and use it as a bridgehead to conquer the rest of the system. My brothers and I saved you from that fate.'

'You destroyed my world,' the boy said, high and shrill with anger. 'You didn't save anything – you burnt us to ash!'

The giant regarded him gravely. 'Yes, we did. But I promise you that the Punishers would have done worse, had they been allowed. Your people would have been cattle to them, mere sport for the vilest appetites imaginable. Those who died quickly would have been the lucky ones. You will rebuild your world – it may take twenty years, but you can do it. Had it been tainted by Chaos, there would have been nothing for it but to scald it down to the very guts of the planet, and leave it an airless cinder.'

The man grasped his son's arm. 'He's young – he knows nothing.'

'Well, consider this part of his education,' the Astartes snapped. 'Now find me something we can use to splint my leg – and something to lean on that will take my weight. I must get mobile – and I need a weapon.'

Their search took much of the day, until finally they hit upon dismantling one of the discarded weapons lying on the battlefield and using the recoil rod within the firing mechanism to splint the Astartes's thigh. As he tied it tight about his lacerated flesh with lengths of wire, the giant ground his teeth, and pus popped out of the hot red wound in his leg. The boy's father retrieved the Imperium weapon his son had found the day before. The Astartes's eyes lit up as he saw it, then narrowed again as he popped the magazine and checked the seat of the rounds within. 'Maybe thirty, if we're lucky. Well, a working bolter is worth something. Now hand me that pole.'

The pole was part of the innards of one of the great biomechanical carcasses which littered the field. The Astartes regarded it with disgust, wiping it clean with wet soil and sand. He used it as a staff, and was finally able to lever himself upright. In his free fist he held the bolter. He found its weight hard to manage in his weakened state however, and so fashioned a sling from more gleaned wire so that he might let it swing at his side. The wire of the sling cut into his shoulder, slicing the skin, but he seemed not to feel the pain.

'It'll be dark soon,' the boy's father said. 'We should perhaps stay here another night and then set off at dawn.'

'No time,' the Astartes said. Now that he was upright he seemed even huger, half as tall again as the man in front of him, his hands as big as shovels, his chest as wide as a dining table. 'I see in the dark. You can follow me.' With that, he set off, hobbling down the slopes of the shattered hillside to the valley below, where the sun was setting in a maelstrom of black cloud and toiling pillars of even blacker smoke, still rising from the stricken city that was their destination.

THEY WALKED HALF the night. The ground they traversed was broken by great bombardments and littered with the wreckage of war machines, some tracked, some wheeled, and some it seemed fashioned with arms and legs. They stopped once beside a great burnt-out carcass which squatted as tall as a building. So shot to pieces was it that its original shape could hardly be made out, but the Astartes limped up to it and carefully, reverently clicked off a metal seal with a tattered remnant of parchment still clinging to it. He bowed his head over this relic. 'Ah, brother,' he whispered.

'What is it?' the boy asked, even as his father tried to hush him.

'One of my battle-brothers; a spirit so bold, so fine, he chose to be encased in this mighty Dreadnought after his own body was destroyed, to carry on the fight, to stay with us, his brethren. His friends. His name was Geherran. He was with my company, and saved us from these–' Here the Astartes gestured at the other wrecks which stood round about, evil, crab-like structures adorned with all manner of ordnance, emblazoned with sickening symbols, '–these defilers. Abominations of Chaos. He broke them, took their heaviest fire upon himself so we might bring them down one by one.'

The Astartes blinked his one eye, then straightened, and limped on without another word.

The boy and his father followed him through a graveyard of the great machines, awed by their size, and the way in which they had been blasted to pieces where they stood. As the planet's two moons began to rise, it seemed they were in the midst of some ancient arena, where the dead had been left forgotten in mounds about them. But the dead were all twisted, snarling, white-faced and putrid. In the moons' light, it did not do to look at them too closely.

They entered the suburbs of the city and began to encounter signs of life. Rats flickered and squealed amid avalanches of rubble, and here and there a dog growled at them from the deepest shadows, eyes alight with madness, luminous foam dripping from its jaws. Once, a stream of cockroaches, each as big as a man's fist, went chittering across their path, dragging some unidentifiable chunk of carrion with them as they went. The Astartes watched them go thoughtfully, hefting the bolter.

'Such creatures are not native to this world, am I right?'

The boy's father was wide-eyed. 'Not that I have heard.'

'Something has been happening here. My brothers would not have left this world again so quickly unless there was a good reason. My guess is something called them out of orbit. A secondary threat of some kind.'

'You think they destroyed all the enemy down here on the surface?'

'We do not leave jobs half done.'

'How do you know?' the boy piped up. 'You were buried under a ton of stone, dead to the world. They left you behind.'

The Astartes turned, and in his eye they could see a light not unlike that in the dog's caught by lamplight. But he said nothing. The boy was cuffed across the back of his head by his father.

They moved on, more slowly now, for the Astartes was straining to keep his massive firearm at the ready. An ordinary man would struggle to lift, let alone fire it. His metal staff clicked against the plascrete underfoot, and stones skittered aside as his feet found their way. Watching him, the boy realised that the giant was near the end of his strength, and now he noticed also that the Astartes was leaving a thickly stippled trail of dark liquid in his wake. He was bleeding to death. He pointed this out to his father, who grasped up at the giant's arm.

'Your leg – you must let me look at it.'

'My systems should have taken care of it. I am infected. Some kind of bio-agent. I can feel it in my skull, like red-hot worms writhing behind my eyes. I need an Apothecary.' The Astartes was panting heavily. 'How far to the spaceport?'

'Another four or five kilometres.'

'Then I will rest, for now. We must find somewhere to lay up until daylight. I don't like this place, these ruins. There is something here.'

'No bodies,' the boy said, making his companions stare at him. He shrugged. 'Where are all the dead people? There's nothing but vermin left.'

'Lean on me,' the boy's father said to the ailing giant. 'There are houses on our right, up ahead, and they look more intact. We'll find one with a roof.'

By THEY TIME they bedded down for what remained of the darkness the Astartes was shivering uncontrollably, though his skin was almost too hot to touch. They gathered rainwater out of puddles and broken crockery and sipped enough of the black, disgusting liquid to moisten their mouths. The air was full of smoke and soot which left a gritty taste on the tongue and there were sparks flying in the midst of the reek.

'The fires are up north, towards the spaceport,' the boy's father said, rubbing his aching shoulder.

The Astartes nodded. He stroked the bolter in his lap as though it comforted him. 'It may be best if I go on alone,' he said.

'My other shoulder is still good enough to lean on.'

The giant smiled. 'What are you, a farmer?'

'I was. I had cattle. Now I have rocks and ash.'

'And a son, who still lives.'

'For now,' the man said, and he looked at the filthy, pinched face of his son, who lay sleeping like an abandoned orphan, wrapped in the charred rags of a blanket on the floor.

'Think of him, then – you have accompanied me far enough.'

'Yes,' the boy's father said dryly. 'And you are in such tremendous shape. You want rid of us because you think something bad is up ahead, at the spaceport, and you want to spare us.'

The giant inclined his head. 'Fighting is my life, not yours.'

'Something tells me this thing is not over. Your brothers overlooked something when they left. This is my world we are on – I will help you fight for it. There is nothing behind me but burnt earth, anyway.'

'So be it,' the Astartes said. 'At daybreak we will walk out together.'

DAYBREAK DID NOT come. Instead there was only a slight lightening of the darkness, and in the sky ahead, a glow which had nothing to do with the colour of flame. The two moons were setting amid oceans of smoke, and the smoke itself was tinted on its underside, a colour like the underbelly of a maggot.

The Astartes rose unaided. His remaining eye seemed to have sunk into his skull, so that it was but a single gimlet gleam in his soot-blackened face. He cast aside his iron staff and stood upright as the pus ran yellow and pink from his swollen leg. The agony of it brought the sweat running down his forehead, but his face was impassive, at peace.

'The Emperor watch over us,' he said quietly as the boy and his father rose in turn, rubbing their smarting eyes. 'We must be quick and quiet now, like hunters.'

The three set off.

THE SCREAM BURST ahead of them like a fire in the night, a tearing shriek which rose to the limits of human capacity, and then was cut off. There was a murmur, as of a distant engine, heavy machinery moving. And when it stopped they heard another sound, murmuring through the heavy smoke and the preternatural darkness. Voices, many voices chanting in unison.

The three of them went to ground in a burning house as the gledes and coals of the rafters spat and showered them. Some hissed as they landed on the sweat of the Astartes's back, but he did not so much as twitch.

'Cultists,' he said, listening. 'They're at the work of the warp, some ceremony or sorcery.'

His two companions stared at him, uncomprehending.

'Followers of the Dark Powers,' he explained, 'gulled or tortured into subservience. They are fodder for our guns.' Carefully, he unloaded the magazine from his bolter, eyed the rounds, and then kissed the cold metal before reloading. He eased back the cocking handle with a double click, like the lock of a door going back and forth.

'How far to the spaceport now?'

'We're almost on it,' the man told him. He was gripping his son's shoulder until his knuckles showed white. 'Up ahead the road turns to the right, and there's a gate, and walls – the spaceport is within.'

'I doubt the walls still stand,' the Astartes said with grim humour.

'There's a guardpost and a small barracks for the militia just within the gate – and an armoury out back, by the control tower. Ammunition, lasguns.'

'Lasguns,' the Astartes said with a kind of contempt. 'I am used to heavier metal, my friend. But it may be worth checking out. We need something to up our killing power. From here in, you stay close to me, both of you.'

He sprang up, and was off with barely a limp. With astonishing speed he sprinted to the end of the street and disappeared into the shell of the last house on the right. After a moment's hesitation, the man and his son got up and followed him.

He was right – the walls had been blasted away. In fact most of the buildings on this side of the spaceport lay in ruins, and the landing pads themselves were cratered with massive shell-holes and littered with the debris of all sorts of orbital craft. At the western end, three tall towers of twisted wreckage stood out, the smoke wreathing them, fires still burning deep in their tangled hulls.

'Punisher drop-pods' the Astartes said. 'We got all three.'

'There's another one,' the boy spoke up, pointing.

They peered together, squinting in the smoke. The boy was right. A fourth, undamaged drop-pod was squatting to the east, where the damage to the landing pads was less severe. Infantry was marching down its ramps.

The Astartes's face creased with hatred. 'It would seem my brothers and I were not as thorough as we thought. We must get word to my company, or your planet will fall to the enemy after all. We must have comms!'

'It'll be in the control tower, out yonder – if it's still intact,' the man said, jerking his head to the north. Dimly through the smoke they could make out a pale white pillar with a cluster of grey plascrete buildings around its foot. There seemed to be no enemy activity out in that direction, but with the smoke and gathering darkness it was hard to be sure.

'Then that is where we go,' the Astartes said simply. 'My brothers must be brought back to this world to cleanse it – or else they will have to extinguish it from space – get down!' This last was in a hiss. A troop of enemy infantry marched past. Strange, angular bald-headed men with heavily tattooed faces. They wore long leather coats adorned with studs and chains and what seemed to be human body parts. They bore lasguns, and chattered and snarled incessantly as they passed by.

'Their talk hurts my ears,' the boy said, rubbing his head.

'The warp infects them,' the Astartes told him. 'If we cannot cleanse this place, then it will begin to infect the remainder of your people.' He lifted a hand to the wound where his eye had been, then dropped it again. 'To the tower, then.'

THEY RAN, RIGHT into the heart of the foul-smelling smoke. The boy became dizzy, and found it hard to breathe, and the distant chanting of the cultists seemed to cloud over his thinking. He faltered, and found himself standing still, staring vacantly, aware that he was missing something.

Then he found himself lifted into the air and crushed against an enormous, fever-hot body. The Astartes had picked him up and tucked him under his free arm, still running.

Out of nowhere a cluster of pale faces appeared in the smoke. Before they could even raise their weapons the Astartes was upon them. A kick broke the ribcage of one and sent him hurtling off into the darkness. The heavy bolter was swung like a club and smashed the heads of two more into red ruin, almost decapitating them. The fourth got off a red burst of lasgun fire that spiked out harmlessly into the air, before the Astartes, dropping the boy, had him by the throat. He crushed the man's windpipe with one quick clench of his fist, and tossed him aside.

'Get the weapons,' he said to the man and the boy, panting. 'Grenades, anything.' He bent over and coughed, and a gout of dark liquid sprayed out of his mouth to splatter all over the plascrete landing strip. He swayed for a second, then straightened. When his companions had retrieved two lasguns and a sling of grenades from the bodies he nodded. 'Someone may have seen that las-fire. If we run into more of them, do not stop – keep running.'

They set off again. The giant was hobbling now, and left a trail of blood behind him, but he still set a fearsome pace, and it was all the man and his son could do to keep up with him, as they fought for air in the reeking hell that surrounded them.

At last the white pillar of the control tower appeared out of the smoke – and a band of cultists at its foot. They saw the shapes come running out of the darkness at them and set up a kind of shriek and began firing wildly. Las-fire came arcing through the air.

In return the Astartes halted, set the bolter in his shoulder, and began firing.

Short bursts, no more, two or three rounds at a time. But when the heavy ordnance hit the cultists it blew them apart. He took down eight of them before the first las-burst hit him, in the stomach. He staggered, and the bolter-muzzle dropped, but a second later he had raised it again and blew to pieces the cultist who had shot him.

The boy and his father lay on the ground and started firing also, but the heavy Chaos lasguns were unwieldy and hard to handle – their shots went wild. The boy fumbled with the sling of grenades

and popped out one thumb-sized bomb. There was
a tiny red button at the top of the little cylinder. He
pressed it, and then tossed the thing at the cultists. It
clinked on the base of the tower and lay at their feet.
One looked at it with dawning horror on his face,
and then the grenade exploded, and splattered him
in scarlet fragments across the white painted wall of
the control tower, along with three of his comrades.

The rest broke and ran, quickly disappearing into
the toiling darkness. The Astartes sank to one knee,
leaning on his bolter. His other hand was bunched
in a fist where the lasgun had burnt a black hole
through his torso from front to back.

'You need my shoulder again, I think,' the man
said, helping up the maimed giant. 'Not far to go
now. Lean on me, my friend. I will get you there.'

The Astartes managed a strangled laugh, but said
no more.

They found the door ajar, a tall steel affair whose
command-box had been blown out. The man made
as if to enter but the Astartes held him back.
'Grenade first,' he rasped.

The boy tossed another of the little explosives
inside. He was smiling as he did so, and when the
thing went off, he laughed.

'I am glad everyone finds this so amusing,' his
father said, as he stepped inside.

Two dead bodies, blown to pieces in the confined
chamber at the base of the tower. There was an ele-
vator, but the boy punched its buttons in vain.

'No power, Pa,' he said. 'The whole place is dead.'

'Stairs,' the Astartes gasped.

'Listen,' the man said. 'Outside – can you hear it?'

A confused babel, a roaring, bellowing sound of voices, some shrill, some deep. Even as they listened, it grew louder.

'Get the door closed,' the Astartes snapped. 'Block it, jam it – use anything you can.'

They slammed the heavy steel door shut, and piled up whatever they could find in the way of wreckage and furniture against it. The Astartes, with an agonised cry, wrenched a stretch of iron piping free of the wall and wedged it against the steel. Seconds later, the cacophony of voices was right outside, and they were hammering on the door. Gunfire sounded, and shells rang loudly against the metal.

'That won't hold them,' the man said. He and his son were white-faced, and sweat was cutting stripes down the grime on their faces.

'Up,' the Astartes said impatiently. 'We must go up. You first, then your boy. I will hold the rear. Any sounds ahead of you, start firing and keep firing.'

'We're trapped here,' the man said unsteadily.

'Move!' the giant barked.

The stairs wound round the inside of the tower like the thread of a screw. They laboured up them in almost pitch darkness, the sound of their own harsh breathing magnified by the plascrete to left and right, their feet sounding hollow on the metal steps. Several times the Astartes paused to listen as they ascended, and once he ordered them to halt.

'Anyone got a light?' he asked.

'I have,' the boy said. There was a whirring sound, and then a feeble glow began, yellow and flickering. It strengthened as the boy kept winding up his torch.

'Good for you,' the Astartes said. 'Give me those grenades.' He popped one out of the sling and peered at it.

'They copy us in everything – these are just like Imperium charges. They have three settings: instant, delay and proximity. The most obvious one is delay, the red button on top – give thanks to the Emperor you picked that one back outside. You twist the top of the cylinder for the other settings.' He did so. 'Move up the stairs.' He set down the little cylinder upright, pressed the red button on its top, and then followed them. Behind him there were three tiny clicks, and then silence.

'The next thing to approach that is going to have a surprise. I just hope there are no rats in here. Move out.'

Round the tower they went by the flickering glow of the boy's clockwork torch. Finally they came to another steel door. It was very slightly ajar, and there were voices on the far side. The boy reached for the grenades, but the Astartes stopped him. 'We need this place intact. Get behind me.'

He kicked open the door and there was a roar of bolter fire, a stuttering series of flashes, and then a click as the bolter's magazine came up empty. The Astartes roared and lunged forward.

Behind him, the boy and his father burst through the doorway, coughing on the cordite stink that filled the space beyond. They were in a large circular room filled with consoles and monitors, with huge windows that overlooked the entire spaceport. A trio of cultists lay dead, their innards scattered like red streamers across the electronic wall-consoles of the tower. On the far side of the room, a titanic battle was raging, smashing back and forth, sending chairs flying, filling the air with broken glass. The Astartes was struggling with a dark, armoured figure almost as massive as himself, and the two were grappling with each other, bellowing like two bulls intent on mayhem. The boy and his father stood staring, lasguns almost forgotten in their hands.

The Astartes was knocked clear across the room. He crashed into the heavy blast-proof glass of the tower and the impact spidered it out in a web of cracks. His adversary straightened, and there was the sound of horrible, unhinged laughter.

'Brother Marine!' the voice gargled, 'You have not come dressed for the occasion! Where is your blue livery now, Dark Hunter? Can't you see you are on the wrong world? This place is ours now!'

The speaker was clad in power armour similar to that they had found the Astartes wearing, but it was bone-white in colour, and a black skeleton had been picked out upon it with ebony inlays. Its bearer wore a helm adorned with two great horns, and the light from his eye sockets glowed sickening green. The many-arrowed star of Chaos had been engraved on his breastplate, and in his hand he held a cruel monomolecular blade which shone with blood.

'How many of you are left now, heretic?' the Astartes spat. 'My brothers will wipe you from this system as a man wipes shit from the sole of his boot.'

'Big words, from the mouth of a cripple,' the Chaos warrior snarled. He drew a bolt pistol from its holster and aimed it at the Astartes's head.

The boy and his father both raised their lasguns and fired in the same moment. The man missed, but his son's burst caught the enemy warrior just under the armpit. The fearsome figure cried out in pain and anger, and dropped the knife. The pistol swung round.

'What are these, brother– pets of yours? They need chastising.'

He opened fire. The pistol bucked in his hand and the impact of the heavy rounds sent the boy's father smashing back against the wall behind, ripping open his chest and filling the air with gore. The Chaos warrior stepped forward, still firing, and the bolter shells blew open the wall in a line of explosions as he followed the flight of the boy, who had dropped his lasgun and was scrabbling on hands and knees for the shelter of the consoles. The magazine clicked dry, and the warrior flicked it free, reaching in his belt for another one. 'Such vermin on this world – they must be exterminated to the last squealing morsel.'

'I agree,' the Astartes said.

The Chaos warrior spun round, and was staggered backwards by the force of the blow. He fell full length on his back. Dropping his pistol, his hands came up to his chest to find the hilt of his knife buried in his own breastplate. There was a thin, almost inaudible whine as the filament blade continued to vibrate deep in his body cavity.

The Astartes, his face a swollen mask of blood, dropped to his knees beside his prone enemy.

'We have two hearts each, you and me,' he said. 'That is how we are made. We were created for the betterment of Man, to make this galaxy a place of order and peace.' He gripped the knife blade, slapping his struggling adversary's hands aside, and pulled the weapon free. A thin jet of blood sprang out, and the Chaos warrior grunted in agony.

'Let me see if I can find that second heart,' the Astartes said, and he plunged the knife downwards again.

THE BOY CREPT out of his hiding place and crouched by the mangled remains of his father. His face was blank, wide eyes in a filthy blood-spattered mask. He closed his father's staring eyes and clenched his own teeth on a sob. The he stood up and retrieved his lasgun.

The Astartes was lying by the wall in a pool of his own blood, his dead enemy sprawled beside him. His body was white as ivory, and the blood leaking from his wounds had slowed to a trickle. He looked up at the boy with his remaining eye. They stared at one another for a moment.

'Help me up,' the Astartes said at last, and the boy somehow climbed behind him and pushed his immense torso upright.

'Your father–' the Astartes began, and then there was a dull boom from below them.

'The grenade,' the boy said dully. 'They're on the stairs.'

'Toss another one down there and then lock the door,' the Astartes said. 'Bring me over that bolt pistol when you're done.'

'What's the point?' the boy asked, sullen. His eyes were red and bloodshot. He looked like a little old man, shrunken and defeated.

'Do as I say,' the Astartes cracked out, glaring. 'It's not over while we live, not for us, not for your world. Now toss the grenade!'

The boy looked round the door.

'There's movement on the stairs,' he said, calm now. He pressed the red button on the explosive and threw it down the stairs. It bounced and clinked and clicked as it went down the steps. He shut the heavy metal door and slid the bar-lock in place. Another boom, closer than the first. There were screams below them, and the floor quivered. The boy handed the Astartes the bolt pistol, and the giant ripped the ammo belt off the fallen Chaos Marine, clicking in a fresh magazine and cocking the weapon.

'I've found the comms,' the boy said, across the room. He flicked several switches up and down. 'At least I think so – it looks like a comms unit anyway. But it's dead. There's no power.'

The Astartes laboured over to the boy on his hands and knees. Blood dripped out of his mouth and nose and ears. He sounded as though he were breathing through water.

'Yes, that's it. Old-fashioned. But it still needs power.' He sighed deeply. 'Well, that's that then.'

The boy stared at the dead lights on the console. He was frowning. He did not even start when the first battering began on the door to the control room, and a slavering and snarling on the other side of it, as though a herd of beasts milled there.

'Power,' he said. 'I have power – I have power here.' His face quickened. 'My torch!'

He drew it out of the bag of oddments at his waist. 'I can attach it – I can plug it in and get it running!'

The Astartes drew himself up and sat on the creaking chair before the console. 'A fine idea, but you'll never crank up enough power with that little hand-held dynamo.'

'There must be something!'

They stared at the dead array of lights and switches before them. The comms unit was a relic, a patched up antique for use on a far-flung border world. The Astartes's good eye narrowed.

'Plug in your torch and start winding,' he said.

'But–'

'Just do it!' He scrabbled open the wooden drawer below the console, while behind them both, blow after heavy blow was rained down on the door to the chamber. The lock-bar bent inwards. A chorus of cackles and growls sounded on the other side, like the memory of a fevered nightmare.

'Sometimes they hang on to the most obsolete of technologies on worlds like yours,' the Astartes said. He smiled. 'Because they still work.' From a tangle of junk in the drawer, he produced a contraption of wires and a small knobbed device. He stared at it, considering a moment, and then set it up on the bench, plugging it into the adaptor socket. Immediately, a small green light came on within it.

'Built to last,' he muttered. He closed his eye, and then began tapping down on the device. A high series of clicks and tones was audible. He adjusted the frequency with an ancient circular dial, and there was a faint crackle.

The two of them were so intent, the boy turning the handle on his creaking torch, the giant tapping away on the strange device, that they were almost oblivious to the grinding and banging at the room's door.

'Is it working?' the boy asked.

'The signal is going out. The code is ancient; a relic of old Earth, but we still use it in my Chapter, for its simplicity. It is elegant, older even than the Imperium itself. But like many simple, elegant things in this universe, it has endured.'

The Space Marine stopped his tapping. 'Enough. We must see if we can get you out of here.'

'There's no way out,' the boy said.

'There's always a way out,' the Astartes told him. He turned and fired at the plexi-glass of the control tower. It shattered and cascaded in an avalanche of jagged shards. Then he reached into the console drawer with a fist and produced a long coil of dull coppery wire.

'It will slice your hands as you go down,' he said to the boy, 'but you must hold on. When you get to the bottom, start running.'

'What about you?'

The Space Marine smiled. 'I will be on the other end. Now do it.'

THE DOOR BURST open, and was flung back against the wall with a clang. A huge figure loomed out of the darkness, and more were behind it.

The Astartes was slumped by the huge broken maw of the plexiglass window, a glint of wire wrapped round one arm, disappearing into the smoky vacancy beyond. He bared his teeth in a rictus.

'What kept you?' he asked the hulking shapes as they advanced on him. Then he raised his free arm and fired a full magazine from the bolt pistol into the intruders. Screams and yowls rent the air, and the foremost two shapes were blasted off their feet.

But more were behind them. The howling mob in the doorway poured into the room, firing bolters as they came, the heavy rounds blasting everything to pieces.

AWAY FROM THE tortured little world, the vastness of hanging space was utterly silent, peaceful, but in the midst of that peace tiny flowers of light bloomed, white and yellow, lasting only an instant before lack of oxygen snuffed them out. From a distance – a great distance – they seemed minute and beautiful, brief jewels in the blackness. Closer to, the story was different.

There were craft floating in the blackness, immense structures of steel and ceramite and titanium and a thousand other alloys, constructed with an eye to utility, to endurance. Made for destruction. They looked like vast airborne temples created for the worship of a deranged god, kilometres long, their flanks bristling with turrets and batteries. About them, smaller craft wheeled and dove like flycatchers on the hide of a rhino.

Within the largest of these craft an assemblage of giants stood clad in shining dark blue armour, unhelmed, their pale faces reflecting back the distant infernos that were on the viewscreens to their front. All around them, travesties of man and machine worked silently, murmuring into their stations, hands of flesh working in harmony with limbs of steel and muti-hued wiring. Incense hung in the air, mixed with the unmistakable fragrance of gun-oil.

'You're sure of this, brother?' one of the giant figures said, not turning his head from the scenes of kinetic mayhem on the screens about him.

'Yes, captain. The signal lasted only some forty-five seconds, but there was no doubting its content. Several of my comms-techs know the old code, as do the Adeptus Mechanicus. It is a survival from ancient days.'

'And the content of the message?'

'One phrase, repeated again and again. Captain, the phrase was *Umbra Sumus*.'

At this, all the standing figures started and turned towards the speaker. They were all two and a half metres high, clad in midnight-blue armour. All had the white symbol of the double-headed axe on one of their shoulderguards. They carried their helms in the crook of their arms, and bolt-pistols were holstered on their thighs.

'Mardius, are you sure – that is what it said?'

'Yes, captain. I have triple checked. The signal was logged and recorded.'

The captain drew in a sharp breath. 'The motto of our order.'

'*We are shadows*. Yes, captain. No Punisher would ever utter those words – the hatred they feel for the Dark Hunters is too great. It is my belief one or more of our brethren sent it from the surface of the planet; he was contacting us in the only way he could. Or warning us.'

'The signal cut off, you say?'

'It was very faint. It may have been cut off or it may merely have passed out of our range-width. We are too far away to scan the planet. The signal itself took the better part of ten days to reach us.'

'Brother Avriel,' the captain snapped. 'Who was unaccounted for after we left the surface?'

Another of the giants stepped forward. 'Brother Pieter. No trace was found of him. We would have searched longer, but–'

'But the Punishers had to be pursued. Quite right, Avriel. No blame is attached to my query. It was the priority at the time.' The captain stared up at one of the giant screens again. Within the massive nave of the starship, there was almost silence, except for the clicks and muttering of the adepts at their posts.

'No other communications from planetside?'

'None whatsoever, captain. Their infrastructure was comprehensively destroyed during our assault, and it was a backwater to begin with. One spaceport, and nothing but suborbital craft across the whole planet.'

'Yes, yes, I am aware of the facts of the campaign, Avriel.' The captain frowned, the studs on his brow almost disappearing in the folds of scarred flesh there. At last he looked up.

'This engagement here is almost concluded. The Punisher flotilla has been crippled and well nigh destroyed. As soon as we have finished off the last of their strike craft we will turn about, and set a course for Perreken.'

'Go back?' one of the Astartes said. 'But it's been weeks. If it was Pieter–'

'Avriel,' the captain snapped, 'What is our estimated journey time to the planet?'

'At best speed, some thirty-six days, captain.'

'Emperor guide us, that's a long time to leave a Brother-Marine alone,' one of the others said.

'We do this not just for our brother,' the captain told them. 'If any taint of Chaos has remained on the planet then it must be burnt out, or our mission in this system will have utterly failed. We return to Perreken, brothers – in force.'

* * *

THE CEREMONY WAS almost complete. For weeks the cultists and their champions had danced and prayed and chanted and wept. Now their mission was close to its fruition. Across the plascrete of the landing pads, a dark stain had grown. This was no burn mark, no sear of energy weapon or bombardment crater. Within its shadow the ground bubbled like soup left too long on a stove. It steamed and groaned, cracking upwards, segments of plascrete floating on the unquiet surface. The screaming chant of the cultists reached a new level, one that human ears could barely comprehend. Hundreds of them were gathered around the unquiet, desecrated stain of earth.

'HOLD YOUR FIRE until I give the word,' the boy said, and up and down the line the order was passed along. In a series of impact craters to the east of the spaceport scores of men and women lay hidden by the broken rubble. They were a tatterdemalion band of ragged figures weighed down by bandoliers of ammunition and a bewildering assortment of weaponry, some modern and well-kept, some ancient and worn-out. Once, a long time ago it seemed now, they had been civilians, non-combatants. But now that distinction had ceased to exist on Perreken.

A black-bearded man who lay beside the boy was chewing on his thumbnail nervously. 'If we've got this wrong, then all of us will die here today,' he said.

'That is why I didn't get it wrong,' the boy said. He turned to stare at his companion and the black-bearded man looked away, unable to meet those eyes.

Almost three months had passed since the boy had slid down a piece of wire held by a dead Space Marine. In that time he had broadened, grown taller, and yet more gaunt. The flesh of his face had been stripped back to the bone by hunger and exhaustion, and his eyes were blank with the look of a man who has seen too much. Despite his youth, no one questioned his leadership. It was as if his fellow fighters recognised something unique in him, something none of the rest of them possessed.

The boy held an Astartes bolt pistol in his hands, and as he lay there in the crater with the rank sweat of fear filling the air around him, he bent his head and kissed the double-headed eagle on the barrel. Then he fumbled in the canvas satchel at his side and produced a mess of wires and a little control panel. A green light burned on the heavy battery still in the satchel.

'Send it,' he said to the black-bearded man. 'It's time.'

His companion began tapping clicks out on the elderly wired contraption. 'May the Emperor smile on us today,' he muttered. 'And may His Angels arrive on time.'

'When the Astartes say they will do something, they do it,' the boy said. 'They gave their word. They will be here.'

* * *

ACROSS THE LANDING fields, the cultists were dancing and stamping and screaming their way into a frenzy. Some of the madly cavorting figures had once been smallholders and blacksmiths and businessmen, friends and neighbours of the ragged guerrillas who lay in wait among the craters to the east. Now they had been turned into chattels of the Dark Gods, worshippers of that which drew its strength from the warp. And now the warp had stirred them into a kind of ecstasy, and it fed off their worship, their blood-sacrifices. The patch of ground which they circled darkened further, popping and undulating as though cooked on some great invisible flame.

And inside that roiling cauldron, something stirred. There was a momentary glimpse of something breaking the surface, like the fin of a great whale at sea. The earth spat upwards, as though trying to escape whatever writhed beneath it. The cultists went into paroxysms, prostrating themselves, shrieking until the blood vessels in their throats burst and sprayed the air with their life fluids. Farther back from the edge, the armour-clad champions of their kind stood and stamped and clashed power swords against their breastplates. The darkness thickened over them all like a shroud.

The boy lay and watched them with his face disfigured by hatred and fear. Up and down the line there was a murmur as his fellow fighters brought their weapons into their shoulders. Some were priming homemade bombs, others were checking magazines. They were an underfed, rancid, ill-equipped band, but they held their position with real discipline, waiting for their young leader's word.

I did that, the boy thought. I made them like this. I am good at it.

He could barely remember a time now when he had been a mere farm boy, living on a green planet where the skies were blue and there was fresh food to be had, clean water to drink. He could barely even remember his father. That boy who had known a father was someone else, from another time. All he could remember now was the endless smoke-shrouded landscape, the constant fear, the explosions of bloody violence, the carnage. And the face of the Astartes who had died while helping him to live. That, he could not forget.

Nor could he forget the moment of sheer bubbling joy and relief when the ancient comms device he had found in the city had proved to work as well as that which they had found in the control tower. One of the older men knew the ancient code by heart and taught it to him. When the first message had come clicking back at them from a far-flung starship on the other side of the system it had seemed like a benediction from the God-Emperor Himself. It was enough to engender hope, to help him recruit fighters from the shattered survivors of the population. They had lived like rats, scavenging, scurrying for weeks and then months in the ruins of their world. Until today. Today they would stand up and take it back.

That was the plan.

The boy clambered to his feet just as the battery-fed contraption in the satchel clicked by itself in a sharp staccato final message.

An incoming message.

The boy smiled. 'Open fire!' he shouted.

And all around him hell erupted.

The chanting of the cultists faltered. They looked up, distracted, angry, shocked. The first volley cut down almost a hundred. Then the ragged guerrillas followed the boy's lead and charged forward across the broken plascrete of the landing field, firing as they came and yelling at the top of their voices.

The ring of cultists opened up, fraying under the shock of the assault. But there were many hundreds more of them further west by their drop-pods. These now set up a cacophony of fury, and began running eastwards to meet the attack.

The boy went to one knee, picking his targets calmly, firing two or three rounds into each. The enemy formation had splintered – they were confused, scattered, but in their midst their champions were restoring discipline quickly, shooting the more panicked of their underlings, roaring at the rest to stand fast.

Now, the boy thought. *It must be now.*

In the sky above the spaceport, eye-blinding lights appeared, lancing even through the heavy smoke and the preternatural night. With them came a sullen, earth-trembling roar.

In an explosion of concrete and soil, a behemoth thundered to earth. It was dozens of metres tall,

painted midnight blue, and on its multi-faceted
sides was painted the sigil of the double-headed axe.
It scattered the cultists through the air with the force
of its impact, and in its wake came another, and
another, and then two more. It was as if a series of
great metal castles had suddenly been hurled to
earth.

With a scream of straining metal, long hatches fell
down from the sides of these monstrous apparitions, as though they were the petals opening on a
flower. These hatches hit the ground and buried
themselves in earth and shattered stone and the
bodies of the screaming cultists, becoming ramps.
And down the ramps came an army, a host of
armour-clad warriors blazing a bloody path with the
automatic fire of bolters, melta guns, plasma rifles
and rocket launchers. In their midst hulking Dreadnoughts strode, picking up the cultist champions in
their clawed fists and tossing them away like discarded rags. They belched flame as they came,
incinerating the cultists, boiling their flesh within
their armour, making of them black desiccated statues.

And overhead the engines of destruction swooped
down to unloose cargoes of bombs on the unholy
stain which the Chaos minions had inflicted upon
the tortured planet. As they went off, so in their brilliant light something bestial and immense could be
seen twisting and thrashing in its last agonies. It
sank down below the level of the plascrete launch
pad as though below the surface of a lake, bellowing,

and as the missiles rained down on it, so the blackened earth became solid again, and the stain became that of normal charred earth and stone, the desecration lifted before it could be consummated.

THE BOY STOOD with his bolt pistol forgotten in his hands, staring at that great storm of fire, a scene like the ending of a world. He felt the concussion of the shells beat at the air in his very lungs, and the heat of them crackled the hair on his head, but he stood oblivious. Tears shone in his eyes as he watched the obliteration of those who had destroyed his home, and in that moment there was only a single thought in his mind.

He stared at the massive, fearsome ranks of the advancing Space Marines, and thought: this is me – this is what I want to be.

THUS DID THE Dark Hunters Chapter of the Adeptus Astartes return to the planet of Perreken, to save a world, and to retrieve the remains of one of their own.

THE TRIAL OF THE MANTIS WARRIORS

CS Goto

A FAINT MIST of light hung in the darkness, casting the vaulted chamber into a grimy and spectral half-life. Specks of dust danced suspended in the twilight, hazing the shadows with interference. From the apex of the central dome a single cone of light cut clarity into the heart of the gold-edged Imperial aquila that was etched into the deck. The hall seemed to fade away from this shining pillar of truth, retreating into the heavy shadows of its circular perimeter, where hints of grave faces haunted the darkness. Standing between the wings of the double-headed eagle, as though entrapped by the single column of light, Chapter Master Neotera's eyes shone with fierce resolve and disbelief. How had it come to this?

His bearing proud despite the humiliation, Neotera held his gaze directly ahead, showing no signs of listening to the whispers of accusation and allegation that hissed around the dark recesses of the Council of Judgement. Held in the beam of light, his armour glittering like a polished emerald, he could not see the faces of the ghostly, shadow-veiled judges. But he knew who they were. They could not disguise their voices from him, and they did not try. This was a court of honour, and the purpose of the darkness was not to hide their identity from him, but rather to hide them from his shame. It did not matter who they were; it mattered who he was, and what he had done.

The Chapter Master of the Mantis Warriors wore no shackles; nobody feared that he would attempt to escape his fate. Under one arm he held his helmet, so that his long, black hair cascaded freely down his back. The tendrils of his elaborate tattoos could be seen reaching around his neck, and his pale blue eyes glimmered aquamarine in the spotlight. Hanging at his other side was *Metasomata*, his revered and elaborately curved blade, celebrated throughout the Religiosa Realms as the *Venom of Tamulus*; it seemed to shimmer with control and restraint just fractions from the hand of its master. Amongst the legends of the Mantis Legion, only the account of the Maetrus's *Foundation of the Mantidae* rivalled in glory that of the *Purgation of Mordriana*, in which Neotera was reputed to have purified the overrun jungles of the home world in the discipline of the Old Way, with no armour and only his blade strung across his back and devotion in his heart.

The members of the Council of Judgement knew him well, and they acknowledged him as a Space Marine of peerless honour. None feared his lethal weapon or his celebrated skill at bladed combat. Many had fought at his side in previous campaigns, and more than one owed him their life. The auto-cannons embedded into the walls as precautions against the criminal, the violent, or the deranged lay dormant and inactivated. Yet the great Neotera stood before them now as their prisoner. They could see how he held his gaze directly ahead, firm and unwavering, not insulting them by looking at them as he awaited their judgement on the charges of treachery and rebellion. He waited, already resolved to die at their word, to take his shame before the Emperor himself, and to purge the sins of his battle-brothers in the fires of a pyre. No others would suffer for his crimes.

'Do you have nothing to say, Master Neotera?'

Will you say nothing?

The impersonal voices from the shadows were firm and unyielding, yet Neotera could feel the compassion in them. He knew that many in the council wanted to understand what he had done. They wanted him to *explain*, as though explanations were possible or helpful. There were those in the council who would have once called him brother, who would have followed him into the depths of the Maelstrom itself, taking the righteous fury of the Emperor into the heart of Chaos. They had seen *Metasomata* carve venom-tinged light into the darkness of the worlds lost in the fringe of the Maelstrom. They wanted to believe that his fall had a reason, that he had lost himself to some kind of irresistible sorcery, that he was no longer the Space Marine he once was. They wanted to find something of him in his explanation, a part of him or his story that could be salvaged for the archives or even for their own personal reassurance. Yet their compassion was underscored by fear, fear that there might be no such explanation, that others might be tempted to make the same choices that he had made. Fear that there was actually nothing wrong with Neotera at all, and that he could be any one of them.

Fear provoked denial. And denial brought anger into the words of others.

'Do you ridicule this council, Mantis Warrior?'

Do you find us unworthy even of your words?

'Do you hold us in contempt even now?'

The voices and thoughts swirled around him, challenging his pride, daring him to break his silence and to attempt to argue. The psychic interrogations probed at his mind, making him dizzy and nauseous. His soul cried out in anger and horror, demanding that he turn the indignance back at his accusers but simultaneously pleading for them to stop asking for words and to simply condemn him. He had nothing to say to them. There was nothing that words could undo.

The silent Chapter Master meant no further offence to this revered and ghostly council, and he refused to be drawn into a contest of words. His crimes were clear for all to see; he had denied nothing. He would not make things worse for his battle-brothers or for the honour of the Mantis Warriors by engaging in the cheap competition of excuses and explanations. He was Adeptus Astartes, one of the Emperor's chosen servants, and he would not play the grubby word-games of servitors, Arbites or inquisitors. History would judge him harshly for his silence, but nobody could judge him more severely than he judged himself. For history, he cared not one iota. For himself, he had given up all hope of salvation – he had taken steps from which there was no returning, and he would not shame his name further by scrambling hopelessly for the last pathetic phantasms of deliverance. He accepted his damnation, and so the condemnation of this revered council held no greater horror for him. Once the fall begins, there is only flame and sword.

Your crimes are heinous beyond our understanding.

'You must help us to understand, Mantis Master.'

Will you say nothing, Neotera? Will you not help us?

'If you say nothing, we can offer no mercy.'

There was a long, resigned silence as the judges waited without hope of hearing a response. The hearing had been in session for three days already, and the Mantis Warrior had not yet spoken, other than to acknowledge his name and rank when he had first been brought before the council. He had not even taken advantage of his right to know whom he faced; which great Chapters the Masters and senior Librarians had been drawn from to compose this Council of Judgement. For three entire days, he had not moved, not a finger or a flicker of an eyelid, and a fine sprinkling of dust had settled out of the air onto the broad, emerald shoulders of his ceremonial armour. He was a statue, the very icon of the immaculate and devoted warrior. And yet he stood before a punitive court that had not been convened for countless centuries; he stood with no defence against the charges and no hope of emancipation.

He was guilty.

For the last three days, his mind had gradually turned in on itself. A question spiralled and spun through his thoughts, but it was not one of those thrown at him by his judges.

How had it come to this?

The question obsessed him, as though it had woven itself into the very fabric of his being. He had been sure. He had been right. And yet, how had it come to this? Not for the first time in his long and brutal life, Neotera recognised the potential of his soul to embrace the kind of fanatical focus and devotion of the Mantis Religiosa. He could feel how easy it would be to release the last vestiges of his sense of self, undeserving as it was, and to lose his will in the vast and blinding brilliance of the Emperor's terrible magnificence. The Religiosa lived as the lost and the saved, having no sense of their own needs and only a pure devotion to the Imperial Will.

The intrepid and pious Captain Maetrus of the 2nd Company had only recently discovered a possible source of this tendency in some Mantis Warriors; he hypothesised that it was connected to a uniquely altered neuro-toxic function of the preomnor implant in the Chapter's gene-seed. However, rather than seeing it as a curse that condemned its victims to the life of fanatical devotion of the Mantis Religiosa, Maetrus argued that it was a reward for faithfulness. The heightened sense of focus and the contracted perception of space and time that accompanied it sharpened a Space Marine's reflexes to an unprecedented degree, sometimes even giving the impression of mild precognition. During the last years of the war, Maetrus had sought Neotera's permission to develop a specialist cadre of Space Marines able to harness this blessed curse, claiming that they might tip the balance in the seemingly interminable battles with the Star Phantoms and the Novamarines. He had wanted to call them the Praying Mantidae, but the demands of the war had stretched resources to breaking point – before they had finally broken in such spectacular fashion – and Neotera had not been able to spare the Space Marines that Maetrus requested.

Neotera wanted to close his eyes and swim in his regrets and laments.

How had it come to this?

The temptation to surrender himself to the light was almost overwhelming. He had felt it before, and it had helped him in situations even more lethal than the one he was in now. For the tiniest and most horrifying moment, Neotera wondered whether this descending battle-haze would be enough for him to unleash the *Venom of Tamulus* on those who sat in false judgement over him. There were only twelve of them – he had beaten worse odds before. Perhaps it was they who sinned against the Emperor? Perhaps he had been right after all – it was his righteous duty to cut down these heretics and hypocrites who dared to stand in judgement over him.

But the moment passed in a heartbeat, and then the appalling shame of the thoughts crashed even more weight into his overburdened soul. He knew he had been wrong, that his war against the agents of the Imperium had been mistaken, that his own judgement had failed him, and that in his failure resided the damnation of all his battle-brothers. It was he, and he alone, who should bear the fury and the agony and the shame. Clinging to even the faintest hope that he had been right and that the edifice of the Imperium of Man itself was mistaken just compounded his crimes with egregious arrogance. He could not even stand to let the idea enter his head; it violated the very foundations of his being.

Even hidden within the confines of his own thoughts, Neotera felt his crimes worsening and his soul screaming in anguish. Yet, to the judges around him, he was a statue of control and composure. His eyes unblinking and his breath all but indiscernible. The certainty of his guilt hardened in his resolve, and his jaw clenched imperceptibly.

How had it come to this?

While his eyes kept Neotera crisply and painfully in the spotlight on the aquila, his thoughts searched desperately for answers. He didn't want explanations for the Council, but part of him needed to know when it had all gone wrong. Why hadn't he *seen* it?

He realised that Maetrus had seen the truth first. The brilliant captain had sent a communiqué to Neotera just before the Star Phantoms had finally broken the defensive barricade around Badab itself. Even as the Phantom drop-pods thundered down into the Palace of Thorns, Maetrus had known that Huron's heart was black and filled with the taint of Chaos. At the same time, Neotera was fighting desperately to hold position in his battle-barge, engaged in the endgame of the war against the Astartes coalition that had turned on Commander Huron's Astral Claws. Neotera had watched Maetrus break formation and turn the guns of his cruiser, *Tortured Soul*, against the ships in the collapsing defences of the Astral Claws. Maetrus had turned his fire against his own allies, breaking the Mantis Warrior formation in two by joining his guns with those of the Star Phantoms and breaking open a corridor for their drop-pods. And Neotera had only been able to bellow his disbelief at this insubordination and treachery – he had not seen the truth even then. In the heat of the battle, Maetrus had offered no explanation but had simply said that he 'trusted that Master Neotera would do the same.' Finally, when Lord Huron's own cruiser punched out of the atmosphere and cut through the Exorcists' blockade,

Neotera had watched with slowly dawning understanding as Maetrus threw the *Tortured Soul* into pursuit and charged into the Maelstrom with guns blazing in the tyrant's wake. It was then, and only then, that Neotera understood what he had done. The horror had been beyond his capacity to comprehend, as though the galaxy had suddenly collapsed around him, leaving him standing alone and desolate in the ruins. He had fallen to his knees and gazed up into the heavens to see the constant, brilliant light of the Emperor, but he had seen only darkness.

The exit-ramp crashed down to the ground, kicking up a great cloud of dust from the moon's surface. As the mist of dirt billowed around him, Shaidan stood on the ramp and scanned the scene, his doubled-bladed Mantis Staff held vertically in one hand by his side. He had not been back to this place since the forging of his staff in the hidden and half-forgotten furnaces of the moon's core. But this was not the return he had expected.

Beyond the rim of the crater that provided cover for his Thunderhawk, Shaidan could see flashes and streaks of bolter fire and energy discharges. Explosions shuddered through the shifting dust, making the ground ripple like a grey, liquid desert. Giant plumes of powder erupted into the thin atmosphere, obscuring the stars, marking impacts over the tightly arcing horizon. Banks of Space Marines were dug into cover in improvised bunkers to the right, forming a steadfast siege of the obscured Astartes facility in the cave at the foot of the mountain to the left. Above the trenches in the plain, standards of quartered blue and bone shook erratically in the airless atmosphere as the ground trembled beneath them. Icons of the Novamarines' twelve-pointed star were clear to see, proudly and defiantly planted on this husk of a moon orbiting Badab Prime.

As his gunship had descended towards the moon, Shaidan had quickly identified the heavily camou-flaged entrance to the cave, which had long ago been blown into one of the volcanoes that peppered the surface of the perpetually dark side of the moon. Despite the efforts of the Astral Claws to keep the location of their base hidden, Shaidan's keen eyes could detect the dull red light and the constant wisps of heat that seeped out of the cave mouth. The tunnels ran straight through to a lattice of magma chambers, from which the base and the mine beneath it had drawn its power for centuries, and then down into the bowels of the moon and the now-abandoned mines. The Mantis Librarian could remember the labyrinth of red-shadowed passage-ways from all those years before. And now a barrage of fire hailed in and out of the cave mouth, trans-forming it into a vision of a flame-breathing dragon emerging from the ancient and fiery depths, lighting the entrance to the secret base like a beacon.

Three squads of Mantis Warriors charged out of the Thunderhawk, filing past Shaidan on either side and fanning out to make a line along the lip of the crater. As Shaidan himself stepped off the ramp into the wake of the Space Marines, the engines of the Thunderhawk roared and the gunship pivoted as it rose out of the crater, bringing its main guns around to cover the Mantis Warriors. Great gouts of fire erupted from the Thunderhawk's lascannons and heavy bolters, spraying the ground around the dug-in formations of the siege forces of the Novamarines, forcing them into cover for just long enough for the Mantis Warriors to crest the crater and begin their charge.

As Shaidan clambered over the lip of the crater, with threads of bolter fire searing over his head, he saw the Mantis Warriors already braced into formation. They had come to this little moon for a rendezvous with a detachment of Astral Claw allies, who had assured them that Badab Prime was being virtually ignored by the coalition arrayed against them. Back on the *Tortured Soul*, Captain Maetrus had been characteristically suspicious and had dispatched Shaidan with three heavily armed squads; they would not be caught unaware because of the naïveté or over-confidence of their allies.

For a moment, Shaidan watched the Devastator squad brace themselves in the low gravity for heavy fire from their missile launchers and plasma cannons, throwing force into the mix of shells and las-fire from the Thunderhawk and rendering the makeshift barricades of the Novamarines into banks of flame and raw energy. As the torrent of fury pounded the enemy line, the two Mantis assault squads blasted off the ground, spilling flame from their jump packs as they screeched over the lunar surface, spluttering staccatos of bolter fire and hurling grenades over the barricades into the trenches beyond. In the thin atmosphere, the assault squads seemed to flash with unnatural speed, and they were over the battered siege line in an instant.

But something was wrong. The attack of the Mantis Warriors had been smooth and by the book; they had hit the formation of Novamarines with sudden and overwhelming force, and they might have expected to be mopping up the fringes of the skirmish by now. Instead, there was an eerie quiet in the theatre as the assault squads hovered over the barricades, their bolt pistols silent and their chainswords still holstered.

From his position on the edge of the landing crater, Shaidan could see Sergeant Treomar of the first assault squad drop out of the sky into the unseen trench. A few seconds later, the sergeant reappeared above the barricade, hovering easily, and turned to face Shaidan. The vox-unit in his ear hissed.

'Librarian Shaidan. The trench is deserted. The treacherous Novamarines have fled.'

Shaidan turned on his heel, immediately realising what had happened. 'The mines! This moon is riddled with tunnels just under the surface; they've dropped into the mines!'

Even as he spoke, he saw a great plume of moon dust erupt into the sky from the crater behind him, directly beneath the low-hovering Thunderhawk. A hole opened suddenly in the ground and a squad of Novamarines stormed out, their bolt pistols coughing and their chainswords brandished. As Shaidan spun his force staff and vaulted down into the crater to check their advance, he saw a team of Novamarines, carrying missile launchers, emerging behind the vanguard. Behind them, labouring through the dust, came the trundling weight of a Thunderfire cannon and the elaborate profile of a Techmarine in its wake. Despite himself, Shaidan found himself admiring the execution of the Novamarines' plan.

With just a few strides and one low-grav leap, Shaidan was down amongst the Novamarines. Immediately his Mantis Staff ignited with coruscating force as the Librarian spun it in a smooth arc around him, slicing one of its twin blades through the abdomen of one Space Marine while punching a burst of lightning from his other hand into the helmet of another. The two Novamarines recoiled under the assault, their bodies suddenly sagging as they tumbled backwards in the faint gravity, crashing into their battle-brothers, who brushed them aside and took their place between the Librarian and the emerging Devastator squad.

Meanwhile, the Mantis assault squads roared into view over the edge of the crater, charging back from the abandoned barricades in the plain. They opened fire with their bolt pistols but were unwilling to throw grenades while Shaidan remained engaged. But the Novamarines had moved with great efficiency. The

Thunderfire cannon was firmly planted on its tracks
and its quad-barrels were already fully adjusted,
angled down into the curving walls of the crater. There
was a sudden and abortive blaze from the barrels and
then silence; for a moment it seemed that the cannon
had misfired. But then the ground convulsed and
shuddered, as though the moon were suddenly
wracked with agony, and a huge subterranean
detonation shattered the side of the crater and the
landscape beyond. The lip of the crater crumpled and
collapsed beneath the hovering figures of the assault
squads. Great cracks ripped into the lunar surface
around the Mantis Devastator squad in the plain,
swallowing three Space Marines whole, as clouds of
dust were ejected into the atmosphere and jets of lava
pulsed up from the ruptured magma chambers
beneath the volcanic region.

Under cover of the tremor shells, lines of missiles
streamed out of the Novamarine launchers and
punched into the underbelly of the Mantis Thunderhawk as it banked and pitched in an attempt to get
clear of the crater. The missiles punched relentlessly
into the gunship's armour, one after another slamming into the same spot beneath the engine block.
The armour was not designed for such extreme,
close-range punishment and Shaidan could actually
see the crack open in the adamantium just before
the next flurry of rockets split the armoured panel
away and crashed into the engine.

For a long, agonising second, the Thunderhawk
shook and started to pitch. Tendrils of smoke

escaped from the stern and intensifying flickers of flame started to lick out from between the cracking armoured panels. Then the gunship pitched abruptly and rolled sharply to the side; it lost its altitude in less than a second and crunched into the lunar surface just beyond the crater, smashing down next to the Mantis Devastators. The impact shook the already unstable ground, and the landscape convulsed. After a fraction of a second, the downed Thunderhawk shifted and seemed to settle, but then the ground beneath it collapsed and it fell a hundred metres down into roiling lava streams below, bringing half of the remaining Devastators with it. As it sunk into the pyroclastic flow, the heat finally detonated the engine core, and the Thunderhawk shattered into an explosive ball of fire.

FROM THE BRIDGE of the *Tortured Soul* the atmosphere of Badab seemed to be on fire. The planet blazed like a small star as the oxygen in the ozone layer raged with flame. Captain Maetrus watched the ships that vied for superiority in different levels of orbit. His own cruiser was caught in between two banks of blockades: the defences of the Astral Claws in low orbit, barely above the thermosphere and supported by volleys from ground-based artillery on the planet below, and the siege line of the Exorcists that sought to cut Badab off from the rest of the segmentum. The two massive bulks of tonnage unleashed constant broadsides across the intervening space, lacing the fire-tainted darkness with searing lines of lance-fire and torpedo trails. Rapid strike vessels and destroyers darted through the theatre, manoeuvring around each other and attempting to approach enemy cruisers closely enough to launch boarding actions.

The 1st Company led the reserve companies in the defence of the home world, where battle with the Novamarines and Howling Griffons had been joined. Meanwhile, about half of the dwindling Mantis Warrior fleet had been pulled into the last-ditch defence of Badab, the final stronghold of the rebellion and the seat of Lord Lufgt Huron, Master of the Astral Claws and most loyal servant of the Emperor. The 2nd Company, as usual, was in the vanguard, engaged where the fighting was most fierce. The *Tortured Soul* had been in almost constant battle for the last eight years – Maetrus had been on the bridge when they had captured the *Rapturous Flame* from the Fire Hawks and plunged the Mantis Warriors into war all those years before. But not even this ancient and venerable vessel could withstand the kind of hammering that it was receiving now. The ship's great spirit remained unbroken and determined, but its systems were gradually collapsing under the relentless strain. The decks shuddered with impacts and the halls echoed with bootfalls as servitors and Space Marines strove to control damage and effect repairs. Whole sections of some decks were constantly and irrevocably ablaze, while others had been torn open to the absolute cold of space.

Over the years of battle, most of the ship's components had been cycled through a system of redundancy to ensure that it was always fully functional and able to withstand even the most formidable assault, but now there was nothing left in reserve. A serious hit on the control systems, life support, or even the engine block would leave the glorious ship all but dead.

A new warning light pulsed on the control deck and a siren sounded, unheard amidst the other alerts and noise. Maetrus flicked his eyes away from the fiery planet on the viewscreen and noted the warning. They were being boarded. With the number of gaping holes in the hull, it had only been a matter of time before one of the Exorcist or Star Phantom ships had found a breach through which to deploy a boarding party.

'Sergeant,' muttered Maetrus almost inaudibly, as though the words didn't really need to be spoken, 'take two squads down to the breach and repel boarders. When Librarian Shaidan returns from Badab Prime I'll send him to support you. Now go.'

Sergeant Audin's helmet tilted slightly, indicating his comprehension; then he turned swiftly and marched out of the bridge. As the door slid open a thin gust of smoke and the smell of charred metal wisped onto the deck.

Maetrus turned his attention back to the viewscreen. A formation of frigates was manoeuvring into an intricate assault pattern around the *Piercing Nova*, one of the Astral Claws' strike cruisers. The *Nova* was ill-equipped as part of a defensive blockade and its crew could hardly be accustomed to repelling this kind of battering – Astartes strike cruisers were designed to seize planets, not to hold them. But the Astral Claws had no choice as Badab's planetary defences were gradually being hammered into the ground by the bombardment canons of the besieging coalition.

The battle for Badab was all but over; it was just a matter of time now. There were no supplies or reinforcements coming through the Exorcists' blockade: the Executioners had basically abandoned their posts and fled back to their home world in an attempt to hold it against the vengeance of the Imperium, and the will of the Lamenters had been crushed in an ambush by the Minotaurs nearly four years earlier – they had done the unthinkable and surrendered. The Axis of Badab was shattered; the Mantis Warriors were now Lord Huron's only hope of survival, and Maetrus knew that this faint hope depended on his 2nd Company.

It was the kind of sight that an Adeptus Astartes might dream about. The heavens were full of war, with massive and terrible forces aligned against each other, and nothing but heroism and devotion lay between death and glory. An entire planet lay in ruins, its atmosphere a blazing inferno enwrapped in flaming clouds. In the mire was a desperate last stand, and spiralling around it was an overwhelming and malignant force bent on the destruction of a people, of a Chapter. Maetrus could see little hope of victory in the theatre before him, and he had no intention of seeking a retreat, even if he could somehow escape the immovable line of Exorcists that held the system in isolation. But his mind was no longer engaged in thoughts of victory or defeat. He had not entered this war believing that it could be won, but only believing that it should be fought. Sometimes honour was not about winning, but merely about dying the right way. For him, realised Maetrus, this war had always been about dying. It had been a long and blood-drenched pathway towards his death.

A great, stuttering explosion broke Maetrus's reflection. One of the capital ships of the Star Phantom deployment convulsed and then blew apart, scattering debris and spinning shards of metal through the Astral Claws' faltering line and into the atmosphere of Badab. It was the *Spectre of Fear*, the cruiser to which Maetrus had despatched his last squad of Mantis Religiosa. He had known that they would not return, but had also been certain that they would not die without glory. The death of a strike cruiser was no less of a testament than those devoted Space Marines deserved. The Religiosa had somehow managed to board the hobbled vessel and presumably fought their way to the engine core, where they had probably triggered a critical overload, staying to defend their sabotage until the engine finally blew. It would make no difference to the outcome of the battle.

'Give me a dozen squads of those Space Marines, and I will give you victory in any battle,' he muttered to himself, his eyes glittering with resigned admiration.

'If we gave you a dozen squads of Religiosa, captain, the Mantis Warriors would quickly go extinct.' The response from Shaidan was unexpected.

'Then we must find a way of harnessing that power without losing the minds of our Space Marines to such unquestioning devotion, my friend. Imagine a Religiosa who *returned*. Shaidan, when did *you* return?' asked Maetrus, finally turning on his heel at the unexpected sound of the Librarian's voice.

'This moment, captain. I bring news from Badab Prime.' Shaidan had removed his psychic hood and his long black hair hung loosely over his shoulders. His face was lined with grime and blood, but his piercing green eyes seemed to look into Maetrus's weary soul as he inclined his head to show his respects. He had never seen the captain's spirit so morose.

'I would prefer bad news,' replied Maetrus. 'The battle is on the brink of a spectacular finale, Shaidan. Good news may simply delay something glorious. Unless you have a miracle, give me bad news.'

'My news may have no bearing on the outcome of the battle, captain. But I think you might call it bad news nonetheless.'

Maetrus considered the face of the Librarian before him, old beyond its years and aching with the wisdom of power. 'You will tell me that Huron has surrendered?' He laughed without humour. 'And that he requests his allies to stand down?'

'I bring no such message, captain. Rather, I bring a report.' Shaidan's friendly tone stiffened. 'I rendezvoused with the squad of Astral Claws on a moon of Badab Prime, as you requested, captain. They were right that the Star Phantoms and the Exorcists are now so focused on breaking the defences of Huron's home world that reaching the minor planet should have been relatively simple.'

'Should have been?'

'Yes, captain. You were also right to note that other forces are at work in this theatre. We met with some inconvenience due to a small contingent of Novamarines. They were... persistent.'

'I think we should skip to the point, Shaidan,' mocked Maetrus gently, inclining his head back towards the viewscreen and the raging battle it showed. He liked this Librarian, and saw in his careful manner the promise of high command one day. But not today. 'There are some other things that require my attention today. And you are needed by Audin, who is repelling a boarding party even as we speak.'

Shaidan nodded, seeing the sad mixture of respect and resigned urgency in Maetrus's face. 'Lord Huron's will is unbroken. He will fight until his Chapter is no more.' Despite the need for rapidity, Shaidan paused to collect the correct words. 'Yet the Astral Claws are no longer themselves, captain.'

'No riddles, Librarian. This is not the time.'

'Maetrus, I almost failed to recognise the squad that I had been sent to meet. In place of the proud colours of the Astral Claws, each Space Marine had painted over his armour in random ways, obscuring their Chapter insignia and even covering the Imperial aquila.'

'These were renegades? Deserters?'

'No captain, this was one of the elite squads employed by Huron as his palace guard. This was the squad that he entrusted to rendezvous with me.'

Maetrus stared. 'What are you saying, Shaidan?' There was anger in his voice; his lack of comprehension fuelled his frustration. 'Has all discipline in the ranks collapsed? I cannot believe it.'

'I cannot be sure, captain, but I believe that this is a new discipline. It seems that Huron has instructed his battle-brothers that the Siege of Badab is evidence that the Emperor has forsaken them at last. He claims that the Emperor's gaze has been corrupted by the bureaucrats of the Imperium and that it can no longer differentiate between loyalty and tyranny. Rumours spread that Lord Huron had gouged the aquila from his shoulder, and vowed to continue his fight for truth *for the Emperor,* even if no longer in the Emperor's name. The Space Marines related a rumour that Huron had insisted that since the Emperor could no longer recognise friend from foe, he would demonstrate his loyalty by ending his service to a muddled mind and by showing it the clarity that it has lost. This, he is supposed to have said, would be the ultimate and most selfless kind of service – risking his own damnation to bring the Emperor himself back into the light. Hearing this, it seems that units in the Astral Claws have desecrated their armour in similar – or not so similar – ways.'

Maetrus stared as his mind raced to process the information. Hearsay and stories were always rife during war, and this war had dragged on for a decade, pitting the Astral Claws against the corrupt and hypocritical Imperium of Man itself. He could understand that tensions would be incredibly high within that Chapter, but he had never heard of the will of a Chapter being broken so completely by battle fatigue or stress. For the sake of the Emperor, Space Marines were not mere Guardsmen! The Adeptus Astartes were built for perpetual war; this was their very reason for being. He could not believe that Huron or his Claws had broken. It was simply not possible. They should be relishing the prospect of their glorious and righteous deaths, not bleating about being forsaken.

Unless… hesitated Maetrus, unless Huron knows that he's wrong.

As soon as the thought hit him, he felt the power of its truth. Huron *is* wrong. And he *knows* that he is wrong. He has deliberately misled us for his own self-serving ends. He has… Maetrus could hardly finish the thought. He has turned us against the Emperor! And we *believed* him… We were too credulous to see the truth – we wanted to help this Chapter, in whom we thought we saw something of ourselves, striving for perfection in a galaxy that misunderstood and feared us. We mistook them for us, and so lost ourselves forever. And Huron knew what he was taking from us. He knew, and he took our souls without even the decency to reveal his claws. Even the agents of Chaos have more honour than this kind of power-mongering and politicking; at least they have the decency to tempt you with the promise of supernatural power.

Suddenly it was all very clear and unambiguous, and Maetrus realised that this rebellion had never felt right to him. He had assumed that the sinking terror in his heart had simply been because of the way that the war was tearing the segmentum apart, but now he realised that the horror was more simple and direct: the rebellion was wrong.

'Captain?' asked Shaidan, watching Maetrus's face gradually set into fury.

'Librarian, you will assist with the repulsion of the boarding party. You should know, however, that if either you or Sergeant Audin wish to avert a mutiny, you will need to be back on the control deck in less than ten minutes to commit your own.'

'You will inform Master Neotera before you act, captain?' Shaidan's question was formal and procedural, as though he were simply going through the motions. The observance of protocol calmed his spirit, which roared for action. His soul felt the perfect righteousness of Maetrus's decision, in a way that it had not felt for a decade.

'Of course.' Maetrus's gaze was level. His fury had settled into a fierce resolve.

'Then we will return to receive further orders once the boarding party has been destroyed, captain.'

With that, Librarian Shaidan nodded curtly and turned to leave. Spinning his ornate, double-bladed force-staff in his hand he marched from the bridge without a backward glance.

'Ruinus!'

An attentive Space Marine stepped forward from his position guarding the doors to the control deck.

'Captain?'

'You heard Librarian Shaidan's report, sergeant?'

'Yes, captain.'

'You will understand that I need to get a message to the Chapter Master. I do not require a response, and there is no time to wait for one. I trust that you will transmit my communication in due time?' Maetrus eyed him carefully.

'Yes, captain. Of course.' There was no flicker of doubt. Maetrus even thought he saw a flash of relief and pride, as though a painful and debilitating wound had suddenly been healed.

'Inform Master Neotera that the *Tortured Soul* will be turning its guns against the Astral Claws imminently. Request no permission and ask no pardon, but please explain that I trust he would do the same in our position. Indeed, I trust he will do the same.'

Neotera turned away from Ruinus. 'Sergeant Soron! Train the starboard weapons batteries onto the *Piercing Nova* and prepare the bombardment cannon to hit the planetary defences. We are going to make this into the right death if it is the last thing we do.'

* * *

As THE THUNDERHAWK exploded, the ground in the crater began to crumble away. Shaidan strode forward over the faltering dust, pushing into the squad of Novamarines that clustered around their heavy weapons in the heart of the crater, trying to defend their retreat back down into the subterranean tunnels and mineshafts of the ageless moon. His Mantis Staff blazed with green, phosphorescent venom, reminiscent of the lethal aura of the Hottentota itself. He lashed and stabbed with the glorious weapon, pushing it through plates of blue and bone power armour in a fury of indignation, righteousness and vengeance. As he advanced through bolter fire and lashing chainswords, he muttered an ancient machine curse, spitting his thoughts towards the Thunderfire cannon just as it teetered clumsily back into the tunnel. It seemed to pause and twitch, as though it had been slighted by the insult. The Techmarine behind it snapped his head around as though struck. And then the cannon simply stopped, whining to a halt in the mouth of the Novamarines' escape route.

As his assault squads dropped down into a semicircle around the far side of the crater, forming an enveloping firing line on the more stable ground of that bank, Shaidan took aim and launched his staff like an ethereal javelin, sending it searing through the remnants of the Novamarine squad and piercing into the great barrel of the Thunderfire cannon. There was a flash and the inaudible crackle of an unspeakable energy discharging, and then the cannon exploded, radiating superheated shrapnel and high-explosive shells like a giant scattergun. The remaining Novamarines took the full force of the detonation, and the Techmarine who had been tending to the cannon was all but incinerated in the blast. The escape tunnel, the Novamarines' only path out of the crater, collapsed completely.

As the Novamarines finally fell under the disciplined volleys of bolter fire from the assault squads, Shaidan focused his thoughts for a moment of quickening and seemed to flash across the disintegrating crater in a blur of emerald light. A moment later, he was lifting his unblemished Mantis Staff out of the ruins of the cannon, and the next he was back across the crater before the last standing Novamarine.

The Mantis assault squads ceased fire and all eyes turned to Shaidan as he stood imperiously before the defeated foe. The Novamarine before him wore the insignia of a veteran sergeant, and his armour was scored with the evidence of countless battles. He stood with proud defiance before the Mantis Librarian, meeting his eerie, emerald gaze through the implacable shield of his helmet's visor.

Shaidan inspected him, a faint psychic light flickering around the nodes in the hood that covered the back of his head. The Wars of Badab, the Liberation Wars as they were known to the righteous, had cost the Astartes so many lives. He had killed countless of the Adeptus himself, and he had seen so many of his sacred brethren fall. Yet he found it hard to believe that any of the Adeptus Astartes could take this lightly or find any joy in their victories. Every victory meant the loss of valuable gene-seed and each death was a cut in the flesh of the Emperor himself.

Yet, it was a consequence of the nature of the Astartes that battles rarely resulted in prisoners. It was not that Space Marines lacked mercy or compassion – indeed, the Mantis Warriors prided themselves on their compassionate natures – but rather they lacked the will to surrender. No matter what the odds or the chances of survival, a Space Marine found his very being in fighting. Without the fight, how could he demonstrate his devotion to duty, and without duty a Space Marine was nothing, perhaps worse. Compassion was for others; for the self there was nothing.

So, Shaidan inspected the last of the Novamarines on Badab Prime with interest, quite willing to accept his surrender, but fully prepared for the likelihood that this sergeant would still believe he could win some kind of victory, despite the dozen or so guns trained on him and the magnificent Librarian standing before him.

The Librarian gazed into the Space Marine's eyes, seeing straight through the opaque visor of his helmet as though it weren't even there. He saw no fear and no desperation. There was no frantic scheming for an escape. The gaze was level and calm, and the eyes shone with deepest sincerity. But there was also something else: this sergeant hated him. He was repulsed by the Mantis Warriors, as though they represented something horribly corrupt and disgusting. For a fraction of a second, Shaidan recoiled from the force of the hatred, shocked to see it in the eyes of one of the Astartes. Composing himself, the Librarian probed a little further, reaching through a null zone into the sergeant's thoughts, where he found unending stories of the horrors and perversions perpetrated by the Astral Claws and their allies in this war. The sergeant felt that the Emperor was on his side.

Shaidan nodded to the sergeant, understanding his reasons, misguided by the lies of war as they may have been, and he turned his back on the Space Marine. In that instant, the Novamarine snatched his bolt pistol from its holster and squeezed a shell into the Librarian's back.

But Shaidan was gone before the shell could impact. With the lightning speed of the quickening, the Librarian flashed out of sight. The first the sergeant knew of where Shaidan had gone was when he felt the burning cold of the twin-bladed Mantis Staff slice effortlessly through the back of his neck. Instinctively, the Novamarine tried to turn to face his foe. Even as the twin blades severed his spinal column he managed to twist the grip of his bolt pistol around and fire one last shot. As his head fell to the ground, the shell punched through his own armour and abdomen and cracked into Shaidan's chest plate, where it stuck, lacking the power to break through another layer.

As the sergeant's crimson life spilled into the grey lunar dust at his feet, Shaidan could feel his surprise and gratitude. The Novamarine had not expected such honour, and his death was sullied by his own sudden but deep-seated doubt. For his part, Shaidan mourned the fact that one of the Astartes could expect so little from the Mantis Warriors.

How has it come to this?

The vox-bead in his ear hissed suddenly. 'Mantis Warrior. We have been expecting you.'

Shaidan looked up to the rim of the crater and saw a contingent of Space Marines assembling, silhouetted against the starry sky. He looked over to Sergeant Treomar on the wall of the crater, who nodded an acknowledgement and signalled that these were the Astral Claws they had been sent to meet. But his signal seemed hesitant, as though he were not immediately sure who the newcomers were.

'It is good of you to join us, Astral Claw,' replied Shaidan as he climbed towards his hosts. He wondered why the Claws had neither warned nor helped them, but it was not the way of the Mantis Warriors to complain or reprimand, and certainly not to suggest that they would have benefited from assistance in a battle that they had already won without it. 'Your timing is impeccable, friend,' the Librarian said sarcastically.

'We have much to discuss, Librarian,' came the voice again. 'And time is short.'

As Shaidan climbed out of the crater he got his first clear look at the Space Marines of the Astral Claws. Despite himself, he stared at them with disbelief. They were arrayed before him in the great

splendour of the ancient armour of the Adeptus
Astartes, which glinted like multi-coloured jewels in
the starlight. And yet there were too many colours.
The splendid golds and blacks of the House of
Huron, about which Maetrus had told him so much
after his visit to the Palace of Thorns, were obscured
and hidden, peeking furtively out from beneath
gaudy daubs of colour, blacks and crude, bloody patterns of red. They were like the perverted progeny of
Astartes and eldar Harlequins, if it were not heretical
even to imagine such things. And even stranger,
Shaidan could see that the Imperial aquila had been
prised off the armour of some and obscured or desecrated on others.

He stood on the very brink of the collapsing crater,
looking between the detachment of bizarre Astral
Claws and the honourable corpses of the Novamarines that littered the dissipating lunar dust. He
could feel Sergeant Treomar and the assault squads
shifting uneasily, as though unsure about the next
move. They were tense and ready for anything.

'Yes, time is short, friend,' said Shaidan at last, 'and
I can see that you must have a great deal to report to
us. First, you will permit us to reclaim the gene-seed
of our fallen brethren, then we will talk.' He nodded
over towards the mouth of the cave that held the
base they had been trying to reach, and he winced
when he saw that the double-headed eagle carved
into the rock above the cave had been decapitated.
'We will also thank you if you can spare a Thunderhawk or other transport for our voyage back to the

fleet. I'm sure Captain Maetrus and the Chapter Master will be eager to hear my report.'

'MASTER NEOTERA, THIS council need hide nothing from you, and we should tell you that we are fully aware of the events of the war that you unleashed on this sector. You need not trouble yourself to tell us the details of how you finally surrendered before the gathered might of the Novamarines, the Exorcists and Star Phantoms after the Lamenters had crumbled against the Minotaurs, how you routed the Marines Errant on Kalibus IV, how you miraculously escaped the formations of the Salamanders at the Siege of Corusil, or even how you managed to capture the *Rapturous Flame* from the Fire Hawks back in 904. We do not need this information from you – it is already a matter of record. The gaps, such as they are, can be filled in by any number of observers. We do not ask for a confession of these acts, for they are undeniable. The blood has been spilled, the Space Marines have been slaughtered, and whole planets have been ravaged. All at your command. We do not seek denials or descriptions.

'What we cannot judge is *why*. What we require of you is *explanation*. What did you seek to achieve? Why would you desert the light of the Emperor and forge an allegiance with this Tyrant of Badab? And what could have driven you to launch those first attacks against the Fire Hawks, knowing that such acts would drag the Legions into the kind of war unknown since the Heresy itself? Even Huron himself dared not strike at his fellow Space Marines – it was only with you that the petty insurgency became a war. How were you convinced to turn away from the honour and devotion of the Astartes? What kind of promises could buy the soul of Khoisan Neotera, Chapter Master of the Mantis Warriors and guardian of the realms of Mordriana and Ootheca?'

What did the cowardly shape-changer offer you, Mantis? Did he promise you a seat at the right hand of a tyrant or liberty from the discipline of the Adeptus? Did he taunt you with the artefacts of his xenos allies, or tempt you with the forbidden knowledge of his corrupted brethren? How did he turn your will against the father of us all, and twist your spirit into treachery? Or would you have us believe that he did nothing… that you were already lost, and that you found a kindred spirit in this Blackheart? Is the great legacy of the Mantis Warriors nothing but an illusion, a cover to hide your own tainted gene-seed? Have you been hiding like cowards for a thousand years, living in pretence and hypocrisy and treating us all like fools? Are you to be damned as well as condemned, Mantis Lord?

'You must *explain*, Neotera. We are not beyond mercy here.' The shadow-veiled words were not without kindness.

Do you not know me at all? The thoughts stayed inside his head. Of course you do not know me. I cannot even recognise myself. I have no answers to your questions, and I would offer none even if they burned like firebrands in my mind. We are beyond these words and reasons now. Deeds are done; we must be measured by them just as we must be held to account for them. How can you taunt me with the *threat* of mercy? Do you think I want your mercy or your forgiveness? Do you think I can go on knowing what I have done, what I have allowed myself to do? Your mercy mocks me and offends yourselves; do not belittle us all with this kind of talk. I am undeserving of your kindness, and you should know even the Emperor in His infinite wisdom would offer me nothing less than condemnation. In the fall, there is only flame and sword. Speak your judgement and rid yourselves of me.

'I seek no mercy.' Barely more than a breath, he wasn't sure if he had spoken the words out loud, yet they wisped around the hall like the scent of poison.

Ah, the silent Mantis speaks after all. Venom was laced through the disembodied thoughts; they ridiculed him, as if certain that he would be broken. *We just offer you a little selfish hope and your resolve shatters. Mercy and treachery are such an exquisite pair. Did Huron offer you mercy? Did you hear the whispered echoes of Horus himself, offering to bring you back into his fold? Was this all it took, feeble-minded insect? Can your soul be bought for a little mercy?*

I seek no mercy, he repeated in his mind, clenching his jaw in the agony of self-betrayal. He had not meant to speak, but his resolve was so powerful and consuming that it had vocalised almost by itself. *I seek no mercy* – the thoughts spiralled around inside his head like a mantra, and just once in three days had they leaked out into the air. It was as though he were becoming the words; he was giving them physical meaning through the remains of his life.

Yet see how easily even those four brief words could be twisted and contorted. Their purity was sullied and despoiled as soon as they left his mouth. Before they had even reached the ears of his judges, their psychic resonance had already been distorted by the noxious mind of the nameless Librarian who wanted nothing more than for the Mantis Warriors to fall into the abyss, to leave them dishonoured and desecrated by the judgement of history. There was genuine hatred in that mind, and it oozed toxically into Neotera's head. The Chapter Master could feel a hunger for profit and spoils in those psychic intrusions, and he realised that not all of his judges were here for vengeance, justice, or knowledge; some were in pursuit of ships and worlds.

'So you are unrepentant, Neotera?'

Even the voices of reason misunderstood him. How could they find him unrepentant when his very being screamed in torment at his deeds? If only he could take back those four simple words and let his devoted silence remain unbroken. But the words could not be revoked, no more than the actions that had brought him to this place. Words could not explain what he had done, and any words that he uttered would only pervert even further the faith that remained in his heart; they would be twisted and tortured until they no longer resembled themselves and he could not see truth from lies. He knew when his choices had been made, and it was becoming clear to him that he had been wrong for many years. But he knew – deep in his soul he knew – that his intentions had been pure.

Intentions are nothing. A servant is judged by his deeds. I seek no mercy. I offer no words and no excuses. I stand ready to bear the unendurable.

THE PALACE OF Thorns was everything that they had been led to expect. It was the ostentatious seat of power on the home world of a proud Space Marine Chapter, full of the pomp and regalia of military exploits and glory. Great statues towered over the gates and reached their arms into arches over vaulted ceilings. Ornate frescoes filled the walls, depicting the most awesome and legendary victories of the Astral Claws: the Purification of the Badab system itself, the Scouring of Tesline, and the Reclamation of Mundus IV. The Chapter Master's honour guard stood sentinel in the corridors and halls, resplendent in their radiant gold and black striped ceremonial armour, like majestic tigers surveying their realms. And the Imperial aquila, the universal sign of devotion and loyalty to the Emperor, held pride of place on each of the grand spires that pushed up towards the heavens.

The contingent of Mantis Warriors was unfazed by the grandeur as they swept through the corridors on their way to the throne room. Their own fortress monastery on Ootheca was no less glorious, and even the jungle palace of Mordriana III could inspire awe. However, their delegation to Badab was understated. Four squads of Space Marines acted as honour guards for a command squad of unusual austerity and gravity: the Chapter Master himself strode through the hallways of the Palace of Thorns. His guards shone in emerald battle armour, polished to the point of ceremonial splendour, yet they moved with the kind of focused caution that spoke of veiled distrust. As a special token of good faith, Lord Huron had permitted them to enter his palace fully armed; and not quite willing to return the confidence, the Mantis Warriors had taken full advantage of his offer. On the landing field beyond the gates, a group of deep green Mantis Thunderhawks held heavy reinforcements.

On their approach to the Badab system, the Mantis Warriors had seen for themselves the evidence of Huron's recent activities. They had heard the rumours and reports, but seeing the evidence gave the official accounts of insurgency and revolt more power and resonance. The adjoining space-lanes were littered with debris and the ruined masses of raided freighters, damaged beyond salvage or repair. Before they had agreed on the rendezvous on Badab, Huron had warned them what they might see and how it might appear to them. He had not sought to deny anything, but had invited the Mantis Warriors to bear witness to the facts.

He had explained that many of the apparently civilian ships had been unmarked, covert Imperial gunships, sent to spy on the Badab system. He claimed that he had discovered that such ships were normal parts of all mercantile convoys to Adeptus Astartes controlled systems, and he had challenged them to forcefully inspect the shipping lanes around their own system of Ootheca if they doubted him. He argued calmly that there were powerful factions in the Imperium that hated and distrusted the Astartes, jealous of their intimacy with the spirit of the Emperor and their resemblance of his body. These factions were now in the ascendant at the Terra-bound end of Segmentum Ultima, where fear of the Maelstrom mixed with distrust of the glory of the Astartes to produce officiousness and insidious suspicion. Huron had told Master Neotera that the Mantis Warriors were also being watched.

As the *Venomous Blade* had cut its way into the outskirts of the Badab system, Neotera had seen the torn prow of an Imperial light cruiser tumbling through the wreckage of a group of freighters. In amongst the debris, he could see the twisted remains of weapons batteries and the charred icon of the aquila. It seemed that Huron was telling the truth about the presence of the Imperium's eyes in this sector.

On the edge of the star-system, the *Blade* had registered a wide spread of signals on its long-range scanners. A fleet of battleships was assembling in the interstellar space between Badab and Rigant. Most of the signatures were too indistinct to be accurately discerned, but those at the vanguard had the solid and menacing echo of Space Marine strike cruisers and frigates. The unusual shape of the *Rapturous*

Flame, the legendary Fire Hawks strike cruiser that had survived the destruction of the Chapter's home world of Zhoros more than five millennia before, was at the heart, as the formation slowly shifted and manoeuvred. They were less than a warp-jump away, but probably several days under normal power. They were waiting for something, and their presence suggested that their attention was fixed on Badab. Perhaps Huron's paranoia was not without substance? Would the Imperium really send Space Marines against their own again? What kind of Chapter would heed such a call?

In one of his first communiqués, before the trouble had exploded into bloodshed in the region of Sfantu, Huron had asked Neotera about the frequency with which the Mechanicus demanded a sample of Mantis Warrior gene-seed. At first, Neotera had not understood why another Chapter would request such information; it had seemed disrespectful to the point of being insulting. He had been suspicious of Huron's motives, and then fearful that rumours about the Mantis Legion were spreading to neighbouring systems. Captain Maetrus of the 2nd Company, the Prophet Captain as he was known, had cautioned many times about the suspicions that could be raised about the Chapter if the mental state of the Mantis Religiosa were to be misunderstood as some kind of genetic anomaly. Maetrus was especially concerned that the condition, which sometimes enhanced a Space Marine's reflexes to such an extent that they seemed to develop mild precognitive abilities, might appear to represent the spontaneous onset of psychic tendencies. Given the proximity of the Mantis Warriors' realm to the Maelstrom and the conditions of constant internecine war on some of its core systems, such as Mordriana, it was not beyond imagination that the Mechanicus would seek to police their gene-seed even more vigorously than that of other Chapters. Yet Maetrus was adamant that the condition was a normal state of mind, and was determined to develop a training programme that would enable all Mantis Warriors to harness this natural ability.

In any case, Neotera had not been willing to share information about the frequency contact from the Mechanicus until Huron had openly admitted that he had made a decision not to submit the gene-seed of the Astral Claws for inspection any more. He had spoken passionately about the ways in which the Mechanicus had lost their legitimacy when they had reinterpreted themselves as a form of genetic police, monitoring the Astartes and holding over them the threat of disestablishment should they fail to meet some arbitrary criteria. Huron had called this oppression. He had labelled it as an evil against the spirit of the Emperor – nobody had ever monitored the Emperor's genetic make-up to try and restrain his development. The Imperium needed the free development of the Astartes, just as it had once needed the free development of the Emperor to give it form, whether it was willing to admit this or not.

Even worse, Huron had attempted to convince Neotera that there were corrupt Space Marine Chapters that knew of this agenda, and which sought to exploit it for their own selfish advancement. He worried that the Imperium was not above turning these lackey Space Marines against their fellow Adeptus Astartes, turning one Chapter against another in a horrible civil war in order to prevent the truth being realised. With barely disguised disgust, Huron had named the Ultramarines and the Imperial Fists, with their intimate ties to the Administratum, as the most likely to turn against the most free-thinking Chapters – those that held the true legacy of the Emperor in their genes.

Neotera had listened to Huron with a mixture of horror and empathy. His words were not without truth – the Mantis Warriors knew the angst and insecurity of dark secrets, like many other Chapters – but he did not dare to trust them. However, the presence of the Fire Hawks just beyond the Badab system seemed to confirm Huron's suspicions.

And now, as the heavy, illuminated doors to the throne room pushed slowly open, Neotera stood before Lufgt Huron himself for the first time. The Chapter Master sat on the far side of the hall, raised on a dais and seated in the most elaborate throne Neotera had ever seen. Fanned out behind him were the twelve Space Marines that comprised his personal guard, each holding their bolters formally across their chest-plates. Along each side of the long room, arrayed as though for inspection, were twin lines of Space Marines in full battle armour. The chamber was brilliant with gold and black.

Neotera paused in the doorway, genuinely admiring the awesome scene. His pause slowly lengthened into a hesitation as he calculated the mass of firepower that was assembled before him and weighed it against the reports of Huron's insurrection. Despite the evidence en route to the planet, Neotera was not quite convinced that he could trust this Huron, the alleged Tyrant of Badab. But behind him were assembled the finest thirty Mantis Warriors from the 1st and 2nd Companies, veterans and heroes all, and Neotera knew that they would not be cowed by this attempt at intimidation. However, he also realised that this display of power effectively nullified any 'trust' that Huron had claimed to show by permitting them to enter his palace armed for battle.

'Chapter Master Khoisan Neotera, Master of the Mantis Warriors and guardian of the realms of Mordriana and Ootheca, I bid you welcome to my hall.' Huron rose as he spoke, his formal words echoing slightly in the high room, and started down the steps of the podium, as though to meet Neotera on the level floor. 'I am grateful that you made the journey. Communications are insecure, and it is no longer easy for me to travel far out of this system, as you will appreciate.'

'Master Huron,' acknowledged Neotera with less exaltation, 'your reception honours us.' He strode across the marbled floor while the rest of the Mantis Warriors fell into line behind him.

'We have much to discuss, Khoisan,' began Huron as they faced each other and bowed slightly, his eyes burning with a deep and hidden light. 'Grave matters of concern for the whole Imperium. The salvation of our brother Astartes rests in our hands – we are the Emperor's last hope. Can I count on you, brother?'

NEOTERA WAS NO longer sure how much time had passed. He was beginning to feel the effects of sleep deprivation; his head felt heavier than usual, as though he were concussed, and his thoughts moved like wraiths through smoke. He was not tired, but over the years he had learned to recognise the slight hazing of his mind as the activity of his catalepsean node as it shifted his fatigued consciousness around his brain to keep him functioning without sleep. Judging by the mist that had settled over his thoughts, like the dust that was gathering on the shoulders of his armour, he had been standing on the aquila for nearly seven days. He had not moved in that time, and he could only recall speaking four ill-judged words. His mind was full of the questions and accusations of the council of judges – their persistent and powerful siege of his psyche had gradually permeated his staunch resolve, and he could feel a dizziness caused by the internalisation of his interrogators' combination of malice and mercy. But he knew that he could not break, not again.

The questions had thrown his thoughts back into reflection, and he had lost himself in the past for a while. But for how long? And how many of his thoughts could the judges see? Were they simply prodding his mind into recollection and then watching his thoughts betray him? There were certainly a number of powerful Librarians in the shadows amongst the faceless judges, but Neotera was not attuned enough to know exactly what might be the dimensions of their powers. Perhaps his resolve not to speak was serving no purpose after all. Perhaps the council could recover the answers it sought without the crassness of language. But then why ask the questions? Why go through the motions of a trial if they could simply empty his brain and sift through his memories themselves?

Unless it was a test. They wanted to see what he would say, whether he would crack, how he would attempt to justify himself, and then measure his words against the inner voice of his soul. Did he believe his own words? Was there deceit in his heart? Did he seek to excuse himself or to blame others? Was there any honour left in him, even after all the horrors he had perpetrated on the galaxy, even after he had violated his most sacrosanct oaths of loyalty?

But he had said nothing. Just those four words: I seek no mercy. He had not tried to *explain*. Although, he knew, his mind had been racing constantly, questing for answers to the questions they posed, for the questions were his own as well: how had it come to this? Did they have the answers? Had they managed to discern the truth from his fevered reflections? Could they *explain* it to him? He needed to know as much as they did. More. For it was his soul that was falling into the inferno, not theirs.

If they could see into his mind, he should be told. He needed to know. He deserved to know. His soul screamed for the knowledge.

How did it come to this? I deserve to know. The thoughts hissed out, like gas from a cracked tank.

You deserve nothing, Mantis Lord.

The bitter thoughts mocked his indignation and seeped with disgust. But he knew that they were right: he deserved nothing. His protests, although intended only for his own thoughts and not for the minds of the council, were unworthy of him and the Librarian's derision was fully justified.

Once again, the pain of self-betrayal wracked his soul, vying with the bottomless horror of his treachery against all that he held to be true and just. It was unbearable, yet he endured. He wasn't even sure that he recognised himself anymore. How had it come to this? How had *he* come to this?

A heavy grinding sound told him that the main doors to the hall were sliding open. Keeping his eyes directly ahead, he traced the movement of footfalls as they fanned out into the shadows of the vaulted ceiling around the edge of the chamber. As far as he was aware, this was the first time that the door had opened and anyone had entered or left since the hearing began. But, he realised, he could not even be sure of this petty little fact – he had lost faith in the integrity of his mind. Was he actually being driven mad? Had he been mad from the start? Had he ever truly been loyal to the Emperor?

'Khoisan Neotera, Chapter Master of the Mantis Warriors and guardian of the realms of Mordriana and Ootheca, this council finds you guilty of the most terrible crimes imaginable to the Imperium of Man.' The voice, deep and raw and unused to diplomacy, washed over Neotera like a dark tide. The horror of its words soothed him like a balm: he was guilty; he would not be forgiven. The relief was real and almost physical.

'You have plotted against the light of the Emperor Himself. You have spilt the blood of His most loyal servants, and you have brought Chaos into the very heart of our Empire. You have offered no defence of your actions, no explanations of your deeds, and you have asked for no leniency. It was the intention of this council that you should be executed for your crimes, and that your gene-seed should be cast into the void. In addition, we intended to dismantle the Mantis Legion, to strip your Space Marines of their armour and weapons, to quarantine your home world of Ootheca, and to condemn the remaining Mantis Warriors to live as servitors, rebuilding the worlds that they have destroyed.'

The voice paused, and Neotera could feel a dozen pairs of eyes studying him. He did not flinch or even blink. He bit down on his jaw and focused his mind on the words: he needed to be clear-headed to hear the verdict and he realised that there was more to come. There was a sudden and sinking panic that the judge would revoke his condemnation, and then a shock that he was feeling panic for the first time in his life, since the Blood Trials on Ootheca when he was first inducted into the Mantis Warriors. What had become of him? Had his treachery really pushed him into madness?

We will take Ootheca, insect lord. Your kind will never pollute its forests again. Now it is mine. The unidentified thoughts were faint and torn, as though shredded by malice. Even in his fevered state, Neotera could sense the presence of a self-serving spite once again.

'And yet, Khoisan, there are those on this council who do not believe that your silence shows a lack of repentance. Some who do not find your bearing arrogant. Some, indeed, who believe that your egregious deeds were not motivated by hatred or self-interest, but rather that you were misled by the cunning of others.'

The words seemed like flames. What were they saying? Were they trying to find a way to save him after all? Did they really retain the faith in him that he had even lost in himself? They had used his personal name – nobody had called him Khoisan for over a hundred years. Did they seek to show *affection* to him?

I am a Mantis Warrior. I need no love from you. I seek no mercy. The thoughts whispered desperately through his mind.

'Nonetheless, Chapter Master,' came another voice, 'your actions speak eloquently and terribly for themselves. In the end, your intentions do not concern us, except in so far as they help us to understand how one such as you might be turned so completely from the light. And you have offered us no help in that regard.'

I seek no mercy.

'Mantis Master,' came yet another voice, the female voice of an inquisitor or Sister Sororitas, 'it is the opinion of this council that the Mantis Warriors are not beyond salvation – that they followed dutifully and loyally the commands of their Master, and that their Master was himself convinced that his commands were in accord with the will of the Emperor. The Chapter shall be excommunicated for one hundred years, during which time we expect that they will demonstrate penitence and loyalty enough to be brought back into the sight of the Emperor. As for Ootheca, Mantis Lord, it will never again give birth to your kind – it is yours no longer. The rights of the Mantis Warriors to that place are forfeit forever; should they survive their penitence, they must begin again elsewhere. They must seek rebirth as well as redemption.'

It is mine.

Neotera's gaze did not waver and he said nothing. An image of the great fortress monastery of Ootheca flickered through his mind, engulfed in an inferno of flames as the emerald banners of the Mantis Legion turned to cinders and blew away in the wind. The loss of his home world tortured his soul, piercing to the very foundation of his almost-forgotten humanity. Yet it was not a terminal end; he could see through the conflagration of horror to the tiniest glimmer of hope that survived the flames. Despite himself, the redemption of his loyal battle-brothers brought him profound relief and happiness. Barely perceptibly, a single tear trickled slowly over the scar on his cheek.

I seek no mercy. For myself, nothing. I seek no mercy. Already this is too much.

But then there is you, Mantis. Even if you were deluded and confused, like a civilian fool being tempted into Chaos with promises of riches, of power, or of fame, then you are little more than a despicable excuse for an Astartes, with a pathetic will and a clouded mind. Your credulity offends the Emperor. His light is not ambiguous or unclear – it is brilliant, pristine and untarnished by doubts or interpretations. Even if you are not evil by intent, your naïveté provides a space for it to grow. This is worse: you make others do evil unknowingly. Your leadership is what dragged your brothers into this war and turned them against themselves. In the end, even the devoted Captain Maetrus mutinied against you.

Consider this, Mantis Lord, your judgement tore your entire Chapter from the fold. You mutinied against the Emperor Himself – this is more than mutiny, it is heresy. And then your most celebrated captain mutinied against you. Civil wars within civil wars. How should we interpret these actions? Should we see Maetrus as evidence that there is yet integrity in your Chapter, despite his disappearance? Or should we conclude that credulity is a flaw in the gene-seed of the Mantis Warriors as a whole? Are you genetically untrustworthy, Mantis? Do you have any place in the Imperium of Man? Can the Emperor gaze on you with anything other than pity, derision, or disgust?

'You will not be executed, Master Neotera.' The voice seemed somehow familiar, but Neotera's mind was reeling with such nausea after the psychic charges that he could not call a name to mind. And now the vocalised words struck horror into his heart. A terrible despair sank upon him, as though a world had fallen onto his shoulders. Were they going to offer him mercy?

'You will be stripped of your armour and imprisoned in the Penitentiacon. There you will live out your life in darkness and isolation. You will have no distractions from your own conscience, and you will find the truth of your treachery or you will die without ever understanding it.'

Neotera's mind staggered. The world fell onto his shoulders and crushed him through the aquila at his feet. His constant and resolute gaze began to swim, before he pulled his will together though sheer self-discipline and screaming anguish. He gritted his teeth against the horror of disbelief: he would not be executed for his deeds, but how could he go on living like this?

You asked for no mercy. We offer you none.

ORPHANS OF THE KRAKEN

Richard Williams

I AM NOT yet dead.

I am only on the brink. I cannot tell anymore how long I have been here. My first heart begins its beat. I count the minutes until it finishes and begins again. I clutch at the sound as long as I can. It is my only reminder that I am still alive.

It is not fear that holds me from the edge. I see what is ahead and it welcomes me. But I have made an oath. Until I have held to my word, I cannot allow myself to fall.

THE TYRANID HIVE ship drifted silently in space. I watched it through my window. It was vast and it was an abomination, ugly beyond description, organic but no creation of any natural god. It was also, as best as we could determine, very, very dead.

My name is Brother Sergeant Tiresias of the Astartes Chapter Scythes of the Emperor, and I came here searching for legends.

I command the 21st Salvation Team, and if that sounds like a grand title then let me correct you now. It is not. There were eight of us at the beginning, myself and seven neophytes. Battle-brothers in training, youths, juveniles, children. I am told that they are our future. I know better; we do not have a future.

By that day I had been in their company, and they in mine, for over two years. Our time together had not been easy, nor without loss. The three empty seats beside me were testimony to that. But the three we had left behind had not disappointed me nearly as greatly as the four who remained. They had slunk to the far end of the assault boat, gathered around one of their number who was making some small adjustment to the squad's heavy bolter. They spoke softly, thinking they would not be heard.

'There… I think it'll work better that way.'

'Are you sure, Brother Narro? It is not Codex.'

'Of course he's sure, Hwygir. Who're you going to trust? Your brother here who's been slicing up these vermin as long as you have, or a book written by some hoary old creaker? These bugs weren't even around back then so the codex is as much use as a–'

'Show some respect, Vitellios,' the fourth of them interrupted. 'The sergeant can hear you.'

'Pasan. I tell you, after all he's put us through, I don't give a scrag if he does.'

It had not always been like this. At the start, in our first few insertions, their voices had been full of hope and they had spoken of what we might find. They had repeated the stories they had heard during their training: rumours of Space Marines wearing the insignia of the Scythes still alive inside the tyranid bio-ships; stories of naval boarding parties surrounded, nearly destroyed, before being saved by such warriors who then disappeared back into the depths; stories of bio-ships convulsing and crumpling in the midst of battle, though untouched by any external force. Stories. Legends. Myths.

They believed, though. They fantasised that, in every dead bio-ship we sought, whole companies of Astartes waited. That they had not been annihilated in the onslaught of Hive Fleet Kraken at all. That Hive Fleet Kraken, that almighty judgement upon us which had destroyed fleets and consumed worlds, might have simply overlooked them. And so they had survived, forgotten, until these seven brave neophytes arrived to rescue them and become heroes to the Chapter, and become legends themselves.

Myths. Fantasies. Lies. As I already knew and they, once they stepped aboard a bio-ship for the first time, quickly discovered.

'Ten seconds!' the pilot's voice crackled over the intravox. 'Brace! Brace! Brace!'

I braced. Here we went again. Another legend to chase, another myth to find, another lie to unmask. How many more before we finally accept it? How many more until we finally decide to end it all?

MY WARDS ADVANCED cautiously from our insertion point into the ship. They fell into their formation positions with the ease of long experience. The hivers, the up-spire Narro and the trash Vitellios, took turns on point and edge. The trog savage Hwygir carried the heavy bolter on his shoulder further back as snath. Pasan, one of the few of the neophytes to have been born, as I, on noble Sotha, walked in the tang position to allow him to command.

If our auspices and scanners had not already told us that the hive ship was dead, we would have known the instant we stepped aboard. The corridors were dark; the only light our own torches. As they illuminated our path ahead we could see the skin of the walls sagging limply from its ribs, its surface discoloured and shrivelling. The door-valves gaped open, the muscles that controlled them wasted.

We waded through a putrid sludge. Though it moved like a sewer it was no waste product, it was alive. It was billions of microscopic tyranid organisms, released by the bio-ship at the moment of its death and designed solely to consume the flesh of their dead parent, consume and multiply. More creatures, gigantic to the microbes, tiny to us, floated amongst them, eating their fill, then were speared and devoured by larger cousins who hunted them.

The hive ship was dead, and in death it became filled with new life. Each creature, from the sludge-microbe up, was created to feed and to be fed upon in turn, concentrating the bio-matter of the ship into apex predators that would bound gleefully aboard the next bio-ship they encountered to be re-absorbed and recycled. In this way, the tyranid xenoforms transformed the useless carcass of their parent into another legion of monsters to take to the void. The carcass of their parent, and any other bio-matter foolish enough to have stepped onboard.

'Biters! To the right!' Vitellios called. The lights on the gun barrels swung around in response. I heard the double shot as Vitellios and Pasan fired and then the screech of their target.

'Step back! Step back!' Pasan ordered automatically. 'Narro!'

Scout Narro had his bolter ready and triggered a burst of fire at the creatures. The shells exploded in their midst, bursting their fat little bodies and tossing them to the side.

The shots would alert every active tyranid nearby. Pasan swivelled his shotgun with its torch across the leathery walls of the chamber, searching for more. Vitellios simply blasted every dark corner. There was another screech for his trouble. The Scouts swung their weapons towards the noise, illuminating the target with blazing light.

There was nothing there. The corner was empty. The sludge rippled slightly around the base of the armoured buttress supporting the wall, but that was all.

I waited for Pasan to order Vitellios to investigate. I saw the acolyte's helmet turn to the hiver, his face shining gold from his suit lights. I waited for him to give the order, but he did not. He turned his head back and started to move out of position himself.

'Scout Pasan, hold!' I ordered angrily. 'Scout Vitellios, assess that area.'

Vitellios, expecting the order, stepped forward with a confidence no one in his situation should have. He enjoyed it, though, defying the others' expectations, claiming that places like this reminded him of home. Though having seen myself the lower hive levels on the planet where he was born, I would not disagree.

Vitellios prodded the floor beneath the sludge to ensure it was solid and then stepped right into the corner. He shone his torch up to where the armoured buttress ended just short of the roof.

'Vitellios!' Narro whispered urgently. 'It's moving!'

Vitellios had an underhiver's instincts. He did not question. He did not waste even a split-second to look at the buttress that had suddenly started shifting towards him; he simply ran.

'Hwygir!' he called as he sprinted clear, kicking up a spray of sludge behind him.

Hwygir pulled the trigger on the big gun. The hellfire shell sped across the chamber and smashed into the buttress even as it launched itself at the Scout fleeing away. The sharp needles within the shell plunged into the creature's body, pumping acid, and it spasmed. It tore itself from the wall, revealing the tendrils and sucker-tubes on its underside and collapsed into the sludge, there to be recycled once more.

What it revealed, what it had slowly been consuming, was even more horrific. Three metres high, even collapsed against the wall, was a tyranid monster the size of a Dreadnought. Its skin was armoured like a carapace, its limbs ended in claws like tusks, its face was all the more dreadful for having been half-eaten away.

'Fire!' Vitellios shouted, and he, Pasan and Narro poured a half dozen rounds into the juddering, foetid corpse.

'It is dead already, neophytes. Do not waste your ammunition.' Shaking my head, I rechecked the auspex for the beacon's signal. 'This way.'

I HAD BEGUN with seven neophytes under my command. On the hive ship identified as #34732 *Halisa*, we stumbled across a colony of dormant genestealers and Neophyte Metellian was killed. On #10998 *Archelon*, Neophyte Quintos lost an arm and part of his face to a tyranid warrior corpse that had more life in it than he had assumed. It almost bested me before I caught it with my falx and finally put an end to it. On #51191 *Notho*, Neophyte Varos slipped through an orifice in the floor. When we finally located him in the depths of the ship, he had been crushed to death.

We have inserted into over a dozen dead hive ships now. We Salvation Teams have probably stepped aboard more bio-ships than any other human warrior. Perhaps more than any alien as well. When I speak it is with that experience. For all the vaunted diversity of the tyranid fleet, for all that Imperial adepts struggle to catalogue them into thousands of ship classes; the truth is that once you are in their guts they are all the same: the same walls of flesh, the same valve portals; the same cell-chambers leading to the major arteries leading to the vital organs at the ship's heart.

But for all the now routine horrors I have witnessed within these ships, on occasion they can still surprise me.

'GOD-EMPEROR...' NARRO WHISPERED as he looked out across the expanse.

The beacon had taken us up, but the tubule we followed did not lead into another cell-chamber, nor even into an artery. Instead it dropped away into a cavity so vast that our torches could not reach the opposite wall. At our feet, the sludge slovenly poured over the ledge in an oozing waterfall into the darkness on the floor. To our left, one side of the cavity was filled with a row of giant ovoids; each one as big as, bigger even, than our mighty Thunderhawks. They glistened with a sickly purple sheen as we shone a light upon them. Several of them were split open. One was cracked. Inside, emerging from it, still clenched tight upon itself in a rigor of death, I saw the creature these birthing sacs contained.

Bio-titans.

Bio-titans. Massive war-engines that, even hunched like spiders, towered over our heaviest tanks on the battlefield. Screaming, hideous, living machines bristling with limbs, each one a weapon, which had carved apart so many Imperial lines of defence.

'There... there's another one,' Pasan said and I shone my torch after his. It wasn't just one. The cavity was filled with these monsters, every one collapsed, knocked aside, dead. Their bloated bodies and scything limbs were barely distinguishable from the flesh of the hive ship beneath them.

It was Narro who finally broke the silence.

'Hierophants,' he concluded as he peered at them. 'Immature, judging from their size.'

'You mean these are runts?' Vitellios exclaimed, his usual cocksure manner jolted from him.

'Oh, indeed,' Narro replied, 'certain reports from defence troopers quite clearly–'

'Of course they are, Scout Vitellios,' I interrupted. 'Do not underestimate our foe in the future. Acolyte Pasan, the beacon leads us forwards, organise our descent.'

Pasan stepped along the cliff-face, examining the floor far beneath. The other neophytes watched the path or checked their weapons.

'Honoured sergeant… could you… could you look at this?' Pasan asked me quietly.

Throne! Could this boy not even command as simple a task as this by himself?

'What is it, acolyte?' I said, biting down on my irritation as I went over to him.

'The floor…' He lay down flat and angled his torch to the base of the cavity directly beneath us. 'They look… they're biters, aren't they? It's covered with them.'

I looked; he was right. What appeared to be solid ground was indeed the segmented backs of a thousand biters packed together as though they were crammed in a rations can.

'And what will you do about it, acolyte?'

Pasan hesitated. Vitellios did not.

'We should head back, we can find a way around–'

I cut him off. 'An Astartes does not retreat in the face of common insects, neophyte. He finds a way through.'

I turned back to Pasan and watched the youth think. He finally produced an answer and looked at me for approval. His plan was sound, but still I was unimpressed by his need for my validation.

'What are you waiting for, acolyte? That is your plan, issue your orders.'

'Yes, sergeant. Culmonios, load a hellfire shell and deploy here.'

Hwygir nodded with all the eagerness of one who knows his inferiority and only wishes to be accepted. He had been birthed Hwygir, most certainly on some dirt rock floor on Miral. He had chosen the name Culmonios when he became an Astartes, I found it distasteful to address a stunted savage such as he with such a noble appellation. I used it in speech at first, but I could never bring myself to think it. Only Pasan still used it now.

The trog hefted the bulky heavy bolter to the lip of the ledge.

'He'll need bracing,' Vitellios muttered.

'I was just coming to that,' Pasan replied. 'Vitellios, dig in and brace him. Narro too. Have the next shell ready as soon as he fires.'

Finally I saw something of command coming to Pasan. He organised the squad into a firing team slowly and methodically. He even carved into the tubule wall itself to provide a steadier base to shoot directly down at the floor and strapped the heavy weapon to Hwygir tightly to ensure the recoil at such an awkward angle did not tear it from his hand.

'Fire!' Pasan ordered finally. The squad braced and Hwygir pulled the trigger. 'Reload. Adjust aim. Fire. Reload. Adjust aim. Fire. Reload.' Pasan continued, the squad following along. 'Halt!'

He and I looked over the edge. The flesh scouring acid of the hellfire had eaten into the biters and, without a foe close by, they had scattered away from the wall and started to feed instead on the corpses of the bio-titans, leaving a path clear across the cavity. It was as I had expected.

What I had not expected was what had now been revealed, the food on which the biters had been feasting. I looked down, my throat tight in horror, at the field of damaged and pockmarked power armour now on display, black and yellow like my own. The feast had been my brothers.

I HAD ONLY ever seen such a sight before in my dreams, my nightmares of Sotha's destruction. I was there at the fall, but I did not witness the worst of it. By the time our last lines were being overrun, I was already aboard a Thunderhawk, unconscious, my chest and legs a mess of cuts and bio-plasma burns. A sergeant had pulled me from the barricade as I fell, thrown me upon an exhausted ammo-cart returning for fresh supplies and then stepped back into the battle. None who survived knew my rescuer's name.

I do not know how I made it from the ammo-cart onto one of the escaping Thunderhawks. I do remember how the Thunderhawk spiralled and dropped as it desperately sought to dodge through the rain of landing spores still pouring down, now unopposed, upon my home. I was awake in time to feel the last tug of Sotha's gravity upon me as we left it to be consumed by our foe, and to know that we had failed our holy duty.

WE CLEARED THE bio-titan birthing cavity of the biters and lesser xenoforms. It took nearly a full day, with the mysterious beacon still a steady pulse upon our auspex, but it had to be done. This place was no longer a simple obstacle to be surmounted in our larger search; it was sacred ground. We called back to the boat and ordered our retainer workers despatched to join us. When they arrived they added their firepower to our own in the final clearance of the cavity. My wards stayed on watch while our retainers began their work to recover our fallen brothers. We counted, as best we could, the armour of thirty-seven battle-brothers. Over a third of a company had died in this place, battling the fledg-ling bio-titans as they burst from their sacs. What a fight it must have been.

The armour bore the markings of the 5th Com-pany. They had not been on Sotha when Kraken came. They had fought and died months before. Chapter Master Thorcyra had despatched them to the very edges of the sectors the Scythes protected, responding to reports of rebellion and xenos incursion, while he himself led a force to counter an uprising to the galactic north. He did not know then that those incursions were the mere tip of the emerging Hive Fleet Kraken. We received a few routine reports back from the 5th, garbled by psychic interference, and then they were swallowed by the shadow in the warp.

By the time another company was free to go after them the truth of the Kraken had emerged, as had the threat it posed to Sotha itself. A general recall was ordered, every battle-brother was called back in defence of our home. And so the 5th became just another mystery, a hundred warriors amongst the millions who had already died at the talons of the Kraken and the billions more who were to follow.

'SO IT'S TRUE,' Senior Retainer Gricole said as he approached me in the birthing cavity. 'Another mystery solved.'

'Get your men working with all speed, Gricole. Secure the area so I can lead my wards on. We are here for the living more than the dead.'

Gricole ordered his men to their tasks, as I did my wards. But then he returned to my side and regarded me sceptically.

'You have something you wish to say?' I asked.

A Chapter retainer, a servant, would never consider questioning a full battle-brother. But not Gricole. I had found him on Graia, a hydropon-sprayer turned militia captain in the face of the hive fleet. His woman was long dead, spared the sight of the tyranid assault, his children died fighting under his command. He had seen the worst that the galaxy held; he was not going to be intimidated by me. He spoke his mind when it pleased him. I respected him for that.

'You can't think there's any chance they're still kicking,' Gricole said in his broad Graian accent. 'That they've been living, battling, inside one of these monsters all this time?'

I looked down at him. 'You are human, Gricole. I know it is hard for you to understand. The human soldier needs regular supply: food, ammunition, shelter, sleep, even fresh orders from those of a higher rank to reassure him that he has not been forgotten. Without any one of those the human soldier cannot function. He weakens and breaks. We are Astartes; we are not the same as you. We can eat what you cannot, sleep yet still be on our guard, and to give an Astartes a mission is to give him a purpose which he will seek to fulfil until ordered to stop or until the Emperor claims him.'

Gricole listened to me closely, nodding in thought, then he spoke again. 'So d'ya think there is a chance?' he repeated.

Gricole was being wilful. 'Consider for whom we are searching here.' I assented. 'This is the 5th Company: Captain Theodosios, Commander Cassios, Lieutenant Enero, Ancient Valtioch. If anyone could survive it would be warriors such as these.'

'I understand.' Gricole nodded. 'And so… do you think there is a chance?' he asked a third time. He smiled, bearing his stained brown teeth. Such stubborn impertinence, if it had been from a neophyte I would not have stood it for a moment, but unlike them Gricole had earned such familiarity with blood.

'The truth then?' I drew breath and looked away. 'Of course not. Death is all we will find in this ship. It is all we will ever find on these missions. You have seen the same as I. Even dead, these ships consume all within them. How can there be survivors? Master Thrasius's Salvation Teams are a fool's errand.'

I had let my bitterness against the new Chapter Master show again. It did not matter in front of Gricole, however; I trusted his discretion.

'He told me he called us Salvation Teams for we will be the salvation of the Chapter,' I continued, still angry at the far distant commander. 'Do you know what the brothers of the battle company call us?'

Gricole shook his head gently.

'Salvage Squads,' I said.

'Hmph,' he muttered. 'Catchy.'

Salvage Squads. It was meant as an insult, but I found the name more fitting with each new insertion. Despite our efforts, we had found none of our missing. None living, at least. What we did find was salvage. The tyranid xeno-species can plunder every last atom of use, but their booty of choice is biological material. Our flesh. This they choose over any other.

The fruit of our own labours then were those items a hive ship, especially if crippled by an assault party's attack, might overlook. Weapons, armour;

our tools of destruction. It did not come only from fellow Scythes; the Astartes equipment we found came in an array of colours: yellow and red, blue, silver, black and green. Irrespective of whether those Chapters might consider it sacrilegious, we took it. Our orders were precise: salvage it all.

GRICOLE'S MEN WORKED quickly and with determination. Like Gricole himself, they were born on worlds that had fallen to Kraken: Miral, Graia, and others, worlds that we had tried to defend in our long retreat from Sotha. The Chapter's original retainers all died defending Sotha; no matter how young, how old, how injured or frail, they had picked up a weapon and given their lives to buy a few more seconds for their masters, for we Astartes, to escape.

We did escape, but at that time our flight appeared only to delay our destruction. The survivors of Sotha stumbled back to the Miral system, there to report the loss of our home to our returning Chapter Master. Thorcyra was stunned, near-shattered by the news. Some advised further retreat against such overwhelming odds, but he rejected the notion and led us all in oaths of defiance. The Kraken was approaching and we would stand and die in the jungles of Miral.

The Kraken came, and we made our stand on the rocky crags of a place named the Giant's Coffin. We fought hard, and we died once again. I do not know if Thorcyra believed some miracle would save us, that perhaps his faith alone might bring the blessing of the Emperor upon us and grant us some astounding victory. It was not to be. Thorcyra fell, torn apart by his foes, and Captain Thrasius ordered the retreat. And, once more, I survived.

If you think I was grateful for my life, you would be mistaken. To leave behind so many brothers once was a tragedy that cut deep into my soul. To have to do so again was more than any man could endure. My body survived Miral, but my spirit did not. As I watched Captain Thrasius swear the oaths of a Chapter Master on the bridge of *The Heart of Sotha*, I was certain that my next battle would be my last.

But after Miral, I am ashamed to say, we grew more cautious. Thrasius did not believe any other world worth the extinction of our Chapter, short of Holy Terra itself. We were told no longer to contemplate the possibility of victory, only of what damage we could cause before we would retreat again. Thrasius planned our withdrawals to the last detail and demanded their precise execution. Brothers died, but none without reason. But I felt the dishonour burn inside me each time the order was given to abandon another world to the Kraken, to retreat while others fought on. I obeyed, but I rejected Thrasius's orders to leave all other defenders to their fate and I brought back with me those I could who had proven themselves worth saving. I was not alone in such actions and those brothers and I shamed Thrasius into allowing such noble men as Gricole to remain with us.

* * *

THE SIGNAL FROM the beacon led us deeper into the ship. We located one of the major arterial tubes, but we found it packed with biters. They were not feeding, rather they had fed themselves to bursting and were dragging their distended bodies along the ground, all heading into the ship. A few hellfire shells here would not have made a dent in their number, and so reluctantly I ordered the Scouts to find another route. The hard muscle wall of the artery cut across all the chambers on our level, barring any further progress, until Pasan noticed the sludge draining in a corner. There was a valve in the floor, kept from closing by the thick sludge's flow. It was too small for us, but we wedged it open wider. I should have sent one of the Scouts first, but I did not wish to be trapped above a panicking neophyte who had lost his nerve. I stowed my pistol, drew my falx, and plunged headfirst straight down into the tight shaft.

At once, I felt that the sludge might suffocate me as I forced myself down. I had only my helmet light to shine ahead of me, but there was nothing to see except the sludge seeping ahead. I moved slowly, leading with my falx and levering the shaft open, then deliberately pressing the wall back and widening the area as I went. My only comfort was the thought that any tyranid xenoform who might have lurked in such a place would have been dissolved by the sludge long before.

The line about my waist pulled tight and then went slack as my wards climbed down after me.

* * *

WORLD AFTER WORLD fell to the Kraken, but under Thrasius we small remnant of the once proud, once brave, once honourable Scythes of the Emperor survived. But then, against such odds, I told myself still that it was solely a matter of time. The absolution of a violent death would still be mine. Then came Ichar IV.

The tendrils of the Kraken had concentrated against that world and there, ranged against them, amidst a great gathering of Imperial forces stood the Ultramarines. Together, they smashed the body of the Kraken. The planet was nearly destroyed, its defenders were decimated, but the tyranids were scattered.

It was the victory for which we Scythes had prayed so fervently, the victory that Thrasius had told us we could no longer achieve.

And we were not there.

Word of the victory at Ichar IV filtered through to the latest planet on which we had taken refuge. Bosphor, I think its name was. Still, even then we did not know the extent to which the Kraken had been cast back. We continued to prepare the planet's defences, trained their wide-eyed troops in the combat doctrines we had learned at bitter cost. We waited for the Kraken to come and turn the skies red with their spores. But the bio-ships never came.

It was only then that I realised that I had survived. That I would survive, not just a few more days, a few more weeks, until the next battle, but decades more. It was only then that we counted the cost and the truth of our plight struck home. Of all my battle-brothers, only one in ten survived. One in ten.

Our officers, who had stood and fought even as they ordered others to retreat, were wiped out nearly to a man. Our vehicles, our machines of war, had been abandoned; our own blessed ancestors in their Dreadnought tombs had been torn to pieces by the Kraken's claws. Their voices and memories, our connection to our legacy and that of the Chapter before us, were lost to us forever.

Thrasius told us that it was not the end. That the dead would be honoured, but that their ranks would be filled, that we would rise once more and be as we once were.

I knew, even as I stood listening to his words, how wrong he was. More youths might be recruited, more Astartes might wear the colours, more mouths might shout our battle cries and recite our oaths. But it would not be us. Everything that had made us a Chapter of Space Marines, everything beyond the ceramite of our armour, the metal of our weapons, the cloth of our banners, was gone.

THE TERMAGANTS SCUTTLED across the slope. The tendrils that covered the area, the curved floor, the walls, even hanging from the roof, would normally have reached out at any movement and grasped at it, but instead they lay flaccid. One of the termagants paused and lowered its head, sniffing; it turned quickly to the rest of its brood and they changed direction. They moved with purpose, they sensed an intruder. They saw a light ahead of them and closed in around it. The leader reached down with one of its mid-claws to pick up the torch, while the others sniffed closer, discerning that the scent-trails had divided. It was then that the trap was sprung.

The half-dozen tendrils closest to the torch suddenly burst as the frag grenades tied to them detonated. The termagants howled as the shrapnel tore into their bodies. Narro, Pasan and Vitellios rose up from their hiding places on to one knee and targeted those few creatures still standing. When the last of them fell, hissing and jerking, I ordered ceasefire and had the Scouts cover me as I approached the carnage. The termagants appeared dead: their weapon-symbiotes hung limply from their claws, limbs were severed and all were covered in their own tainted ichor. I took no chances and raised my falx and cut the head off each one. It was little victory. I felt no more revenged for having done so. I never did. Soon the biters would move in and begin to eat, and through them the dead flesh of these 'gaunts would be reformed into the next generation.

'These freaks wouldn't last a minute in the underhive,' Vitellios said as he lit his helmet light and swaggered over to admire his handiwork. 'Even a yowler would scope a dome before picking up a piece of trash. These 'gaunts are not too smart.'

I looked down at the torch. In the midst of the violence it was still shining. I picked it up and switched it off.

'Extinguish your helm-light, neophyte,' I ordered. 'Pasan, form a watch. Don't assume that these were alone. Narro, come here.'

The Scouts followed my orders instantly, even Vitellios. He was an arrogant upstart, but not when his own neck was on the line. He had been picked out from amongst the scum pressed into service as militia in the defence of the hive-world Radnar. Barely into his teens, he was already the leader of several gangs of juves who had run rampage through a few underhive sectors. The Scythe Apothecaries had removed his gang markings, tattoos and the kill-tags of the dozen men he claimed to have bested, but they could not extract the smug superiority he carried with him. His training record identified him as a natural leader. I disagreed. To lead, one must first learn how to follow, a task he continually failed. He may have been born to lead a gang of hive-trash, but never command Astartes.

'What do you think, Narro?' I asked, indicating the tyranid bodies. Unlike Pasan, Scout Narro always grasped instantly whatever task I had for him. He had been recruited from Radnar as well and he, at least, had come from one of the noble families. He had already been tapped for additional training that would lead him to become a Techmarine when he became a full battle-brother. He picked up one of the severed heads and peered fascinated at its sharp and vicious features.

"Gaunt genus, obviously. Termagant species.'

'Correct,' I replied. 'Go on.'

'Strange, though, to see them here...'

'Within a hive ship? Yes, truly bizarre, neophyte,' I directed him back. 'Are they fresh? Have they just been birthed?'

We had learned the hard way that newborn xenoforms were one of the danger signs. Even within a dead ship, certain vestigial reflexes might induce fresh tyranid fiends from their sacs if an interloper triggered them. Yet another defence against grave robbers such as us. If these termagants were freshly hatched then more of them might descend upon us at any moment.

'It is…' Narro murmured. 'It is not easy to say conclusively.'

'Then give me your best guess,' I replied curtly. 'Show me that Forge Master Sebastion's efforts with you were not wasted.'

Narro put the head down and ran a gloved hand down the flank of the slug-body, examining the texture of the flesh. I grimaced in disgust at such contact.

'No. They are not,' he said finally, and I let a fraction of the breath I had held escape. 'You see this scarring, and the skin, and this one here has lost part of its…' he began to explain.

'Thank you, neophyte,' I dismissed him before he could digress.

'But what Sebastion said was…' he began with fervour, then faltered when he saw my expression. But then I relented and nodded for him to continue.

'Master Sebastion, in his teachings, speaks of how in the assault upon Sotha and Miral and the rest, the

ships of the Kraken released millions of such creatures and expended them as... as a company of
Marines would the shells of their boltguns. Yet we
Salvation Teams have rarely encountered them. He
believed that, because they must be so simple to produce and had so little purpose once their ship was
dead, that they were the first to be reabsorbed...'

Beneath my gaze, his voice trailed away.

'Thank you, neophyte,' I told him clearly. 'That is
all.'

I looked towards our path ahead. If the auspex
could be trusted then the beacon was close. Once it
was recovered I could quit this insertion and leave
the ship to rot. I did not want to delay any further,
but then, out of the corner of my eye, I saw Narro
reach down and grasp something. He had picked up
the 'gaunt head again and was about to stow it in his
pack.

'Drop it,' I told him.

He fumbled to explain: 'But if it is rare I only
thought it might provide insight, if I could study–'

'Drop it, neophyte,' I ordered again. It had been
Narro's affinity with the holy ways of the machine
that had first brought him to Sebastion's attention,
but his curiosity had bled from the proper realm of
the Imperial enginseer into the living xenotech of the
tyranid. I had overheard him speak to his brothers of
his fanciful ideas of where such study could lead; to a
weapon, some ultimate means to destroy the Kraken
and its ilk and drive them back into the void. He did
not understand the danger. The young never did.

'And consider in future to what infection or taint such trophies may expose you and your brothers. Save your thoughts of study until you are assigned to Mars. Until then, do not forget that you are here to fight.'

Shamed, Narro released it and the snarling, glassy-eyed trophy rolled a metre down the slope until it was lost in a knot of tendrils.

'There is an explanation for why these 'gaunts may have survived,' he said.

'And that is?'

'This ship... It is not dead.'

IT WAS A ridiculous idea, but even so I felt the briefest chill at the thought. Every scan we had done of the hive ship before insertion told us that it was exactly as it appeared to be: a lifeless husk. But what if...? Could it still...?

No, I told myself as we continued on. I was no whelp neophyte. I would not fall prey to such paranoia. Every instinct I had, instincts honed from two long years of such expeditions, told me that this ship was dead. If it had been alive, we would never have made it this far. We would have been surrounded and destroyed within the first hundred steps. We certainly would not have been able to ambush those 'gaunts; some creature, some tiny insect would have been watching us and through it, the ship would have seen through our design.

We went deeper, the atmosphere thickening as we went. We climbed ridges of flesh and traversed the crevices between, squeezed our way through tiny capillaries and valves, and down passages ribbed with chitinous plates or covered with polyps crusted with mucus. We passed over caverns crammed with bulbs on stalks so that they resembled fields of flowers, and under roofs criss-crossed with lattices of tiny threads like spiders' webs. And everywhere we saw the same decay, the slow deconstruction of this grotesque, complex organism back into raw bio-matter by the biters and the smaller creatures they fed upon.

'THERE IT IS!' the cry finally went up. Vitellios shone his torch into a wall-cavity and there it was indeed, driven into the flesh-wall like a service stud. A piece of human technology, bound in brass and steel, as alien in this place as any tyranid xenoform would be aboard a human craft.

Excited, my wards crowded in to see. I batted them back, telling them to set watch. I did not wish to be taken unawares now of all times. Narro scraped away the translucent skin that had grown over the metal. I saw him instinctively reach to deactivate the signal and I grabbed his hand away. He looked at me askance and I slowly shook my head. He nodded in understanding and levered open the beacon's cover, exposing its innards. He groaned in dismay.

'What is it?' Pasan backed towards us, shotgun up, and glanced at the beacon.

'The data-slate,' Narro explained. 'Acid. It's been burned through.'

There was something more though. I looked closer. There were markings on the interior of the casing, distorted by the acid-damage, but still recognisable. They had been scratched by human hand and not tyranid claw.

'But it doesn't make sense...' Narro thought out loud.

'What doesn't make sense?' Pasan replied, the concern clear in his voice.

VIDESUB, it read. Vide Sub. It was not code. It was High Gothic. An order. A command.

'Why would they destroy the message and leave the beacon transmitting?'

Look down.

The floor burst into a mass of scythes and talons as the monster exploded from its hiding place. The force of its eruption launched me into the air and threw me to the side. I smashed headfirst into a flesh-wall and slumped down to my knees.

'God-Emperor! Get back!' I heard someone cry as I slipped to the ground.

I forced myself onto my back. The gun-torches danced across the chamber as the Scouts moved. Pasan's was stationary, skewed at an angle, far to the other side. Vitellios's jumped as he sprinted away. One still remained in the centre; Hwygir was turning, bringing his heavy weapon to bear. His light caught the monster for an instant; it reared, jaws and mandibles gaping wide, as it swept two scything claws above its head to cut down the diminutive figure standing in its way. The Scout pulled the trigger and the monster's black eyes sparked orange with the ignition of the shells.

The first bolt clipped the bone of the claw even as it cut down towards him and ricocheted away. The second passed straight through the fleshy arm before detonating on the other side. But the third struck hard between two ribs of its exoskeleton. The explosion jolted the monster from its attack even as its blowback blinded Hwygir for a critical moment. The injured claw retracted early, the other was forced off its line and carved a bloody streak down the side of the Scout's leg instead of chopping his head in two.

Both Hwygir and the monster stumbled back for a moment. The savage dropped the sights of the heavy bolter, trying to blink his eyes clear, and his torch swivelled away from the monster just as it sprang and flipped over, digging back underground. Its thick snake-tail shot from the darkness, puncturing the casing of the heavy weapon on Hwygir's shoulder with such force as to knock it into the side of his head and leave him stunned.

'Burrower! Get clear!' It was Vitellios, shouting from cover.

Vitellios on one side and Pasan on the other desperately flashed their torches in every direction, hoping to catch a glimpse of the creature before it struck again.

'There!' Vitellios shouted.

'There!' Pasan cried.

They were facing in different directions. Vitellios had already fired; the hollow bark of a shotgun blast hitting nothing but the empty air echoed back to us. I pulled the torch from my pistol and twisted it in my hand. It blossomed with light in every direction.

'Quiet, you fools!' I hissed at them, drawing my falx as well. 'It's a ravener. It goes after the vibrations!'

They both stopped talking at that. I looked about the cavern in the dim, grey light. There was nothing on the surface to suggest any movement beneath. Hwygir was moving slightly beside the hole from which the ravener had burst. I saw Narro as well; he was lying beneath the beacon, smashed between it and the ravener's first attack. Hwygir saw him too and started slowly to crawl over to him, leaving the heavy bolter where it had fallen.

'No, you...' I cursed, but the trog did not hear me. Pasan did though. He suddenly stepped forwards, then picked up his feet and started to run. Great, booming, heavy steps. Not towards the heavy weapon, but away from it. I sensed, rather than saw, the ravener below us twist within the ship's flesh to go after him.

'Pasan! I order you–' I called after him, but I knew he was not going to stop.

I jerked my head around to Vitellios. 'Get the bolter. I'll get him.' I snapped, and powered after the running Scout.

Pasan knew both I and the ravener were after him now and quickened his pace over the leathery surface. In a shower of flesh and fluid, the ravener burst not from the floor, but from the wall. Pasan leapt and rolled, but the tyranid beast caught his leg in one of its grasping hands, flicked him around and hammered him against a chitinous strut. The shotgun flew from Pasan's hands as his body went limp, and it drew a claw back to slice him in two.

I bellowed at the beast as I ran and fired my pistol as fast as it allowed. My snap-shots blew the flesh from the walls and the beast indiscriminately and it twisted in pain. It coiled, ready to burrow again, and I dropped my pistol and raised my falx with both hands. The ravener leapt. I swung. The falx's tip pierced its carapace and hooked inside. I was yanked off my feet as the ravener dug down at an extraordinary rate. It dragged me on and I braced as I sped towards the hole it had created. My body hit the ground splayed across the hole and went no further. The ravener threatened to pull my weapon from my hands, but my grip was like steel. It thrashed beneath me, churning up the ship-flesh around it. Its tail, still in the air, whipped back and forth, battering at my side. I held on. It strained even harder against the hook of the falx and I felt it begin to tear itself clear. The next time the tail struck, I seized it with one arm, then released the falx and grasped it with my other.

'Vitellios!' I called. He was already running towards me, the heavy bolter cradled in his arms.

Beneath me, the ravener spiralled in my grip to try and escape; its scythes lashed up and punctured my armour, but I was too close for it to cut deep. Vitellios, only a few steps away, brought the bolter up, ready to fire. With a heave, I wrenched it out of the ground to give Vitellios a clear shot and, as I did so, it coiled into the air. Part of its thorax came free and I saw it grow an ugly pyramid-like cyst. It was a weapon, and it was pointed straight at me.

Vitellios and the ravener fired at exactly the same instant. The hive-trash pumped the beast full of bolt-shells that burrowed down along the length of its body and exploded. The bio-weapon shot a burst of slugs into me that burrowed up into my body and did nothing more.

I collapsed over the tyranid's remains. I did not know then what had hit me, only that my armour had been pierced. There was pain, but it was not incapacitating. I had seen brothers hit by tyranid weapons go mad or be burnt from the inside out, but as my hearts beat all the harder to race my blood around my veins I felt neither come upon me.

'How do, sergeant? You okay?' Vitellios had fallen to his knees beside me, his tone even more self-satisfied in victory. 'Caught ourselves a big one today.'

'Coward,' I replied coldly.

'What?' He looked shocked. 'Coward? I just saved your–'

'After you ran. After you fled.'

'I… That wasn't…' He was incensed. Almost ready to reload that bolter and use it on me. I did not care. 'That was doctrine! You're ambushed, you break free! Then you look to strike back!'

'Leaving your brothers to fend for themselves? Do not use doctrine to try to excuse that.'

Pasan had come round and was struggling upright. I heaved myself to my feet; my blessed body was raging, fighting to repair the damage done to it, but I would not show these neophytes even a hint of my weakness.

'You're pathetic. Both of you,' I told them. 'Pasan, get yourself up. Vitellios, go back. Check on the others.'

Vitellios stomped away and called after his brothers.

'Narro! Hwygir! If you're dead, raise your hands…' After a moment's pause, he turned back to me: 'They're good.'

Then he made a gesture in my direction that I am certain would have meant something to me had I been born amongst hive-trash like him, and continued away. Pasan was on his feet now, his helmet facing shattered, his face cut, bruised and crumpled.

'Honoured sergeant–' he began.

'Later,' I said. 'You will explain your actions later. Let us just get ourselves off this piece of thrice-damned filth.'

We hobbled back to where Narro and Hwygir had fallen. In spite of Vitellios's ignoble sense of humour, both still lived. I caught sight of the beacon again and the order scrawled there: VIDESUB. Look down. Another joke.

But it wasn't. For Vitellios spoke up again, and this time his voice was neither smug nor bitter. It was in awe.

'Sergeant Tiresias.' He shone his torch down into the hole below the beacon where the ravener had hibernated. In the violence of its awakening, however, it had scratched open a cavity even further beneath. Down there, glinting back in the light, shone the shoulder armour of a Space Marine. And upon that armour was inscribed the legend:

CASSIOS

THE SPACE MARINE'S vital signs barely registered on our auspex. His metabolism was as slow as a glacier. He might easily have been mistaken for dead, but we knew better. Even in suspended animation, he was an impressive figure. His chest was the size of a barrel, his armour was crafted and worked with a pattern of lamellar, festooned with images of victories and great feats through the owner's life. The neophytes stood, slack-jawed, gaping at him. For once, I shared their sense of wonder.

We dug him from his cradle and commenced the ritual to rouse him there. It was not worthy of a survivor, a hero such as he, to be borne back to his home as though he were an infant. I would not have the retainers see him in such a state. I would give him the chance to stand alone, if he willed it, and return as a hero should.

We waited on guard, expectant, for an hour or more. Tending our own wounds, but staying silent aside from checking the auspex readings. Then, finally, his chest heaved. His eyes opened.

COMMANDER CASSIOS STEPPED from the darkness of the tunnel and into the beams of the powerful floodlights set up by the retainer crews working within the cavern of the bio-titans.

Gricole saw him at once and called his workers to order. They stood, hushed, as Commander Cassios walked amongst them. He, in turn, acknowledged them, and appeared about to speak, and then he saw what their work was. He dropped to his knees, resting his hands upon the armour of his men. His head was bowed, he was praying. Gricole ordered his men away and I did the same with my wards. A warrior such as Cassios deserved to be allowed to keep such a moment private.

After they had cleared away from the cavity, he stood and moved through the rest of the armour and possessions that Gricole's men had been carefully storing.

'Valens. Nikos. Leo. Abas. Tiberios. Messinus. Herakleios.' Names; he could name each one just from what little remained.

'Theodosios. He was my captain.' I realised that Cassios was addressing me. 'It was so hard for him to ask me to lead the diversionary attack. I volunteered. I insisted! I knew that our company only stood a chance of escape if he was leading the way…' his voice trailed off.

I brought Cassios out with me and took him back to the boat. Only Gricole was waiting for us there. He looked at me, concerned. He tried to see to my wounds, but I waved him away. My Astartes physiology had started healing me from the moment I was wounded; whatever poison the ravener had pumped into me, my body would defeat that just as I had overcome the beast. In any case, I had a more pressing task to address, though it was one I would have given my life not to have to fulfil.

The 5th Company had fought and died against the Kraken before the rest of us had even known it had emerged from the void. Cassios had been here ever since. He believed he had lost his men. He did not know he had lost so much more.

THE DAYS AND weeks after Ichar IV were ones of celebration for the militia defenders of Bosphor, who had never fought the Kraken and now never would. My brother Astartes and I were in no mood to join them and we retreated to our ships.

Some of us immersed ourselves in prayer, others in rage. A few, gripped by madness at what they had seen and what they had lost, rampaged around the ship until they were forcibly restrained. There were accidents. At least, we called them accidents. We Astartes have no word for the act where a brother chooses to end his service in such a manner. It is not spoken of, but his gene-seed is sequestered, marked as potentially deviant, as though it was a disease of the body and not of the soul.

I thought I had seen every reaction there was to the tragedy of our Chapter. I was wrong. When I told Cassios of the battles, of the losses, of what we had been reduced to, he showed me something different. He showed me the response of a hero.

* * *

CASSIOS HAD HAD his eyes closed, standing perfectly still, for nearly a minute. Then his face screwed up in rage, but he did not shout, he breathed. He took great heaving breaths as though he could blow the emotion out from his body and into the air. Then his eyes opened.

'And what is being done?' he asked.

'About what?'

'What is being done to revenge ourselves against this abomination? What is being done to strike back? What is being done to rid our space of this bastard xenos curse for good?'

I placed my hand upon his shoulder.

'As soon as we return to *The Heart of Sotha* they will tell you all. We will leave at once. Your brothers will be most eager to see you again.'

I smiled at him, but he did not return it.

'We cannot leave before we are finished here.'

'Before we are finished?' I asked. 'You are here with us. What more is there?'

Cassios tilted his head a fraction, indicating out the window. 'This ship, nearly half my company, it killed them, feasted on them.'

'And it is dead now,' I reassured him.

'We did not kill it.'

'No, but perhaps our brother-Chapters did on Ichar IV or perhaps it was the servants of the Navy. I understand you want satisfaction, commander. Believe me, I want that for every brother we lost. But our service is done. You cannot kill it again.'

'You misunderstand me, brother-sergeant. It was never killed. The ship still lives.'

THRASIUS DISAPPEARED FROM our midst then; for several days we were told he had secluded himself to meditate upon the Emperor's will for our Chapter, but then we discovered he had left us entirely on some secret task. He had told us before that we would take the time to rebuild, restore ourselves, and there were many who disagreed with that intention.

I do not expect you to understand. We are Astartes. We are not like you. We do not wake in the morning and muse upon what our purpose may be that day. We know. From the day we are chosen to the day that we die we know what our purpose is. We fight in the name of the Emperor. If we are ordered, then we go. If we are struck, we strike back. If we fall, then we do so knowing that others will take our place. We do not pause, we do not hold back, we do not relent.

We fight. That is our service to the Emperor. That is what we are. If we do not fight, then we do not serve Him. If we do not serve Him, we are lost. One might as soon as tell a mechanicus not to build, a missionary not to preach, a telepath not to think, a ship not to sail. How can they? What use are they without it? And yet that was what Thrasius was asking us to do because if we were to suffer the casualties of even the most minor of campaigns, it would be enough to finish us for good. If we wanted to survive, we could not lose anymore. We could not lose anymore, so we could no longer fight. And for how long?

Our armoury, our training grounds, a whole world of our recruits that had been lost with Sotha, perhaps those could be restored. But what of the gene-seed? Both in our living brothers and in our stores lost with Sotha, both now devoured by the Kraken. Without gene-seed there could be no more Astartes, and gene-seed can only be grown within an Astartes, from the progenoid glands implanted in us as youths. There were barely more than a hundred of us left. Most had already had their glands taken when they had matured, to be kept safe in the gene-banks of Sotha. Those few of us in whom they had still not matured… how many new generations would it take to recover our numbers? How many years would the Chapter be leashed, unable to put more than a bare company into the field? Fifty? A hundred? Could we ever recover or would we just fade into ghosts of what we had been? A cautionary tale: the Chapter that feared its own end so greatly they placed themselves above their oaths, their service to Him.

No, better to end it all with a final crusade. That is what my commander, Brother-Sergeant Angeloi, said to me, and I agreed as many others did in the corridors of *The Heart of Sotha*. When Thrasius returned to us we would tell him what his men had decided and we would require his acceptance. This was not for glory, this was for our souls. We had been great once, let our story end well in a great crusade that would end only when the last of us fell. Other Chapters would then stand forward to take up our duty and our spirits would join His light as His proud warriors and our names would be spoken with glory as long as mankind endured.

'TRUST ME, COMMANDER–' I raised my voice higher, trying to make him see sense.

'You may trust me, sergeant. I have been aboard that monster for nearly three years. Do not doubt what I say.'

'The auspex–'

'The auspex is wrong. Our technology, blessed be His works, has been wrong as often as it has been right. We are not some dependent xenos like the tau, we rely on human flesh and blood, and there is a spark of life there, I know it.'

'Even so,' I declared, 'it does not matter.'

Cassios blinked. That had surprised him.

'It does not matter?' Cassios raised his eyebrow. 'Explain yourself, sergeant.'

'So it lives, despite the auspex, despite what we saw aboard, the ship lives. It does not matter. We will still leave. We will send a despatch to the battlefleet, they will send a warship and destroy it for good.'

'You said yourself, sergeant, the battlefleet is fully engaged with the hive fleets splintered from Ichar IV. There will be no warship, and this abomination will heal and be the death of further worlds. It is not befitting an Astartes to pass his duty on to lesser men.'

'Then we will return with all our brothers. With *our* warships. We shall destroy this beast ourselves.'

'We are here now. We shall finish it now. Make your preparations for reinsertion. That is my last word on the matter.'

'But it is not mine…' I told him.

'Are you challenging my authority, sergeant?'

'No,' I replied calmly. 'You are challenging mine, commander. This team is mine. This mission is mine. And you… are not permitted to command.'

'What?'

'You have been aboard that ship three years, brother,' I spoke softly. 'Surrounded by the xenos, one of them just centimetres from you. We do not know what has happened to you. *You* do not even know. Doctrine is clear. Until you return with us, until you are examined by the Apothecary and purified, you have no authority to hold.'

To that, Cassios had no answer.

I LEFT CASSIOS to himself and started walking back along the narrow corridors of the assault boat. I headed for the Apothecarion. I was sick. I did not know if it was the other injuries or the infection of the ship, but whatever war was being waged inside me against the ravener's venom, I was losing. My guts burned, my head felt as though it was floating above my body. I stumbled on a step and, at that noise, the neophytes appeared from the next cabin. Concerned, they rushed to my side, but I waved them away. No weakness. No weakness in front of them.

'Get away… get away…' I tried to push them off, and stagger on. I saw them back away as my vision dimmed. I did not feel the deck hit me.

* * *

EVEN IN MY poison-fever, I could not escape my wards. They plagued my mind as the toxin did my body. In my dreams I saw them clearly. I saw how each would add to the slow disintegration of my Chapter; to its reduction to a shadow of its former self. Hwygir was unable to step beyond the feral thinking of the savage world on which he had been born. Was that the purpose for which the Astartes were created? To be unthinking barbarians? No.

Narro was the reverse, his mind too open. His young fascination with the xenos was a danger he did not comprehend. He thought to save humanity by studying the technology of its enemies, using such xenotech against them, integrating it within our own forces, within ourselves. His path would lead us to create our own monsters, corrupt our blessed forms and thereby our spirits. We Astartes may have bodies enhanced to be greater than any normal human, but our souls remain those of men. The only knowledge an Astartes needs of a xenos is how it may be destroyed. Anything more is heresy.

Vitellios, I could see however, was destined for a different kind of heresy. Years of training, hypno-conditioning in the ways of the Chapter, and still he clung to his old identity. His arrogant presumption of self-importance. That he might be right and the Chapter might be wrong. Our history lists those Astartes who doubted the Emperor, and each of their names is blackened: Huron, Malai, Horus, and the rest.

Pasan, though, was my greatest disappointment. Every advantage that could be offered, a destiny nigh pre-ordained, and this lacklustre boy was the result. Insipid, full of self-doubt, unable to grasp the mantle of leadership even when presented to him. If half-men like him were to be the future of the Scythes then, Emperor help me, I would have rather the Chapter have stood and died at Sotha.

'GRICOLE,' I CROAKED when next I awoke. 'How am I?'

Gricole raised the dim light a fraction and bent to study the readings from the medicae tablet.

'Your temperature is down. Your hearts are beating slower. And your urine… is no longer purple. I would guess you are through the worst.'

I coughed. It cleared my throat. 'Good,' I said, my voice stronger. 'Too much time has been wasted already.'

I levered myself up and off the tablet. I felt a touch of weakness in my legs.

'The time has not been completely wasted,' Gricole began. 'We have been making some progress–'

'We have set out for home?' They should have waited until I was conscious again, but in this instance I would forgive them. 'How far have we gone?'

I looked into Gricole's stout, troubled face. I pushed past him, out of the Apothecarion, and to a porthole. The hive ship filled my view.

I turned back to my retainer, my thoughts gripped with suspicion. 'They have not gone onto the ship without me?' I strode across the room, my weakness vanishing before my anger. 'I expressly forbade it!'

I stalked out into the antechamber. My four wards were there. Startled, they stumbled to attention.

'Who was it?' I demanded. 'One of you? All of you? Who here did not understand my orders?'

I looked pointedly at Vitellios, but he stared straight ahead, not moving a muscle.

'You will find your tongues or I will find them for you,' I said sternly.

'Honoured sergeant.' It was Pasan. 'Your orders were understood and followed. We have not left this craft.'

His words were bold, but the slightest quiver in his voice betrayed his nervousness. I stepped close to him and studied him carefully.

'Then explain to me, Neophyte Pasan, what is this progress that you have made?'

I saw his eyes flick for an instant behind me, to Gricole, and then away. He blinked with a moment's indecision.

'We found a–' Narro started.

'Quiet,' I overruled. 'Neophyte Pasan can speak for himself.'

'We have… we have been mapping the surface,' he spoke, gaining confidence with each word. 'We found an aperture that we believe will lead us straight to our target.'

'Is this impertinence, Pasan? We recovered the beacon. What target is this?'

'My men,' Cassios said from the entrance hatch. He stepped into the antechamber. 'My apologies, brother-sergeant, we could not make you aware during your indisposition. These Scouts were fulfilling my instructions.'

'It is a second beacon, honoured sergeant.'

I looked from Cassios to Pasan. 'Another beacon? Our auspex read only the one.'

Vitellios chipped in. 'It signalled only once, at the exact time we discovered the commander's beacon.'

'It makes sense, sergeant,' now Narro spoke again. 'If some of the xenoforms can detect the beacon's signal you would not wish to lead them to all your hiding places. You would wait until a rescue party might be close, close enough to reach a primary beacon. Then once we accessed that, it must have sent a signal to all the secondary beacons to begin transmitting.'

'And one replied. Once.' I looked back at Cassios, but he was concentrated upon the neophytes' explanation. 'Our auspex did not detect a second signal at that time.'

'Not our squad auspex, no,' Narro continued, 'but the one on the boat did. It is noted within the data-log. It is at the far end of the ship, so deep inside we would not have detected it.'

'Very well. Commander?' I fixed my gaze upon Cassios. 'Do you know what we may find?'

'Our boarding parties struck all across the ship. There are several for whom I have not accounted.' He shook his head sadly. 'I only pray they were as lucky as I and that we may reach them in time.'

My wards appeared convinced, but I was not. Yet if more of our brothers were still sent abourd that abomination, I could not leave them behind.

'So, Scout Pasan, tell me. What is this aperture that you have discovered?'

'ARSE!' VITELLIOS SWORE as he took another grudging step along the dim tunnel. 'I can't believe I have to climb up this bio-ship's arse.'

His overblown irritation elicited a smattering of laughter from the other neophytes.

'Keep the chatter off the vox!' I snapped at them all, my patience worn thin. There was no atmosphere in this part of the ship so we were fully encased within our armour with only the squad-vox to keep in contact. I was still not recovered, I felt weak, uncomfortable, and my discomfort frustrated me even further. Such petty inconveniences should be nothing to an Astartes. My body should be healed fully, not still ailing. I pushed on, the temperature rising and my temper shortening with each step.

How had I come to this? Reduced to a haemorrhoid on a hive ship's backside! Was this what heroes of the Astartes did? Would, one day, a new generation of battle-brothers listen in hushed tones to the tale of this adventure?

'Brother-sergeant?' Cassios's voice came through to me. He had set it to a private channel. Cassios, though, would be my salvation. When we returned home after this insertion, we would not be met by a Techmarine adept to catalogue our salvage. No, we would have an honour guard fitting for the hero we would restore.

'Commander?'

'I asked the neophytes, during the days you were inconvenienced, of the circumstances of my rescue.'

'With what purpose?' I had intended my query to be polite, but as I heard it back through the vox it had the tinge of accusation.

'No more than to further my understanding of them. It struck me that Scout Pasan in particular showed considerable courage in leading the ravener away, allowing the heavy bolter to be retrieved.'

'It would have shown considerable courage had I ordered him to do it,' I said, my voice sounding testy, 'but in the midst of battle, you must act as one. You cannot have a single person deciding to act alone, expecting everyone else to understand his meaning.'

'And yet at other times you have remarked on his failure to use initiative. That he has waited for orders.'

'He must learn to judge between the two. That is also part of leadership; when to act and when to listen to others.'

'You truly believe he is the right one to groom as acolyte?'

I knew to whom Cassios was referring, but I held firm in my opinion. 'Pasan is Sothan. Like you and I. One of the last. He has it within him. He merely needs to discover it.'

The conversation ended shortly after that. Cassios did not understand; he had spent two days with the neophytes. I had fought alongside them for over two years. My mind dwelt on Cassios's behaviour. It had been the neophytes who had pushed for this second insertion yet I knew it was exactly what he wished. There are reasons why any Space Marine discovered still living aboard a hive ship must be examined by the Apothecarion before returning to duty. It is not the constant danger and warfare, our minds are enhanced so that we may fight without rest, but it is the unknown influence of the greater tyranid consciousness that bears down on each and every living thing within its grasp. No one yet knows what effect that may have.

There is another reason as well. Not all tyranid xenoforms are created simply to destroy their enemies. Many are designed to infiltrate their minds, turn them against their friends and lead them into traps to be devoured. Cassios's behaviour seemed normal, but then perhaps that was a sign. How normal should a man be after such an experience?

I led them on in silence. The torches on our suits illuminated only a fraction of the gloom ahead of us. In truth, we did not know what function this part of the hive ship performed. Pasan had found the entrance at the stern of the vessel; it had been small, shrivelled, but the tunnel had widened out considerably after we had penetrated the initial portal. The bio-titan birthing cavity was nothing to the size of this cavern. Walking along the middle, the lowest point, we could see neither wall nor roof. We might as well have been walking upon the surface of a planet, the only difference being that the ground sloped upwards rather than down as it disappeared into the darkness on either side. It was desolate; there were no remains here of any of the lesser tyranid creatures that we had waded through in our earlier expeditions. The floor was bare, a series of shallow crests as though we were on the inside of a giant spring, and the footing was firm. It appeared as though we had found the one part of the vessel where nothing had ever lived.

Or I may have spoken too soon. I noticed to my right Cassios stop suddenly, he kneeled and held his gauntleted hand on the ground.

'Something's coming. Take cover,' his commanding voice coming through the vox crackled around the inside of my helmet. What cover? I asked myself, but Cassios was already breaking to one side.

'To the right,' I ordered my wards after him. They responded instantly, ready to follow him. We ran for a minute until the rising wall hove up into view, soaring above our heads into the shadow. Cassios climbed the slope until it was as steep as we could manage and then stopped there, looking further ahead.

'What is it?' I asked him. The auspex showed nothing.

'Do you not see them?'

I peered into the gloom. 'No,' I said.

He bade us wait, however, and within a few moments I saw what he had seen. A ridge emerged ahead of us, stretching across the horizon, as though a mighty hand had gripped the ship from the outside and was squeezing it up towards us. I heard my wards gasp as they saw it too.

'Holy Throne...'

'God-Emperor...'

'Sotha preserve us…'

'What in the name of a hive-toad's spawn-baubles are those?'

The ridge was no muscle contraction: it was a phalanx of huge tyranid creatures of a sort I had never seen before. Each as big as a tank, as big as a Baneblade, packed tightly together so there was not a centimetre between them, and moving as a line slowly towards us. Their armoured eyeless heads were down, so low as to be ploughing over the surface in front of them, dragging their bulbous bodies behind. Their limbs had atrophied so they oozed their way forward like snails. I did not know what their slime would do, but their weight alone would crush us. I looked to the left, to the right, there was no way around; they ringed the circumference of the cavern, somehow sticking to the walls even as they arched round and became the ceiling. I doubted whether all the weaponry we had to hand would be enough to stop one of these brutes in its tracks.

I looked down the line, searching for a tank-beast that appeared smaller or weaker. If we targeted one with concentrated fire there might be a chance, but my attention was dragged away when my wards suddenly let out a great cheer. Cassios was advancing, climbing the curving slope as he went. He had gone mad, I realised, the sight of his foe had driven his wits from him.

'After him!' I ordered the Scouts. I would be damned if I would let him die now, after all he had survived, before he could be welcomed back home.

We chased him as quickly as we could, struggling at the steep angle this close to the wall. He charged ahead of us, not even drawing his weapon. Scrabbling higher, he leapt from the cavern wall onto the top of the nearest tank-beast's head. Then, balanced precariously as the beast chomped forward, his power sword appeared in his hand and he stabbed down.

The tank-beast did not seem to notice.

'Back!' I shouted, appalled, to the others. 'Back! Firing positions!'

The beasts' pace had appeared slow from a distance, but up close they ground forwards with surprising speed. On such a slope, it was as if a Land Raider was barrelling towards us, teetering on a single tread.

'Stay on the curve! Stay high!' Cassios's voice blasted into our helmets as we fell back and he stabbed down again. I glanced behind, this time the beast acknowledged the strike with a flicker of its head that nearly threw Cassios off, but then it returned to its path and he regained his grip.

The Scouts stood ready to fire, but I hesitated, fearing the volley would hit the commander.

'Fire above me!' Cassios ordered, and we fired a battery of shells and shot over Cassios's head as he ducked and swung again. He cut to the right side of the beast's head, on the underside of where he was crouching. This time the beast shied slightly away from the barrage, but again returned to its course.

'Again!' He cut. We fired, the beast looming before us as though we were insects.

'Again!' he cried one last time before the beast steamrollered over us. We fired and he jammed the sword in as deep as it would go. The beast reacted. It squirmed away from our shot and lazily snapped towards the pinprick causing it pain. Its weight shifted and the upper edge of its body detached from the wall. For the first time we glimpsed the immense pores and suckers that had held it fast. As those came away from the surface, its weight shifted even further and more suckers came loose. With the inertia of a battleship ramming another, it slowly toppled down upon the tank-beast to its side and both monstrous creatures halted for a moment in confusion. Above them, their collision had left a gap. None of us needed to be told what to do.

We raced forwards to pass through before the tank-beast recovered. As we crossed into the valley we had created in the advancing ridge, it regained its grip and lumbered back. The valley's wall closed in upon us and I willed every last jolt of energy to my legs. The walls slammed shut as we shot from them and skidded upon the deep coating of mucus the tank-beasts left behind. I gained purchase for an instant before Hwygir, out of control, knocked me flying. We slid down the curved wall of the cavern right back into the centre until we finally stuck where the mucus was pooling.

I cut through the groans on the vox, demanding my squad to report. Haltingly, they did so. Slowly, trying not to fall again, I picked myself up from the laden ground and then checked the others. Cassios was rising as well. Hwygir was holding the heavy bolter high in the air, keeping it dry. Narro and Pasan were scraping the fluid off themselves as Vitellios just stood there, a look of horror on his face as he stared down at the mucus dripping off from every part of him.

'I've been slimed,' he said.

I forwent commenting that such dross reminded me of the grime-swamp where he'd been birthed; I had more pressing concerns.

'Neophytes, get yourselves up. Check your weapons, check your weapons!' I chivvied Vitellios. 'Straighten yourselves and get ready to move.'

I stepped away a little to check my own pistol and could not help but reflect once more on the new depths to which my command had sunk. I saw Cassios stepping around the neophytes, congratulating them individually. It did not matter, as soon as I returned him to *The Heart of Sotha* I would request transfer to the battle company and no one would be able to deny me.

'What is this place anyway?' I overheard Vitellios ask the rest.

'A no good place,' Hwygir concluded.

Narro was already working on hypotheses. 'Maybe some kind of alimentary canal, maybe a funnel or blow-hole.'

'Maybe the barrel of a bio-cannon?' Pasan queried.

'One big cannon,' Vitellios said.

'Either way, I just hope there's nothing bigger coming up out the pipe.'

I allowed them their inane chatter this once. I had checked my pistol and by His grace it still functioned. Our weapons last hundreds of years for a reason. I holstered it and then punched the auspex back to life to check the path ahead. I looked at its readings and then punched it again. The readings did not change. My body still moved, taking a few steps forward, but my brain, for this moment, had frozen. There *was* something bigger coming up the pipe. It wasn't a tank-beast or a carnifex or even a bio-titan. It was the spark of life that Cassios had claimed to sense. Ahead of us, growing, feeding, ready to be born, was a creature far larger than any we had encountered. It was the Kraken's offspring. It was another hive ship.

'Brother Tiresias?' The lieutenant stopped me as I walked the corridors of *The Heart of Sotha*.

'Brother Hadrios,' I responded, surprised. 'I thought you were away with Master Thrasius?'

'We have just returned,' the lieutenant said flatly, his eyes heavy. 'He wishes to see you. You will come with me.'

He turned away, expecting me to follow. After a moment's hesitation, I did. The lieutenant offered no further conversation and so we walked in silence. He led me to the Master's chambers and left me there. The chambers were still dark, the mosaics along its walls unlit, unprepared for their master's return, much as the rest of us. This was not how I expected matters to unfold. We imagined we would have forewarning when Thrasius reappeared, to gather our strength so that we might confront him together and demonstrate our collective will. Instead, he had stolen back like a thief in the night and taken us off-guard.

A line split down the panelling on one side and the chamber filled with light. Hidden in the light, Master Thrasius stood. I imagine that I have already created in your mind's eye a character for Master Thrasius. A careful man, a smaller man; lesser than those who came before him. Desperate, perhaps. Petty. Failing. Let me dispel that character from your mind now. No man can become an Astartes without the potential for greatness, and no Astartes can become the master of a Chapter without a part of that greatness realised. Thrasius was no exception and he was to achieve even more over those next few years. He was big, big even for one of our kind, but his face had stayed thin. His long hair was still black where Chapter Master Thorcyra's had turned grey, and he wore his beard shorter. He was wearing a simple robe in the Chapter's colours and beneath it a vest of ceremonial scale armour, fastened loosely across his chest. I knew him to be a fierce warrior, a master tactician, and brave without question, but at that moment I saw him only as the obstacle to our Chapter finding the destiny it deserved.

I bowed; he bid me stand.

'Brother Tiresias, welcome. I regret that my absence had to be of such great duration,' he spoke. 'I understand that Brother-Captain Romonos has kept the battle company busy.'

Busy, yes, with small raids, petty battles and hasty withdrawals.

'I am told that you brought honour upon the Chapter by your actions during the campaign upon Tan.'

'My thanks, Master.' I nodded without emotion, but I relaxed a little. So this was merely to be a little perfunctory commendation. I would humour him and then find Sergeant Angeloi and tell him that our opportunity had come.

'What did you think of that campaign?' he asked.

'It was a great success. A significant victory,' I spouted what I knew I should say and bit my tongue on the rest.

The Chapter Master regarded me. 'I have read the reports, Tiresias, I asked what you thought.'

'Master, I have said already what I think. I do not know what you require from me.'

'That is an order,' he said calmly.

Well, if that was what he wished, that is what he would have. 'The campaign on Tan…' I snorted. 'The campaign on Tan was a joke. No, worse, it was a travesty. A few skirmishes, and standing guard throughout an evacuation. Providing support to others instead of leading from the front, where an Astartes should be. It does not even deserve to be called a campaign, let alone a victory.'

I stopped then. I had said too much, far too much. I had breached protocol, discipline, even simple good judgement. I looked at the Master, but his face was without expression.

'Did we lose any of our brothers?' he asked quietly.

I knew he knew already, but he wanted me to say it. 'No, no brothers lost. A few injured. Most minor. One more serious.'

'Brother Domitios, yes, but he will recover. I know also, Tiresias, that when he fell it was you who went to his defence. It was you who skewered the xenos beast that threatened him. It was you who saved his life.'

I nodded again. It was true, but I did not think it remarkable. Astartes are trained to do nothing less.

'You acquitted yourself well, brother. Very well,' the Master continued. 'You have always done so, even when you have had misgivings about the orders you have been given. That is why I wished you to speak your mind. Why I am talking to you now.'

'Do not mistake my words, Master.' I countered. 'I understand the value of restraint, of retreat when circumstances dictate. We defended the orbital stations, but we did not even try to save that planet. We did not even step foot upon the surface. Before we even entered the system we were defeated in our hearts.'

I paused. Thrasius let the silence hang in the air between us for a long moment. 'You wish for it to be as it was.' he said.

'Yes!' I gasped. 'Kraken is broken, its fleets are scattered. We do not need to sell our lives merely to delay their advance. If we commit ourselves in force we can win a victory, a true victory. As Calgar did on Ichar IV, as we did at Dal'yth Tertius, and Translock. Yes, I wish to fight as we did, with every weapon, every muscle, every sinew at our command. Come victory or death, to fight as an Astartes should.'

I had not expected to burst out with such sentiments now, to anticipate the statement that Sergeant Angeloi was readying to give him. I expected Thrasius to roar back at me, but his reply was very quick.

'One day, Tiresias, we shall fight like that again. But for now it cannot be. For now, any action where no brother is lost must be victory enough,' he said simply. 'I know that it is far easier to say than it is to accept in one's heart. That is my challenge, one of them at least, to help us understand what has happened to us. How we must change. So many brothers dead; Sotha gone, mere rubble in space. The noble Scythes of the Emperor, loyal reapers of mankind's foes, cut down ourselves by the great devourer. It is not a fate we deserved.'

He stepped away from me, his robe brushing lightly over the polished floor.

'I understand your frustration, but you must have hope in our future. And that is what I left you to acquire. Here.'

He keyed a sequence into a control and the mosaics along the walls rose smoothly, revealing pict-screens behind. They all displayed images of one of the ship's hangar bays. It had changed greatly. The fighters had gone; the machinery had all been stripped away. In their place, a bizarre maze had been constructed. Plasteel walls covered and painted to resemble the corridors of a tyranid bio-ship. Inside the maze I could see Space Marines advancing in their squads; not Space Marines, no, they were too small. They were neophytes.

As I watched, one of them trod upon a pressure-switch. A trapdoor in the floor opened and he vanished before even catching his breath to shout.

'Traps, creatures, combat servitors programmed with tyranid attack patterns. It is as real as we can make it. We have paid close attention to the data we gathered fighting these monstrosities, after all, it came to us dear.'

'How many?' I asked, my voice a whisper.

'Three hundred in total, and more to come. Young, untested, but keen. All orphans of the Kraken like ourselves. All ready to be baptised with tyranid blood.' Thrasius placed his hand upon my shoulder then. 'They only need leadership, guidance, from brothers like you. Sergeant Angeloi recommended you specifically, Tiresias. Promotion and this, your first command.'

I opened my mouth, but found for once no words were waiting there. Thrasius continued:

'You see, Tiresias, one day it shall be as it was. And it shall not take a hundred years, or even fifty. When the next hive fleet comes to plague these sectors we will be ready to answer the Emperor's call.'

I stepped back a little, and Thrasius's hand fell from me.

'I will… thank you, Master. I will be sure to thank my sergeant when I–'

And then I saw a look in Thrasius's golden eyes.

'I will ensure you will have the chance to send a message after him,' he interrupted. 'Brother-Sergeant

Angeloi has already departed to join the xenos hunters of the Inquisition, the fabled Deathwatch. Given our experiences, they requested as many brothers as we could spare to help spread the knowledge of the forms of the tyranid blight and how each may best be destroyed. I granted him, and a few others, the honour of carrying our name and our teachings to the galaxy.'

A few others, Thrasius said, but in truth over forty brothers had gone already, reassigned to the Deathwatch. They were nearly a third of our strength and each one of them was one of Angeloi's crusaders. And the chance to compel Thrasius to order one last, glorious campaign had gone with them.

'Now rest a moment, brother,' Thrasius directed me to sit, 'and allow me to share with you how your new command will aid our Chapter's Salvation.'

I never discovered the truth behind the creation of the neophyte companies. The recruits themselves I knew were, just like Gricole and our retainers, from the worlds of the long retreat. Even before the hive fleet arrived in the Sotha system, even while my squad-brothers prepared the planet's defences, plans were being made so that the Scythes might rise again.

The best of the youngsters of Sotha had already been secretly evacuated. Each place we turned to make our stand, Miral, Graia, and the rest; while my brothers fought and died, the most promising youths were recruited and rescued. Harvested by us, I suppose, while those left behind were harvested by the xenos.

But the gene-seed, that was the question. Three whole companies of neophytes and more to come, Thrasius had promised. How was it possible? There were many theories. A few were sensible; that Thorcyra had been forewarned of the attack on Sotha and ordered the gene-seed to be removed in secret, or that the old Chapter Master had struck an agreement with the Inquisition to return our gene-tithe and whether the Deathwatch Marines were the only price he had had to pay. Other theories were darker, that Thrasius had found or purchased arcane or alien tech that allowed progenoids to develop artificially far faster than in a Space Marine, or that most of the neophytes did not receive true gene-seed, they were merely bio-engineered and would never mature into true Astartes. I even heard a whisper that the gene-seed was not ours; that before the Salvation Teams there were squads designated Reaper Teams. I do not credit such thoughts, however; no Astartes would stoop to such measures even if the future of the Chapter depended upon it.

But then, I have had cause to wonder, can you ever be sure what lengths a creature will go in order to ensure the survival of its children?

'A KILOMETRE AND a half long, millions of tonnes, and a face only a hormagaunt could love...' Vitellios murmured, watching the muscles of the hive ship's offspring ripple beneath its hull-skin.

'And it's trying to get out,' Pasan said.

This was it then, the source of the 'gaunts we had encountered, the spark of life that Cassios had sworn existed. The bloated biters we had seen were not venturing inwards to wait; they were coming here to feed this offspring on the bio-matter of the corpse of its parent.

'Very well,' I decided. 'As soon as we return to the boat, we will send a despatch to the closest battle-group, Ultima priority. They will respond to that.'

'No,' Cassios said.

I scoffed. 'I assure you, commander, they will!' But then, through the visor of his faceplate, I saw the expression in his eyes.

'They will still be too late. We are the only ones who are close enough and we are here to kill that creature.'

I had had enough of him. He had challenged my command once already and I was not going to waste my breath diverting him from such vainglorious stupidity.

'As you wish, commander,' I told him and gave the signal for the Scouts to gather and follow. 'I will ensure your final action is recorded with the proper honour.' I had walked several steps before I realised my wards were not with me.

'Ensure it is recorded for all of us,' Vitellios spoke up.

I should have seen it. I should have seen it as soon as I saw them standing with Cassios as he convinced me there were others within the ship that may be saved. They were not looking at me to lead them; they were looking at me to see whether I believed their lie.

'A second beacon?' I did not look at Cassios, but rather at Narro. He knew I would have trusted him to double-check the auspex readings.

'It was not his idea,' Pasan said. 'Nor was it the commander's. It was mine.'

'Yours?' I shot back at my acolyte.

It was Cassios who replied. 'I would have left you back there. It is clear to me that you have failed as their teacher and you have failed even as their leader. But Brother Pasan wanted you here.'

I looked away from him; there was nothing he could say to me. Two days it had taken him, two days to take the loyalties of the wards I had cared for for two years. I looked back at Pasan. 'Why did you want me here? So that you may see my face as you disgrace me?'

'No,' Pasan said. 'So that you may have the chance to join us.'

'Join you?' I exclaimed. 'For what purpose would I do that? What do you offer but the futile waste of your lives?'

Pasan replied, but the four of them may as well have spoken as one.

'To know what it is to fight as an Astartes.'

I could not credit this from such youths. 'You do not know,' I told them. 'You have never seen the full Chapter deployed in battle. Squad after squad standing proud in their armour, bolters raised. Reciting your battle-oaths with one voice and then marching forwards, knowing your brothers are there for you as you are there for them. You draw such strength from them, being not one warrior fighting alone, but one of a thousand fighting together. Ten hundred bodies forming a single weapon. Until you have experienced that… you do not really know what it is to fight as an Astartes.'

The neophytes were silent. I felt my words had reached them at last.

'You are right, honoured sergeant,' Pasan said. 'We do not know. We have never experienced that. But then, when will we?'

'When you are full battle-brothers,' I said.

'Will we? Even if we do as you say. We leave here now, with you; we survive to take a place in the battle company,' Pasan glanced at his brother-Scouts for support. 'When will we ever march into battle a full Chapter strong? How long will it take us to recover before we do anything more than nip and pinch at our enemies? A hundred years, two hundred? How much more will be lost to the devourer by then?'

Pasan stood forwards and Vitellios stepped with him.

'I know you think little of me,' the hive-trash said. 'That I don't take being a high and mighty Astartes seriously. But there's one thing I am serious about. My life. I joined to scour our galaxy of the alien bastards that slaughtered my world. I didn't raise myself up from hive-trash, put myself through all the trials to be chosen as a Scythe so I could dig through the dead and grow old training the next generation. I didn't do all I've done just to become an antiquated relic…'

'As I am, you mean?' I snapped back. I was beyond anger, I was furious. I raised my hand and Vitellios braced himself for the blow, but Pasan stepped in front of him.

'Why are you against us?' he cried. 'We all know that this is what you truly want. We've heard you rail to Gricole often enough.'

'Now you are spying upon me as well?' I said, incredulous.

Hwygir grunted in the corner, 'A small craft, our transport.'

'You are not the only one with an Astartes' senses,' Vitellios chipped in, but Pasan cut him off.

'No excuses, honoured sergeant. You wanted us to hear. You wanted us to know how much you resented this mission, resented us for what we took you from. Now here is your chance. There is the enemy. We can reach it. We can kill it. Yes, some of us, all of us may die. But is this not the chance for glory you want?'

All four of them were standing now, united against me, yet united in favour of everything I believed. The anger that had flared inside me vanished.

'Yes, it is,' I agreed with them. 'More than you know. Every sinew and muscle in my body craves to carry the fight to the xenos without caution, without restraint. To serve as an Astartes should serve.'

'Then you are with us!' Pasan shouted.

'But then…' I continued. 'I look deeper than my muscle, I look into my bones. And there, inscribed a thousand times, is the oath I took to the master of this Chapter to obey his orders and the Emperor's word therein. It is an oath that I have never broken, and never will. As for the rest… I give it up.'

I swept my arm up and pointed at them. 'You are my witness! You hear me now! I give up my glory, I give up my revenge, I give up my hope of what I could have been,' I shouted even though they were close, but I knew I was not addressing them. 'I accept it cannot be as it was! A battle where no brother falls is glory enough!'

I saw their faces, they thought me mad, but in truth I was healed. The weight of the loss of my brothers, the weight of my rage that I had survived when they had not was lifted. I took a breath and breathed free for the first time since Sotha.

'No glory,' I finished quietly, 'is greater than the future of our Chapter. We are not greater than it, none of us. Any Astartes who thinks they are… there is a word for those…'

'Renegades,' Cassios said from behind me. 'But which of us is the renegade, brother? You, who defend our Chapter's crippled body or I, who defend its soul?'

'It's starting to move…' Narro reported.

'Then we shall as well,' Cassios gestured to the Scouts, once my wards, now his men, then turned back to me. 'I offer you the chance to fight as a Scythe should, with his hand, his oath on his lips and his brothers by his side. If you do not come, let it be upon you.'

'It shall be upon me,' I stated, 'but I shall come. I take this oath now: you may take these children to their deaths but I shall bring them back again.'

* * *

It was to be the final insertion of the 21st Salvation Team. The ship, the offspring, was grinding itself forward down the lifeless channel. We blew a hole through the young, unhardened skin as close to our target as we could manage. If the offspring noticed our pinprick at all its reaction was lost amidst the wild throes of its agonising birth. The chambers inside could not be more different than the dead, dark halls of its parent. Luminescent algae lit our path, the ground was springy beneath our boots, the wall-skin taut, the door valves firm, and the noise... each chamber and tunnel vibrated with the screeching noise as the offspring pulsed and squirmed out into space, but below that you could hear the hum, the pulse, the beat of its life all around you. The life the Scythes were here to take.

We moved quickly. Cassios led the way, allowing his warrior instincts to draw him towards the creature's heart. The Scouts followed a step behind; their excitement, their fear did not dull their skill. They moved easily, not in a single formation, but always shifting from one to another, running, covering. First Vitellios would run, as Pasan protected him, then Narro as Vitellios did the same, then Hwygir would charge up, bursting as ever with pride at being entrusted with the vital heavy weapon. They protected one another. For two years I had tried to find one amongst them suited to be their leader; at that moment I realised that they did not need one. They fought as one: as Hwygir reloaded, Narro shot into the tyranids to keep them from recovering; as Narro was caught by a tendril,

Pasan forced his gun down into its maw and blew its brain out; as Pasan forced open a door-valve, Vitellios destroyed the creature lurking above it; as Vitellios ran quickly back from a new rush of 'gaunts, I lent my fire to his to halt them where they stood.

Our foes were not the fearsome monsters of Macragge and Ichar IV. The ship had grown only its most basic defenders: termagants, other 'gaunts and the like; and it itself was focused on its struggle towards freedom. However, its plight, its vulnerable state, triggered a response from the creatures barring our path that was all the more visceral. Cassios did not care, he simply battered them aside. These tyranids, who had overwhelmed countless star systems with force of numbers, now found themselves overwhelmed in turn by Cassios's simple force. Every chamber we encountered he stormed, every 'gaunt in his way fell to the shells of his pistol or the curved edge of his power sword. He gave them no chance to gather, but charged into the thick of them, relying on his speed to spoil their aim and his thick armour to protect his flesh. That it did for him, but it did not for the rest of us and we suffered our first loss.

'Brother!' Hwygir shouted after Narro as he stumbled. One of the shots of bio-acid aimed too quickly at Cassios had flown past the commander and struck Narro. Across the vox, I heard him clamp down on his scream. Hwygir had already raised the heavy bolter and was struggling across to check on him.

'Keep us covered!' I yelled at him and shoved his weapon around to face the closing enemy. I heard his frustrated roar as he fired, but my focus was on the stricken Narro. He was still breathing. I rolled him and saw his arm clutching his side. Without ceremony I pulled the arm away to see the wound and discovered that the arm ended at the wrist. His hand had been eaten away.

His eyes snapped open, he looked down in shock at his stump and breathed in to holler in pain. I punched him sharply in the chest and he gasped instead, winded.

'Overcome it!' I shouted into his ear. 'You shall build yourself a new one.'

He struggled to nod as his Astartes metabolism kicked in and dampened the shock and the pain. I took his weapon and handed him my pistol.

'Sergeant!' Hwygir called back as he released the trigger for a moment. 'How is–'

I looked up as Hwygir turned his head to ask after his brother. I saw the shot hit the back of his helmet and the blood splatter on the inside of his face-plate as the tiny beetles of the bio-weapon bored through his skull and ate the flesh of his face from the inside. The savage fell and, in that instant, I felt the loss of a brother.

I dived towards his body firing wildly to force his killers to scuttle back. I cannot claim any sentimentality – I had fought too long to allow such feelings cloud my reactions – it was solely his weapon I was after. I rose and aimed the heavy bolter. I had not fired one in battle since the long retreat from Sotha. I pulled the trigger, felt the reassuring recoil and watched as its shells blew a line of bloody death across the 'gaunts' first ranks.

The offspring lurched suddenly to one side and all of us, tyranid and Space Marine alike, were knocked from our feet. Hwygir and the 'gaunt bodies rolled away. I hefted the cumbersome gun and scrambled back where Cassios and the rest of the squad had regrouped.

'It's accelerating,' Cassios said without a glance back towards where Hwygir had fallen. 'We have to move faster.'

'Does it matter?' Vitellios asked. 'We're inside it now, it's not getting away!'

'Every second we delay gives it time to call in more beasts.'

'Then what are we waiting for?' he jumped up, ever the fearless one, and smashed the butt of his shotgun against the next door-valve. The valve shrank back and he led us through. He made it a single step before a set of jaws within the valve snapped shut, razor-sharp teeth puncturing the length of Vitellios's body from his ankle to his head. I grabbed his arm, wedged the barrel under his shoulder and fired into the darkness, into whatever monster lay beyond. The door-mouth rippled in pain and slid back into the walls. It was too late, though, for Vitellios. His face was fixed in an expression of surprise, no last witticism to give. The hive-trash fell and I felt the loss of a brother.

It was then that we truly understood that it was not just these 'gaunts: every single piece of flesh around us wished us dead. The wall algae blazed brightly as we came near to draw the beasts, bulbed stalks burst and covered us in spores that sought to burrow into our armour, cysts showered us with bio-acid, even the muscles of the floor rippled as we fired, to disrupt our aim. It would have been enough to stop any human warriors, but we are Astartes. The Angels of Death. And all the offspring's efforts could not keep us from our quest's end.

'We are close,' Cassios declared, as another 'gaunt lay in pieces at his feet.

'How close?' I shouted as I delivered another volley of fire against the creatures pursuing us.

'Can't you hear it?'

I could hear nothing over the explosions of the bolt shells and the roar of the offspring's progress. It must be close to birthing now, but I did not care. Gricole would see it as soon as it emerged, he would know to carry a message back to the fleet. Others would know, they just would not know what had happened to us.

'I hear it!' Pasan cried, and then I heard it too: a deep throbbing sound.

'Brothers!' Cassios announced. 'I give you the heart of the beast!'

The single organ, if it was just one, filled the chamber beyond. It was a giant column, surrounded by red bloated chambers. From the top of each chamber split massive leeches that surmounted the top of the pillar and descended into the centre. It looked as though eight great Sothan phantine beasts were drinking from a pool. The entire structure constantly pulsed and shifted as gallons of fluid pumped through it each second. It was the energy cortex, and it was covered by tyranids. Smaller 'gaunts with bio-weapons, larger ones with great scything claws, a few at the top even had wings.

'It's a trap,' Pasan gasped. 'It let us get this far…'

'It's not a trap if we know it's coming,' Cassios told him.

No, it's insanity. I glanced at Cassios again; his eyes were at peace. Perhaps he really had been tainted, perhaps all he had done was in service of some xenos impulse inserted into his brain. Perhaps all the while we had been inside the offspring, the offspring had been inside him.

'Why don't they attack?' Pasan whispered.

'Maybe… maybe…' Narro's mind raced, he was feeling the disorientation worst of all. 'Maybe they did not wish to risk fighting here, risk damaging the cortex.'

But then the great thundering of the offspring as it climbed out the channel of its parent reached a crescendo and went silent. It was out. It was into space. My faith was with Gricole. He would do what needed to be done. It just remained for me to do the same, call this assault off, to save the lives I could. But Cassios was already advancing, a brace of mining charges in his hand. I stopped him and held one of the charges up.

'It's set to instant detonation,' I told him.

'Of course,' he replied and we locked gazes for the last time.

'Then we stay here. They deserve the chance, Cassios. Give them that.'

He shrugged, uncaring. This was to be the epic of his death; whether others were with him did not matter. I looked at my last two wards – Narro quickly nodded agreement with me, and so too, slowly, did Pasan.

'Cover him,' I told them, as Cassios raised his power sword high and cried:

'For Sotha! For the Emperor! Death! Death! Death!'

My wards and I fired in unison: heavy bolter, bolt-gun and pistol together, blowing holes in the ranks of the tyranid. The tyranids responded in kind, releasing a volley of borer-beetles, bio-acid and toxin-spines against Cassios as he charged. Cassios slammed to a halt and flinched, drawing his cloak around him. I saw his mighty frame collapse under the onslaught.

'No!' Pasan shouted and sprinted after him, spraying fire wildly as he went. The hormagaunts had already leapt from the energy cortex and were surging towards the downed commander. I did not call to bring Pasan back, I saved my breath, he would not come. I had lost him long before. Instead I trained the heavy bolter to clear his path. The first of the hormagaunt wave exploded as my shell hit home, the one behind stumbled and was knocked down by those behind it, pushing forwards, the third leapt and my next shell caught its leg and its body cart-wheeled away in pieces. The fourth reached Cassios and took the brunt of

Pasan's fire. The next rank sprang, arcing high to clear the bodies before them. Two fell to my shells, one to Narro's, but three fell upon the son of Sotha. One sliced through his gun and then his arm, the second caught his knee and cut deep into his side and the third split his head straight down the middle. The son of Sotha fell and I felt the loss of a part of myself.

Then, in a crackling arc of light, the three 'gaunts were carved apart themselves. Cassios rose, his cloak dissolved, his armour cracked and scarred. Blood streamed from the split in his armour at the neck. He spun to face the approaching horde and threw himself into their midst.

He was beyond our help now. I might have only seconds to fulfil my oath and save who I could. I turned to Narro, the last of my wards, and told him:

'I never thought it would be you. But it is best that it is.'

He looked at me, confused. I shook my head and pointed to our escape. This one at least I would save, I thought, the most brilliant of them. Perhaps, I thought, that would be enough. But I was not to be allowed even that. Above us, I heard a familiar bestial scream, first one, then a second. Without thinking, I brought the heavy bolter up straight into the ravener's face.

The brutal claw carved through the heavy bolter even as I pulled the trigger. The round rocketing down the barrel suddenly struck bone and exploded. Shrapnel burst through the barrel-cover and flew at me. I stumbled back, dropping the useless heavy weapon and clutching my face. I pulled the ruined helmet off, blinking to catch the ravener's next attack. I looked and saw it collapsed on the ground, its claw blown off, its face a mass of blood and bone. The second still held Narro's body impaled upon its scythe-claws as it twisted towards me. I drew my falx. This was to be the end.

The second ravener leapt, its two scythe-claws high. I dove forwards. The scythes came down but I was inside their reach and they glanced off my shoulders. My falx was already embedded through its chestbone. Its mid-limbs plunged through my armour and unloaded its venom as I twisted and pushed it off my blade. I staggered back, holding my guts inside my body, I was still not dead. Neither was it. It flew at me in one last attack, my falx came up and caught its scythes as they came down and pushed them to one side. As its blades went down mine cut back across its gaping mouth and sliced its head open.

I felt its ichor splatter my face, I tasted it as my mouth opened to roar my defiance. At that moment, somewhere behind me, a dying hand released its grip upon the mining charges and the chamber was filled with the Emperor's wrath.

I WOKE ABOARD a dead ship, a ravener my bedside companion. I rolled the corpse away. I dragged myself to my feet and began to search about the dark and lifeless chamber. Whether the tyranids had fled or died on the spot from the psychic shock I did not know. I was searching for something else. I found it.

I thought it impossible for any one, any Astartes, to live through that. I was right. The body of Commander Cassios was a shell. But I was not there for sentiment, I did not do that. I was there in the hope that something inside him survived. I grimaced in pain as I felt the bite of the ravener poison. A stronger dose this time, from a young beast, rather than a stale relic. I took the carnifex from my pack and placed it first against Cassios's throat and then against his chest, and took from him the Chapter's due.

MY SECOND HEART finishes its beat. My recollection concludes, as it always does, with the memory of dragging myself into this hole and, even as the bio-poison burned its way around my body, focusing on my training, slowing my mind, suspending my system and halting the poison's spread. It was too late for me; I know that. I will die when I wake. Pasan, Vitellios, Narro, Hwygir; Cassios had taken them in, but I will carry them out again. I know they are dead, their bodies lost, perhaps more bio-matter for the devourer, but their spirits live on. Two of them in the carnifex in my hand, in the progenoid glands of Commander Cassios from which new gene-seed and two new Astartes would arise. And two of them my own shell. The glands in my throat and in my chest that would bear two more. Cassios and I are lost, as we should have been long ago. These four are the future of the Scythes now, and I will live and bear the pain of poison until I deliver them back home.

* * *

'SERGEANT! OVER HERE!' the neophyte called.

Sergeant Quintos, commanding the 121st Salvation Team, strode over to his ward. The neophyte gestured down with his torch into a crevice in the floor of the dead bio-ship. Sergeant Quintos activated the light built into his bionic arm. He had lost the original years before when he himself had been a scout in a Salvation Team. Down there, glinting back in the light, shone the shoulder armour of a Space Marine. And upon that armour was inscribed the legend:

TIRESIAS

AT GAIUS POINT

Aaron Dembski-Bowden

I

THE MEMORY OF fire. Fire and falling, incineration and annihilation.

Then darkness.

Absolute silence. Absolute nothing.

II

I OPEN MY eyes.

There before me, outlined by scrolling white text across my targeting display, is a shattered metal wall. Its architecture is gothic in nature – a skeletal wall, with black steel girders like ribs helping form the wall's curvature. It is mangled and bent. Crushed, even.

I do not know where I am, but my senses are awash with perception. I hear the crackle of fire eating metal, and the angry hum of live battle armour. The sound is distorted, a hitch or a burr in the usually steady thrum. Damage has been sustained. My armour is compromised. A glance at the bio-feed displays shows minor damage to the armour plating of my wrist and shin. Nothing serious.

I smell the flames nearby, and the bitter rancidity of melting steel. I smell my own body; the sweat, the chemicals injecting into my flesh by my armour, and the intoxicatingly rich scent of my own blood.

A god's blood.

Refined and thinned for use in mortal veins, but a god's blood nevertheless.

A dead god. A slain angel.

The thought brings my teeth together in a grunted curse, my fangs scraping the teeth below. Enough of this weakness.

I rise, muscles of aching flesh bunching in unison with the fibre-bundle false muscles of my armour. It is a sensation I am familiar with, yet it feels somehow flawed. I should be stronger. I should exult in my strength, the ultimate fusion of biological potency and machine power.

I do not feel strong. I feel nothing but pain and a momentary disorientation. The pain is centralised in my spinal column and shoulder blades, turning my back into a pillar of dull, aching heat. Nothing is broken – bio-feeds have already confirmed that. The soreness of muscle and nerve would have killed a human, but we are gene-forged into greater beings.

Already, the weakness fades. My blood stings with the flood of adrenal stimulants and kinetic enhancement narcotics rushing through my veins.

My movement is unimpeded. I rise to my feet, slow not from weakness now, but from caution.

With my vision stained a cooling emerald shade by my helm's green eye lenses, I take in the wreckage around me.

This chamber is ruined, half-crushed with its walls distorted. Restraint thrones lie broken, torn from the floor. The two bulkheads leading from the chamber are both wrenched from their hinges, hanging at warped angles.

The impact must have been savage.

The… impact?

The crash. Our Thunderhawk crashed. The clarity of recollection is sickening… the sense of falling from the sky, my senses drenched in the thunder of descent, the shaking of the ship in its entirety. Temperature gauges on my retinal display rose slowly when the engines died in exploding flares that scorched the hull, and my armour systems registered the gunship's fiery journey groundward.

There was a final booming refrain, a roar like the carnosaurs of home – as loud and primal as their predator-king challenges – and the world shuddered beyond all sanity. The gunship ploughed into the ground.

And then… Darkness.

My eyes flicker to my retinal display's chronometer. I was unconscious for almost three minutes. I will do penance for such weakness, but that can come later.

Now I breathe in deep, tasting the ashy smoke in the air but unaffected by it. The air filtration in my helm's grille renders me immune to such trivial concerns.

'Zavien,' a voice crackles in my ears. A momentary confusion takes hold at the sound of the word. The vox-signal is either weak, or the sender's armour is badly damaged. With the ship in pieces, both could be true.

'Zavien,' the voice says again.

This time I turn at the name, realising it is my own.

ZAVIEN STRODE INTO the cockpit, keeping his balance on the tilted floor through an effortless combination of natural grace and his armour's joint-stabilisers.

The cockpit had suffered even more than the adjacent chamber. The view window, despite the thickness of the reinforced plastek, was shattered beyond simple repair. Diamond shards of the sundered false-glass twinkled on the twisted floor. The pilot thrones were wrenched from their support columns, cast aside like detritus in a storm.

Through the windowless viewport there was nothing but mud and gnarled black roots, much of which had spilled over the lifeless control consoles. They'd come down hard enough to drive the gunship's nose into the earth.

The pilot, Varlon, was a mangled wreck sprawled face-down over the control console. Zavien's targeting reticule locked onto his brother's battered armour, secondary cursors detailing the rents and wounds in the deactivated war plate. Blood, thick and dark, ran from rips in Varlon's throat and waist joints. It ran in slow trickles across the smashed console, dripping between buttons and levers.

His power pack was inactive. Life signs were unreadable, but the evidence was clear enough. Zavien heard no heartbeat from the body, and had Varlon been alive, his gene-enhanced physiology would have clotted and sealed all but the most grievous wounds. He wouldn't still be bleeding slowly all over the controls of the downed gunship.

'Zavien,' said a voice to the right, no longer over the vox.

Zavien turned from Varlon, his armour snarling in a growl of joint-servos. There, pinned under wreckage from the collapsed wall, was Drayus. Zavien moved to the fallen warrior's side, seeing the truth. No, Drayus was not just pinned in place. He was impaled there.

The sergeant's black helm was lowered, chin down on his collar, green eyes regarding the broken Imperial eagle on his chest. Jagged wreckage knifed into his dark armour, the ravaged steel spearing him through the shoulder guard, the arm, the thigh and the stomach. Blood leaked through his helm's speaker grille. The biometric displays that flashed up on Zavien's visor told an ugly story, and one with an end soon to come.

'Report,' Sergeant Drayus said – the way he always said it – as if the scene around them were the most mundane situation imaginable.

Zavien kneeled by the pinned warrior, fighting back the aching need in his throat and gums to taste the blood of the fallen. Irregular and weak, a single heartbeat rattled in Drayus's chest. One of his hearts had shut down, likely flooded by internal haemorrhaging or burst by the wreckage piercing his body. The other pounded gamely, utterly without rhythm.

'Varlon is dead,' Zavien said.

'I can see that, fool.' The sergeant reached up one hand, the one not half-severed at the forearm, and clawed with unmoving fingers at the collar joint beneath his helm. Zavien reached to help, unlocking the helmet's pressurised seals. With a reptilian hiss, the helmet came free in Zavien's hands.

Drayus's craggy face, ruined by the pits and scars earned in two centuries of battle, was awash in spatters of blood. He grinned, showing blood-pinked teeth and split gums. 'My helm display is damaged. Tell me who is still alive.'

Zavien could see why it was damaged – both eye lenses were cracked. He discarded the sergeant's helm, and blink-clicked the runic icon that brought up the rest of the squad's life signs on his own retinal display.

Varlon was dead, his suit powered down. The evidence of that was right before Zavien's eyes.

Garax was also gone, his suit transmitting a screed of flat-line charts. The rangefinder listed him as no more than twenty metres away, likely thrown clear in the crash and killed on impact.

Drayus was dying, right here.

Jarl was...

'Where's Jarl?' Zavien asked, his voice harsh and guttural through his helm's vox speakers.

'He's loose.' Drayus sucked in a breath through clenched teeth. His armour's failing systems were feeding anaesthetic narcotics into his blood, but the wounds were savage and fatal.

'My rangefinder lists him as a kilometre distant.' Even with its unreliability compared to a tracking auspex, it was a decent enough figure to trust.

The sergeant's good hand clenched Zavien's wrist, and he glared into his brother's eye lenses with a fierce, bloodshot stare. 'Find him. Whatever it takes, Zavien. Bring him in, even if you have to kill him.'

'It will be done.'

'After. You must come back, after.' Drayus spat onto his own chest, marking the broken Imperial eagle with his lifeblood. 'Come back for our gene-seed.'

Zavien nodded, rising to his feet. Feeling his fingers curl in the need to draw weapons, he stalked from the cockpit without a backward glance at the sergeant he would never see alive again.

Jarl had awoken first.

In fact, it was truer to say that Jarl had simply not lost his grip on consciousness in the impact, for his restraints bound him with greater security than the standard troop-thrones.

In the shaking thunder of the crash, he had seen Garax hurled through the torn space where a wall had been a moment before. He had heard the vicious, wet snap of destroyed vertebrae and ruined bone as Garax had crashed into the edge of the hole on the way out. And he had seen Zavien thrown from his restraint throne to smash sidelong into the cockpit bulkhead, sliding to the floor unconscious.

Enveloped in a force cage around his own restraint throne, Jarl had seen these things occurring through the milky shimmer-screen of electrical force, yet had been protected against the worst of the crash.

Ah, but that protection had not lasted for long. With the gunship motionless, with his brothers silent, with the Thunderhawk around him creaking and burning in the chasm it had carved in the ground, Jarl tore off the last buckles and scrambled over the wreckage of what had been his power-fielded throne. The machine itself, its generator smoking, reeked of captivity. Jarl wanted to be far from it.

He glanced at Zavien, stole the closest weapons he could find in the chaos of the crash site, and ran out into the jungle.

He had a duty to fulfil. A duty to the Emperor.

His father.

ZAVIEN'S BLADE AND bolter were gone.

Without compunction, he took Drayus's weapons from the small arming chamber behind the transport room, handling the relics with none of the care he would otherwise have used. Time was of the essence.

The necessary theft complete, he climbed from the wreck of the gunship, vaulting down to the ground and leaving the broken hull behind. In one hand was an idling chainaxe, the motors within the haft chuckling darkly in readiness to be triggered into roaring life. In the other, a bolt pistol, its blackened surface detailed with the crude scratchings of a hundred and more kill-runes.

Zavien didn't look at the smoking corpse of his gunship in some poignant reverie. He knew he would be back to gather the gene-seed of the fallen if he survived this hunt.

There was no time for sentiment. Jarl was loose.

Zavien broke into a run, his armour's joints growling at the rapid movement as he sprinted after his wayward brother, deep into the jungles of Armageddon.

III

THEY CALL IT Armageddon.

Maybe so. There is nothing to love about this planet.

Whatever savage beauty it once displayed is long dead now, choked under the relentless outflow of the sky-choking factories that vomit black smog into the heavens. The skies themselves are ugly enough – a greyish-yellow shroud of weak poison embracing the strangled world below. It does not rain water here. It rains acid, as thin, weak and strangely pungent as a reptile's piss.

Who could dwell here? In such impurity? The air tastes of sulphur and machine oil. The sky is the colour of infection. The humans – the very souls we are fighting to save – are dead-eyed creatures without passion or life.

I do not understand them. They embrace their enslavement. They accept their confinement within towering manufactories filled with howling machines. Perhaps it is because they have never known freedom, but that is no true excuse to act as brain-killed as a servitor.

We fight for these souls because we are told it is our duty. We are dying, selling our lives in the greatest war this world has ever known, to save them from their own weakness and allow them to return to their lightless lives.

The jungle here… We have jungles on my home world, yet not like this.

The jungles of home are saturated with life. Parasites thrive in every pool of dark water. Insects hollow out the great trees to build their chittering, poisonous hives. The air, already swarming with stinging flies, is sour with the reptilian stench of danger, and the ground will shake with the stalking hunts of the lizard predator-kings.

Survival is the greatest triumph one can earn on Cretacia.

The jungle here barely deserves the name. The ground is clinging mud, leaving you knee-deep in sulphuric sludge. What ragged life breathes the unclean air is weak, irritating, and nothing compared to the threats of home.

Of course, the jungles here possess a danger not even remotely native to the planet itself. They swarm with the worst kind of vermin.

With the planet locked in the throes of invasion, I am all too aware of what brought down our Thunderhawk.

A pack of them hunted up ahead.

As soon as he heard their piggish snarls and barking laughter, Jarl's tongue ached with a raw, coppery urgency. His teeth itched in their sockets, and he felt his heartbeat in the soft tissue around his incisors.

His splashing sprint through the jungle became a hunched and feral stride, while the chainblade in his grip growled each time he gunned the trigger. Small arms fire rattled in his direction even before he cleared the line of trees. They knew he was coming, he made sure of that.

Jarl ignored the metallic rainfall of solid rounds clanging from his war plate. The trees parted and revealed his prey – six of them – hunkered around a tank made of scavenged, rusted scrap.

Greenskins. Their fat-mouthed pistols crashing loud and discordant, their brutish features illuminated by the flickering of muzzle flashes.

Jarl saw none of this. His vision, filtered through targeting reticules, saw only what his dying mind projected. A far greater enemy, the ancient slaves of the Ruinous Powers, feasting on the bodies of the loyal fallen. Where Jarl ran, the skies were not the milky-yellow of pus, but the deep blue of nightfall on ancestral Terra. He did not splash through black-watered marshland. He strode across battlements of gold while the world ended around him in a storm of heretical fire.

Jarl charged, his scream rendered harsh and deafening by his helm's vocalisers. The chainsword's throaty roar reached an apex in the moment before it was brought down onto the shoulder of the first ork.

The killing fury brought darkness again, but the blackness now was awash with blessed, sacred red.

ZAVIEN HEARD THE slaughter. His pace, already at a breakneck sprint through the vegetation, intensified tenfold.

If he could catch Jarl, catch him before his brother made it to Imperial lines, he would avert a catastrophe of innocent blood and the blackest shame.

His red and black war plate – the dark red of arterial blood, the black of the void between worlds – was a ruined mess of burn markings, silver gougings where damage in the crash had scored away the paint from the ceramite's surface, and mud-spattered filth as he raced through the swamp.

Yet when one carries the pride of a Chapter on one's shoulders, necessity lends strength to aching limbs and the false muscles of broken armour.

Zavien burst into the clearing where his brother was embattled. His trigger fingers clenched at once – one unleashing a torrent of bolter shells at his brother's back, the other gunning the chainaxe into whirring, lethal life.

'Jarl!'

Treachery.

What madness was this? To be struck down by one's own sons? Sanguinius, the Angel of Blood, turns from the twisted daemons he has slain and dismembered. One of his own sons screams his name, charging across the golden battlements while the heavens above them burn.

The primarch cries out as his son's weapon speaks in anger. Bolt shells crack against his magnificent armour. His own son, one of his beloved Blood Angels, is trying to kill him.

This cannot be happening.

And, in that moment, Sanguinius decides it is not. There is heresy at work here, not disloyalty. Blasphemy, not naked betrayal.

'What foulness grips you!' the Angel cries at his false son. 'What perversion blackens the soul of a Blood Angel and warps him to serve the Archenemy?'

'Sanguinius!' the traitor son screams. 'Father!'

ZAVIEN ROARED JARL'S name again, not knowing what his brother truly heard. The cries that returned from his brother's vox-amplifiers chilled his blood – a bellowed, clashing litany of archaic High Gothic and the tongue of Baal that Jarl had never learned.

Surrounded by the ravaged bodies of dead greenskins, the two brothers came together. Zavien's first blow was blocked, the flat of Jarl's chainblade clashing against the haft of his axe. Jarl's armour was pitted and cracked with smoking holes from the impact of bolt shells, yet his strength was unbelievable. Laughing in a voice barely his own, he hurled Zavien backwards.

Unbalanced by his brother's insane vigour, Zavien fell back, rolling into a fighting crouch, shin-deep in marshwater.

Again, Jarl shouted in his unnerving, ancient diction – words Zavien recognised but did not understand. As with Jarl, he had never learned Baalian, and never studied the form of High Gothic spoken ten thousand years before.

'Let this not be your end, my son. Join me! We will take the fight to Horus and drown his evil ambitions in the blood of his tainted warriors!'

Sanguinius removes his helm – a sign of honour and trust despite the war raging around them – and smiles beneficently at his wayward son. His benevolence is legendary. His honour without question.

'It need not be this way,' the Angel of Blood says through his princely smile. 'Join me! To my father's side! For the Emperor!'

ZAVIEN STARED AT his brother, barely recognising Jarl's face in the drooling, slack-jawed grin that met his gaze. His brother's features were red; a shining wetness from eyes that cried blood.

A meaningless screed of syllables hammered from Jarl's bleeding mouth. It sounded like he was choking on his own demented laughter.

'Brother,' Zavien spoke softly. 'You are gone from us all.'

He rose to his feet, casting aside the empty bolt pistol. In his red gauntlets, he clutched the chainaxe two-handed, and stared at the brother he no longer knew.

'I am not your son, Jarl, and I am no longer your brother. I am Zavien of the Flesh Tearers, born of

Cretacia, and I will be your death if you will not let me be your salvation.'

Jarl heaved a burbling laugh, bringing bloody froth to his lips as he wheezed in a language he shouldn't know.

'You disgrace my bloodline,' the Angel said with infinite sorrow, his godlike heart breaking at the blasphemy before his eyes. 'The Ultimate Gate calls to me. A thousand of your masters will fall by my blade before they gain entrance to the Emperor's throne room. I have no more patience for your puling heresy. Come, traitor. Time to die.'

Sanguinius unfurled his great white wings, pearlescent and sunlight-bright in the firestorm wreathing the battlements. With tears in his eyes, tears of misery at the betrayal of one of his own sons, he launched forward to end this blasphemy once and for all.

AND I REALISE I cannot beat him.

When we are shaped into what we are, when we are denied our humanity to become weapons of war, it is said that fear is purged from our physical forms, and triumph is bred into our bones. This is an expression, an attempt at the kind of crude verse forever attributed to the warrior-preachers of the Adeptus Astartes.

It is true that defeat is anathema to us.

But I cannot beat him. He is not the warrior I trained with for decades, not the brother whose every move I can anticipate.

His chainblade, still wet with green gore, arcs down. I block, barely, and am already skidding back in the sulphuric mud. His strength is immense. I know why this is. I am aware of the... the genetic truths at play. His mind cannot contain his delusional fury. He is using everything he has, *everything*, powering his muscles with more force and expending more energy than a functioning mind can allow. I can smell the alkaline reek of his blood through the damage in his armour – combat narcotics are flooding his system in lethal quantities. In his madness, he cannot stem the flood of battle narcotics fusing with his bloodstream.

His strength, this godly power, will kill him.

But not quickly enough.

A second deflected slice, a third, and a fourth that crashes against my helm; a blocked headbutt that crunches into my bracer and dulls my arm; a kick that hammers into my chestplate even as I lean aside to dodge.

A thunderclap. My vision spins. Fire in my spine.

I think my back is broken. I try to say his name, but it comes out as a scream.

Rage, black and wholesome, its tendrils bearing the purest intent, creeps in at the edge of my vision.

I hear him laughing and damning me in a language he shouldn't know.

Then I hear nothing except the wind.

Sanguinius lifts the traitor with contemptuous ease.

Held above his head, the blasphemer thrashes and writhes. The Angel of Blood stalks to the edge of the golden battlements, laughing and weeping all at once at the carnage below. It is a tragedy, but it is also beautiful. Mankind using its greatest might and achievements as it attempts to engineer its own demise. Titans duel in their hundreds, with millions of men dying around their iron feet. The sky is on fire. The entire world smells of blood.

'Die,' the Angel curses his treacherous son with a beauteous whisper, and hurls him from the battlements of the Imperial Palace into the maelstrom of war hundreds of metres below.

Freed of his burden and his bloodline's honour restored, the Angel in gold makes haste away.

His duty is not yet done.

IV

CONSCIOUSNESS RETURNED WITH the first impact.

A jarring crunch of armour against rock jolted Zavien from his lapse into the murky haze of near-unconsciousness. Feeling himself crashing down the cliff side, he rammed his hand down hard into the rock – a claw of ceramite clutching at the stone. The Astartes grunted as his arms snapped straight, taking his weight, arresting his tumbling fall.

Damage runes flicked up on his retinal display, a language of harsh white urgency. Zavien ignored them, though it was harder to ignore the pain throughout his body. Even the injected chemical anaesthetic compounds from his armour and the nerve-dulling surgery done to him couldn't entirely wash it away. That was a bad sign.

He clawed his way back up the cliff, teeth clenched, gauntlets tearing handholds into the stone where nature hadn't provided any.

Once at the top, the Flesh Tearer retrieved the chainaxe that had flown from his grip, and broke into a staggering run.

HE ALMOST KILLED me.

That is a hard truth to swallow, for we were evenly matched for all of our lives. My armour is damaged, operating at half capacity, but it still lends me strength as I run. Behind me, the wrecked greenskin tank remains alone, its crew slain, the rest of its missiles aiming into the sky with no one to fire them.

Curse those piggish wretches for bringing down our gunship.

I run on, gathering speed, slowing only to hack hanging vegetation from my path.

I recall the topography of this region from the hololithic maps at the last war council. The mining town of Dryfield is to the east. Jarl's rage-addled mind will drive him to seek out life. I know where he is going. I also know that unless something slows him down...

He will get there first.

SISTER AMALAY D'VORIEN kissed the bronze likeness of Saint Silvana, and let the necklace icon fall back on its leather cord. The weak midday sun, what brightness penetrated the gauzy, polluted cloud cover, was a dull presence in the heavens, only occasionally reflecting glare off the edges of *Promethia*, the squad's Immolator tank.

Her own armour was once silver, now stained a faint, dull grey from exposure to the filthy air of this world. She licked her cracked lips, resisting the desire to drink from the water canteen inside the tank. Second Prayer was only an hour before, and she'd slaked her thirst with a mouthful of the brackish water, warmed as it was by the tank's idling engine.

'Sister…' called down Brialla from the Immolator's turret. 'Did you see that?'

Amalay and Brialla were alone while the rest of their squad patrolled the edges of the jungle. Their tank idled on the dirt road, with Amalay circling the hull, bolter in hand, and Brialla panning her heavy flamers along the tree lines.

Amalay whispered a litany of abasement before duty, chastising herself for letting her mind wander to thoughts of sustenance. Her bolter up and ready, she moved around to the front of the Immolator.

'I saw nothing,' she said, eyes narrowed and focused. 'What was it?'

'Movement. Something dark. Remain vigilant.'

There was a tone colouring Brialla's voice, on the final words. A suggestion of disapproval. Amalay's laxity had been noticed.

'I see nothing,' Amalay spoke again. 'There's… No, wait. *There.*'

The 'something' broke from its crouch in the vegetation at the tree line. A blur of crimson and black, with a chainblade revving. Amalay recognised an Astartes instantly, and the threat a moment later. Her bolter barked once, twice, and dropped from her hands to clatter to the dirt. The gun crashed once more from its vantage point on the ground, a loud boom that hammered a shell into the tank's sloped armour plating.

Even as this last shot was fired, Amalay's head flew clear of her shoulders, white hair catching the wind before the bleeding wreckage rolled into the undergrowth.

Brialla blasphemed as she brought the flamer turret around on protesting mechanics, and wrenched the handles to aim the cannons low.

The Astartes was cradling Amalay's headless body, speaking to it in a low snarl. Her sister was already dead. Brialla squeezed both triggers.

Twin gouts of stinking chemical flame roared from the cannons, bathing Amalay and the Astartes in clinging, corrosive fire. She was already whispering a lament for her fallen sister, even as she blistered the armour and skin from Amalay's bones.

It was impossible to see through the reeking orange miasma. Brialla killed the jets of flame after seven heartbeats, knowing whatever had been washed in the fire would be annihilated, purged in the burning storm.

Amalay. Her armour blackened, its joints melted, her hands reduced to blackened bone. She lay on the ground, incinerated.

A loud thud clanged on the tank's roof behind Brialla. She turned in her restraint throne, the slower turret cycling round to follow her gaze. Already, she was trying to scramble free of her seat.

The Astartes was burning. Holy fire licked at the edges of his war plate, and his joints steamed. He eclipsed the sun, casting a flickering shadow over her. His armour was black, charred, but not immolated. As she hauled herself out of her restraints, he levelled a dripping chainsword at her face.

'The Flesh Tearers!' she screamed into the vox-mic built into her armour's collar. 'Echoes of Gaius Point!'

In anciently-accented Gothic, her killer said six whispered words.

'You will pay for your heresy.'

I watch from the shadows of the trees.

The Sororitas are tense. While one of them performs funerary rites over the destroyed bodies of their sisters, three others stalk around the hull of their grey tank, bolters aimed while they stare into the jungle through gunsights.

I can smell the corpses beneath the white shrouds. One is burned, cooked by promethium chemical fire. The other had bled a great deal before she died, torn to pieces. I do not need to see the remains to know this is true.

For now, I hide, crouched and hidden. The jungle masks the ever-present charged hum of my armour from their weak, mortal ears, while I listen to fragments of their speech.

Jarl's trail has grown cold, even the smell of his potent blood lost in the billion scents of this sulphuric jungle. I need focus. I need direction.

But as soon as I draw near enough to see the sisters' steel-grey armour and the insignias of loyalty they each wear, I curse my fortune.

The Order of the Argent Shroud.

They were with us at Gaius Point.

Echoes of that battle will haunt us all until the Chapter's final nights.

'My auspex senses something,' I hear one of them say to her sisters. I make ready to move again, to taste shame and flee. I cannot confront them like this. They must not know of our presence. 'Something alive,' she says. 'And with a power signature.'

'Flesh Tearer!' one of the sisters calls out, and my blood freezes in my veins. It is not fear I feel, but true, sickening dread as she uses our Chapter's sacred name. *How can they know?*

'Flesh Tearer! Show yourself! Face the Emperor's judgement for the barbarity of your tainted Chapter!'

My teeth clench. My fingers quiver, then grip the chainaxe tighter. *They know.* They know a Flesh Tearer did this. Their wretched slain sisters must have warned them.

Another female voice, the one carrying the auspex scanner, adds to the first one's cries. 'We were at

Gaius Point, decadent filth! Face us, and face retribution for your heresy!'

They know what happened at Gaius Point. They saw our shame, our curse, and the blood that ran that day.

They believe I butchered two of their sisters here, and now lay the sins of my brother Jarl upon my shoulders.

Gunfire rings out. A bolter shell slices past my pauldron, shredding vegetation.

'I see him,' a female voice declares, 'There!'

My trigger finger strokes the Engage rune on the chainaxe's haft. After a heartbeat's hesitation, I squeeze. Jagged, whirring teeth cycle into furious life. The weapon cuts air in anticipation of the moment it will eat flesh.

They *dare* blame me for this...

They open fire.

I am not a heretic.

But this must end.

V

ZAVIEN REACHED DRYFIELD just as the sun was setting.

He had left the jungle behind three hours before. The lone warrior's run came to an end at the fortified walls – outside the mining settlement, he heard no sound from within, only the desperate howl of the wind across the wasteland.

Hailing the walls, calling for sentries, earned him no response.

The settlement's gates were sealed: a jury-rigged amalgamation of steel bars, flakboard and even furniture piled high behind the double doors in the wall ringing the village. These pitiful defences were the colony's attempts to reinforce their walls against the ork hordes sweeping across the planet.

With neither the time nor the inclination to hammer the gates open through force, Zavien mag-locked his axe to his back and punched handholds in the metal wall itself, dragging himself to the ramparts fifteen metres above.

The village was a collection of one-storey buildings, perhaps enough to house fifteen families. A dirt track cut through the village's centre like an old scar; evidence of the supply convoys that made it this far out from the main hives, and the passage of ore haulers who came to profit from the local copper mine. Low-quality metal would be in great demand by the planet's impoverished citizens, who could afford no better.

The largest building – indeed, the only one that was more than a hut made from scrap – was a spired church bedecked in crudely-carved gargoyles.

Zavien acknowledged all of this in a heartbeat's span. The Astartes scanned the ramshackle battlements around the village, then turned to stare at the settlement itself.

No sign of movement.

He walked from the platform, falling the fifteen metres to the ground and landing in a balanced crouch.

He came across the first body less than a minute later.

A woman. Unarmed. Slumped against the wall of a hovel, a blood-smear decorating the wall behind her. She was carved in half, and not cleanly.

The wide streets between the ramshackle huts and homes were decorated with trails of blood and the tracks of weight dragged through the dirt. All of these led to the same place. Whomever had come here and slain the colonists had dragged the bodies to the modest church with its shattered windows and corroded walls of flakboard and red iron.

Zavien's retinal locator display was finally picking up faint returns from Jarl's war plate. His brother was inside, no longer running. And from the silence, no longer killing.

The Flesh Tearer stalked past the weaponless corpse, limp in its lifeless repose, slain by his own sword in his brother's hands. Zavien had seen such things before – they were images he would never forget while he still drew breath.

He felt cold, clinging shame run through his blood like a toxin. Just like at Gaius Point.

It wasn't supposed to happen.

At Gaius Point.

It was never supposed to happen.

THAT NIGHT, THEY had damned themselves forever.

It should have been a triumph worthy of being etched onto the armour of every warrior that fought there.

The Imperial front line was held by the Point's militia and the Order of the Argent Shroud, who had rallied the people of the wasteland town into an armed fighting force and raised morale to fever pitch through their sermons and blessings in the name of the God-Emperor.

The greenskins descended in a swarm of thousands, hurling themselves at the town's barricades, their mass forming a sea of bellowing challenges, leathery flesh and hacking blades.

At the battle's apex, the Sisters and the militia were on the edge of being overwhelmed. At last, and when it mattered most, Gaius Point's frantic distress calls were answered.

They came in Thunderhawks, boosters howling as they soared over the embattled horde. The gunships kissed the scorched earth only long enough to deploy their forces: almost two hundred Astartes in armour of arterial red and charcoal black. The rattling roar of so many chainblades came together in a ragged, ear splitting chorus, sounding like the warcry of a mechanical god.

Zavien was in the first wave. Alongside Jarl and his brothers, he hewed left and right, his blade's grinding teeth chewing through armour and bloody, fungal flesh as the sons of Sanguinius reaped the aliens' lives.

The orks were butchered in droves, caught between a hammer and anvil, being annihilated from behind and gunned down from the front.

Zavien saw nothing but blood. Xenos blood, stinking and thick, splashing across his helm. The smell of triumph, the reek of exultant victory.

He was also one of the first to the barricades.

By then, he couldn't see. He couldn't think. His senses were flooded by stimuli, all of it aching, enticing and maddening. He tried to speak, but it tore from his lips as a cry aimed at the polluted skies. Even breathing did nothing but draw the rich scent of alien blood deeper into his body, disseminating it through his system. To be so saturated by xenos taint ignited a fire in his mind, tapping into the gene-deep fury that forever threatened to overwhelm him.

Driven on by the ceaseless urge to drown his senses in the purity of enemy blood, Zavien disembowelled the last ork before him, and vaulted the barricade. He had to kill. *He had to kill.* He was born for nothing else.

He and his brothers had been fighting in ferocious hand-to-hand battle for two hours. The enemy was destroyed. The joyous cheers of the militia died in thousands of throats as, in a wave of vox-screams and howling chainswords, half of the Flesh Tearers broke the barricades and ran into the town.

With no foes to slay, the Astartes turned their rage upon whatever still lived.

The Angel mourned the slain.

Their deaths were a dark necessity on the path to redemption. The prayers he chanted to the ceiling of the Emperor's throne room inspired tears in his eyes, and tears in the eyes of the thousands of loyal soldiers staring on.

'We must burn the slain,' he whispered through the silver tears. 'We must forever remember those who died this

day, and remember the foulness that turned their hearts against us.'

'Sanguinius!' a voice cried from behind. It echoed throughout the chamber, where a million banners hung in the breezeless air, marking every regiment ever sworn to fight and die for the young Imperium of Man.

The Angel tilted his head, the very image of patient purity.

'I thought I killed you, heretic.'

'JARL!'

Wheezing, mumbling, with bloody saliva running in strings from his damaged mouth grille, Jarl staggered around to face his brother.

What burbled from his mouth was a mixture of languages, wet with the blood in his throat. The chemical reek of Jarl's body assaulted Zavien's senses even over the smell of his brother's burned armour and the reek of the slain. The combat narcotics flooding Jarl's body were eating him alive.

Zavien did nothing but stare for several moments after he called his brother's name. The dead were everywhere, piled all across the floor of the church, a slumbering congregation of the slaughtered. Perhaps a hundred of them, all dragged here after the carnage. Perhaps many of them had been found here in worshipful service, and only half the village had needed to be dragged. Trails of streaked, smeared blood marked the floor.

'Burn the bodies,' Jarl said in grunted Cretacian, the tongue of their shared home world, amongst a screed of words Zavien couldn't make out. 'Purge the sin, burn the bodies, cleanse the palace.'

Zavien raised his chainaxe. In sickening mirror image, his blood-maddened brother raised his dripping chainsword.

'This ends now, Jarl.'

There was a bark of syllables, a drooling mess of annihilated words.

The Angel raised his golden blade.

He had been so foolish. This was no mere heretic. Had he been blinded all along? Yes… the machinations of the tainted traitors had shrouded his golden eyes from the truth. But now… Now he saw everything.

'Yes, Horus,' he said with a smile that spoke of infinite regret. 'It ends now.'

VI

THE BROTHERS MET in the defiled church, their boots struggling to grip the mosaic-laid floor, awash as it was with innocent blood. The whining roar of chainblades was punctuated by crashes as the weapons met. Jagged teeth shattered with every block and parry, clattering against nearby wooden pews as they were torn from their sockets.

Zavien's blood hammered through his body, tingling with the electric edge of combat stimulants. Jarl was a shadow of the warrior he had been – frothing at the mouth, raving at allies that didn't exist, and half-crippled by the lethal battle-drug overdose that was burning out his organs.

Zavien blocked his brother's frantic, shaking cuts. Every time his axe fell, he'd carve another chasm into Jarl's armour. Ultimately, only one warrior was aware enough to know this would never be settled by chainblades.

With a last block and a savage return, Zavien smashed Jarl's blade aside and kicked it from his grip. Its engine stuttered to a halt, resting on the tiled ground. Jarl watched it fly from his grip with delayed, bleeding vision.

Before he could recover, Zavien's hands were at his throat. The Flesh Tearer squeezed, his hands crunching into Jarl's neck, collapsing the softer joint-armour there and vicing into the flesh beneath.

Jarl fell to his knees as his brother strangled him. His gene-enhanced physiology was poisoned by both the curse and the narcotics, and his sight began to darken as his body could take no more punishment.

Darken, yet clear.

Deprived of air, unable to even draw a shred of breath, he mouthed a voiceless word that never left the confines of his charred helm.

'Zavien.'

Zavien wrenched his grip to the side, snapping the bones of his brother's spine, and still strangling.

He stood like this for some time. Night had fallen before the warrior's gauntlets released their burden and Jarl's body finally slumped to the ground.

There the madman rested, asleep among those he had slain.

'It is done,' Zavien spoke into his squad's vox channel, his eyes closed as only silence replied.

'Jarl is dead, brothers. It is done.'

HE CHOSE TO finish what his brother had begun. Even in madness, there sometimes hides a little sense.

The bodies had to be burned. Not to purify any imagined heresy, but to hide the evidence of what had happened here.

It was never supposed to happen. Here, or at Gaius Point. They had damned themselves, and all that remained was to fight as loyally as they could before righteous vengeance caught up with them all.

As the church burned, pouring thick black smoke into the polluted sky, the sound of engines grumbled from the horizon.

Orks. The enemy was finally here.

Zavien stood among the flames, immune to them, his axe in his hand. The fire would draw the aliens closer. There was no way he could defend the whole village against them, but the thought of shedding and tasting their blood before he finally fell ignited his killing urge.

His fangs ached as the vehicles pulled in to a halt outside.

No.

Those engine sounds were too clean, too well-maintained. It was the enemy. But it was not the greenskins.

* * *

I WALK FROM the church, the broken axe in my hand.

There are twenty of them. In human unison, impressive enough even if it lacks the perfection of Astartes unity, they raise their bolters. The Sisters of the Order of the Argent Shroud. The silver hulls of their tanks and their own armour are turned a flickering orange-red in the light of the fire that should have hidden our sins.

Twenty guns aim at me.

The thirst fades. My hunger to taste blood trickles back into my throat, suddenly ignorable.

'We were at Gaius Point,' the lead sister calls out. Their eyes are narrowed at the brightness of the flame behind me.

I do not move. I tell them, simply:

'I know.'

'We have petitioned the Inquisition for your Chapter's destruction, Flesh Tearer.'

'I know.'

'That is all you have to say for yourself, heretic? After Gaius Point? After killing the squad of our sister Amalay D'Vorien? *After massacring an entire village?*'

'You came to pass judgement,' I tell her. 'So do it.'

'We came to defend this colony against your wretched blasphemy!'

They still fear me. Even outnumbered and armed only with a shattered axe, they still fear me. I can smell it in their sweat, hear it in their voices, and see it in their wide eyes that reflect the flames.

I look over my shoulder, where Jarl's legacy burns. Motes of amber fire sail up from the blaze. My brother's funeral pyre, and a testament to what we have all become. A monument to how far we have fallen.

We burn our dead on Cretacia. Because so many are killed by poisons and beasts and the predator-king reptiles, it is a mark of honour to die and be burned, rather than be taken by the forest.

It was never meant to be like this. Not here, and not at Gaius Point.

Twenty bolters open fire before I can look back.

I don't hear them. I don't feel the wet, knifing pain of destruction.

All I hear is the roar of a Cretacian predator-king, the fury rising from its reptilian jaws as it stalks the jungles of my home world. A carnosaur, black-scaled and huge, roaring up to the clear, clean skies.

It hunts me. It hunts me now, as it hunted me so long ago, at the start of this second life.

I reach for my spear, and…

Zavien clutches the weapon against his chest.

'It is death itself,' he grunts to his tribal brothers as they crouch in the undergrowth. The tongue of Cretacia is simple and plain, little more than the rudiments of true language. 'The king-lizard is death itself. It comes for us.'

The carnosaur shakes the ground with another slow step closer. It breathes in short sniffs, mouth open, jaws slack, tasting the air for scents. A grey tongue the size of a man quivers in its maw.

The spear in his steady grip is the one he made himself. A long shaft of dark wood with a fire-blackened point. He has used it for three years now, since his tenth winter, to hunt for his tribe.

He does not hunt for his tribe today. Today, as the sun burns down and bakes their backs, he hunts because the gods are in the jungle, and they are watching. The tribes have seen the gods in their armour of red metal and black stone, always in the shadows, watching the hunting parties as they stalk their prey.

If a hunter wishes to dwell in paradise among the stars, he must hunt well when the gods walk the jungles.

Zavien stares at the towering lizard-beast, unable to look away from its watery, slitted red eye.

He shifts his grip on the spear he crafted.

With a prayer that the gods are bearing witness to his courage, he throws the weapon with a heartfelt scream.

THE FLESH TEARER crashed to the bloodstained ground, face down in the dust.

'Cease fire,' Sister Superior Mercy Astaran said softly. Her sisters obeyed immediately.

'But he still lives,' one of them replied.

This was true. The warrior was dragging himself with gut-wrenching slowness, one-armed and with a trembling hand, through the dirt. A dark trail of broken armour and leaking lifeblood pooled around him.

He raised his shaking hand once more, dug the spasming fingers into the ground, and dragged himself another half-metre closer to the burning church's front door.

'Is he seeking to escape?' one of the youngest sisters asked, unwilling to admit her admiration for the heretic's endurance. One arm lost at the elbow, both legs destroyed from the knees down, and his armour a cracked mess that leaked coolant fluids and rich, red Astartes blood.

'It is hardly escape to crawl into a burning building,' another laughed.

'He wishes to die among the blasphemy he caused,' Astaran said, her scowl even harsher in the firelight. 'End him.'

A single gunshot rang out from the battle-line.

Zavien's fingers stopped trembling. His reaching hand fell into the dust. His eyes, which had first opened to see the clear skies of a distant world, closed at last.

'WHAT SHOULD WE do with the body?' Sister Mercy Astaran asked her commander.

'Let the echoes of this heresy remain as an example, at least until the greenskins take control of the surrounding wastelands. Come sisters, we do not have much time. Leave this wretch for the vultures.'

ABOUT THE AUTHORS

BEN COUNTER

Ben Counter is one of the Black Library's most popular authors. An Ancient History graduate and avid miniature painter, he lives near Portsmouth, England.

AARON DEMBSKI-BOWDEN

Aaron Dembski-Bowden is a British author with his beginnings in the videogame and RPG industries. He's been a deeply entrenched fan of Warhammer 40,000 ever since he first ruined his copy of *Space Crusade* by painting the models with all the skill expected of an overexcited nine-year-old.

He lives and works in Northern Ireland with his fiancée Katie, hiding from the world in the middle of nowhere. His hobbies generally revolve around reading anything within reach, and helping people spell his surname.

C S GOTO

C S Goto has published short fiction in *Inferno!* and elsewhere. His work for the Black Library includes the Warhammer 40,000 Dawn of War novels, the Deathwatch series and the Necromunda novel *Salvation*.

JONATHAN GREEN

Jonathan Green lives in West London. He is well known for his contributions to the Fighting Fantasy range of adventure gamebooks, as well as his

novels set within Games Workshop's worlds of
Warhammer and Warhammer 40,000, which
include the Black Templars duology *Crusade for
Armageddon* and *Conquest of Armageddon*. He has
written for such diverse properties as Sonic the
Hedgehog, Doctor Who, and Star Wars
The Clone Wars.

To keep up with what he is doing set your
personal cogitator relay to
www.jonathangreenauthor.blogspot.com

PAUL KEARNEY
Paul Kearney studied at Lincoln College, Oxford
where he read Anglo-Saxon, Old Norse and
Middle English and was a keen member of the
Mountaineering Society and the Officer Training
Corps. He has published several titles including
the *Sea Beggars* to critical acclaim, being long-
listed for the British Fantasy Award.

NICK KYME
Nick Kyme hails from Grimsby, a small town on
the east coast of England. Nick moved to
Nottingham in 2003 to work on White Dwarf
magazine as a Layout Designer. Since then, he has
made the switch to the Black Library's hallowed
halls as an editor and has been involved in a
multitude of diverse projects. His writing credits
include several published short stories,
background books and novels.

You can catch up with Nick and read about all of
his other published works at his website:
www.nickkyme.com

GRAHAM McNEILL

Hailing from Scotland, Graham McNeill worked for over six years as a Games Developer in Games Workshop's Design Studio before taking the plunge to become a full-time writer. In addition to many previous novels, including bestsellers *False Gods* and *Fulgrim*, Graham has written a host of SF and Fantasy stories and comics. Graham lives and works in Nottingham and you can keep up to date with where he'll be and what he's working on by visiting his website.

Join the ranks of the 4th Company at
www.graham-mcneill.com

MITCHEL SCANLON

Mitchel Scanlon is a full-time novelist and comics writer. His previous credits for the Black Library include the novel *Fifteen Hours* and *Descent of Angels*. He lives in Derbyshire, in the UK.

JAMES SWALLOW

James Swallow's stories from the dark worlds of Warhammer 40,000 include the Horus Heresy novel *The Flight of the Eisenstein*, *Faith & Fire*, the Blood Angels books *Deus Encarmine*, *Deus Sanguinius*, *Red Fury* and *Black Tide* as well as short fiction. His non-fiction features *Dark Eye: The Films of David Fincher* and books on scriptwriting and genre television; Swallow's other credits include writing for Star Trek: Voyager, scripts for videogames and audio dramas.

He lives in London, and is currently working on his next book.

RICHARD WILLIAMS

Richard Williams was born in Nottingham, UK and was first published in 2000. He has written fiction for publications ranging from *Inferno!* to the Oxford & Cambridge May Anthologies, on topics as diverse as gang initiation, medieval highwaymen and arcane religions. In his spare time he is a theatre director and actor. *Relentless* was his first full-length novel and his latest book is *Reiksguard*.

Visit his official website at
www.richard-williams.com